A RIVER CHASE
OVER PERILOUS RAPIDS

The water hit her face like a slap. A hand grabbed at her ankle, but she kicked loose. She swam in her strong crawl toward the center of the river. After ten or twelve strokes she turned her head sideways and gulped air. Then she headed down.

She breaststroked five or six feet below the surface, eyes open, till she was near the middle of the pool. She came up for air and wondered why she wasn't cold. She sucked her lungs full and made another surface dive.

Ace, she kept saying to herself, are you down here? It's Mommy, angel! *Mommy's coming*. She kicked till she was so deep that the water looked like cold green paint. Suddenly her stomach muscles contracted, and the strength left her arms and legs. The green depths turned gray, then black. A voice screamed, *You've killed the baby...it was your fault...you shouldn't have chased them...you've killed the baby*. She wondered what her mother-in-law was doing here.

JACK OLSEN
HAVE YOU SEEN MY SON?

CHARTER BOOKS, NEW YORK

HAVE YOU SEEN MY SON?

A Charter Book/published by arrangement with
Atheneum

PRINTING HISTORY
Atheneum edition/1982
Charter edition/May 1984

ISBN: 0-441-31825-8

Charter Books are published by The Berkley Publishing Group,
200 Madison Avenue, New York, New York 10016.
PRINTED IN THE UNITED STATES OF AMERICA

For Su again and always

SPRING

1

LAEL FOLLOWED HER son's trail through the house, her scuffs flapping against the scarred oak floor. His sneakers don't miss a thing, she said under her breath. They pick up sand, they pick up tar, they pick up mud. Thank God we don't have horses.

It was time for his lunch. A peanut butter and jelly sandwich was the plat du jour again. Ace was getting leaner every day, and it was the only dish he was sure to eat. Maybe for dinner she could con him into eating some chicken salad, provided she lied about the mayo. He'd caught her white-handed the last time she'd made it. "Mom, that's mayo! *Yuck!*"

His diamond-tread footprints ran from the back door to the front. She wondered what he had been stalking. A killer seal, like the last time? She shrugged. Who could comprehend the five-year-old mind?

As she stood on the sagging redwood porch, an unexpected puff of wind lifted the hem of her faded wraparound skirt and swirled it against her legs. A light April breeze blew from north to south down the four-mile length of the island, soothing her tanned skin like lotion. Out on Puget Sound, a regatta of sail-boats in pastels and stripes moped along, spinnakers extended like cupped hands.

She thought of those last tense outings before the final breakup, how Mike's face had reddened as he'd yanked at the six-horse Evinrude and cursed the wind that had insulted him personally by dying away. What few joys the poor man had! She tried to remember if he'd been more light-hearted before his business had gone under. Not much. His whole family always acted as though God were a sergeant at arms.

She wondered if some small part of herself wanted him back. A clavicle perhaps? No. And anyway, he would never come home after what she'd said. Words: the neutron bombs of marriage. She'd picked over their final scenes again and again and always come to the same conclusion: that something would have cracked the fragile shell of that marriage sooner or later. Sooner was better for everyone, especially the child. She stretched her long bare arms and told herself for the thousandth time to quit belaboring the subject. Eight years of taking blame were enough.

Ace's black hair flashed into sight. He was chasing an enraged mallard drake across the little arc of beach and gathering a new supply of wet sand to distribute through the house. "Acey," she called out, "time for—"

The phone rang. She hoped it wasn't that writer again. *So* persistent. The breakup hadn't been three days old when he'd called and suggested lunch in town. How quickly they picked up the scent. Should she tell him the truth? *Norm, I'm sorry, I'm just not ready for the social whirl. Dating leads to sex, and I'm not planning any for another twenty or thirty years. Call me then, Norm, will you?* Sex still brought memories of Mike in bed, wordlessly kneading her breasts like a pastry chef.

She picked up the phone and heard her husband's voice— think of the devil!—wanting to know if he could borrow Ace overnight. He sounded excited, as though the idea had just struck him. His wants and ideas came in bursts, instanter, like a child's. He'd always claimed that creative minds were different from the rest, but that the difference couldn't be comprehended by noncreative minds.

It was two minutes before noon on a Sunday; she wondered why he wasn't out on the Sound, fishing for salmon, his great passion. Once she'd suggested he name his black-hulled Bay-liner *Bait Noire,* and he hadn't even smiled. Who joked about religion? Maybe the salmon weren't biting today, or maybe he was acting on another impulse. Their third and last marriage counselor had pointed out that impulsiveness was hard on marriage and child-raising. That had been the end of the marriage counseling.

"Come on over and get him," she said, making herself sound more upbeat than she felt. "He loves your pajama parties." Ace had been acting antsy lately. Maybe he couldn't articulate his distress, or maybe he didn't want to sound disloyal to her by admitting he missed his father. For a five-year-old, he had a finely tuned sense of diplomacy.

"Is it okay if we, uh, borrow your truck?" Mike was asking. "We might, I mean—we might take a drive up in the mountains, and you know those log roads." He was talking faster than usual, interrupting himself. Did she still make him as nervous as he made her? After four months apart? Not likely. He'd probably just come in from a long jog. Exercise made him high, filled him with energy and inspiration. She remembered how he would come panting into the house in his sweat suit and stab at his drawing board with his pencil while his ideas were fresh. And then abandon them later, when the self-doubt returned. Oh, Mike, she thought, maybe if I'd given you more support. . . .

"You can use the Luv anytime," she said. "You know that." The truck's four-wheel drive would be safer on the steep roads. She had just changed the oil and filters.

"Can the kid be ready in an hour?" he asked.

Larry Allen, the family cat, added himself to her pale blue blouson like a fur piece, his breath smelling faintly of mouse. "For a trip to the mountains," she said through tickly wisps, "Ace can be ready in one minute and thirty-seven seconds."

"See you, Lael." Her name sounded odd on his lips. He'd always called her baby, babe, or sweetie—never Lael. She pulled her arms tightly across her chest and felt a chill. I love, therefore I am. What's the corollary? I don't love, therefore I'm not? How about—I love not, neither am I loved?

She sighed, annoyed at herself. How could anybody think broody thoughts on a day like this? With Ace gone she could do the paper work that had piled up on her desk while she'd been spring planting. Hold on there, she told herself. This weather's too good to waste at a desk; rain might start tonight and keep up for a week, and then the basil will get black spot and die. Protect the basil at all costs! Hot caps: that's the answer. And after I cap my basil, I'll give my fennel some attention.

She wondered why she'd suddenly started feeling good. Feeling good gave her twinges of guilt, as though it had to be at someone's expense. Another holdover from the years with Mike.

She stepped outside to call Ace again. Far across the Sound, Seattle's new buildings shimmered in the April sun like rock candy. A row of cormorants rode serenely past on a gravel barge; an auklet pecked at a slick. The lovely light-struck scene made her smile. She shut her eyes and sucked in the salty air with a sybaritic hiss. She asked herself if there was life after separation and decided that the answer was yes, provided the weather held up.

2

THROUGH THE WINDOW Lael could see Ace clomping back and forth on the porch in his new climbing boots, waiting for the first sight of his father's car. That crazy Mike, she thought; he'll never change. Expects the world to jump when he calls. If I had a speck of pride, I'd have told him what to do with his last-minute trip to the mountains. But that wouldn't have been fair to Ace. The child's tremulous soprano voice came through the window:

> Fee fie foe fun
> I smell the blood of a Englishmun
> Be him alive or be him dead
> He'll grind my bones to break his bread

Please God, she prayed silently, let him have a good time with his father. And bring my baby home safe and sound. We're in the salvage business now, the two of us, rebuilding our lives on scraps and hopes and expectations. It's *sauve qui peut* for a while, but we'll make it, won't we, Ace? Why shouldn't you go out and have a good time with your dad? You're not the ones getting divorced.

Besides, she thought, I can never pay him enough attention on Sundays. After six days of digging and weeding and harvesting and drying and tying and bagging her herbs, all she ever wanted to do on Sundays was tidy the little shingle cottage, catch up on back copies of *Organic Gardening* and *Sunset*, and maybe read a chapter or two of the Brontës or May Sarton, if she could get Ace to bed early enough. Which was becoming a very large *if.* . . .

No one seemed to understand how much grunt and groan it took to run her Salt-Water Herb Farm. "Oh, your little business," people would say. "How cute." She told herself that anyone who called her job cute should be sentenced to hack cedar roots out of a parsley bed nine hours a day.

It had started as a single raised bed, four by eight feet, and she had kept the business going even in the bleakest days of the marriage, working in the rich black soil that she had mixed with her own hands from compost and fertilizer and sand and seaweed. A week after Ace's birth she had been back on her knees, weeding. Her herbs were tractable, reasonably predictable, fairly consistent. They would never file for divorce.

From the porch her son's high voice threatened her wine goblets: "My country tizzafee, sweet land of liberty. . . ."

Lately his asthma had been augmented by a touch of malapropism—a remembrance of the great-aunt on the Estes side who enjoyed listening to "Medication" by Thaïs. One of his preschool teachers had said there was nothing to worry about: "All bright kids mangle words. It's because they take chances." Lael was grateful for the consolation.

". . . Oh, gimme a home where the buffaloes roam, and the deer and the angelo play—"

When the voice subsided, she noticed the sound of the halyards jingling against the aluminum mast on their little San Juan sloop; the wind had picked up. She tried to decide how long it had been since she'd checked the mooring knots. Too long, at least by her husband's standards. How well she remembered the arguments.

"The boat almost tore loose again today."

"But it's your boat, Mike—"

"Yeah, it's my boat, but somebody always fools with the knots."

"I never in my life—"

"Drop it, Lael, will you?"

She looked out the window and saw his canary yellow Ford Escort turning off the beach road in a swirl of chalky dust. Ace was already halfway up the long driveway, running out from under his blue Seattle Mariners cap.

Once the closeness of her two men had produced small twinges of jealousy, had made her feel left-out, banned from the exalted club of penis wielders. As a parent, Mike had carefully avoided the scut work of child raising. The result was that Ace loved him more like a grandpa or a favorite uncle. His divorce complaint had demanded custody of the child, but both sides knew he would never get it. He seemed to be adjusting to the idea, making the occasional visitation, learning to enjoy his son on an outpatient basis. Was this the beginning of healing—for all of them?

The car bumped down the drive, Ace running alongside in his Oshkosh B'gosh overalls. Every few steps he would break into a skip or jump into the air. Mr. Skippyfrisk! She thought of all the pet names they had called him through the years: Billy Boom Buster, Sonny Sunshine, Eddie the Truck Driver, Mr. Guacamole, Ol' Judge Tate, everything but his real name: Alexander Charles Estes Pritcher. Their intentions had been good, but somehow they'd managed to outfit him with a new nickname every week. And finally, over his grandmother Pritcher's objections, settled on the one suggested by his initials.

Mike climbed out and lifted him, and for an instant their hair blended in a sunlit puff of black. No one looking at them could doubt that they were father and son. Mike nodded in her direction, staring past her in a way she remembered from their recent meetings. The tip of his nose twitched nervously above his wispy black mustache, and the whites of his dark eyes were an unhealthy oystershell white. Was he having trouble sleeping? Who wasn't? "How the hell are you?" he asked.

She swallowed hard and hoped he didn't notice. He had used those same words that first night at the Kappa house at Mount Holyoke. She had thought him nervy but—interesting. Who among the wimps she knew would have barged in and asked "How the hell are you?" in front of that prune of a housemother? Years had gone by before she finally caught on that his brash exterior covered a desperate uneasiness. The first of many discoveries. . . .

"Bring him back on time, Mike, will you?" she asked, speaking lightly so he wouldn't flare up.

"The crack of dawn again?" He was still smiling, but his old mannerism of shifting his weight from one foot to the other gave away his unease. She wondered what gave away hers.

"His car pool gets here at twenty to nine," she said gently. "They hate to wait."

"Don't worry, we'll be on time." He patted Ace where "42" and "PRITCHER" came together on the blue T-shirt. "Hey, Lael, go get his good shoes, will you? And the new suit? The one from Frederick and Nelson's?"

"The flannel? Why?"

His smile flamed out; she wished she hadn't asked. "'Why?'" he echoed in the sharpening tone she remembered so well. "What the hell kind of a question is that?"

"I just wondered why he needs a suit for the mountains."

He looked back and forth between her and Ace. "We might go to dinner later. I like him to be dressed up." Since when?

she wondered. But she knew better than to argue.

"You won't keep him out late, will you, Mike?"

"C'mon, Lael, lighten up. I don't see him that often." The edge was still in his voice; she was sure he was resentful about what she'd said four months ago, and always would be. She felt like shouting, *You see Ace as often as you damn well please. I've never turned you down once. But children need their sleep, especially asthmatic children. . . .*

She held back; she didn't want to put the trip in jeopardy. A piqued Mike was capable of turning on his heel and driving off without a word. "Try not to get him overtired, okay?" she said almost apologetically.

"Jesus, Lael, do you have to orchestrate every little thing?"

"'Kay, guys, time to go," Ace broke in, tugging at his father's leg. "Come on, Dad." He looked back and forth from one to the other with a hopeful smile. He must be remembering those awful last months, she told herself. A wave of love and compassion swept over her. Acey Pritcher, five years old, and square in the middle.

She found his suit and shoes and folded them neatly in a silver box from Nordstrom's. While she was at it, she threw in his hated new pajamas with the tennis racket print. She'd had no idea how opinionated five-year-olds could be about clothes. Someone else would be fighting the pajama wars tonight.

Mike had just backed her black truck out of the garage and started up the driveway when she saw the brake lights go on and Ace's door open. She heard her husband say, "Go on now. *Go on!*"

Please, God, she prayed to herself, don't let the trip be over already. That's where the asthma comes from: all the tension and strain. Never knowing where he stands. The doctor as much as said so.

The child climbed from the truck and ran to her on his skinny legs, his face flushed. He hugged her around the thighs and said, "Love ya, Mom."

She kissed him on the cowlick that had formed when she'd cut the bubble gum from his hair. She felt emotionally overwhelmed, almost teary. "Love *you*, Mr. Guacamole."

"Dad reminded me to tell ya," he explained.

She was ashamed of herself. It was loving of Mike to insist that Ace run back and say good-bye. Just for a moment they were a family again.

She pushed her son's black-rimmed glasses up the slope of his thin nose. He jerked away like a puppy slipping its leash. A giggle, a crunch of gravel, a single wave of a grimy hand, and her only child was gone.

She walked a few feet along the private beach in her weightless Adidas parka, trying to sort out her feelings. She had always drawn strength from the *perpetuum mobile* of the bay: diver ducks diving, puffins puffing, plovers—she tried to remember what plovers did. Plove? She already felt high on the salt air.

An admiring whistle floated down from an unmuffled car on the bluff—teen-agers, probably. She turned and headed back to the house. She had been blessed with a trim but pro-portionate figure, for which she was not ungrateful, but lately she had played down her firm breasts and narrow waist by wearing floppy cardigans or loose blouses or this old nylon parka. Her long legs were usually encased in soft worn jeans streaked with sand and humus. Her face was tanned summer and winter from working outdoors, but the only cosmetics she wore were lip gloss and the faintest touch of eye shadow. She thought of herself as not necessarily attractive—thin nose a little crooked, mouth a little weak—but attractive enough.

Far across the water, a freighter blared its horn as it released its tugboats and headed toward the Strait of Juan de Fuca and the open sea. Attractive enough for what? she asked herself. I was married and a mother; looks were a minor matter. But now I'm back in the cold world. Will I measure up? Another worry. . . .

She reached the straggly salt grass that marked the western boundary of her bayfront acre. Had she spent too much time on her herbs, letting the glamour ebb from their marriage? Glamour: such a vapid word. It brought to mind lacquered hair, inch-long fingernails, skin that couldn't be touched for fear the goo would rub off, women like the Gabors and Elizabeth Taylor endlessly preening. Had all that glamour helped their mar-riages? In her own marriage the failure had been in other depart-ments.

The breeze tugged at her dark blond hair, and she pulled the parka tightly about her. She was trying to put a certain word out of her mind. Had she really been . . . frigid? She told herself she certainly *had* not. He was so damned unreasonable. She could join him in exuberant lovemaking five nights in a row, but if she wasn't in the mood on the sixth, she was frigid. The word lay like a curse on her peace of mind.

She tried to sort out her feelings at seeing Ace and Mike leaving together. Glad and sad, that was it. Glad for Ace but sad that she'd been cast again in the role of good old prosaic mom. All fathers were heroes to their sons. She'd always built him up to the child. A mistake probably. But he'd always been the dominant one, the "important" one, and he'd never been shy about pointing it out. "Sure I'll turn the compost for you," he would tell her, "and then you can design a building for me." But of course she didn't have the talent. He'd emphasized that, too. Well, he was right, wasn't he? Scrabbling about in the earth and making herbs grow—was that a talent?

A small one, she told herself, but mine own.

She walked under the Madame Hardy roses and disturbed a Steller's jay. On sunny days like this her weathered silver gray cottage gave off a scent of cedar from beams and planks that went back a century. It was the last house like it along the bay; the old charm of the island was slowly giving way to subdivisions and condos and RV parks. She guessed Ace and Mike were in Nisbet right now, loading up on ice cream and milk shakes. How typical, she thought. Mike takes him to the Dairy Queen and I take him to the dentist.

She wondered where father and son would go after their mountain trip and asked herself: why am I wasting time wondering? Most likely they'll drive over to the Thunder Bay Inn for dinner, and afterward they'll go to Mike's new apartment and watch the Sunday Night Movie. That's too much stimulation for a child with a breathing problem. By morning he'll be goggle-eyed, and it'll take all my patience to gentle him down for school. But Mike won't have to deal with the problem. Not till the next time the paternal instinct takes him away from his fishing. . . .

She walked into her warm kitchen and groped inside the refrigerator for an orange. A piece of violet construction paper floated to the floor; Ace must have been using the hydrator as a filing cabinet again. She reread the squiggly block letters in blue Magic Marker:

> DeAR MOM I LOV
> e YOU. LOVe
> ACe.

Yes, yes, *yes,* she said to herself. My own sweet son adores me. The rest is unimportant.

3

It was just turning dark—eight-fifteen on this spring evening—when she finished straightening up Ace's room and discovered that he had forgotten his nebulizer. He hadn't had a serious attack of asthma in weeks, but he sometimes woke up wheezing, and nighttimes were the worst.

She had no choice; she had to call Mike's apartment. It was awkward, yes—a strange woman might pick up the phone, or he might fly into one of his Cutty Sark rages at her for forgetting the medicine, as though he himself were unconnected to the problem. He'd always complained that her overprotection made the child's asthma worse. She knew where he got his ideas. Once his mother had told her, "Lael, I know it's none of my business, but you coddle Alex too much, you smother him. *That's* where his asthma comes from."

As the number rang, she rehearsed what she would say.

Hello, Mike? Hate to bother you, but Ace forgot his nebulizer. . . .

Oh, hi, Mike. Listen, this is silly, but. . . .

No, she wouldn't say, "Hate to bother you," or, "This is silly." Why was she always so apologetic? All three of them had forgotten the nebulizer, hadn't they?

A familiar voice answered, *"Mmm yes?"*

The dry nasal tone was so unexpected that it almost made her jump. What should I call her? she wondered. *Mother*, as though nothing has changed? *Catherine? Mrs. Pritcher?*

"Mother!" She hoped she sounded pleasantly surprised. "I didn't know you were on the island."

"Well, now you know." The voice raised bumps on her arms; it had the superior quality common to maitre d's and opera ushers.

She wondered how she had managed to put herself in this position. If Ace began to wheeze, it would take only a few minutes to drive the medicine around the bay. Why anticipate trouble? Now she was forced to talk to her mother-in-law for the first time since the breakup, and what was there to say?

Mother, I didn't mean what I told him. I mean, I meant it, but not the way he took it. I was just . . . mad. Our marriage wasn't working anymore. Yes, yes, I wanted it to, I tried—for Ace. But see, Mother, I—I couldn't. The short-form explanation wasn't heavy enough to explain the break-up, and there wasn't time for the long form. She could imagine the version Mike had provided.

She settled for a simple "How've you been?"

"Getting by," the woman answered. "Was there something you wanted?"

"Oh, uh—"

"How's your little hobby?" Lael held the phone away from her ear as though it had fangs. *Mother,* she felt like saying, *we share the same name, we share your grandson, we shared your only son for eight years, and the first question you ask me after Mike and I break up is—how's my little hobby?*

"It's fine," she said. "Fine."

"Selling lots of mustard greens?"

She felt her face flush. A long time ago Catherine Pritcher had asked her where she expected to find time to take care of Mike and Ace and how she could ever sell enough "mustard greens" to make expenses. Embarrassed, Lael had said, "Just think of it as my little hobby." The woman had settled on that description.

"It's too early for mustard greens, Mother," Lael said, annoyed at herself for giving a serious answer.

"Was there something you wanted, Lael?" the flat voice came back. Evidently the question about mustard greens had exhausted her supply of small talk. Lael remembered so many tense conversations in the past, remembered the tiny points of light glittering like ice crystals in those thin blue eyes as the woman listened without warmth or approval. Good-bye to all that, she said to herself, and managed a smile.

"I just called to say Ace forgot his medicine," she said.

There was a pause. "What medicine?" Catherine Pritcher sounded genuinely puzzled. Was it possible that she had forgotten about her grandson's condition? Yes, Lael realized, it was possible.

"His epinephrine nebulizer. For his asthma."

"Will he be needing it?" The slightest note of concern had crept into the gelid voice.

Lael decided not to risk another lecture on how she was over-mothering Ace and causing his asthma. "Oh, it's probably okay. If you hear him wheezing, call me. He's been fine the last few weeks . . . he probably won't be any trouble—I mean, he won't have any trouble. Okay, Mother?" The words tumbled out. She felt graceless, unworthy, and in an awkward attempt to end the conversation she said, "Is he up? Ace, I mean? Maybe I could just say good night."

There was a silence, then: "Alex is outside playing." Another pause. "With, uh, his dad."

Outside playing? This late? "Well, I won't disturb them then," she said, feeling like a phone solicitor.

"That's probably wise."

"Bye, Mother."

"*Mmm* bye." The dial-tone buzzed instantly, as though a finger had been poised over the disconnect button. Lael thought of Mike and what it must have been like to lose his father at three and be brought up by this humorless praying mantis of a woman.

She flopped onto the threadbare corduroy sofa and berated herself for the way she'd handled the conversation. She was ashamed of her nervousness, the way her heart had sunk at the first sound of her mother-in-law's voice. No family obligation remained; she should be speaking up now, defending her interests. The herb business had cleared nearly $12,000 last year, and a good thing, too, since Mike had always treated money as though it were perishable. Until she had taken over the family accounts herself, they had never put a penny aside, and even now her $2,700 at Island Savings & Loan had come entirely from her herb business. Did that sound like somebody's "little hobby"?

Her shoulder-length hair, freed from its usual bandanna, picked up a sheen from the imitation Tiffany lamp overhead as she flailed away with her bone hairbrush. Except for washing her hair in herb shampoo and lemon juice, fifty brisk strokes a day were the only treatment she ever gave it, but it held its body and its dark blond color. She was always asked who did her hair and was embarrassed when she had to answer, "Me."

At the forty-first stroke it began to dawn on her that Catherine had sounded even more distant than usual. She stopped brushing to reflect. Distant, yes, and wary. A little off-balance. What could the woman have to hide?

She resumed the count at forty-two and told herself to think about something else. If I understood the Pritchers, she thought, maybe I'd still be living with one—and turning to stone an inch at a time. I've lived with Pritchers and I've lived without Pritchers. Without is better.

At least so far.

4

By eight forty-five the next morning, the car pool for the Humpty Dumpty Play School had come and gone and there was no sign of Ace and his father. When Mike finally got around to returning the boy, Lael would have to drive him to nursery school. She might have known.

As she sat drumming her fingers on the kitchen table, Larry Allen jumped up on her lap, and without thinking she brushed him off. He jumped back up, purring. The little gray tiger cat had followed her around like a pup ever since she'd found him half-dead on the highway. When he wasn't rubbing against her ankles, he was out collecting mice and shrews and fish heads that he laid at her feet. She didn't consider herself a natural-born cat lover, but Larry Allen had won her over with his stumpy tail and ratty coat and silly ways.

At nine-fifteen she lifted him off her lap and dialed Mike's apartment. The number didn't ring, and after a second attempt she gave up. They were probably on their way.

Ten minutes later she tried again, with the same result. She wasn't surprised; the island phones were as capricious as the island natives. She dialed "O" and told the operator she knew the phone was in order because she had spoken on the line the night before.

"I'm sorry," the voice said after several trials. "I can't seem to get a ring. Would you like me to connect you with repair service?"

"Uh, no. No, thanks."

She spun her circular index to P and looked up Catherine Pritcher's number in the village of Mansfield, just over the bridge that connected the west side of the island to the mainland. She misdialed, dialed again and tensed when the familiar greeting came across the line: "*Mmm* yes?"

"This is Lael," she said. "I hate to bother you, but Mike and Ace aren't here, and—"

"Why call *me?*"

16

The phone felt cold against her ear. "He, uh—I can't get him at home."

She heard an impatient sigh, then: "I had nothing to do with it!"

"With what, mother?"

"Good-bye, Lael."

Suddenly the coldness of the phone had spread through her body. Still in her apron, she ran from the house to the Ford Escort that Mike had left behind. She sped around the bay road, skidding through corners. His new apartment was on the near outskirts of Nisbit. She banged on the pastel orange door till her knuckles hurt, then rushed downstairs to the super's office and asked him to open the door with a passkey. The instant they entered, she smelled the emptiness. A typewritten note was pinned to the furnished sofa:

> Lael. I'm sorry, but there was no other way. I do NOT intend to lose my son because of your inadequacies as a wife. It will be best if we don't start exchanging calls and letters. A clean break is right for Ace (and for me too). I haven't decided where we'll locate, so there's no point in trying to find us. Ace will be raised in a moral home, a healthy atmosphere. If you want to blame some-body as usual, look in your mirror.

The janitor clenched and unclenched a black and yellow tractor cap that advertised DIESEL POWER. Had he been in on the dirty work, too? She clamped a hand over her mouth and tried to think straight. Ace kidnapped? By Mike, of all people? Oh, God, another one of his impulses. He'll be back before dark, all contrition. Won't he? If the man only knew his own mind. . . .

The note's tone irritated her. A moral home, Mike? A healthy atmosphere? Like the one you created when you treated your wife like a slave and a whore? And let a child suffer from asthma night after night because "it's all in his mind"? Will you raise him in that kind of healthy atmosphere?

It was less than a mile to the county sheriff's Nisbet sub-station. En route she wondered if she should use the Ford's CB radio to summon help; but Mike hated it when anyone else played with his expensive toys, and she had never learned how. Besides, what would she say? "SOS. Be on lookout for. . . ." She wasn't Angie Dickinson.

The substation was empty. She ran across the street to the

squat tan municipal building to find the village clerk, an addled old man with a fringe of white, fluffy hair like milkweed. Her mind raced her body; she strained to keep herself under control. Kidnapping was a serious crime, even when it was committed by an amateur. Every cop in the state would go to work on the case as soon as she turned in the alarm. Mike wouldn't get far. He was miserably miscast as an abductor of children, even his own.

The old clerk began dialing a number before she'd finished her story. He passed the phone across to her with a quaking hand. "Here. Speak up. Don't leave a thing out."

A woman's voice said, "Sheriff's office."

As Lael recited the bare facts, she felt the immensity of her action, its irreversibility. In her mind she could hear teletypes clattering, police sirens, the clank of a cell door closing on the man who had fathered her son. She could imagine the recriminations later, the explanations she would have to make over and over. Poor Mike, she thought, he's so confused. He's lost his marriage, his business, his pride, and when the divorce hearing comes up, he'll lose his son. One blow too many. But a child isn't a bauble to be spirited away in the night. Of all the dumb, impulsive. . . . When they catch him, I can drop the charges.

The female voice asked, "What's your marital status, ma'am?"

"Pardon?" The question flustered her. On the other side of the scarred countertop the town clerk was shuffling papers, but she knew his tufted ears were tuned. Jungle drums would throb tonight from North Point to Schwager's Bight and back. *Mike Pritcher stole his own kid.* You mean that young architect? The guy with the big ideas? *That's him.* Why the hell would he do a damnfool thing like that? *Who knows? It ain't the first crazy thing he ever done. . . .*

The female deputy sheriff said, "I need your exact marriage status."

"Uh, separated," she answered. "I have custody of my son."

"By court order?"

"No. By a separation agreement."

"Between you and your husband?"

"Well, uh, yes. Between our lawyers."

"Oh. Uh, Miz Pritcher, would you hold for just a minute?"

She heard the hollow sound of a hand being cupped over the mouthpiece. Then the voice came back. "Ma'am? I'm sorry.

We can't do thing one." The woman spoke just above a whisper. "I'm really sorry, Mrs. Pritcher. I always feel terrible about cases like this."

"I—I don't get it." She flattened the phone against her ear. "Are you saying you won't—you can't—" Suddenly she was terrified. Ace, Ace, you aren't really gone! "Oh, God, oh, please, oh, *listen,* miss," she said hoarsely. "You've got to help me."

Something brushed the back of her denim skirt; she jumped and turned and almost dropped the phone. The clerk had brought a chair and was urging her to sit. Boneless, she slumped down as the voice on the phone began an explanation that registered only as disconnected fragments: ". . . his own son . . . equal entitlement . . . no crime committed . . . not till you have a decree. . . ."

She was outside turning the ignition key in Mike's little Escort before she realized that she had no idea what to do next. In all that half-heard chatter, one message had come across clearly: Ace's kidnapping was not a police matter.

Driving like a drunk, she aimed the car down the sandy street. She couldn't afford to take legal advice from a voice on the phone—not in a matter like this.

Her lawyer's office was a block away, in the unfinished shopping mall. She squinted at the sun. It was the same sun that had shone the day before and the day before that, but suddenly it looked different. Not for long. Acey Pritcher was coming home to his mother!

Somehow.

5

SHE PARKED TWO feet from the curb and picked a path among the hardened droppings of cement and exposed cable endings and weeds and bitter memories of the uncompleted shopping center. She hated to come to this mall. Mike had designed the place in frank imitation of the Mexican architect Luis Barragan—color as structure, luminous slabs of orange and pink and ocher, walk-in color-field paintings, filtered light—but the island people weren't ready for Edward Durell Stone or Eero Saarinen, let alone an innovator like Barragan. "In this day and age, who else could lose his ass on a shopping center?" Mike had complained afterward. For weeks he'd brooded and stared into space and barely talked.

She stepped around a Jimson weed growing from a crack and came to the only occupied office. A door with a row of black press-on letters said IVAN STEIN, ATTY. AT LAW. A shiny motorcycle rested just outside on its kickstand.

She walked in without knocking, her footsteps muted on the twisted hemp throw rug, the only other sound the *zzzp-zzzp* of a fly. It was a large one-room office, the walls decorated by a framed photograph of an Indian chief, a poster of a raised muscular fist above a field of lettuce, and an artist's rendering of a broken tanker bearing the warning OIL SPILLS—AND KILLS! A stained couch and two fold-up wooden chairs lined the wall. She was glad to see they were empty. Usually they were occupied by Stein's clientele: stoop laborers with stained hands, gillnetters blinking their eyes at the unaccustomed daylight, men with small eyes and skin like sliced bread who looked as though they had just walked away from the penitentiary. Every time she entered this office she fought an urge to scratch. She hoped this didn't make her a bigot.

The lawyer slumped backward in his chair, his feet in sweat socks atop the cheap metal desk, his face concealed by a single sheet of newspaper. He was a tall young man with curly red hair, a ponytail, and a lean body with no backside. For reasons unknown, he had set up shop in the village when just about everyone else was leaving. But he was cheap, and he was here.

She said, "Mr. Stein?" The newspaper slid to the floor, and a face popped into view. One end of his reddish brown mustache pointed up and one drooped. His Ben Franklin glasses hung from an ear. She was sure he'd been nodding out. At their first consultation on the divorce he'd offered her a joint to calm her nerves. What would it be this time? Heroin?

"Do *what?*" he said, shading his eyes.

"I'm sorry," she said. "I didn't mean—"

"'S okay," he mumbled. With his fiery red eyebrows and steely blue eyes he seemed to wear a perpetual glower, but for once she had him at a disadvantage. "Bad night," he mumbled. "Musta dozed. Glad you woke me. Got somebody coming in." He always spoke in hurried fragments, as though late for an appointment miles away. From the beginning he'd handled her case like an afterthought. Now it was time to earn his fee.

"Acey's gone," she said. "He took my son."

"Huh?" He arranged his glasses on a nose that curved slightly downward at the tip like a scimitar. "Oh. Mrs. Pritcher? Who'd you say—*what?* Hey, have a seat."

"My son," she said. "He's been kidnapped."

The back of his swivel chair creaked as he leaned forward. "Kidnapped? Alexander? Who by?"

"Mike. My husband."

He stretched his skinny arm toward the telephone. "I'll call the sheriff—"

"I already did. They said it's not a police matter."

He pitched sideways off his chair and wound up on the bare hardwood floor on his hands and knees. She'd had no idea he was so wrecked. Then she saw that he was peering at a row of greenbound lawbooks that lined his walls at floor level.

"Sit!" he said, motioning behind his back. Why was everybody trying to get her to sit? *This was not time to sit!* A cardboard filing cabinet stood at an angle to the wall; papers overflowed from an open drawer onto the floor. She couldn't imagine how he kept track of anything.

He regained his chair, put down the book he'd selected, and fished a pencil and a pad of lined yellow legal paper from the litter on his desk. "Tell me what happened," he said, yawning behind a freckled hand. "Don't leave a thing out." She had a sudden hope that his lethargy was only temporary, that he would metamorphose into a typical storefront lawyer with ideals and energy.

When she had finished, he slowly shook his head. He looked upset. Or was he nodding out again? She had noticed before that he had a habit of twisting his nose. Lots of dopers did. "I'm sorry," he said. "Whoever you talked to was right about Washington law."

"But he kidnapped Ace!" she said, glaring at him. "This is the United States. There must be something—"

"He's been child-snatched—God, what a scummy phrase. Child-snatched, not kidnapped. You got the right to snatch him back. That's about it."

"What about the separation agreement?" she demanded. "The one you drew up."

"A piece of paper. Means nothing till the court approves it. We could sue, is all."

"What good would that do?"

He shook his head in disgust. "Couldn't even serve the papers."

How she wished she had followed her first instincts. She had wanted to go to Seattle or Bremerton and find the best divorce lawyer to defend her rights. But there'd been next to no disagreement between her and Mike on anything except custody of Ace. So she'd gone to Stein for a preliminary consultation and asked him why Mike would be demanding Ace. "A bargaining ploy, that's all it can be," the red-haired lawyer had answered. "Not a very good one, though, since it'll probably annoy the judge."

He'd sounded so positive that she'd hired him, ponytail and all. Now she was stuck. They'd already blown the first court date—she'd been there bright and early, eager to nail down the permanent custody matter once and for all, but her lawyer hadn't shown up. An irked judge had postponed the trial, and now she had to face the ordeal all over again. This Stein was a total klutz. At all hours of the working day she would see the sign hanging from his door: OUT TO LUNCH. He certainly was.

Now all six feet several inches of him began pacing the room, the tips of his long red mustache quivering. He consulted with himself as though she weren't there: "Knew he wouldn't get custody, so he pulled this . . . what a scumbag . . . goddamn criminal. . . ." He punched his palm. "We'll catch that son of a bitch." For once he wasn't rushing her out, the way he usually did. He glanced down at his notes. "What'd you say he was driving?"

"The Chevy Luv. The one I use in my business."

His eyes narrowed. "Your business?"

"The Salt-Water Herb Farm."

"I forgot." She wasn't offended. She knew it wasn't Exxon.

He circled his desk like a basketball player trying to get into position and stopped at her chair. "How's it registered?"

"What?"

"The truck. *How's it registered?*" He shot the questions like a TV district attorney. Why were they talking about her truck? She'd already tried to give the description to the sheriff's office, and no one there had wanted to hear about it.

"It's registered to the business," she answered.

"How'd he get it?"

"I lent it to him. For the mountains. It's got four-wheel drive."

He did a deep-knee bend alongside her chair and crinkled his long, thin nose. His eyes were a vivid shade of blue that she had never seen on a color chart. The only relief from the hot intensity of his face was a dimple that came and went in the middle of his chin and a small gold Star of David at his throat. "That's our shot," he said. For the first time she caught a hopeful note in his voice. "You sure you don't have your cars confused?" he asked.

"Don't you remember the separation agreement? Mike got the car and I got the truck."

"No more joint ownership?"

"I reregistered it under my business. For the tax write-off."

"Who the hell gave you *that* advice?"

"You."

"Oh." He looked away, and his eyes turned up in his head as though he were trying to remember the date of an unimportant event in ancient history. Then he whirled and said, "Okay, pay attention. I'm gonna dial the state police. You get on and tell 'em your truck was ripped off."

"But—"

"It's our only chance. If Pritcher gets out of this jurisdiction, you may never see your kid again. Tell the cops you woke up this morning and the truck was missing."

"But it wasn't missing! I *lent* him the truck. I—"

"He took off with your truck! That's auto theft. Don't confuse the issue by telling the cops you lent it to him."

The fool was telling her to lie to the police. A penitentiary offense for sure. He finished dialing and shoved the phone at

her. She hesitated, then accepted it. When they came to arrest
her, she could claim that she'd been too distraught to think
straight. She knew that was a cop-out, but she had no intention
of going to jail for following the advice of an irresponsible
lawyer.

While she was busy lying to the deep male voice on the
other end of the phone, Stein reached into a portable cooler in
the corner of the office. He opened two amber bottles of Anchor
Steam beer, set one in front of her, and took a long swig of
the other.

"I feel like the world's biggest liar," she said when the call
was finished. She hated beer, but she took a sip. "That officer
asked me if I had any idea who stole my truck."

"That's when you said, 'Not the slightest'?"

"Yes."

"Perfect."

She ignored the compliment. "What happens now?"

He wiped his mustache with the sleeve of his green flannel
shirt. "Go home and stay by your phone. If the truck's still
around, there's a chance the cops'll find it. Especially with
those business decals on the doors. If he took the kid out of
state, we'll try something else." He spun in his chair playfully.
"Like putting Saint Jude on a retainer."

"Saint Jude?" she asked. "Aren't you, uh, Jewish?" She
realized it was a stupid question.

He smiled. "Where's it say Jews can't do business with the
saints?"

"Which one is Jude?" she asked nervously.

"The patron saint of impossible causes."

6

AT TEN O'CLOCK that night Lael was sprawled atop her bedspread trying to find sleep. She tried reciting poetry from memory but found that snippets were the best she could do: ". . . God, I can push the grass apart . . . Buffalo Bill's dead, defunct. . . . April is the cruelest month. . . . Oh, God, yes, April *is* the cruelest month. Now I know.

Clenching her fists, she babbled from the works of Robert Frost. A reliable tranquilizer. She was halfway through "The Death of the Hired Man," backing and filling to get the lines straight, when the phone rang. She grabbed it in the middle of the first ring. "Ma'am, this is the sheriff's office in Port Angeles. You the party that reported a stolen black Chivvy Luv?"

She tried to think of a safe answer. Port Angeles was sixty miles west, a small seaport on the Strait of Juan de Fuca. It was the last northwestern city before the Pacific. Why were they calling her from there? "I reported it, uh, missing," she said.

"We have it here." She took a deep breath. Was that *all* they had there? She tried to ask, but the words stuck in her throat. "The driver says he's your husband, ma'am." The voice sounded critical. "Is that true?"

She wished her lawyer were around to whisper advice. "No," she said. "Uh, well, he *was* my husband. But we're . . . separated."

"He says you lent it to him."

She yelled, "DO YOU HAVE MY BABY?"

"We've got a boy here, yes, ma'am. He's resting. He was a little, uh, under the weather."

Of course he was. Asthma. And no medicine. He could have died. "He's okay?"

"Fine. Drank a few too many pops, maybe."

"God in heaven," she mumbled. The phone felt like a barbell. "That's my Ace."

"Excuse me?"

"My son. Ace. Uh, Alexander. Please, where is he?"

"Here. In the courthouse building."

"I'll be right there."

"Don't hang up! I need help right now. Got a very annoyed taxpayer sitting outside my office. Talking lawsuit." The scene wasn't hard to imagine. "Mrs. Pritcher," the deputy went on, "you put out a stolen vehicle report on this truck, and he says it wasn't stolen. You see the problem?"

"He was kidnapping my son," she said blankly.

"His son, too."

"But I have custody."

"Why isn't there a missing persons report?"

"The sheriff here wouldn't take one. They told me it was a—"

"A domestic matter, yeah." There was a pause. "Well, it is."

"Wait, Officer, please!" She had a vision of losing the connection and racing to Port Angeles to find that Mike and Ace had just left. "Can you wait a few minutes while I get my lawyer?"

"Lady, my neck's out a mile."

"Please!"

"A few minutes?"

"I promise." She scribbled his name and phone number and dialed Ivan Stein at home. *Please answer,* she prayed as the phone rang over and over. *Please. Answer answer answer! I'll lose my son if you don't answer. ANSWER, YOU DAMN HIP-PIE, ANSWER ME THIS SECOND . . . !*

"This is Van."

"Mr. Stein? This is Lael—uh, Mrs. Pritcher."

"Lael! Hey, sorry. I was watering the goats. Hold on a sec." *Watering the goats?* "Hey!" His voice came back. "Don't tell me they found the truck?"

"In Port Angeles."

"You're kidding!"

"No. They just called me."

"All . . . *right!*" He said it like a high school cheer.

She told him what she knew, and he said, "What a piece of dumb luck! Hey, you're gonna have to go out there—"

"I know, I know. But I'm afraid they'll get away." She felt a squeeze at her waist and saw that she was twisted in the phone wire. Quickly she spun the other way, as though in great danger. Everything was so frightening now.

"Hang up and wait right there," he said. "Don't leave! I'll get right back."

She dialed her twenty-year-old sister in Nisbet. Julie would still be up studying; she majored in pharmacology at the University of Washington and worked parttime at the herb farm. "I'll be right over," her sister said. "Don't waste time explaining." Exactly the response Lael had anticipated.

She was just buttoning the last button on her most conservative suit when the phone rang. "Relax," the lawyer said. "We get a hearing at ten o'clock in the morning. Clallam County Courthouse, Port Angeles. Don't forget to bring your separation agreement."

"What—what happened?"

"The schmuck got stopped for speeding. The cops ran the license number and got a hit on the truck. I love it!"

"I, uh—*huh?*" He talked so fast.

"The car theft won't stick, but who cares? I called a lawyer out there and he woke the judge at home and we scored a quick hearing on the kid. Courts always jump when there's a minor involved. Hey, meet you there in the morning."

"I'm going now," she said.

"Got a place to crash?"

"In the car if I have to."

"Drive slow," he said. "The kid's not going anywhere till we get there."

"I hope to God you're right."

7

LAEL YANKED THE wheel to avoid a black-tailed deer meandering along Highway 101. Her sister Julie, riding as co-pilot and best friend and backup emotional support, gasped but said nothing. Out on the strait the moonlight lay in luminous slicks. A large bug flashed in and out of the headlights like a spark.

Lael made a U-turn in front of the red-brick courthouse building and parked the little yellow Escort with one wheel over the curb. She took the wide stone staircase three steps at a time and shoved through the heavy glass doors. In the fluorescent-lighted sheriff's office her eyes darted about till she saw Ace lying on a cot alongside a desk, an old gray blanket pulled up to his neck.

She fell to her knees beside him. His breathing was deep, rhythmical. She looked for signs that he had been crying but found only pale, undisturbed skin around his eyes. She resisted an urge to lift all forty-one pounds of him, to crunch him in her arms and spin him around and hold him high above her in the light, but she reminded herself that he needed rest. Ace, oh, my baby....

She tried to blink her eyes dry. Honeybug, she said under her breath, what did they put you through? She knew she must look like the smothering mama that Catherine Pritcher had always decried, but she couldn't keep her shoulders from trembling. A middle-aged deputy patted her back with a hammy red hand and said, "You're his mom?"

"Yes."

"Somebody owes us two bucks for pop." She looked up. He displayed a lopsided grin, as though expecting a smile in return. She gave it a try but felt too intimidated, out of place. The office smelled of guns and leather and fresh-pressed pants: a man's world. Ruby-colored lights scanned a dial; a computer screen glowed as pale green letters rose to the surface and drowned. Down a long hallway she could see a barred door. Was that where they were holding Mike? He would never forgive her. A scratchy voice recited some numbers over the radio, and another said, "*Received.*" Coptalk. She felt like a poseur, an intruder. She had to collect her son and run before they found out.

His possessions lay on a chair that had been pushed against the cot: his black-rimmed glasses, a half-eaten Kit Kat bar, a small bone, a dirty handkerchief, three nickels, two balloons, and a package of fruit-flavored Chewels. "What happens next?" she asked.

"He's your boy, isn't he? Sign this paper and drive on home."

A wall clock jumped one tick to 2:08. "My lawyer said something about a hearing in the morning?"

"Mr. Pritcher's parked in back, waiting to switch cars with you. He waived the hearing. The boy's all yours."

"The rotten thing knew he couldn't win," Juliet muttered. Lael had forgotten she was there. She held a finger to her lips. This was no time to antagonize the male power elite.

"Will I be needing this?" she asked, sliding the separation agreement across the counter top.

The deputy squinted at the first page and handed the crackling paper back. "No, ma'am. It's all settled. Nolo contendere."

She left her sister to watch over Ace and went with the deputy to move the Escort. She drove it around the building and pulled up next to the familiar shape of her black Luv, parked in a spot marked "Commissioner."

Her husband's shock of black hair pushed through the open window of the truck. He blinked and stared as though he had never seen her before. Her first impulse was to scream "Why?" at him a few dozen times and then kick him in the shins. She wondered why he had waited in the truck instead of taking a motel room for the night. Was it to be near Ace till the last possible second? To sort of watch over their son? Probably. How much simpler it would be just to hate him.

Without a word he untied a tarpaulin from the sides of the Luv and lowered the tailgate. Out on the bay a ship's bell clanged dully. The unexpected sound and the strangeness of the setting gave her the impression that she was dreaming. When she awoke, would Ace be gone again? She wished Mike would hurry.

He slid his typewriter, a tackle box, and two suitcases out of the truck bed and arranged them in the back of the Escort. There were still more shapes in the truck. She stepped closer in the shadows and saw six or eight sealed cardboard boxes, some fishing rods, Ace's good shoes. They had planned a long trip. Where? At the bottom of the hill a morning ferry would leave for Canada; they'd often taken it as a family. Why else would he have brought Ace to Port Angeles? She shivered when she realized how close he'd come to getting out of the country.

He stacked the rest of the load on the walkway. "I'll pick this stuff up in a while," he told the deputy. He stepped into the light from the courthouse window. "Sorry for the inconvenience." Lael recognized his tone and his look, part shame, part anger—his wounded-animal role. Oh, Lord, she said to herself, what kind of man would he be if he didn't despise himself? Then she realized that he was talking to her.

"Excuse me?" she said.

His voice was low: "... upset ... couldn't think ... Hope you understand."

She would have preferred his customary sullen silence or even an attack. He was always throwing her off-balance; it was one of the reasons she couldn't live with him. "You don't have to explain," she whispered.

The light caught his twisted face, and she could have cried for him. Now *he* was losing a son; she knew what that did to the pit of the stomach. As he drove off, she hated herself for being so soft, hated herself for the bovine forgiveness she granted so freely. He *was* sorry; she knew that. He was genuinely sorry; he was sincerely, truly, emphatically, grandiosely, lachrymosely sorry. He always was. She remembered all the 3:00 A.M. scenes when she would wake up to find him on his knees alongside the bed, being sorry. And she had always forgiven. Can a marriage succeed with the wife as confessor? She knew the answer to that one.

She followed the deputy into the office. Ace sat next to Juliet on the cot, rubbing his brown eyes with his knuckles. "Hi, Mom," he said as though they were meeting at the Streamliner Diner for lunch. "Me and my dad rided out here." When she rounded the counter, he ran three or four steps on wobbly legs and hugged her so hard his nails dug into the small of her back.

"You okay, Mr. Guacamole?" she asked.

"'Kay, Mom."

"My baby." She bit her lip and held him tight.

*   *   *

Juliet was at the wheel, driving home through the thin night-haze. Ace slept in the middle, huddled against his mother. Passing through Sequim, Julie said something softly.

"What?" Lael asked.

"I said, 'Why do you let him walk all over you?'"

"I don't," she said, and wondered if she did. Yes, of course she did. But old habits were hard to break, and she had been the obedient wife for eight years. Would it take another eight years to get rid of the reflex?

"I mean, what does it take to make you mad?" Julie was asking.

"Hmm?"

"Oh, never mind!" Her sister was never at her best without sleep.

By the time the Luv reached the Hood Canal, a climbing chrome sun had reduced the haze to wisps and patches. Down on the water, Lael saw a flash and a splash. A gull arrived to clean up the remains. Ace raised his head at Lofall and made a sleepy announcement: "You know what?"

Both sisters answered, "No, what?"

"I can spell policeman. Want me to show you?"

"Yes," Lael said.

"C-O-P." He snorted lightly and let his head drop back in her lap. "The man teached me." A few minutes later he was sleeping again.

My son, she thought, my baby boy. My trickster, my punster, my songster, my angel. . . .

My Ace.

8

WHEN SHE ENTERED the office, Ivan Stein was slouched behind his desk in a "No Oil Pipeline" T-shirt. It made him look like a food stamp applicant, but on the whole she preferred it to other shirts she'd read this summer. "Nuke the Whales," for example, and "Anybody That Don't Skydive Ain't Worth Shit." What next? One of her classmates from Mount Holyoke was working in San Francisco copyreading T-shirts. The world was becoming unrecognizable.

"I won't lie to you," Stein said. "We almost lost the kid."

"I know," she said, squeezing a balled-up handkerchief. "I could tell." She wanted to lash out at somebody for not warning her in time, but she also wanted to be fair. Who on earth could have predicted Mike's action? She remembered how nervous he'd sounded on the phone. She should have sensed something was up. A typical impulse, to steal his son and run. He'd had wild ideas like that every second week of their marriage. Schools of silver salmon would show up in the ocean, and he would dash out of the house. "Gotta go!" he would say, and be gone for days. A man at the mercy of his whims. A *family* at the mercy of his whims.

"I'll push the divorce," the lawyer was saying as he rearranged the venetian blind to lift the light from her face. He seemed calmer than usual, less harassed. "Then you'll have some legal papers that'll mean something."

"What'll they mean?" She caught the faint cynicism in her voice and regretted it, but never again would she take legal documents at face value. Her separation agreement had turned out to be worthless.

"Once you get permanent custody, he can't lay a finger on the kid. If he does, we can bring in state cops, local cops, FBI, everybody but the Hundred and First Airborne. This time we were just lucky."

Oh, Lord, yes, she said to herself. Lucky and reckless and stupid. I could be sitting in a cell right now, charged with filing a false report, listening to the ship's bells in the harbor at Port

32

Angeles. She remembered how he had instructed her to lie to the police. It was hard to fault a plan that had brought back her son, but neither could she put much faith in a lawyer who flouted the law. And forgot court dates. If he'd shown up on the day the case was called, she'd have won permanent custody of Ace a long time ago, and Mike would have thought twice about defying the courts.

She recalled her first visit to the storefront law office months ago and how bored Stein had seemed—yawning, nodding, tapping his teeth with a pencil, and turning to stare out the window while she'd spun out the painful tale of her failed marriage. It had been like talking to a wall. Just another island bitch shedding a husband, that was how he'd made her feel. Julie had said later, "He can't relate to you, Lael. He's not that kind of lawyer. You're not a cause."

Cause or not, she needed hard answers right now. "If Mike tries this again, could he be charged with kidnapping? I mean after the divorce goes through?"

He peered at her over the top of his wire glasses. "Nothing that heavy. Custodial interference or maybe contempt—something like that."

"And he'd go to jail?"

"Maybe. Maybe not. But for sure you'd get the kid back."

"Right away? From any place? From *any* state?" She was going to cover the possibilities if it took the rest of the afternoon. Three other clients waited on the old couch. If there was a dress code, she was the only one violating it. She hoped she didn't look pompous, but she certainly looked out of place in her plum cardigan jacket and shirred cream skirt. Next time she'd wear her grubbies. Protective coloration.

"Federal law says states are supposed to honor each other's custody orders," Stein said, "but there's always a way to stall. Possession is still the main thing."

"The laws make no sense."

He smiled and touched his ponytail in a curiously feminine gesture. She noticed that it was held by a beaded Indian circlet. She still found it hard to believe that she was represented by a lawyer with a ponytail. Aesthetically it didn't bother her— it hung neat and clean and copper red down his back—but it just didn't seem a responsible hairdo. At least once in a while he must have to appear before conservative old judges who would be prejudiced against a freak lawyer. The ponytail seemed too defiant, too glaringly self-indulgent. She thought of the difficulties she'd had with self-indulgent men.

"So you figured out that the law sucks, eh?" he was saying, the trace of a smile on his face. "Aren't you gonna quote Mr. Bumble?"

"Is he the one that said—?"

"'The law is a ass, a idiot.' *Oliver Twist*. A lawyer hears that his first day in law school and twice a day for the rest of his life. Not that it isn't true."

At least they agreed on something. She leaned forward on the wooden chair. "Tell me exactly what to do next."

"Don't let the kid out of your sight till we get permanent custody. Your husband's shown his hand. Knows he's gonna lose the kid at the divorce hearing, so he's trying to snatch him ahead of time. Personally I think he's short a few buttons, but that doesn't help us right now. Where is he, by the way?" She shrugged. "No relatives around?"

"His mother lives in Mansfield, right across the bridge," she said. "I phoned her. She said, 'Do you realize Michael could have gone to jail?' Then she hung up."

"Order a butterfly net. For two." He ran a hand through his red curls and disarranged them a little more. "Okay, just remember, protect the kid at all costs."

She sighed. "Do me one favor, will you?"

"Sure."

"Don't call him the kid. That's his father's expression. Call him Ace if you want to. Anything but the kid. Nothing personal." She hoped she didn't sound rude.

"Oh. Uh, sure. No problem." He looked at her through narrowed eyes. "Now do *me* a favor, will you? My last name's for court. Call me Van."

She tried to smile politely. "Why not Ivan?"

"My mom's the only one ever called me that. She was crazy about Tchaikovsky."

"His first name was Peter, wasn't it?"

"Mom thought it was Ivan." She waited for a more detailed explanation, but none was forthcoming. So he'd been misnamed after a Russian composer. Spacy mother, spacy son.

He beckoned to a pregnant woman on the couch and stood up, as though Lael's interview were ended. "If you send the kid— if you send *Ace* to school, make sure he's in good hands. People you trust." She tilted her head up to see his expression. It was somber. "There's plenty of cases where kids were grabbed off the school steps. Or out of their own yards. Till the divorce you're vulnerable."

"I've got no legal rights till then?"

"You've got Ace. Hang onto him."

She saw the days stretching endlessly ahead. Living in a state of siege. Wondering who was behind the next bush. Jumping at sounds. Sleepless nights. How could she run the herb farm? Maybe they'd have to hide out somewhere, at least till the divorce came through. Where could they go? "What a prospect," she said, mostly to herself.

The lawyer twisted his gently downturned nose to one side and sniffed. "I'm not worried," he said. He took her by the arm and led her politely to the door. "Not to rush you," he apologized.

No, no, go right ahead, she thought. Ease me out so you can work on your causes. What is it this time, Aid for Mauritanian Refugees? I'm glad you're not worried about my case; the rest of us are worried sick.

A small-boned Oriental boy walked in as she walked out. He smiled politely at her and then reverted to a worried frown that seemed to fit his face. He was carrying an armload of schoolbooks and a sack that gave off the odor of deep-fried fish. Just before she shut the door, she heard him say, "Hi, Dad, here's lunch."

9

A WEEK AFTER the trip to Port Angeles the sisters sat in Lael's warm kitchen, blinking their identically warm brown eyes against the sunlight that dappled the copper pots and the braided stalk of red peppers and the silken strands of asparagus fern. "I can't believe it's Mike," Lael said.

"But it is!" Juliet insisted. "Who else would hang up without talking? Who else needs to know if you're home alone?"

"A breather?"

"Does he breathe at you?"

Larry Allen jumped on her shoulder and made his food-begging purr as she tried to recall. "No. He doesn't do anything *at* me. The phone rings and I pick it up and there's no one there. What would you do, Doc?" Now that Julie was closing in on her pharmacology degree, the family had renamed her.

"How many calls have you had?"

"Let's see. Uh, three. All in the early afternoon."

"Me, I'd call the sheriff."

"Look what that got me the first time."

"This is different."

"I hate to bother them." Lael got up and pulled a sick leaf from the jade plant and straightened the sampler on the wall. "Herbs," it read. "The friend of physicians and the praise of cooks." Words by Charlemagne, needlework by Maude Estes, her mother.

"You always put yourself last," Julie said. "Sometimes that's nice. Sometimes it's asinine."

"Drop the subject, will you, Jules?" She threaded her fingers through her blond hair and pulled till her scalp hurt.

"Mike has a score to settle. If you give him an opening—"

"Does it look like I'm giving him an opening? Ace is either here with me or at school with sixteen kids and two teachers. He's never alone." Enough, Sis, she was thinking. *Enough.*

"He won't give up."

"He's not within *miles,* Doc. He moved. Nobody's seen him." She wondered where he could be. She did *not* miss him. Definitely not. But she wished she could pin him down.

She watched Julie dab thick pats of butter on a piece of

36

homemade raisin bread and resisted the temptation to nag. When her sister watched her diet, she had a nicely rounded Bavarian milkmaid's figure, but every extra calorie traveled south. Lael marveled at the differences between them. She herself could eat the entire smorgasbord at Inge's and not gain an ounce. The fashionable word was *slender*, but she had to admit that *skinny* fit her better. She was nearly five feet nine and had never been able to get her weight above 115. She looked forward to the time when her metabolism would slow and she could enjoy the luxury of a weight problem. "How's my nephew holding up?" Julie asked, munching.

"Ace? You mean his asthma?"

"His . . . adjustment."

"Oh, that. Nothing's changed. He asks me, 'When's Dad coming? Why do I have to run inside if I see his car?' I try to explain, but he doesn't want to hear about it. He loves his dad."

"They're bound to be close," Juliet said. "They're the same mental age."

Lael topped their mugs with steaming boneset tea and held her tongue. Cracking wise about Mike seemed as pointless as cursing the wind. Past offenses had become irrelevant. She had a business to run and a child to protect and no energy left for reviewing Mike's past sins. Maybe she'd committed a few herself. What difference did it make now?

Julie refused to be silenced by her silence. "How can you be so—so indifferent? Everybody knows how he treated you."

No, they don't, Lael thought. And never will. She had been brought up to keep her troubles to herself. "Let's bag the subject," she said, rubbing her tired eyes. She hadn't slept much: night noises again. "We're repeating ourselves."

Julie looked apologetic. "I didn't mean to—"

"Look, Doc," Lael said, touching her sister's arm, "the divorce is in the process. What more can I do? Don't ask me to hate the man. He's my son's father. He's high-strung, disturbed. I know his faults better than anybody. He's touchy; he can't take criticism; he thinks the world's out to get him. But he's had a lot of bad breaks, too, and Ace loves him. Every child needs. . . ." She let her voice fall away, uncertain what Alexander Charles Estes Pritcher needed that his father could provide.

"A role model?" Juliet asked slyly.

"Oh, Julie, *shush!*"

10

LAEL SAT AT the roll-top desk in her living room, working on withholding tax forms while Larry Allen tried to lick her bare toes with his No. 3 sandpaper tongue. Two of the part-time employees of her Salt-Water Herb Farm were schoolboys on minimum wage, and the third was Julie at $4.40 an hour; but the tax forms were as complex as though they were oil barons.

In the nearly total silence of the old house she heard waves slapping against the weathered dock that Mike had rebuilt. The familiar sound gave her a twinge of fear, and she found herself thinking about a subject she had vowed to avoid.

So much darkness out there.... So many places to hide.... Will he come by land or sea this time? Will he try to trick me again or turn to force? Damn Julie for reminding me!

The ultimate upsetting thought made her clutch her throat: *Will he get away with it this time?*

And a few seconds later: *Could I go on if he did?*

She rammed the deskchair backward and tried to imagine her creaky house without Mr. Guacamole running and yelling and tracking his footprints through it. The plants would die. The wallpaper would peel. The place would go as flat as a pricked balloon.

She wondered how people held themselves together after personal tragedies. EIGHT BURNED TO DEATH IN FIRE...MURDERER KILLS PARENTS...FOUR DEAD IN HEAD-ON CRASH. But those were headlines, abstractions. They were about other people, therefore unreal. The loss of Ace would be so tangible she could already feel it in a spasm in her stomach and a quiver in her hand. He was five years old and spoke very peculiar English, but he was her life.

She slumped in the thin ladder-back chair while Larry Allen looked up and purred expectantly. Even without disquieting reminders from her sister, she'd found herself waking four or five times every night in a wet-pack of twisted sheets. It wasn't like her to worry so fervently. That had been one of Mike's habits: obsessive brooding, endless premonitions of disaster. How many more of his characteristics had rubbed off on her?

His pessimism had squeezed the joy from their lives. A slow form of suicide. Or murder.

She switched off the print-out calculator and pushed the chair under the desk, put the reluctant cat out, checked Ace's breathing once more, and went to bed. Around midnight she awoke with Van Stein's warning tumbling through her head like a Moussorgsky dirge: "Don't relax . . . not for a second. . . ."

The wind hummed and soughed, preening the garden, snapping branches, rattling the shake shingles like a magician with a deck of cards. She went back to sleep by sheer force of will and didn't know what time it was when something made her sit straight up and listen. The wind again. She slid under the warm sheet and pressed the pillow around her ears, but blowing fragments tapped at her bedroom window like fingernails.

There! That sound was different from the others, more like a footfall, stopping and starting, shuffling, sliding. She cleared the tangled hair from her eyes and combed it with her fingernails, thinking: I'd better look good if company's coming. She tilted her head and listened hard.

Maybe it was raccoons. Last fall they had visited her porch every night, but the patter of their feet had been more like raindrops, not like this *sneaky* noise. She remembered Julie's warning: "He'll be back, Lael." Oh, God, don't let it be Mike. Let it be a robber, a rapist. Let it be *anybody* but Mike.

She glided through the dark hall on the balls of her bare feet, avoiding squeaky boards. Ace's breathing was normal. He had kicked off his Daffy Duck cotton sheet; she straightened out one matchstick leg and tucked him in again. She turned and tiptoed back through the hall and across the fading Oriental rug in the living room toward the porch that enclosed three sides of the house.

She found the big front door locked but the screen door open. Had she left it like that? Probably. There were so many security measures; it was hard to remember each one. Hard, but *necessary*. She'd have to do better.

She jerked her gray velour housecoat across her bare thighs— in those last tense months with Mike she'd had to relearn the reflexes of modesty. When would she stop reacting as though he were still around? *Ever?* She had a separation agreement, an alarm system, a faithful watchcat, a pondful of chorusing frogs that went silent when anything approached the house. All she lacked were a moat and a detachment of marines. And still she slept in instalments and sat up at the slightest sound. She couldn't understand her own reactions. As far as she knew, Mike hadn't been near the house, hadn't been near the island, since the abduction. Surely he wouldn't try anything like that again.

She walked out on the open porch and cocked her head. A sound like chalk against a blackboard made her whirl. It was those same loose floorboards rubbing together, reminders of the cottage's driftwood origins. She used to hear that peculiar squeak whenever Mike tried to come in late without waking her. It was one more alarm system.

The wind nipped at the dormers. She instructed herself to stand fast. This was her house; she knew every inch. Let intruders be afraid. She separated the night sounds like strands in a skein. An air horn brayed from the Coast Guard station at North Point, four miles away. In the near woods a pair of owls exchanged calls, finishing in faint ascending hoots that trailed away in the upper reaches of the swaying firs and cedars. Was it mating time again? Mike would know. It was the sort of information that he accumulated: interesting, sometimes even fascinating, but of no commercial value. Like his drawings and designs, browning at the corners next to the stacks of *Architectural Digest* in the attic.

The torn canvas on their light-footed San Juan sloop flapped and snapped at its sagging dock. Wind or not, Mike would have stomped onto the sea-slickened boards in his clogs, raging about the goddamn weather, and checked the boat from bow to stern. He valued his possessions above all else.

She stepped back inside and eased the front door shut. She marveled at the familiar *poof* as the heavy slab sealed. This house that had been built almost a hundred years ago still breathed like a human.

She had just returned to tepid sheets when she heard a thump from Ace's room.

The wind in his shutters? Once she could have made that assumption, but no more. She rushed naked to his room. He hadn't moved. In the glow of a night light his round face gleamed with innocence. With each breath a wisp of fine black hair rose and fell on one cheek. Oh, baby, she thought, why can't you always be so sweet, so manageable? In a few short hours he would race through the hall and perform his customary grand jeté from the end of her bed to her stomach. Then he would resume his infinite supply of unanswerable questions:

Is there real butter in butterflies? But there MUST be. Then it's a damn lie to call them butterflies. Why can't I say damn? Mike says it. . . .

She lifted a few loose hairs from his mouth, lowered her ear gently to his chest, and heard a slight wheezing, not enough to matter. The doctor said he was showing signs of outgrowing his asthma. Hang in, Acey! She brushed his pale cheek with her lips. Then she heard the thump again. It seemed to come from his window.

She peered through the glass into the night. As she watched, one side of the outer shutters began to fold open. She waited for it to catch the wind like a loose sail and slam against the wall, but the dark green shutter stopped abruptly, as though restrained by a hand.

She leaned forward till the tip of her nose almost touched the cool glass.

A woman's face stared back.

She lost her balance and squatted hard on the vinyl floor. She crawled to the edge of her son's bed and took a deep breath. The gun, she thought. I've got to get the gun. Mike's .38 Chief's Special was still in the bottom of her locked dresser drawer. She'd sworn never to lay a hand on it.

She stood up and took a few steps and stopped in her tracks. She clenched her fists and told herself for God's sake to stop jumping at shadows. Of *course* she'd seen a woman. The window was made of glass, wasn't it? What a ridiculous reaction.

It was bad for the child, all this jumpiness and worrying and panicking about nothing. Why, she'd been ready to unlock the gun! And do what—shoot down her own reflection? Griping at herself, she slid the window open and locked the loose shutter.

Behind her a small voice chirped, *"Run!"* Ace must be dreaming about monsters again. What could she do to make him more secure? She nudged him awake to disconnect the dream and smoothed his black hair. "Night, dad," he mumbled.

She waited till his chest rose and fell evenly under the Superman pajama top and then returned to her bedroom. As she punched her pillow into shape, she swore a solemn oath that she wouldn't get out of bed again unless she smelled smoke and saw flames. It was after two. She instructed herself to be asleep in minutes—five at the most. Up in the filigreed eaves the wind howled like an animal in pain. She gave the clock a final look and pressed her eyelids closed.

11

"I WHISTLED. Hey, Mom, I whistled!"

She heard the news, but she was too tired to open her eyes.

"Mom, listen!" Sound filtered through the pillows that covered her head. *Fttt fttt fttt*—it came to her ears like a teakettle leaking steam. She lifted a pillow and opened one eye. Daylight. Larry Allen, the cat, was licking his paw on the night table. A small vertical primate stood by her bed. His tiny lips were puckered and his forehead creased in concentration. A line of crumbs ran down the front of his pajamas. Each night, before she went to bed, she laid out a gourmet's snack to greet him in the morning: a couple of bran crackers, a rose-hip wafer, and two chewable vitamin tablets in the shape of the Flintstones. Apparently he had popped his pills already.

She pulled the sheet over her head. Maybe the black-haired tyrant would turn benevolent and allow her another thirty or forty seconds of sleep. "Time's it?" she muttered.

"Seven-one-five," he read off the digital clock. Seven-one-five was past time to get up. She shut her eyes for a few seconds, and when she opened them, he was gone.

She reached back over her head and banged the wall three times with her fist, their secret signal. She nodded with relief when she heard him clomping in from the kitchen. "Say the password!" he called out.

Who could say that password on an empty stomach?

"Say it, Mom! Come *on,* Mom! I can't talk to you if you don't say the password." He sounded upset. You never knew what was crucial to them.

"Okay, *okay.* 'Rotten rabbit guts.'"

"Rotten rabbit guts," he echoed, and ran toward her bed.

"Stop!" she said. She didn't feel like being jumped on this morning.

For once he obeyed. He pulled up and repeated the news of his latest triumph. "I can whistle! Listen, Mom!" His cheeks puffed out and his face reddened. *Fttt fttt fttt.*

She said, "You *whistled!*" and pulled him down.

42

"No kissing," he squealed. "Hey, Mom, I didn't whistle to be kissed!"

"I had a wooden whistle," she said, letting him go, "but it wooden whistle."

He laughed, showing his straight white teeth. "Hey, Mom, that's funny."

Yes, she thought, and highly original, too. She wondered what would happen when the old lines didn't break him up any more. For now, any joke would do. "Why does a downy-breasted merganser swim the canal?" she asked.

"Aw, Mom, you told me that a hundred dozen times."

Oh. Sophistication has set in. Terrible disease. "Well, uh, do you know what bus crosses the ocean?"

"Colum-bus."

"You heard that one, huh?"

"From you."

"No! When?"

"Today before yesterday."

"You mean *the* day before yesterday."

"Right." He walked across the room and stood in front of the mirror, *ffttt*ing at his reflection. "Hey, Mom?" he said. "Know what?"

"No, what?"

"I learned a rhyme in school."

She pulled on the sloppy wool socks that served as slippers. "That's nice, Acey. Who taught you? Susan?"

"Big Jeremy."

"Which one is Big Jeremy?" She could never keep them straight.

"The one that's five going on six. Little Jeremy's four going on five. C'mon, Mom, you know that."

She sat corrected. "Well, come on, say it."

"Say what?" He had probably forgotten already. The TV programmers were right: A five-year-old's attention span could be measured in seconds.

"The new rhyme."

He recited in singsong rhythm:

> As I was going to Saint Ives,
> I met a man with seven wives.
> Uh, every wife had seven sacks.
> Uh, every sack had seven ducks.
> The husband didn't give a fuck.

Without changing her expression, she looked at his face. It was as guileless as ever. The infamous F word was just a sound to him. She told herself to stay calm. It had to start sometime. Dear God, a chaplain's grandson. Entrusted to her care. If he ever uttered a word like that in front of her parents, all the saints and angels would converge on the house like bees. So far she'd been lucky. The worst he'd ever said in front of them was "cow pie," and her mother hadn't known what it meant. "Uh, Ace?"

"Yeah, Mom?"

"Uh, that one word, uh—that's not a word for nice boys. I mean, that's a kind of a—you know—a *naughty* word." Who was the embarrassed kid here? *"Ummm,* maybe you shouldn't say it anymore." The power of gentle suggestion. So much more effective than rude commands or orders.

"You mean 'fuck'? What's it supposed to mean anyway?"

"Baby, *please.* I told you not to say it."

"Why?"

"Because it's . . . vulgar."

She wished she could start the conversation over. It was important not to inhibit his word-gathering powers, prodigious at the moment, and it was important not to make him feel guilty and dirty, but it was also important to steer him away from words that could get him into social trouble.

Ace looked up at her, his face clouded over. Lately it had been easy to upset him. "I said sumpin dirty, huh, Mom?"

"Heavens, no! What gave you that idea?"

"Susan putted Big Jeremy in the corner when he said it."

"Well, I'm not putting *you* in the corner, Mr. Guacamole. No sirree. I love you toooooooo much! I'm gonna grab you and tickle you silly!" Another of their rituals. He pretended to pull away while she played his conspicuous rib cage like a xylophone. He leaped back and she caught him and they rolled over and over till they fell from the bed in a giggling heap and made Larry Allen scoot away with a bushed-out tail.

Over poached eggs and oranges and wheat toast served on plastic dishes embossed with bas-reliefs of Oscar the Grouch, he asked, "Mom, when can I have my dad back?" Another tough question. He asked it often, and usually in an admonitory tone, as though she were withholding his father like a toy or a treat.

The truthful answer was "I don't know," but she didn't want to sound so hopelessly uninformed. She still hadn't heard from

Mike—not since the scene in Port Angeles two weeks earlier. He could be in Hong Kong or Tierra del Fuego by now, or a few houses away on the island. He didn't operate on logic, and his actions couldn't be anticipated. She had learned that much in eight years.

What could she tell Ace? The poor kid missed Mike as a playmate, not as a father. If only the unpredictable father hadn't also been an unpredictable husband, she thought, we might still be together. She wondered when she would feel ready to explain the situation to Ace. Ever? Who could describe the acid rains of love?

She ate quickly, but not as quickly as her son. He was straddling a chair in front of the TV and watching a frog-on-the-street interview with the big bad wolf when she finished. "Time to get dressed," she said. "Your ride'll be here."

It took fifteen minutes to prepare him for the car pool. A family of mallard ducks waddled away when mother and son walked out on the porch. "I wish she'd hurry," he said, his head pressed against her thigh.

"What brought on the change? Last week you wanted to stay home and watch quiz shows."

"The man's gonna be there today."

"Not that magician again?" An amateur performer had appeared before the class and inspired Ace to spend two weeks trying to turn water into wine and wine into water, spattering the kitchen walls. Surely that troublemaker wasn't due back so soon.

"The man with the pointy hat and the big nose," the child said. She stabbed at the last buttonhole on his sweater, a moving target as always. "He hides. But we can see him. Then he runs away."

He had her full attention. "Runs . . . away?"

"Yeah."

"When?"

"Lots of days."

She held him by both shoulders and stared hard at his eyes. "Where does the man hide?"

"In the woods behind the school."

Oh, God. . . .

12

Susan, the teacher, was trying to put down a tag-team wrestling match when Lael led Ace into the Humpty Dumpty Play School. She had waved off the car pool driver and questioned the child for ten or fifteen minutes, getting nowhere, and then decided to take him to school herself. If someone was lurking in the woods, she didn't want him out of her sight for a second, especially since she had a good idea who the someone might be.

"Don't get physical!" Susan shouted. "Noah, let go of Josh's hair."

"He fighted on me first!" Noah said, his yellow curls bouncing. "My daddy said—"

"I'm in charge here, Noah, not your daddy."

All those Bible names, Lael thought. They should call it the Humpty Dumpty Divinity School. It always jarred her to hear the teacher say things like "Rebecca, you and Jonathan stop teasing Luke and go play with Isaiah!"

Ace went off to join his friends, and Lael glanced at late items on the bulletin board: "East Island car pool group has a dropout. Call Rhonda." Somebody must have got sick of waiting ten minutes every morning for the McCollum kid. "Creative dance class: Students will experience rhythm through body movement, acting out songs, and rhythm activities." Translation: The kids will shuffle around while the teacher bangs the piano and looks at her watch.

She took a seat on the inside steps and watched Susan turn from the wrestlers to a scene of interplanetary war: David Cohn was poking Kyle Angstrom with a plastic laser sword, and Kyle was defending himself with a papier-mâché globe. Ace had dropped from sight. Now where *was* he?

She went downstairs and checked the playroom. It was empty. A familiar fear took her by the throat. How long would she react like this? Till he went to grammar school? *College?* She had seen him a few minutes ago. He had to be there. But where?

46

She hurried upstairs and heard his voice: "Tim is sad. The fat pig is bad. Tim ran and ran." Cross-legged atop the masonite table, as highly visible as the Great Pyramid of Cheops, he was absorbed in *Primary Phonics: The Tin Man*. How had she missed him? Maybe the magician is back, she thought, making little boys disappear. Then she thought: That's *not* funny!

Susan Sievertson, her auburn hair already rumpled fifteen minutes into the school day, came over. She was an energetic woman, barely five feet tall, with a yell leader's voice and manner. "Hey, what's up? You sounded scared on the phone."

"I feel a little better now," Lael said. The two women walked to the church office, where Susan sat behind the desk and Lael on the couch. There was a smell of furniture oil and piety in the air.

"Listen, we all know what you went through," the teacher said. "What's this about a prowler?"

"Ace says a man's been hanging around the school."

Susan frowned. *"Here?"* She repeated the word two or three times, her voice picking up volume.

"Outside. During fresh-air time, I guess."

"Jesus, Lael, what next? Jerry and I moved to this island because we thought it was safe. Now I don't know."

"I worry that it's Mike again. I know it sounds crazy, but—"

"Wait right here."

A few minutes later the teacher came in with Ace on one hand and his constant companion, Big Jeremy, on the other. Jeremy was deliberately stubbing his salt-water sandals on the rag rug. Despite his nickname, he was small for his age, with enough wiry black hair to supply another boy of his age. The two of them looked like shampoo ads as they came into the office. "What'd I do?" Jeremy asked, frowning up at Susan. "Jake's the one said 'poop.'"

"Sit!" the teacher snapped. The boys sat on the couch on either side of Lael, eyeing each other warily.

"Ace just told me the two of you saw the man together, Jeremy," Susan said softly. "Is that true?"

"What man?" the boy asked.

"The man in the woods," Ace said, leaning across his mother's body toward the other boy. "The one that waved and runned away? Remember?"

Jeremy looked disgusted. "That was supposed to be a secret."

"A secret?" Susan asked.

The older child smiled knowingly. "We see that guy every day. He's—" He paused. "Why do you want to know?"

"Because it's very, *very* important," Susan said.

Jeremy nodded like someone who appreciated degrees of importance. "That's just Rumpelstilkins," he said.

"Rumpelstiltskin?" Susan said.

"Yeah. Rumpelstilkins. He spins his gold back in our woods. He gived us some."

Lael wondered if she had been taken in by her son's vivid imagination again. When would she learn? "Is that true, Ace?" she asked.

His liquid brown eyes turned toward the other boy, and both nodded.

"There's no *real* man out there?" Lael asked. Both boys nodded again solemnly.

"A strange man, eh?" Susan said, looking at the sagging ceiling. "Well, I guess you could call Rumpelstiltskin strange. With that funky hat and all." She rolled her eyes at Lael and patted her on the shoulder, and teacher and students returned to class.

Lael felt strangely unrelieved. Ace had seemed so definite about the way the man had beckoned and run. Of course, he could be just as definite about robbers and space pirates and monsters.

The difference, she said to herself, is that no space pirate ever tried to kidnap him. No, the difference is *me*. Old paranoid me. I'm turning a normal kid into a nervous wreck. Did I really think Mike was hanging around the Humpty Dumpty Play School waiting to strike again? How stupid! I've got to get it together before Ace weirds out like his mom.

She walked back to the classroom. The two boys were in conference in a corner. Susan and Ann Leopardi were showing little Cyndy Hogg how to tie a bowknot on a mock-up of a shoe. "One more favor and I'll go," Lael said to the teachers. "Who has the duty this afternoon?"

"Driving?" Susan said, looking up. "Ann again."

"Annie, do something for me," Lael said, turning to the pretty mother who helped out at the school. "This afternoon I'll be in Seattle buying herb starts, but my sister'll be at the house. I know it's silly, but make sure you hand Ace over to her, will you?"

"Don't worry, Lael, I already know—"

"I mean, take him right to the front door, okay? And make sure he gets inside?"

"We know the situation, Lael," Susan said gently.

"I'm sorry," she said. "Maybe I'll relax after tomorrow."

"What's tomorrow?"

"The divorce hearing. I'll get legal custody. At last." She didn't mention that the divorce should have gone through a long time ago; she might have been spared a lot of anxious days and nights if it had. Something to thank her space-case lawyer for. "Till then—well, I'll just be a pest, I guess."

"Not a pest," Ann Leopardi said, laying her hand on Lael's arm.

"What then?" Lael asked. "A—"

"A mother," the woman answered.

13

HER BUYING MISSION completed, Lael waited impatiently for the four-thirty ferry back across a lumpy Puget Sound to the island. Her little black truck was first in line; she'd missed the three-forty by seconds. She phoned her lawyer from the booth on the pier. For once there was good news. Mike had dropped the demand for permanent custody of Ace, and the divorce would go through in the morning. "Not that we ever had a thing to worry about," Stein said.

She thanked him politely and called home to inform her sister, who already knew. It was disheartening to learn that the Salt-Water Herb Farm was getting by without the presence of its chief executive officer: Julie was weeding the comfrey beds, Ace was on slug patrol, and the two young hired hands were turning compost and listening to The Who on their portable stereo with the six million watts.

Momentarily content, Lael climbed back in her parked truck, shut her eyes against the brightness of the water and the sky, and thought about her neatly arranged beds of herbs from anise to yarrow, smiling alphabetically at the sun. Hold on there, she told herself. Can plants smile? That's—what's the phrase?— the pathetic fallacy. So much for grammarians: *My plants smile!*

Maybe it was self-deception, but she believed that her herbs missed her almost as much as Ace, and she made it a habit to hurry home from her business trips. She believed in the secret life of plants and the nurturing caring touch, at least her own. Of course, five years of coolie labor hadn't hurt her plants. Hard work and a loving thumb, that was the secret of raising herbs—and never, *ever* raising your voice.

She knew her ideas were unscientific; Mike had told her often enough. He'd kidded her so much about her plants that she'd stopped talking about them, one more breakdown in their communication. She could hear his voice. "For God's sake, Lael, drop those scissors! I can't bear to hear the rosemary scream!" But she knew that the herbs responded to her. Like Ace.

Deep in reverie in the waiting line, she asked herself if she was on her way to becoming an eccentric, a little old lady in tennis shoes. At twenty-eight? It did seem early. Would Ace like an oddball for a mom? He hasn't complained yet. That little dickens! He's an oddball himself.

She closed her eyes and smiled. In less than an hour she would be home to give him a squeeze, always assuming that His Lordliness was in a mood to accept such familiarities. When she looked up from her thoughts, the incoming ferry was sliding into its slip. The big green and white boat didn't seem to move as much as expand, growing broader and taller until it shut off her view of the water and sun and enveloped her truck in its shadow.

She drove aboard at the head of the pack, imagining herself in a pace car leading a field of snarling racers to the starting line. She would cross everybody up by driving off the far end of the deck and the caravan would follow her, six fathoms deep, emitting clouds of bubbles. The cars would speed across the floor of the sound to the island, climb up the beach, shake themselves dry, and proceed to their destinations.

She decided she needed a nap. She'd been fantasizing too much lately. A loud blast signaled the ferry's intention to depart. A minute later it bobbed upright like a bathtub toy, shuddered its length and breadth, and inched ahead.

She slumped sideways to try to squeeze into four feet of front seat. Something in the mirror caught her eye, a figure climbing out of another black truck eight or ten rows back.

For a second she felt as though she were watching herself in Ace's bedroom window again. The woman had a slender build and wore a familiar outfit: jeans and a sweat shirt and a white snapbrim tennis hat like her own. She waited for a better look at the face, but the woman walked briskly toward the passageway and disappeared.

She tried to doze and couldn't. Too much on her mind. Why do I keep seeing myself? The other night in the window— well, that was just a reflection. But this? What's happened to good old steady Lael?

She yawned and stretched and stepped out on the car deck, breathing in the moist air as it rushed from bow to stern through the great hollow core of the ferry. Halfway back she realized she had been keeping her eyes open for the woman in the tennis hat. How silly! She walked by the woman's black truck. It was a Luv, but much newer than hers. The bed wasn't littered with

peat pots and dirt, the cab was immaculate, and the truck bore
dealer's tags. There must be hundreds of black Luvs around.
No big deal.

She climbed the double flight of metal stairs to the upper
deck, looked around the cafeteria, and decided it was calorie
day on the SS *Rick Anderson*. A barker must have stood on
the dock shouting, "All women over two hundred pounds half
fare!"

She got back to her truck in time for the ferry's landing
signal—a long and two shorts—and stared resolutely ahead.
A cluster of weathered pilings came in sight, legs dressed in
pantaloons of blue-gray mussels that showed only at low tide.
The dark water surged with foam and spray from the reversing
engines. Home again.

She couldn't resist one last peek in the mirror. White Hat
was back, but a burst of glare covered the other Luv's windshield. Enough, Lael, she told herself. The ferry crunched
sideways against the pilings and bumped to a stop.

She eased the Luv up the ramp and drove to the market in
Nisbet. The narrow aisles, the familiar smells, the bright
colors—all helped return her to reality. She waved at a checker
and exchanged greetings with a bagboy who once had pulled
weeds at her herb farm. The butcher called out, "Hi, Lael. Got
some nice organic chickens." She smiled and shook her head
and passed him by. Thank the Lord for this island, these friends.
They seemed to say: Lael Pritcher, you *belong*.

The store freezer was stocked with Häagen-Dazs chocolate
chip, Mike's favorite. She reached inside and pulled back her
hand. Who cared if it was Mike's favorite? She wondered how
long she would see the world in terms of Mike.

There was a supply of farm-fresh fertile eggs—a rare treat—
and she picked up a carton and thought how nice it would be
to make a thick nog for Ace's dessert tonight, help fatten up
those silly bony legs. Against all reason, she couldn't wait to
see her son, couldn't wait to reassure herself that he was safe.
Juliet was taking care of him. Good old reliable Doc. If Mike
ever showed his face, Julie'd take the ax to him, split him like
a piece of cordwood. Now what brought on *that* bloodcurdling
thought?

She came to a pyramid of honeydews, topped by one with
a cutout wedge—cool and green. That devilish produce man—
he arranged everything to make the dumb suggestible shopper
load up on items she didn't need. The dumb suggestible shopper
added a melon to her armload.

She was halfway to the milk counter when a sudden realization almost crumpled her knees. She stopped and looked wildly toward the door, the groceries unsteady in her hands.

The Luv, the woman, the hat....

What other reason could there be? Today was Mike's last chance.

She lurched toward the exit. The melon hit the floor with a splat. She slid the egg carton into a vegetable bin and ran outside to her truck.

She was in second gear before she cleared the parking lot. Speeding along the beach road, she peered at every oncoming car, but there was no sign of the other Luv. If she were right— God forbid, oh, please, God, *make it be a fantasy again!*— the other truck would probably escape by the back way, over the bridge to the west. Port Angeles again? No, they'd try someplace else this time....

She was halfway down her long driveway when she saw Juliet standing on the lawn with the two high school boys.

"Ace!" Lael said as she jumped from the truck. "Where—?"

"Lael, oh, *Lael,*" her sister said through fingers that covered her mouth. "Wasn't that you?"

14

THE MANTEL CLOCK tolled midnight, but Lael ignored the sound and its implications. She looked at her parents, huddled on a sofa in a corner of her living room like mourners exchanging the warmth of their bodies. Her father was still in his khakis with the tiny gold cross on the collar—he must have been on duty when Julie had called him at the base. His gray hair was raked back in a pompadour. Not that the senior chaplain at Bremerton followed White House fashion; he had combed his hair exactly the same for as long as anyone could remember.

The light from the driftwood lamp glinted in the circles of rhinestones at the ends of her mother's swept-wing glasses. She looked tired. Her fingers joined and rejoined as though she were working on another project: a shawl, a blanket for a new baby. She believed in busy hands, arthritic or not.

Juliet was sprawled on the floor like a tired teen, her head propped on one of the throw pillows from Guatemala. Her eyes were half-shut, but one foot kept wiggling. Father, mother and sister all seemed angled toward the phone. The last time it had rung, all three had lifted upward in one motion and just as quickly subsided, her father shaking his head a fraction of an inch as though to say, no, no, let Lael take it, Lael is the commanding officer of this ordeal. . . .

The deputy and the lawyer had come and gone. Now there was nothing to do but wait for word. An arrest. A sighting. Anything. She tried to remember the police interview, to recall if she'd been of any use. She'd still been in shock when the plain-clothes deputy had arrived: a rangy chain smoker with creased skin like parchment. She had answered his questions with the verve of someone just out of surgery.

". . . And then what did this woman do?"

"She, uh, she drove to my mailbox and stopped, the way I always do. At the head of the driveway? Then she—she reached through the truck window for the mail. Right, Julie?"

"Right."

The deputy had said, "But couldn't your son tell—?"

"It's fifty yards," Lael had answered.

"Something wrong with his eyesight?"

"No. I mean, yes. He wears glasses."

"Didn't he have them on?"

"Didn't he, Julie? Yes. He can see fine with his glasses."

"Why would he break away from your sister and run up the driveway to a stranger?"

Ivan Stein had broken in angrily, "Goddamn it, Sears, you've been over that three times!" She'd never seen him look so annoyed. "Look, the kid thought the woman was his mother. She was dressed like her, wore the same hat, drove the same truck, stopped at the mailbox the same way. That's premeditation, Sears. Did you call the FBI?"

The deputy had sniffed and looked sheepish.

"Well, call 'em, God damn it! This isn't a child snatch; this is a kidnapping!"

Kidnapping.

Lael remembered the lights fading from yellow to gray as the full weight of that awful word had sunk in, remembered her sister rubbing the backs of her hands and her mother laying a damp washrag across her forehead and her father kneeling alongside with his chaplain's look of concern.

She felt stronger now, hours later, but her family wouldn't leave. "Don't you think you should go to bed?" Ralph Estes asked. "It only takes one of us to answer the phone."

"I couldn't, Dad. Why don't you and Mom drive on back to Bremerton and—?"

"We'll leave soon enough," her mother said, smiling sweetly. "Do you think we could sleep?" No, you poor things, Lael said to herself. You suffered every time Julie or I scraped a knee or had our feelings hurt at school. And you loved Ace the same way. How you must be suffering now.

A silence settled on the room, broken only by the frog chorale outside. She walked to the front door and opened it slowly. Larry Allen slipped out through the first few inches of crack, and the frogs went silent as though on cue.

Sinuous ribbons of mist hung over the lawn. She stared into the darkness, not knowing what she was looking for. A miracle? Her son, skipping across the grass? "Hi, Mom, the lady taked me for a ride. . . ." She eased the heavy door shut and sat on her pine rocker, drawing up her legs. Maybe she should take Stein's advice and petition Saint Jude.

"That damned Mike," Julie said softly.

"Who, baby?" her mother asked over the top of her tea cup.

Juliet looked up as though surprised to be heard. "Just thinking out loud," she said.

"Where do you suppose he found the woman?" Lael asked.

"Mike's a good-looking man," her father said. "He could
talk women into things."

"But why steal Ace?" she asked, trying to keep her voice
down. "Dad, he could see Ace anytime he wanted. All he had
to do was call. You know what the divorce papers say? That
he can have Acey any weekend of the year plus two months
of his own choosing plus he can see him here at any time on
twelve hours' notice. *Twelve hours' notice at any time!* I never
tried to cut him off. Ace *loves* him. They need each other."

"It's hate we're dealing with here," her sister said.

"Hate and love are close," her father mused, the chaplain
now, the professional. "You can't always tell where one leaves
off and the other begins."

"He has no reason to hate me!" Lael said, ashamed at the
way she spat the words but unable to control herself. She
wondered if she had spoken the truth. They'd had some terrible
screaming sessions, had flung unforgivable insults back and
forth like the bloodiest blood enemies. . . .

Lately she'd been having dreams in which Mike ended up
crying in her arms. She knew that dreams often meant the
opposite of what they seemed, like her father's equating hate
and love. Did it mean she still wanted Mike—or hated him
more than ever? It was all too confusing for a lit. major. She
had always thought of psychology as the science of opposites:
Love is hate; sickness is health; up is down. She remembered
a line of Shakespeare: "Men have died from time to time, and
worms have eaten them, but not for love." She wouldn't trade
that sentence for the whole literature of psychology.

"He's not a normal man, honey," her mother was saying,
as though a statement like that would be a comforting thing to
tell a woman about her son's father. "You can't expect him to
have normal reactions." That had always been her mother's
thesis; more than once it had produced strained feelings between
them. "I remember all those times when he. . . ." The tired
voice trailed off, as though she realized she had said too much.

In the silence, a year-old conversation came back to Lael
word for word.

"Mike, are you mad about something?"

"No."

"Sure?"

"I was thinking about last night. Remember what you said?"

"You mean, in bed?"

"You said, 'Let's get it over with.'"

"I'm sorry. I was tired. It went on too long. I'm sorry."

"Got any idea how that makes a man feel?"

"I said I'm sorry!"

It's hate we're dealing with here. Julie must be right. What else could explain the impulse to kidnap his own son? But where did so much hate come from? Just because I didn't want to do things his way? Night after night, year in, year out?

After that conversation, he hadn't talked to her for two days, sitting at meals with his face buried in a magazine, saying *hmmm* and *uh-huh* when she tried to make conversation, leaving messages with Ace: "Tell your mother I'm going to Seattle." The ordeal had ended, as always, in bed: another ordeal. Where was the love? Where was the closeness, the warmth, the *talk?* He'd made breakfast for her the next morning, and she'd felt like a prize whore. Again.

She looked across the shadowed living room at her father and mother. He was talking softly into her thinning gray hair. She caught a few phrases: ". . . came home and found her with the quartermaster . . . said he'd take care of it . . . swore the child was black. . . ." He must be telling one of his my-wife-she stories; they always began with an upset sailor barging into his office and saying, "My wife, she. . . ." Was Mike off somewhere reciting his own my-wife-she stories to friends? To Ace? Did he have a legitimate case against her? Maybe. So much depended on emphasis and nuance and on who was testifying and who was sitting in judgment.

She remembered how he came home long after midnight on their last night together, how he reached between her legs the instant he slipped under the covers. His fingers were like bare bones. *Was this what passed for love, this silent groping in the dark? Couldn't love speak?* Something broke in her. "I—I can't," she said, a note of hysteria in her voice. "Not now. Please, Mike, just this once."

"C'mon, babe," he said softly.

She pushed his hand away and sat up in bed. "I—can't."

"C'mon, sweetie!" His voice took on a whiny tone.

She slid from the bed and walked to the far side of the room. She couldn't do it tonight. She was beyond choice.

"Baby," he asked, "what's the matter?"

"I don't know. I wish I knew."

There was a long silence. His face was working—the eyes blinking slowly, the corners of his lips twisting down. He bounced out of bed and began pulling on his shorts. "I've seen it coming a long time," he said. "Let's face reality, Lael. You got problems."

"Why don't you come out and say I'm frigid?"

"I didn't say that."

"No, but you think it."

"Goddamn right I think it."

Sitting in her dimly lighted living room, she remembered the shouting scene that followed, the final exchange when there was nothing left but the need to hurt:

"My mother has you pegged good. She says you're a career girl, not a wife."

She was livid. "Then why don't you go home and sleep with her? Isn't that what all you mama's boys want? *To fuck mommy?*" It was as though someone else had spoken. She'd never used that word before.

His face turned the color of flour, and he dressed and left. Two weeks later a deputy sheriff drove down her long driveway and served the divorce complaint. She accepted it in a strangely tranquil mood. Something had been killed in her, and it no longer mattered whether it was suicide or murder.

Now she wondered if what she'd said that night justified the revenge he was taking. Stealing Ace? Putting an asthmatic child through such an ordeal? The vindictiveness seemed out of proportion.

She started another pot of coffee for her parents. When she returned to the living room, their eyes were closed and their heads had nodded together, barely touching. Half asleep, there was a rigidity to her father's posture, a natural dignity. He hadn't even loosened his shirt; he was in uniform. Lael was moved by their oneness, by their fidelity to her and each other, by their love. She thought of all the times her mother had packed up their books and dolls and furniture and moved the family thousands of miles to live as close to him as the navy would allow. *Till death do us part*. They had always been so out of touch with the times.

The four of them, the parents and two daughters, sat together through the night. No one called.

15

THE RAINS CAME. *Après Ace,* she thought, *le déluge.* God, another silly quote. Her mind had been strangely active lately, busy, erratic, reeling with quotes, puns, Ace's famous malapropisms, street addresses from her childhood, general nonsense. A phrase would enter her mind—"rotten rabbit guts"— and play for hours. She decided that this must be the way the brain coped, filling the folds and whorls, leaving no space for loneliness or self-pity.

She had done everything she could: made herself a pest around the sheriff's office; hired a detective agency; put tracers on credit-card transactions and bank accounts; consulted almost daily with her lawyer. Her first phone call to Catherine Pritcher had brought a stiff reply: "The deputies have been here three times. Get off my back." Later calls had brought only a loud click. For a few days she'd hoped for another miracle of Port Angeles, but as time passed, she began to realize that this kidnapping was different.

The rattle of the spring rain was so hard and steady on the old shake roof that it caught her attention only when it stopped. Willow branches flailed sideways. The borage leaves drooped like a wet cocker's ears. Radio announcers gave up on the sun and prattled about drybreaks, as in "Seattle's enjoying a lovely drybreak right now." Seconds later the drybreak would be over.

She interpreted the violent weather as nature's comment on the abduction. Everything she saw or did seemed to relate to Ace: wrong-number phone calls, innocent comments by friends, talk-show blatherings, changes in the weather. Her life was now defined by his absence.

The divorce went through, and she won permanent possession of a piece of paper awarding her custody of her missing son. "Does this mean the cops'll look for Ace?" she asked Van as they left the courtroom.

"I only wish it did," he said, patting her elbow.

The ancient bookseller from Nisbet, a neat vertical mummy with the smell of earwax about him, dropped by with a volume on child snatching. "Heard about your case, thought this might be a help," he said, standing in the steady drip from the roof. He wouldn't take money.

The book made her sick. While the days had been passing, she had held to the irrational hope that Mike and Ace would surface somewhere and she would hop in her truck and wave her all-powerful legal papers and reclaim her son. The book taught her that others had labored under the same delusion for years. But she didn't dare stop reading. If there was a single piece of information that would help her find Ace, she had to winnow it out.

She read of children dragged around the world by parents who refused to obey court orders. There was even a phrase for such offenders: custody kidnappers. Husbands (wives, too) had dyed their hair, undergone facial surgery, obliterated their fingerprints, learned new languages, lived out their years without hearing another word of their native tongues, just to thwart custody orders. The trouble they'd taken! She recognized Mike's personality in more than one of the case histories.

She couldn't understand the violence some of these people committed against their own children. She read about infants spirited away in burlap sacks, chloroformed, dosed with sleeping pills; parents pulling on each arm of a baby, screaming curses over the heads of the children they professed to love. "Mike's playing hardball," her lawyer had told her when Ace was first stolen. But how hard would he play? *How hard would she?*

Her feverish mind called up pictures of Ace imprisoned in a lonely cabin, climbing over deadfalls in a dense forest, sinking into jungle swamps, lost and afraid without her, sobbing in panic, sneaking away from his father and being caught and dragged back like an escaped murderer. Five years old! In calmer moments she imagined them hiding out in nearby mountains—the Cascades, the Canadian Rockies, the Olympics, places where Mike could fish. She imagined Ace striking out for home like a lost cat, following streams and roads, brought to his knees by fatigue, barely able to breathe through constricted bronchial tubes, and finally falling through the front door into her arms.

Between her dreams and imaginings she had to survive. It was all she could offer him. Each day became an exercise in fending off hysteria. She locked the door to his room and hid the key so she wouldn't wander in. On a corner of the porch she found his music box—"Lara's Theme"—and eyed it as though it were a cobra. One tinkling note would demolish her reserve. She clutched the enameled box in a viselike grip to keep the lid from activating the sound and stuffed it in a locked cupboard along with some of his other possessions: crab shells, a greasy pack of cards, a chipped amber marble, the dried jawbone of a small animal, a corroded nickel.

She couldn't get used to the new silence around the house, especially when clouds and fog came down and shrank the outer world. She would be doing the accounts, or cooking one of the meals she ate to live, or dusting or washing or shaking out rugs, when suddenly she would stop, frozen in position, the first faint acceleration of heartbeat signaling an anxiety attack. *Acey! Where is my Ace?* She would shake and tremble and look around for something strenuous to do. Usually she would grab the ax and split logs; cords of fir and ash filled the shed.

Friends phoned, but she found them small consolation and felt guilty about it, felt that she wasn't satisfying their need to be appreciated. Alicia Tate seemed to call every two hours. Cassandra Loomis of the lumber mill Loomises sent weekly flowers and cards and then stopped communicating altogether, as though the whole thing had become too tacky. Van Stein called almost daily, usually after she had come in from the herb garden for the evening. He was full of chatter about his work: lawsuits against clear-cutters, injunctions against polluters, campaigns against the "Californicators" of the northwest. She hadn't expected him to take much interest in the case, and she was almost sorry he did. He was too closely connected to the kidnapping.

"Any news about Ace?" he would always say at the end of the conversation.

"Nothing. You heard anything?"

"No, Lael. I'm sorry. Hang in, hon."

Once she caught a peculiar break in his voice, as though he were disturbed by her words. She had been telling him how Mike often ignored or forgot Ace's medicine and how the child desperately needed the weekly shot program that had been relieving his asthma. "Gotta find him," the lawyer said in a hoarse voice. "It's a sacred goddamn responsibility. Listen, kids are . . . the main thing."

She wondered if she'd heard right. Why this sudden intensity about a subject he'd never mentioned before? *Kids are the main thing*. Had children become his latest cause?

After three weeks had passed with no word, she told him about the book on child snatching and asked if it was exaggerated. "Every lawyer's had cases like that," he said. "When I was with Legal Aid, a man brought his daughter in. Still wore a sling from a dislocated shoulder. His wife had—"

"Please!"

"Oh, jeez, I'm sorry. I wasn't thinking. . . ."

Juliet moved in, temporarily between apartments. Her mother and father dropped by with parental advice and tokens of love: a leather-bound tome from her father, *Never Alone*, telling of Christ's special love for the bereft; a box of prize kiwi fruit from her mother. Close friends like Susan Sievertson and Ann Leopardi were in and out almost daily, but like the telephone callers, they really didn't want to hear the sordid details, at least more than once. While they were urging her to "get it all out," a film would settle over their eyes. She understood. There was nothing more boring than troubles that were here today and here tomorrow. They belied the natural order: beginnings, middles, and ends.

She finally took Stein's advice and bought a telephone recording device; she hadn't wanted to take so drastic a step because it was an admission that Ace might be gone for good. She spoke her message onto the continuous loop of tape: "Ace, if it's you, this is Mom. I love you, angel, don't hang up. Tell Mommy where you are, what city, what street. And if you don't know, Ace, tell Mom what it looks like, how you got there. In a car? In a plane? Okay? Tell Mom when you hear the little beep. Okay, angel?" She turned the recorder on whenever she left the house, even when she walked to the mailbox.

On the twenty-fifth morning without word, she was sitting at the kitchen table with Julie when a car turned in at the driveway. She looked at the clock: eight forty-five, pickup time for Ace's car pool. An empty Volkswagen van came down the drive ahead of a roostertail of shell dust. The driver stopped and tapped the horn twice. Lael went out and recognized Bette Stinson, one of the mothers. "Ace ready?" the woman called out cheerfully.

Juliet shoved past Lael and said, "Ace was kidnapped, Bette. Didn't you hear?"

The woman's mouth fell open. "Mother of God," she said.

Lael smiled and said, "It's okay, Bette."

"I didn't know. Forgive me, Lael. We've been in Alaska.

Oh, God. I didn't know. I'm so sorry."

She took an ad in the *Island Review*—"Anyone who has seen my son Alexander C. E. Pritcher, also known as Ace...." together with a description and a picture and the key word, "reward"—but the only response was useless calls: a psychic in Port Townsend claiming that she'd had a clear vision of Ace riding in a car with a license plate that said "Great Lake State"; a note from a self-styled crime researcher in West Seattle, offering his services at a "special discount rate"; a suggestion by a preacher in The Dalles, Oregon, that "we sit down and council together."

She went to the print shop in Nisbet to have a poster made. Mr. Stitchberry, the offset printer, handed her a large sheet of stiff white paper and said, "Make up something personal, so people can get a feeling for the little fella. Nowadays they see so many wanted and missing signs, it's nothin' anymore."

She sketched in a title: HAVE YOU SEEN MY SON? Underneath a face shot of Ace she put a message and her signature. She ordered five hundred posters and placed them herself all over the island and Bremerton and points between, wherever a store owner was sympathetic, then ordered another five hundred to spread on the east side of Puget Sound from Everett through Seattle and down to Tacoma. When she went back to the print shop for her third set, she suddenly realized that she hadn't paid a cent and hadn't been billed. "No, and you ain't gonna be," the bald-headed printer said. She thanked him and left, feeling like a mendicant.

She wrote letters endlessly—to news editors, foster homes, county agencies in Washington and Oregon, any place where Ace or information about him might turn up. There was no response to her frantic mailings except for a few sympathy notes. A local radio newsman called to tell her he felt bad about what had happened—he had known Mike and was surprised he would pull a stunt like this—but there were thousands of divorced parents in her position, and it was an old story to everyone in the news business. The information wasn't consoling.

One afternoon a guest arrived uninvited, a middle-aged man with patches of white hair dotted about his skull and a flamingo scarf that leached the color from his face. "You poor lady," he said, embracing Juliet by mistake. "I went through the same thing myself. Let me tell you...."

He raved for an hour about his missing wife and daughters.

Every Christmas and birthday, he said, he bought presents for the three children and placed them in the attic in front of their portraits. He talked to their photographs, kept their rooms dusted and neat. "Now what kind of scum would treat a loving husband like that?" he asked, spitting the words as though Lael and Juliet had been co-conspirators. His hands trembled and his eyes rolled in their sockets as he called his wife "the whore of Babylon" and insisted on leading a prayer for the missing children of the world.

"How long have they been gone?" Julie asked as he was walking out to his car.

"Nineteen years this June seventh. Oldest'll be twenty-five August ninth. But I still see 'em in their cribs. Teeny-tiny things. I look into every baby buggy I see. Out of habit, ya know? Sounds crazy, don't it?" He turned his face away.

Yes, Lael agreed silently, it sounds crazy. Was this what nineteen years of waiting did to a human being?

She hoped she wasn't looking at her future.

SUMMER

16

ONE AFTERNOON IN mid-June the phone rang as she was pinching off basil buds. Stein spoke even faster than usual. He said that an anonymous caller had informed him that she'd just returned from a Canadian vacation and had seen Mike and Ace on the *Coho*, the ferry to Victoria, British Columbia. Mike had been reading aloud from tourist pamphlets, and Ace had looked flushed and excited. The caller had last seen them disembarking in Victoria.

Lael peeled a purring Larry Allen from around her neck and tightened her grip on the phone. "When?" she asked.

"Just a few minutes ago."

"No! I mean, when did she see them?"

"Oh. Early May."

"That's . . . let's see . . . that sounds right. Oh, God, this could be—Van, do you know when the next ferry leaves for Victoria?"

"I looked it up. Eight-thirty in the morning. From Port Angeles. Listen, Lael, don't flip out about this, okay? People make mistakes. Victoria's another country—"

"You don't understand," she said, eager to hang up and pack. "This rings true! I mean, British Columbia was one of our favorite places. Vancouver, Campbell River, Harrison Hot Springs. . . . We went to Victoria a couple times and Ace loved it. He was crazy about Miniature World and the Wax Museum, places like that. I can just *see* them sitting on the *Coho* reading those pamphlets. Nobody could have made that up."

"Sure they could."

She hardly heard. She was already in Canada, running through a long empty passageway to her son, squeezing him and stroking his glossy black hair and patting the tears on his cheeks. "Lael," the lawyer said, "how about holding off awhile? Let me make a few calls to Victoria. I won't bill out the time. I'm just curious."

"I've got to go."

"Think about it a minute. What can you do alone?"

"Look for Ace."

"In a city of a hundred thousand?"

"Anyplace. Will the Canadians honor my custody order?"

"Huh? Yeah, I think so. We have comity."

"Comedy?" She wondered what comedy had to do with anything. A typically spacy Ivan Stein remark.

"Comity," he repeated. "C-O-M-I-T-Y. Means each country honors the other's rulings."

"So they'll send Ace back?"

"Yeah. Eventually. Listen, Lael, why don't we sleep on this?"

"I couldn't sleep now."

"Over-reacting?"

"That's better than sitting around."

He kept insisting that she was building herself up for a letdown. She said it was time somebody did *something*. He said she'd drop from exhaustion if she acted on every tip. She accused him of insensitivity. He said she was subconsciously seeking ways to suffer. She asked him why he didn't learn his own profession instead of practicing psychiatry without a license. He asked what the hell she meant by that. She told him he'd messed up her case from the beginning. There was a long silence, then: "That was a lousy thing to say, Lael."

"You cost me my son." She knew she was overstating, but the words flew out.

"How—how the hell'd I do that?" He sounded shaken.

"By missing that court date and dragging out my divorce. You told me yourself, if I'd had legal custody instead of that phony separation agreement, Mike never would've dared—"

"Hey, I already apologized six times. That was a bad day. One of my Indian clients—"

"Don't explain. I realize I'm not a cause. I'm not even a minority."

"Oh, for Christ's sake. Look, it was a simple divorce action. How the hell was I supposed to know I was dealing with a nut case? Did you ever warn me about him? Did you ever drop the least little hint?"

"I certainly—"

"You certainly did *not!* You kept saying, 'Let's keep it calm, let's keep it amicable.' Telling me what a wonderful guy he was, what a wonderful father. Went out of your way to make me think it was a routine no-fault divorce. And then Mr. Wonderful turns out to be a goddamn child snatcher. Why—"

"Don't call him names!"

"What? Why not? How about—asshole?"

She hung up and sat perfectly still till her fingers stopped trembling. She wondered why she had defended Mike, of all people. Habit, she decided. Loyalty doesn't end overnight. Even misplaced loyalty.

She picked through her clothes closet, then decided to call back and apologize. She wished she knew what made him irk her so much. His spaciness? Or was it simply that she depended on him, and she'd always hated to be dependent? No, she *wouldn't* call. He was in the wrong. He had mishandled her case. It was original sin. Let him stew.

She laid out a two-piece khaki outfit with a bush-jacket top—drip-dry, light, functional, abounding in pockets—and felt a moment's trepidation about her trip. Would the Canadians answer her questions? Hotel managers, bellboys, clerks? Policemen? She wished Julie could go with her for moral support, but somebody had to stay behind to take care of the Saturday customers. Once her mother had filled in and sold all the chive starts.

She tried to catch a few hours' sleep, but her mind raced. So Ace was in Victoria. Or *had been* in Victoria. The more she thought about it, the more sense it made. Mike had tried to take him to Canada the first time; more than once she'd thought about going there and looking around, but where? Now she had someplace to start.

The dream crept up on her.

She has just given birth to a son.

She hears herself begging, "Please, please, let me hold him."

A voice answers from far away: "The password—we must have the password."

She cries out, "Rotten rabbit guts!"

The doctor smiles and hands her a doll.

17

SHE DROVE CAREFULLY along the twisting highway that ran between needled peaks of the Olympics to her left and the Strait of Juan de Fuca to her right, through dark tunnels formed by Douglas fir and hemlock, past unexpected rhododendron patches where old cabins had sunk back into the earth, along foaming streams lined with wild roses and scarlet thimbleberries, through tiny habitations with names like Blyn and Carlsborg.

At eight-thirty in the morning she was aboard the gray-hulled ferry *Coho* as it slid from its dock in Port Angeles and headed for Canada. She sat in the small cafeteria in the stern, watching the swells slam broadside into the ship. "Killer water" Mike used to call this passage back in their sailing days. The west wind blew unchecked across eight thousand miles of North Pacific and funneled into the mouth of the strait. She watched the dark blue seas thrashing in rips and whirlpools the size of city blocks. She thought of the six-foot octopus they had snagged, the wolf eel that had snapped at Mike, the lingcod with their double rows of angled teeth that couldn't let go of anything they grabbed.

She pursed her lips and wondered why she was making so many sinister associations. The Strait of Juan de Fuca had always been a playground to her. When had it turned menacing? She was deep in thought when someone said, "Hi!"

She looked up. Ivan Stein was holding tight to the hand of a shiny-faced Oriental boy with straight black hair like Ace's and gleaming white teeth touched with gold. His brown eyes were flush with his facial planes; she guessed that made him Chinese. "Meet Trang," the lawyer said. "My son."

"Please to meet you," the child said, sticking out his hand. She remembered seeing him in the lawyer's office. *My son?* He must be adopted. Unless Stein had an Asian wife with dominant genes.

"I didn't know you were married," she said, motioning them to join her at the Formica table.

"I'm not," he said. "Trang's the boy who came to dinner."

"I come for visit," the boy said. "Two year now. Think I stay." He spoke in fragments, like his "father." The look on his face told her she was hearing well-worn family lines.

She produced a smile that she wished she felt. Politesse at all cost; it was in short supply. Stein slid into the seat next to her. His curly red hair looked as though an attempt had been made to subdue it. He wore a dark pin stripe suit about two sizes too small, a white shirt with a collar button missing, a beige knitted tie with a lumpy knot. His motorcycle boots looked as though they'd been through a war. His ponytail would certainly make a lasting impression on the staid Canadians.

"Lael, listen to me," he was saying. "You shouldn't be doing this alone. If there's a chance Ace is over here—I mean, I want to help, okay?"

"Dad?" the child said. "I think I look around. Okay you?"

Stein slapped the boy lightly on the short pants and said, "Okay me."

She mouthed, *Seasick?*

"Doubt it," he said as Trang walked off. "He spent a long time on the water."

"What water?"

"The South China Sea."

For the first time in days her thoughts veered from Ace. "He was a boat person?"

"Five months. A Malay gunboat sank their barge, and he swam for it."

"His family?"

"Drowned."

She felt like crying for Trang, for Ace, for all the lost and lonely boys. "I'm sorry," she said. How many times had she said those same words lately or heard them said to her? "Van, listen," she said, feeling a flush of warmth and gratefulness toward him, "if you really want to help—"

"I do. *We* do."

She wished she had a master plan, but nothing had come to mind except perhaps to check in with the police juvenile bureau and start looking at faces. The lawyer must have sensed her lack of direction. He said, "How about if I do the uniforms and you do the civilians?"

"What do you mean?"

He pulled a yellow pad from his scarred briefcase and slid it across the table. The top page was covered in small block-lettering. Under "VAN," she read:

Call on:
Victoria PD
RCMP
Immigration
Customs
Hotels

Under "LAEL," she read:

Check out:
Places Ace liked. Wax museum, etc.
Usual restaurants where went before
Waitresses, etc., that knew him
Any shops, etc., where known?
Whatever

Under "TRANG," there was a single sentence:

Stay downtown, cover ground, *eyes on a swivel!!!*

"What's this?" she asked.

"Battle plan," he said. "I'll talk to the cops, Canadian customs, immigration, all the stiff upper lips. You do the humans."

So he'd worked out the exact details of how *she* was going to look for *her* son. He certainly had a way of taking over.

She studied his list. "'RCMP'? The Mounties?"

"Traffic cops nowadays, but they might know something. Can't afford to miss a bet."

She slid the list back across the table. "Efficient," she said. This must be how he worked on his causes.

"Once we get off the boat, we gotta *move*," he said. "We've only got today and tomorrow."

"*You've* only got today and tomorrow."

"How long are you staying?"

"Till I find my son."

"What about the herb farm?"

"Julie's there. It doesn't matter."

He looked out the window and back at her. "Gotta find him fast. I have to be back Monday morning. You bring a picture?"

She handed him one of her duplicates—Ace in his glasses, teaching Larry Allen to beg. He folded it carefully in a sheet of legal paper and slipped it into his briefcase. "We'll have copies made," he said. "There's a passport place on Government Street. We'll paper Victoria with this picture. Looks enough like him, I guess."

She glanced again at the search plan. "What's this mean, 'Waitresses, etc., that know him'?"

"People who might've taken notice when you were here before. 'What a cute little boy,' stuff like that."

"It never happened," she said. "Canadians are reserved. And we were only here twice. Stayed at the Empress. More British than the British."

"I'll check their registration records."

"Mike knows that's the first place I'd look."

"I'll check anyway. No sense doing a half-assed job."

She picked up his legal pad. "What's 'Trang...eyes on a swivel'?"

"He'll mingle in crowds and see what he can see. Loves stuff like that. Thinks he's Fu Manchu."

"You'd let him loose in a strange city?"

"Trang's never been in a strange city."

"What's that mean?"

"He knocked around on his own for so long you could drop him in downtown Novisibirsk and he'd be fine."

"Novisi-what?"

"Novisibirsk. Russia." He slipped off his Ben Franklin glasses and peered at her through watery blue eyes. He looked as though he hadn't slept.

"Trang. Is that his first name or his last?"

"His middle name. Stein's his last name. His first name didn't work out too well at school."

"What on earth was it?"

"Phuoc."

"Oh." She felt herself redden and wondered if she was turning into a prude as well as a grump.

"Want a drink, a sandwich?" he asked. "Looks like they're closing the counter. Coffee?"

"I don't usually drink it." Another negative. Funny how self-conscious and stiff he made her.

He came back with a Styrofoam cup. She realized why he was wearing a suit; he would be interviewing the authorities, and his "Save the Whales" T-shirt might look a little out of place. Maybe he wasn't quite as spacy as he seemed. "Don't waste time worrying about Trang," he said. "In Saigon he burglarized houses. It was steal or starve. Now he's turned conservative. Won't even drink a Coke. Thinks Reagan's a Soviet agent."

She noticed that the ferry had stopped pitching and rolling. She looked through the splattered window and saw a grayish destroyer standing out to sea, a big red flag with a maple leaf rippling from the stern. It looked like a warship her father had served on when she was a little girl. A fleet of sportfishing boats bobbed into view alongside a bed of waving kelp fronds the color of molasses. Then she saw the long graystone Victoria breakwater. The city looked forbiddingly large under the silvery June sun. Was Ace on one of those streets?

The *Coho* slid up the placid tidal river. She felt a chill. She had never been here without Ace. Too many memories were being revived, too many sights: the Seatrain barges brimming with sawdust, the tugs like waterbugs, the red double-decker bus inching along Government Street with its payload of tourists. She turned away and tried to compose herself. This wasn't a pleasure trip; it was a rescue mission. Going to pieces was hardly the way to begin.

Trang returned, smiling. "Let's go, man," Stein said, slapping the boy's shoulder. "Motorcycles drive off first." The three of them agreed to meet later, and father and son disappeared below.

She stepped out on deck as the ferry made its final turn to starboard and the Empress Hotel appeared ahead with its copper-sheathed turreted roof and its carapace of ivy that looked as though it were holding up the building. Other passengers surrounded her on the deck. As she turned to walk inside, she felt a shiver go down her back. She had stretched out her hand for Ace.

The ferry's engines stopped, and the big bulk eased against the wharf. Her eye caught an ungainly floating structure and the sign UNDERSEA GARDENS. One of Ace's favorite places. She dabbed at her eyes and thought she must be the first person in history to be moved to tears by the Undersea Gardens. Oh, Lael, she told herself, what a silly woman you've become. Still missing Ace, even missing Mike. If I could only learn to hate. The women's libbers would throw me out. . . .

She looked up. A hawser snaked through the air. A crowd milled about on the pavement, mostly adults, a few children in bright summer clothing. She studied them carefully and said under her breath, Be there, Acey, be there! End my torture, please, God, end it right now! *You can put him there with a snap of your fingers!*

But Ace was nowhere to be seen. A single black-edged cloud slid under the sun and pressed a shadow on the scene.

18

A LONG DAY'S search produced nothing. She had saved Mother Goose Village for last. It was the one place she was positive father and son would have visited. On their last trip as a family Ace had been crazy about the life-size sets, acting out his dreams and fantasies, his brown eyes alive with excitement.

She shoved three dollar bills through a hole in a big blue shoe that served as a ticket booth. "And the child?" an elderly female's voice said through the hole.

"There is no child," Lael said.

She walked through a door and down a cool hallway lined with unmarked doors, each door blue on a field of blue and therefore intensely disorienting. A part of her brain had decided that she would be able to divine if Ace had been here lately, like a mother wolf sniffing out a strayed pup. She opened a door at random and came to a padded hill where several visiting Jacks and Jills yelled and laughed as they rolled down. Ace wasn't one of them.

She tried another door and found Humpty Dumpty's wall with its foam mat below, but wall and foam were untenanted. She checked out Little Miss Muffet's spider and Mother Hubbard's begging dog and elected to walk instead of jump past Jack Be Nimble's candlestick. She crossed the empty bridge of the Three Billy Goats Gruff with the leering waxen troll and his flashing red eye sockets, opened another door, and saw the lower half of a small boy halfway up a ten-foot beanstalk made of a wooden trunk and green loops of rope. An adult male with his back to her stood guard below. She held her breath and stepped on the set.

Wrong father, wrong son.

Soon the exhibits turned grotesque, leering. She felt frightened as she walked faster and faster, peering into faces, kneeling and squatting for a better look, making one or two children turn away anxiously, until she rounded a corner and jumped backward at the sight of the Big Bad Wolf, its long pink tongue wiggling lewdly in its plastic mouth. Ace's vibrations were gone, if they'd ever been here; now she felt menaced. She noticed that she had circled back to the entrance.

She rapped on the little round window and said, "May I speak to you?"

"Yes, of course."

A door opened in the side of the plastic shoe, and the ticket taker stepped out. The old woman must have been measured for the job; she was barely five feet tall and smelled of rose water. "Excuse me," Lael said nervously. "I'm Mrs. Pritcher? From Washington? I was wondering if you'd seen this child." She held out a picture of Ace.

"There's so many," the woman said, paying more attention to Lael than the picture.

"Yes, but this one is—"

"Special, of course." The old woman smiled sweetly under her bonnet. "Well, he certainly is a fine looking boy. Yours?"

"Yes."

Mother Goose took another look. "I don't remember him," she said. "Was he here?"

"About a month ago."

"I'm sorry. I wish I could help."

Lael thanked the woman and turned to leave. "Would you like to sign our register?" the voice called after her.

The guest book lay open on a desk in the corner. A ball-point pen dangled from a thin chain. "Sign right there," Mother Goose said, and disappeared inside her shoe.

Lael scribbled her signature and pored over the rest. She didn't even know what to look for. "Michael E. Pritcher and stolen son"? It was foolish to come here and more foolish to expect Mike to leave a trail. But she kept on turning pages. Sensible approaches had failed. Maybe it was time to try something foolish.

She had reached the first week of May when she saw it scrawled across the top of a page in inch-high letters:

ACe

She stepped back and blinked. Ace, is it you? *My* Ace? The mad penman who used to mark my walls with indelible ink? She leaned over the page. The three vivid letters were bracketed by names she didn't recognize: Chas. and Julia Campbell of Phoenix, Ariz., and Marie Louise van der Porght of Nairobi, Kenya.

She closed her eyes and tried to imagine the scene.

Mike stands in line to pay. Ace wanders away, full of his usual energy and curiosity. He spots someone signing the guest book. The pen drops to the end of its chain. He grabs it and quickly makes his mark.

She was as close to her son as she'd been in two months. His hand had touched this pen, this paper. She double-checked to see if Mike had signed elsewhere, but he hadn't been that careless.

She walked away with her head down, eager to drive back downtown and share her news with Van and Trang. At the small gift shop she remembered something Van had said about not doing a half-assed job. It was almost 5:00 P.M., but she turned and went in. A middle-aged man with an undersize toupee of metallic reddish brown was making change for a party of girls in greenish uniforms. She waited till the traffic cleared and thrust the picture at him with the same speech she'd been making all afternoon: " . . . just checking . . . my son . . . about a month ago."

"Oh, yes," the man said in a cheerful English accent. "Mr. Pritcher's boy. Alex, is it?"

Her knuckles whitened against the counter. "Uh, yes," she said. "Alexander Pritcher. We call him Ace."

"Ace?" A slight frown.

"Uh, yes." She swallowed an explanation. "He's my son. Do you happen to know where he is right now?"

The frown broadened. "Right now? Well, I would imagine he's home, madam, wouldn't you?"

"But where's home?"

The man patted his outrageous hair and rearranged a pair of gold-rimmed glasses on his face. He gave her a long look and said, "I thought you were his mum."

"I am." She felt uneasy. "I mean, I used to be. I mean we, I—it's a long story."

He pushed the glasses up on his freckled forehead as if he couldn't bear to see her too clearly, sniffed once, and turned to a ledger next to the cash register. "I'm sure I don't want to intrude, madam. If you're his mother, you're certainly entitled to know where he lives. Could I trouble you for a bit of ID?"

She passed over her driver's license and her American Express card, and he studied them slowly. He looked at her through his glasses and again without them. She asked, "Is he—I mean, would he be in your records?"

"He is, madam. His dad paid in advance for our largest set of the Three Bears. Quite lovely, actually." He smiled, showing perfect teeth. "We didn't have the papa bear in stock—one of our young ladies had broken a set—so we had to mail off to Toronto for it. It just arrived the other day, and I sent it round. Here's the address."

Good God, she thought, Mike's first mistake. He must be awfully sure of himself. Maybe he figured the Canadian government would protect him. Stein had said otherwise. She hoped he was right this time.

She extended a shaky hand to accept the slip of paper as the man's little eyes flicked busily across her face. She started to tell him how much the information meant to her, but something told her to hold off. After she and Van collected Ace, they would come back and buy every doll and game and gewgaw in the store.

"It's in North Victoria, missus," the man was saying in the softest of voices, as though he were beginning to sense the intensity of her feelings. "Lovely place to raise a child. Not what it once was, understand, but perfectly respectable."

She thanked him and started for the door. "And madam?" he called after her in perfectly oval tones. "The best of luck to you, I'm sure. Such a nice little lad. I do remember that."

A nice little lad. Yes. She remembered that, too.

19

THE ADDRESS WAS in a tree-lined college neighborhood: ethnic restaurants and theme saloons, sprawling old houses with Greek letters across the front, thick lawns scarred by games of Frisbee and touch football, young people in jeans hauling their books on bikes and scooters. In a transient area like this no one checked on the neighbors. The house itself was a three-story white frame building with scallops of peeling paint and a large glassed-in front porch with one cracked pane.

As Lael watched with Stein from the front seat of her Luv, she tried to will herself not to think. Too many emotions were pressing in: elation that she would soon see Ace, fear that something would go wrong, hope and anxiety and joy and bitterness and trepidation. They had been watching for several hours when the lawyer asked, "Why would he keep a five-year-old out this late?"

"He treats him like an adult," she said. "You know—the daddy's little man number? He always accused me of coddling him by putting him to bed at eight."

"Tell me again what she said."

"The landlady? Just that she hadn't seen them since early this morning."

"Did you ask where they usually go?"

"No. I thanked her and walked away like it was no big deal. Just the way you told me." She turned and touched his arm. "Van, listen, are you sure Trang's okay? Back there at the dock? I mean, it'll be dark soon, and he's only—"

"I told you, don't worry about Trang. You think he'll turn into a pumpkin?"

"He's—what? Seven? Eight?"

"Thirteen."

"Thir*teen?*"

"He doesn't eat much."

A car rounded the corner and slowed in front of the house. She held her breath. The car kept on going. She told herself not to feel let down. Before this night was over, there was every chance she would see her son. For some reason the thought made her tremble. She barely heard Stein's drone: ". . . on his own back in Saigon. Drugs, stealing, hustling. He's probably found himself a nice little opium den somewhere and settled in for the night. With a concubine."

She couldn't help asking, "What'll he do for dinner?" She felt like the self-appointed guardian of every small boy on earth.

"He'll buy it. He's the Bank of Trang. Delivers papers, mows lawns, anything to turn a buck. Still finds time to take care of the house. He's completely self-sufficient—gets himself up in the morning, makes breakfast for both of us, walks down the hill to the bus stop, comes home and studies and makes dinner. Does that sound like somebody we need to worry about?"

She frowned. "Sounds like you turned him into your houseboy." He was bringing out her worst side again. What *was* it about him?

"Hey, I *begged* him, 'Trang, stop cooking for me, man! Spend the time on your homework.' He says, 'No problem, no problem.' Next night there's another hot meal on the table. Course, it's always rice. Rice with a twist. A little sausage, a little fish, maybe a tiny piece of salt pork. Acts like he's paying for the stuff himself. One night it was slugs."

"Slugs?"

"I asked him about the brown bits in the rice, and he said, 'Snails.' I asked him where he bought snails, and he said he found 'em in the garden, and I asked him if they had shells, and he said no, he caught 'em out of their shells."

She gagged. "What did you *do?*"

"I panicked. I tried telling him I couldn't eat 'em because they weren't kosher, but he knows I'm not religious. So—" He jerked forward in his seat. "Look!" A small light-colored sedan had pulled up in front of the rooming house. "Is that it?"

She craned her neck. "It's the right color."

"Looks like an Escort," he said. "Remember, we wait till they're completely parked. Then we box 'em in with the truck and make our move. All they can do is run, and they can't get far. Ready?"

She had already started the engine. Her palms smeared the steering wheel and her pulse beat in her eyes. Now that it was happening, she was afraid. So many things could go wrong. Suppose Mike had a gun, a knife. Or even a tire iron. How far would he go to keep his son?

As she eased the Luv away from the curb, the other car came to a sudden stop in the middle of its parking maneuver. Had her black truck been spotted? The passenger's door opened, and a fat woman in a broad-brimmed crimson hat planted one foot and then the other on the curb. The car pulled away, gears grinding. "A Renault," the lawyer muttered. It was their third false alarm.

She slumped forward and took a deep breath. "I was scared," she admitted.

After she had reparked, he said, "I sure would like to get it over with." He stretched his long legs. "Damn, he keeps a kid out late."

An unanswered question rattled around in her mind. She couldn't remember what it was. Oh, yes. "How do they taste?" she asked.

"What?"

"Slugs."

He laughed. "Not bad, if you got enough tamari sauce."

"You *ate* them?"

"Couldn't hurt his feelings."

She took a long look at a man who would eat slugs to keep from offending a child. He looked hot and tired. In the heat of the late sun he'd been taking off his three-piece suit in installments; she hoped he would stop at the pants.

"What made you adopt him?" she asked.

"I don't know. Guilt, I guess."

"About what?"

"Oh, I don't know. The war, I guess. What we did to his country. . . ." He yawned and said, "Hard to explain."

I wonder why I don't feel that guilt, she asked herself. I never hurt anybody in Vietnam. I went to college and minded my own business. Maybe I *should* feel guilty, come to think of it. Why does Stein always make me feel inadequate? Is he getting even for some of the things I said? He's so *righteous*. The standard disease of the storefront lawyer. I hope it isn't contagious.

The conversation dwindled away as the shadows lengthened in the miniature park a few yards away. Like the rest of Victoria, it was spattered with color: Maiden's Blush roses with delicate pink faces, yellow and brown Gloriosa daisies the size of salad plates, morning glories in the palest purple peeking from deep green hangings that flowed down a limestone wall. She could imagine Ace playing here in the daytime.

She wondered if Mike had hired a permanent sitter. What kind of woman is raising my baby? Is she patient? Every nanny isn't a Mary Poppins. She could hear them bickering.

You didn't say the password.

Password? What password?

Rotten rabbit guts.

Filthy little beast....

"Hey, why don't you take a little walk, get some air?"

"What?"

The lawyer was staring at her. "You look sick," he said.

"I was just thinking."

She wondered what Mike and Ace were living on. He couldn't possibly be licensed to practice architecture in Canada. Maybe he was working as a draftsman or commercial artist. He had a beautiful free-flowing style, the opposite of his personality. Or maybe he was borrowing till things calmed down. From his mother's savings, perhaps. Catherine would give him anything.

The old frame rooming house was still in half-light, but shadows were climbing its front. They had checked the back; there was no garage off the narrow alley and no place to put a car. Mike would have to pull up on the street, where they could see him.

"He loves wild mushrooms," the lawyer was saying. "Comes home with baskets full. Steams 'em with rice."

Lael had only been half listening, but she'd caught enough to make her frown. "Ever hear of *Galerina autumnalis?*" she asked, *"Amanita phalloides?"*

"Who are they?"

"Deadly mushrooms."

"If we go," he said, kissing the Star of David that hung from his neck, "we go together."

There was something pathetic about his remark. Was the orphan his whole family? "Where'd you find him?"

"Singapore."

"What were you doing there?"

"Red Cross."

"How'd you get him home?"

He paused. "There's ways."

"You didn't go through channels?"

He snorted. "Can you imagine me trying to adopt a kid through channels? A hippie freaky backslid Jew?"

She might have known. He was an expert at bending the

law. "How'd you pick him?" There must have been thousands.

"He grabbed me and wouldn't let go, you know what I mean? By the time I was scheduled to go home we were, uh— tight." He sounded embarrassed.

"I understand."

"So I brought him home in the cargo hold of an air force jet. Far-out, huh? Some guys smuggle dope and get rich. I smuggle kids and go broke. Love it!"

"Would they take him away from you?"

"In a second."

She felt a flash of fear for both of them. "Doesn't that bother him?"

"We don't discuss it. He's had enough trauma."

"So you moved to our island to be away—"

"Did anybody ever tell you you're nosy?" he interrupted. She shot him a quick glance. He didn't look angry.

She closed her eyes and sighed. Every time she tried to get some sort of grip on this man—to figure out who he was, *what* he was—he slipped away. Now she had new words to describe him. Guileless—that was one. And trusting. And for a storefront lawyer, almost naïve. But also loyal. Loyal and loving, true to himself in an outlandish sort of way. She felt a sudden surge of gratefulness, another of the girlish emotions that had been welling up in her lately. Someday she would have to tell him how much she appreciated his patience, his steadfastness, how good it felt to have him on her side. Someday. But not today. . . .

Darkness slid over the Luv. A streetlight half a block away bounced sparkles off the glass porch of the old white house and made her think of one of Ace's favorite characters, Tinker Bell. She heard a gasp and a snore. Stein's red head had fallen to one side. It was nearly an hour before he woke up.

"What's the time?" he asked hoarsely. She remembered how he'd been asleep at his desk when she'd first come to tell him Ace had been kidnapped. He mustn't be getting enough rest. Too many causes.

"Five after eleven."

"Damn." He ducked his head and looked through the windshield. "Any lights go out in that house yet?"

"One or two. But there's still one in the front window."

"Hey, why don't you ask the landlady what the hell's going on? She'll be going to bed soon and—"

"She'll suspect something."

He yawned, started to talk, and yawned again. His yawn made her yawn. They looked into each other's yawning faces and smiled. It was late, but their wait would soon be rewarded. Not even Mike could keep the child out much past midnight. As though he knew what she was thinking, he said, "We'll outsit 'em, that's all."

"Thanks, Van."

"But maybe the landlady can help us." One of his long arms brushed against the back of her head as he stretched. "Maybe she's heard something."

She twisted the mirror. Her hair looked like a handful of straw. For once in her life she wished she had a cosmetics kit with blusher and mascara and lipstick.

"Why don't you go up and knock?" he said. "Couldn't hurt."

Lael walked fifty feet to the cracked cement steps. The front door opened before she touched the knob. "Oh, it's you again, miss," the landlady said.

"Yes," Lael said, trying not to sound anxious. "I just wondered. Did Mr. Pritcher—"

"Called some time ago, miss," the woman said, her cheeks shaped into round rose ovals by her smile. "They'll be along any minute. I told him you and the gentleman was waiting in your truck."

20

VAN PICKED UP Trang and the motorcycle and had gone home via Vancouver to keep a court date. Sick with disappointment, Lael had stayed on to hire a Canadian detective agency and then gone home herself. For a long month she heard nothing. The sheriff's office had lost interest; Catherine Pritcher refused to talk, and there were no new responses to her placards. Then one muggy afternoon she answered the extension phone in her greenhouse and heard an intense accent like escaping steam. "Is that Mrs. Pritcher? B.C. Investigations here."

"Who?"

"British Columbia Investigations. In Victoria? You retained us in the matter of young Alexander?"

"Yes?"

"I'm so sorry, Mrs. Pritcher, but I'm afraid we've spent a month getting exactly nowhere. Mr. Pritcher and your son seem to have dropped from sight. Quite remarkable. We'll press on, of course. Sooner or later they'll. . . ."

She barely heard the rest. After a few more words she said "Thank you," and hung up. She'd had such high hopes.

Four days later she received a bill. Her $500 retainer had been eaten up, and $441 more was due and payable. B.C. Investigations Ltd. was pleased to offer a 5 percent discount on accounts paid within thirty days and considered it an honor to serve her. She called them up and called them off. She could not find Ace by going bankrupt.

August came, though not as hotly on her island as inland. The days passed as heavy and dull as stone. Juliet moved back to her own apartment but still managed to spend most of her time at the herb farm. Her mother and father visited as often as ever but seemed less willing to discuss Ace, as though they had decided it was cruel to remind her. The old shake cottage seemed strange: a bed-and-breakfast place she had wandered into by mistake. There were no tracks to clean up, no Magic Marker to erase from the walls. The peanut butter dried in its jar. Once she flicked on the TV and heard a familiar voice:

"There's only one person in the whole wide world exactly like you, and that's you yourself. I like you just—" She slapped the off button with her palm, and Mr. Rogers faded away, tying his shoes.

Cleaning behind the davenport, she found a stiffened handkerchief. A Larry Allen keepsake, dragged in from outside? No, her little bobtailed cat dealt strictly in animal matter, preferably mice. This had to be a memento of Ace. She decided she couldn't handle any more surprises and scoured every corner of the house from attic to basement, finishing in a lather at 3:00 A.M.

Most nights were less eventful. She would lie awake inventorying memories: the morning when he had scampered into their bedroom shouting, "I'm dry! Hey, Mom, I'm dry!" His defeats and triumphs, his adventures, his pets, his totems. The eel he'd kept alive in their bathtub. The corrective shoe he'd worn for three months. The hours he'd worked at his chalkboard till he put together the mysterious arcs and lines and intersects that spelled "ACe." Sometimes, in her dreams, she would hear him beg, "'Kay, Mom? *'Kay?*" as though he were asking for something and she were denying him.

Every morning the pain resumed, a fresh new grief to absorb and assimilate. She had to beat down feelings of uselessness, of guilt. What am I *for?* I'm not healing; I'll *never* get over this. What's the matter with me? I can't stand this dull, boring, uninspiring, vanilla life. . . .

She tried to pick up her spirits by starting a daily letter to Ace, an idea she borrowed from one of the women who called to offer help. She knew the act was irrational—so was love, so was faith—but she had to find relief somewhere, and she couldn't afford to analyze the relief out of existence. "Hi Ace my angel!" she wrote the first day. "The mallards are fine— still as fat and waddly as ever. They wish you were here to chase them. . . . Mommy made your favorite breakfast today: French toast with nutmeg and cinnamon. . . . Guess what! I bought new Crayolas for you—the big box with *forty* colors. You'll *never* be able to use them up. . . ."

Her garden consoled and depressed her. The alternating rains and sun of summer had made the herbs flourish. Sometimes she wondered how the verbena could be so flamboyant, the sage so luxuriant. Didn't they miss him? She tried to overpower her low moods by working fertilizer into the empty beds, hauling wheelbarrows of sand and mulch, yanking blackberry runners and dandelion spikes and thistle roots. She instructed herself not to whine or wallow in self-pity, not to allow herself to be crushed. Women lost children every day to car wrecks, drownings, disease, even to childbirth. It was God's own sexual stereotyping: Men fought wars, and women lost children. And she hadn't lost Ace for good. He was alive, somewhere. She had to keep looking.

At the end of each working day the clothes stuck to her back like tape. She often thought of the old saying: "Horses sweat; men perspire; women glow." Then I'm a horse, she told herself, because I *sweat*. Her body became even more lean and tanned. In the darkness of each pre-dawn she jogged. At night she did the bills and the correspondence and wrote her letter to Ace.

Occasionally she slept.

Stein dropped by now and then, always alone. "Trang's on a field trip to the mastodon site," he explained one day in his breathless style. "What a kid! Last week he...."

She jerked away, unfathomably upset. "Oh, Van," she said. "I want to hear about Trang, I honestly do, but ... I keep seeing Ace. Do you know—he'll be six next month? And he won't even be home?"

He drew her to him on the porch and rubbed gentle circles against her back. She backed away, and he looked embarrassed. "I'm—I'm sorry," she said. She wondered if this would always be her reaction to men. "I try not to think about him," she said, trying to regain her composure, "but—"

"Don't talk," he murmured.

To atone for her coldness, she invited him in for bergamot tea. "This is what the colonists drank after the Boston Tea Party," she said, trying for a brighter subject.

He took a sip. "Interesting," he said.

"You don't like it, do you?"

"I'm anti-tea. My grandmother used to pour it down me every time I got a cold. 'Here, Ivan, a nice glass tea.'"

"Where was this?"

"Oh, she was from Norway."

"I thought you were Jewish."

"My grandmother Perlberg was from Norway. That's where I got my red hair. A Norwegian in the woodpile."

"Lots of Jewish people have red hair." She wondered why

she had to say "Jewish people." Why not "Jews"? Did Jews say "Christian people"?

"Not lots," he said. "Just Woody Allen. And me."

"Did you live in Norway?"

"West of there," he said. "Encino. L.A."

"Isn't that a rich place?" Another dumb question. She was full of them today. He used to make her nervous; now he made her stupid.

"We *wished!*" he said. "Encino's just suburbia. Verily ye shall be judged by the car ye drive, that kinda place. We'd sit *shivah* if the zoysia turned brown."

She decided to stop being nosy, and after a short silence he told her why he'd dropped in. A retired Chicago police lieutenant had just moved to the island. He was a specialist in missing persons.

"How would I pay him?" she asked. "I've got two mortgages and a home improvement loan. My savings are almost gone, and I'm overdrawn. I don't know how to pay *you.*"

"I'm not into money, Lael. You know that."

She wondered how he managed to feed himself and his foster son. No wonder they ate slugs. He still hadn't billed her for the divorce. Maybe it was his way of atoning for missing the first court date.

She asked him what another investigator could do that hadn't already been done. "Well, for one thing he knows how to tie into the national crime computers," Van answered.

"We're already tied in. Don't you remember? The Stovall Detective Agency? 'We Never Sleep'? They promised to feed in everything—Ace's description, Mike's description, car license number, Social Security number, *everything*. That was four months ago, and there hasn't been a single touch—"

" 'Hit.' "

"—A single hit since then."

"Stovall's a general detective agency. This guy's a retired missing persons cop. A specialist."

"You really think I should hire him?"

"Would I come all the way over here and drink this awful glass tea if I didn't think so?"

She drove to Thunder Bay to talk to the detective, Matt Nyren, a big, neckless man of forty-five or fifty with a round stomach like a beach ball. She noticed that his wing tip shoes turned up at the toes, as though he bought them too big.

She tried to recite the facts in order, but by the time she reached the woman in the black Luv she could see that she wasn't holding her audience. His colorless eyes rolled around in his bald head; he sighed loudly; he snaked his little finger deep into his ear with apparent intent to maim, then scrutinized the contents. He chewed the end of his cigar into soggy flakes and pulled them off as though preening a pet bird.

"That's it, huh?" he commented at the end.

"Uh, yes," she said. She told herself that there must be a boring sameness to child-snatch cases. Still, he could have faked a little interest, especially since he had demanded a $100 retainer at the outset.

He asked for a list of every friend Mike had ever had, every business contact, every credit card, every business and personal connection as far back as she could remember. "When ya get home," he told her, "call me back with everything ya can gimme on insurance policies, bank accounts, phone records, voter registration, medical, book clubs, Blue Cross, VA records, anything with a number on it."

She put the information together, phoned it back to him, and heard nothing for two weeks. Then he showed up at her door, folding and refolding a gray fedora hat that looked borrowed from an old G-man movie. "Lady," he said, refusing her invitation to step inside, "I been going night and day, and lemme tell ya—this is the deepest drop I ever seen. Your husband's not using his own name, his own Social Security number, his own driver's license, or his own credit cards. His saving's account's sitting in the Island National Bank, two hundred bucks and change, and it hasn't been touched. I wouldn't be surprised he's even changed his looks: hair color, mustache, beard, plastic surgery, fingerprint mutilation. Nothing would surprise me. *Dead* wouldn't surprise me. Is he, would he, I mean, is he suicidal?"

"No," Lael snapped. *Please,* she thought, *don't feed my nightmares.*

"I musta talked with fifty people," the detective went on, smoothing the wet end of his cigar into an obscene little point. "I sifted his mother's trash two Mondays in a row, and ya know what I found? Trash. I grabbed her mail every day and steamed it, and the only letters she got was bills and a postcard from an aunt in Cincinnati."

"What do you recommend?" Lael asked.

"Me? A brown bag job might help."

"What's that mean?"

He lowered his voice. "A break-in. Safe and clean. The mother's got his address someplace around the house."

"You mean, you'd sneak into Catherine's house?"

"Sneak in, break in, whatever. FBI does it all the time."

"That's a crime!"

"No crap? So's stealing a kid."

There was something especially evil about entering a home unwanted and unasked. It was a violation of privacy, a little rape. She thanked Matt Nyren for his efforts and paid him off with a check: another $380. Her resources were running low, and she had no idea where to turn. She went to sleep on a Tuinal.

The next morning, two weeks to the day before Ace's sixth birthday, she climbed into her cherry-colored Hang Ten warmups and her old gray Nikes with the steel blue swoosh and began her predawn run. She opened at her fastest pace ever and didn't slow till she'd pounded the clamshell ridge all the way to Higman's Point and back, almost fifteen miles. Running down her driveway, her arms and legs flailing, she passed through her usual natural high to the edge of a delirium that made her see double and sent her sprawling on her front porch steps gasping for breath. It was worth the strain. For minutes she'd beaten back the new thought that had entered her mind and wouldn't leave:

Ace was gone for good.

21

EARLY ON AN evening a week later, Lael sat with her sister at the old maple table in the kitchen, trying to concentrate on the cross charts for a hybrid comfrey. The phone rang. "You get it, will you, Julie?" she said. For almost four months she had been jumping at the sound. It wouldn't hurt if somebody else answered once.

Julie said, "Hello," then: "My God!" Her brown eyes opened wide and she whispered, "Lael, it's him."

"Who?"

"*Him!*"

She grabbed the phone. "Hello?" a weak voice said. "Can you hear me?" He sounded as though he were calling from a mine shaft.

"Mike, where are you?" she asked. She entertained the idea that he would say they were on their way home.

"Forget that," he said, sounding out of breath. "Listen, I need. . . ."

The voice faded, and all she could hear was a warble. She remembered rural phones like that. "Mike?" she said. "I can't hear you. Mike, please, I can't hear you!" My God, she thought, will he think I hung up? And never call me back? Damn this phone. *God damn this phone!*

There was a noise like a waterfall, a hollow silence, and the connection died.

She let out a shriek, started to dial "O," then hung up and waited, glaring at the phone.

A few hours later the sky turned black. Rain hit the windows in bursts as though sprayed from a fire hose. She sat at the table with her head resting on her forearms. Her sister hugged her and left at 1:00 A.M.

She tried to imagine why Mike had called. To taunt her? What had he meant, "I need. . . ."? Did it have something to do with Ace? Why else would he call her? *Was something wrong with Ace?*

How simple it would have been to call back, how humane.

92

Maybe he was afraid they could trace a second call. Or maybe he'd been using a pay phone and somebody else had been waiting to use it. For *three* hours? She ticked off the possibilities and ticked them off again. Why would he go to such lengths to make me suffer? Is Julie right? Does he really hate me? *What does he have to hate me about?*

At two-thirty she went outside. The sky was still thick, but the rain had stopped, leaving the air warm and soupy. The lights of Seattle laid a pink blush against the base of the clouds. Down at the pond the watch frogs were repeating their three favorite words: *rivet, orbit,* and *dammit.* It was hard to imagine that once the whole family had enjoyed that nightly racket. *Oh, Mike, what did you want? Why did you call?*

The frogs went silent in the middle of a crescendo, every voice dying at once. They must have sensed a threat, a heron or owl cruising the red-glowing sky on silent wings or a family of raccoons sneaking out of the woods for *cuisses de grenouilles.* She wondered where Larry Allen was spending the night. She needed the little watch cat. She needed her frogs. She needed her herbs and her sister and her parents and friends. But most of all, she needed Ace. The place was unbalanced without him. She put her head in her hands and cried softly. The frogs started up again.

22

ON ACE'S SIXTH birthday she intended to sleep late, shortening the number of hours she would have to get through, but a tapping from the living room woke her before dawn. A robin was challenging its own reflection, rushing along the overhang toward the front window, stopping just short, now and then scratching at the big pane with its claws or tapping with his beak.

She made a broad X across the middle of the pane with masking tape—something she should have done weeks ago. Last year she'd been too late, and a Steller's jay had battered itself to death against the glass. She had found the body days later, a weightless splash of Prussian blue under the rhododendrons. She remembered the night she'd panicked at her own reflection in Ace's window. Maybe she should put an X back there, too. Hysterical birds and hysterical mothers, there were plenty of both around the old house.

By midmorning, she had begun to feel a web of conspiracy drawing around her. Julie arrived with an armful of hydrangeas and mums that must have cost a day's pay. Her mother phoned at 10:00 A.M.—"just wanted you to know I'm on my way over, baby"—and her father called an hour later from the naval shipyard at Bremerton, where he was hearing the latest my-wife-she's. Susan Sievertson, Ace's nursery schoolteacher, phoned and chatted for fifteen minutes, and a trio of neighbors from up on the bluff dropped in with brownies and a thermos of coffee. She thanked them and gave each a little tussie mussie floral bouquet in its own silvered vial.

None of her visitors or callers had mentioned Ace, and she knew why. She imagined them meeting all week in cabals and plotting strategy. *Whatever you do, don't talk about the boy.... Don't remind her.... Just drop in, she needs company right now....*

Stein called at noon. "Hey, how about dinner tonight?"

"We're having quiche," she said, eager to get back to her garden. "Bring Trang." The boy had been riding over on his bike lately, bearing gifts of mushrooms, clams, wild herbs, edible seaweeds. It was as though he felt indebted—or was he acting for Van? It didn't matter. She was surprised to find she had a lot in common with both of them.

"No, no," Stein said, laughing. "I don't mean at home. I mean out. Like—a date."

"A date?"

"Jeez, Lael, don't pass out." She waited for him to say that she needed a change of scene. "Hey, you oughta go into town once in a while," he said. "Sniff some carbon monoxide, hear some noise, get mugged."

She was beginning to find the organized sympathy unsettling. Nobody liked to be ganged up on. The women from the bluff couldn't have known it was Ace's birthday; someone must have solicited them. Stein wouldn't have known either. Julie must have told him. Or her mother. All the solicitude was making her feel like a charity case.

"Why tonight?" she asked, trying not to sound ungrateful.

"Why not?"

"I just wondered. You never asked me to dinner before. Am I a cause now? Is that what's happened?"

"Huh?"

"I just meant, are you asking *me* to dinner or some poor depressed client? Because if—"

"Hey, Lael!" he interrupted. "If you don't want to go, just say so. God, those weird theories of yours. Don't you ever see anything in simple terms?"

Suddenly she felt ashamed. Stein had stood by her. Except for her family, he had been her mainstay. She *owed* him in more ways than one. But how could she go out for dinner on Ace's birthday? "I'd be awful company," she said.

"Impossible."

"It's Ace's sixth birthday, Van. You knew that, didn't you? Come on, tell the truth."

He hesitated. "Yeah, I knew. So what? It just gave me a good excuse."

"I'd wretch you out."

"Hey, what do you think I want from you, Lael, some kind of scintillating performance? Look, we'll take the six o'clock boat, and we'll have a nice quiet dinner and come home early. No strain, no pain. You won't even have to wear your ball gown."

She tried to think of a way out. She had looked forward to

another quiet evening by the phone. She couldn't take a chance
on missing Mike's next call.

"Van, thanks," she said. "But I just can't."

"Look, Lael, you've got a whole bunch of negative feelings,
and you've got to express them. Why not to me?"

"Oh, Van, you're doing your psychiatrist number again."
This time she didn't mean it in an unkind way—just as an
observation.

"*Ja! Ja!*" he said. "Shtein za shrink. *Der Herr Doktor* vill
now eggshplain vot happens ven you hold beck za feelings.
Zay vill come out *in ozzair vays!* Za feelings, zay can—not—
be—rrrrrepressed!" He sounded like someone gargling.

"I haff a friend whose vife split," he went on in a less
raucous voice. "Poor man, he vouldn't talk about it, vouldn't
efen *sink* about it. You know vot happen to zat poor soul? He
got terminal jock itch. *Ja!* Zay hooked him up to za jock itch
machine, but he passed away in za eggspensive care unit. He
vas only thirteen, za poor klutzenheimer. So—"

"Van?" she interrupted.

"—Herr Doktor Shtein—"

"VAN!"

"*Ja?*"

"If you bag the accent, I'll meet you on the six o'clock
boat."

As soon as she hung up, she felt like calling him back. In
the greenhouse she shared her misgivings with Julie. "For God's
sake, go!" her sister insisted. "See a movie, get high—anything
but hang around here."

"But Mike might call."

Juliet's saucer-shaped brown eyes stared hard across a flat
of rocket starts. "You can't sit by the phone forever, Lael.
That's letting Mike control your life. Hasn't he controlled it
enough already?"

"I don't have any choice."

"You don't, huh? Well, I do. I don't have one thing to do
tonight but study my damned history of pharmacology, and I
can do it here as well as anyplace else. So *go!*"

"Sis, I—"

"Go, go! You're bugging me."

She parked the Luv in the terminal lot and walked onto the
green and white ferry. She wore a black silk scarf around her

dark blond hair and a beige Burberry raincoat over a loose black velour tunic and a pair of chocolate brown jeans. She had studied her clothes closet before making the selection, trying to pick out something pleasantly feminine but not misleadingly sexy.

Stein sat at a salon table on the main deck, arranging paper cups. "A spot of Chablis?" he asked in an English accent, raising a sweating green bottle. He was wearing the same three-piece suit and motorcycle boots he had worn to Victoria, but this time his boots were polished, his soft blue tie was neatly knotted, his light blue oxford cloth shirt looked new, and—my God, she thought, his ponytail's gone.

"Van!" she said, pointing to his head. "What did you do with all that hair?"

"Sent it to the Smithsonian. They insisted."

As he began pouring the wine, she noticed again the graceful curve of his nose and his dark blue eyes. She thought: My first date with a genuine Norwegian Jew. We'll eat herring; what else? She was feeling silly even before she took a drink. Maybe he'd been right about needing to get away.

"Just a drop," she requested. As he filled the paper cups, she asked nervously, "What are we drinking to?"

"To Ace," he said. "Six years old today."

She hesitated. "To . . . Ace," she said. She took a cool sip and said, "Thanks, Van. All day everybody's been avoiding the subject. Thanks for understanding."

"What's to understand?" His cheeks reddened a little to match his droopy mustache. "It's his birthday."

"You know something?" she said, reaching across and touching his wrist. "I think people are scared to mention him for fear I'll cry. I think people would rather be punched than cried at. But I don't cry . . . all that much." She suddenly felt tearful and had to stop. A classic example of autosuggestion.

He grabbed her hand. "Cry at me all you want. I've been cried at by experts."

Out of the corner of her eye she spotted a familiar figure marching toward the front of the ferry. She recognized the slightly bowed legs with the highly articulated muscles, the eyes that stared unblinkingly straight ahead, the business suit, the simple gray hat. "Van!" she whispered. "That's Mike's mother."

Stein turned. "So that's the bitch."

"You shouldn't call her that. She can't help herself."

"Lael, people are gonna walk all over you till you learn to hate a little."

"Herr Doktor Shtein shpeaking? What's the next lesson? How to hate?"

He refilled her cup and then his own. "What's her problem?" he asked.

"Oh, God, it goes way back. Mike's dad was knifed to death on Queen Anne Hill. Trying to break up a street robbery."

"When?"

"When Mike was three. Catherine panicked. She packed up and moved to the island, figured they'd be safe."

Stein stared after the disappearing figure. "I've seen her someplace," he mused.

"Thunder Bay Inn. She's been a waitress for thirty years."

Thirty years on her feet, Lael thought. Thirty years of holding the fries, 10 percent tips, grouchy cooks, varicose veins. She disliked the woman but admired her persistence. How many mothers would have put Mike through college and then double-shifted for another year so he could take a master's in design? You couldn't just write off somebody like that.

Stein interrupted her thoughts. "I remember her now. She waited on me one night. All smiles and courtesy. 'Everything all right, sir? *Good!*' Then the busboy dropped a glass, and she really got on his case. I wonder if she was the one who snatched Ace."

"No," Lael said.

"How can you be sure?"

"That woman was taller. And younger."

The ferry hooted its landing signal, and they strolled to the car deck. "It's, uh, cute," she said, anxiously eyeing his black motorcycle. What else could you say about a bike?

"You call a Yamaha three fifty *cute?* With Kerker headers?" When she didn't answer, he kicked a tire. "Cute? With K Eighty-one Dunlops? Manley valves, Sifton cams, magneto ignition—?"

"What's magneto ignition?" she interrupted him. "What're *any* of those things?"

"Please. Don't joke." He helped her onto the seat.

They zipped along the waterfront streets at surprisingly reasonable speeds, crossed the bridge to West Seattle, and parked in front of a nondescript little restaurant called "The Phoenecia." Inside, she excused herself to check in with Julie. There'd een no calls. When she returned to the booth in the corner, a waitress was serving matching bowls of hummous and baba ganooj with hot pita bread, plus a salad scented with pomegranate and another with garlic. "So eat already," Stein said, tearing the bread in half and shoving a hunk at her.

She looked around for utensils. *"Eat!"* he said, holding up his fingers. He dipped a crust into the bowl of baba ganooj.

After a while he asked, "Taste the onion? The garlic? The two feet of Satan."

"Excuse me?" She had been trying to imagine why Mike had never called back, but the mention of Satan caught her ear.

"When the devil ran from the Garden of Eden, onion and garlic shot up from his footprints. Onion from his left and garlic from his right. Or was it the other way around? I missed that one on my finals."

"You studied theology?"

"Four years."

"To become a—a Jewish rabbi?"

"Well, actually I wanted to become a Catholic rabbi, but the bishop said, 'Give it up, my son, it'll never fly.'" He smiled innocently.

"Oh, Van." She was embarrassed, but his smile made her relax. She wondered if he was going to discard Doktor Shtein and switch to this new David Letterman approach. Or was it Richard Pryor? "What really happened?" she asked.

"About what?"

"About leaving theology school."

He licked a smear of hummous from his finger. "Bacon did me in," he said.

She tried to remember the name of the essays that her father was forever quoting. *Meditationes Sacrae.* "It wasn't his *Sacred Meditations,* was it?" she asked.

"Not *Francis* Bacon," he said, faking a disgusted scowl. "*Real* bacon. Like in Cudahy? Hormel? Snap, sizzle, pop?"

"You dropped out of school because of bacon?"

"Had to eat it, yeah. So I quit. For six months I oinked out. Rashers of bacon, BLT sandwiches, hot dogs wrapped in bacon, bacon and eggs, bacon and bagels, bacon and *bacon.*"

"And now you hate it."

"No. I'd quit again for bacon."

"You never went back?"

"Not to rabbinical school."

Ace returned to mind; she was surprised that he had left momentarily. She wondered if Mike had had a little party for him today. Where? *Is he happy?* Stein scooped up some diced pomegranate on a piece of pita bread and popped it into her mouth.

A smiling black-eyed man arrived with a glistening rack of lamb and began carving it with a butter knife. "Tender, eh, Mr. Van?" he said. "You like tender, lady? This lamb *tender!* I pick especially for you!"

For a while they ate to the sound of Egyptian music: all wailing and quaver and hot percussion. "What's Trang doing tonight?" she asked.

"Studying for a test in sex education."

"Do you help him?"

"Help him? He helps *me.*"

Now who was he being? Johnny Carson? David Steinberg? He launched into a stream of light patter, peeking to see if he was having any effect. When he turned to politics, she found herself inspired to challenge some of his more sweeping statements, and by the time the baklava had arrived, oozing butter and honey and a hint of walnut, the two of them were hot and heavy into supplyside economics, which he considered an economic joke. "A rising tide lifts all the boats, huh?" he asked. "What if you're standing on the beach?"

She thought how seldom she'd ever talked to Mike about anything beyond their own limited interests: his drawings and fishing, her herbs and housework. Everything had been so shallow, so limited, the only common denominator a small boy. She wondered what it would be like to live with someone who could work up a rhetorical sweat over Cambodia and Afghanistan and the twelve-year-old berry-pickers of Northwest Washington. And had strong opinions about Bartok and Steve Reich and the proper amount of saffron to put in a paella.

He had quoted Shakespeare twice during the evening. Trying to impress? What difference did it make? Trying to impress was another form of compliment. She'd never found it offensive, as long as it wasn't boring. And when was the last time anyone had mentioned Virginia Woolf to her or quoted Ecclesiastes? She was a lit. major who never talked lit. She'd forgotten the joys of the old fashioned rap, one on one.

But she had to phone home again. This time Julie answered on the first ring. The news was bad.

23

JULIE HAD HAD the presence of mind to push the record button on the Panasonic answering device, and now the sisters and the lawyer leaned into the kitchen counter and listened to the taped conversation.

"Hello? Is Lael there?" Once again the voice was faint and scratchy, mixed with warblings and transmission clatter.

"No. Who's this?"

"It's Mike, Julie. Michael Pritcher. Where's Lael?"

"Out."

"Till when?"

"I don't know."

"Balls." The voice was weak, but not so weak that his petulance didn't carry. Lael wondered what made him think the rest of the world should be at his service night and day and how Catherine had developed this selfishness in her son. Would the pattern be repeated in a grown-up Ace? One more reason to get him back fast.

"Maybe I can help," Julie's loud voice said on the tape.

"You can't. It's about the kid's asthma. It's. . . ." The voice began to fade. Lael leaned forward.

"What about his asthma?" Julie's voice asked.

"His inhaler thing. It isn't working. I got the kind Lael always gets, but it makes his heart beat too fast."

"Is that what you called about last week?"

"Yes."

"Why didn't you call back?"

He hesitated. "Uh, trouble. With the phone, I mean."

"The phone? My God, Lael sat up half the night—"

"Forget that!" He sounded aggravated. "Listen, the doctor says he needs his shot program. He—"

"You took him off?" Julie interrupted. "He hasn't been getting his allergy shots?"

"I—we—there wasn't time."

"What kind of shape is he in?"

There was a pause. Words faded in and out of the waterfall

of static, but Lael caught two frightening ones: "temperature" and "oxygen."

Julie repeated, *"What kind of shape is he in?"*

This time the answer was inaudible.

Oh, God, Lael said to herself, Ace *needs* that immunization program. The inhaler just relieves the symptoms. Mike never bothered to get that straight. She wondered who was sitting up nights with the child, helping him stay calm while he fought for breath. Mike and his mother always considered that mollycoddling.

"Give me a number!" Julie said. "I'll have Lael call you the second she gets in. She knows all about the shots."

"I can't give you a number."

"Why not?"

"We, uh, don't have a phone yet." His voice dropped away and came back weakly. ". . . Pay attention. Lael keeps his allergy chart in her desk. Take it to my mother's house in the morning. The doctors need it. Otherwise, they'll have to do a whole new set of scratch tests."

"Yes, *yes*. Will your mother know where to send it? Can't the Island Clinic mail it direct?"

A click and a pop and a dial-tone came from the recording machine on the kitchen table. "He's admitting that Catherine knows where they are," Lael said, growing progressively agitated as the realization sank in. "We've got it on a cassette. We should put the sheriff on her!"

Van sighed. "Lael, don't—"

"We've got what we need!" she said. Suddenly she felt a rare spasm of joy. Hooray for the home team! She reached out and rumpled her sister's hair. Mike had blown it this time.

"Lael, relax," Van said, standing up and holding her shoulders. "It's illegal to record phone calls in Washington unless both parties consent."

"What's that mean?"

"The cassette's no good as evidence. Inadmissible. If you played it for the sheriff, he could hit you with a gross misdemeanor."

"What's a gross misdemeanor?"

"One that calls for jail time."

"So the tape's—?"

"Worthless. It tells us what we already knew, that's all."

"Oh, God!" Lael said. Another hope gone. She looked to-

ward Julie, then away, her eyes seeking relief and not finding
it.

Stein gave her a reassuring squeeze. It didn't help. She felt
useless, unmotherly. Not only was Ace as far away as ever,
but he was in the hands of a thoughtless man-child who didn't
have the decency to keep up the one medical program that had
helped. How unfair.

The lawyer was talking. "The cassette—we'll have it an-
alyzed."

Lael looked up. "What good will that do?" She felt sick.
Oh, Lord, she said to herself, don't let me lose the first good
meal I've had in months.

"It might give us an idea where he called from," Van said,
flipping the recorder open and removing the cassette.

"By then it'll be too late," she said.

"Can't be sure," he said.

She rushed to the living room. From her desk she extricated
a folder marked "Medical" and looked at Ace's allergy record.
He had registered between 1 and 2 for various foods and pol-
lens, 2 for rabbit hair, 2+ for cedar sawdust and fall leaf
molds, 4 for house dust, and 4+ for "summer grass mix." His
asthma was a minor aggravation most of the year, but an ordeal
in June and July. Here in Washington it was September; the
summer grass mix was mostly a memory. Where on God's
green earth was it still hot summer?

She slumped in front of the desk and tried to make sense
out of what was happening. Of course, she would take the
records to Catherine Pritcher in the morning. But then what?

She tried to anticipate whether the woman would mail the
list or phone it. Maybe we could tap her line, she thought, and
trace the call. But that would take police assistance or a court
order. Even the area code would be a help. Where's "down
here"? South Seattle? Portland? Argentina? God, she thought,
what news. What awful, horrifying, unsettling news. It's enough
to make you give up on the human race.

Except for a few.

24

THE NEXT MORNING she drove two miles through a light rain to the subdivision where Catherine Pritcher and her only son had fled to escape the perils of the mainland thirty years ago. Lael thought of these eight or ten blocks as Time Warp Heights. The asphalt streets were lined with post-World War II tract houses, rectangular boxes in decorator colors—Gulden's yellow, Tijuana turquoise, buttermilk white, cranberry red—no two painted the same, each set back from the sidewalk to provide small front yards in which no children played. Carved street numbers were the style, complete with misplaced quotation marks and apostrophes. She found the right one. "FORTY THREE PARK DRIVE. THE PRITCHER'S."

The arbor vitae in front of the one-story house had been allowed to grow thicker since her last visit almost a year ago. Bushes behind the wooden fence filled in the interstices so that the house, unlike its neighbors, was shut off from the view of passersby. The mailbox sat at an angle on a splintered post. The gate in the middle of the front fence was closed and locked, both hinges flecked with rust. The place looked like a small run-down fortress, as though the subjects of a minor queen had just completed a war and were too exhausted to prepare for the next.

Catherine came out behind a frozen smile, sweatered arms halfway extended, just as though she hadn't broken off their relationship months ago. "Lael!" she called from halfway down the short walk. "How nice!" She's being a Pritcher, Lael thought, predictably unpredictable. Any second her demeanor could change.

"I have his allergy record," Lael said in her most business-like voice. If Ace were in bad shape, speed mattered more than courtesy. The mail delivery would be slow enough as it was.

"Come on in," the woman said, and Lael heard, Good morning, your table will be ready in just a moment. The slightly nicotine-stained teeth behind the painted red lips reminded Lael of the day she and Mike had returned from their elopement

"I'm *so* glad you're in the family now," Catherine had said that morning eight years ago, flashing a grin that gleamed like sunlight off a dirk.

She noticed that the inside of the compact house had changed since her last visit. The surfaces still overflowed with junk and memorabilia, but an entire wall of the living room was covered with pictures of Mike: looking happy at birthday parties, fiercely determined in his football sweater, stern in his National Guard uniform, proud holding up a fish, furtive in the full-color photo that had come with the wedding package at Reno. Lael's picture was nowhere to be seen. She was sure she'd been cropped from at least two or three. She wondered if the wall display had been put up for her. A subtle message: *See? I love him more.*

Another wall held pictures of Catherine and her doomed husband, heads together, watch-the-birdie smiles, and a faded sepia photograph of a tall squinting man and a slender young woman: Mike's grandparents perhaps. The only books were *The Handyman's Encyclopedia* and the four-volume supermarket edition *History of the U.S.* in faded green and gold.

Hanging from the wall of an alcove was something else new to Lael: a Christ on the cross so lifelike with its painted red bloodstains that she halfway expected a cry of pain. On a nicked brown table a plastic Infant of Prague was juxtaposed behind a lighted red candle in a votive glass. It had always disturbed Catherine that her son had married out of the faith. Maybe she was sending up home prayers that it wouldn't happen again.

She hoped she wouldn't be asked to make the complete tour. Mike's room had been preserved intact like a pharaoh's, and she remembered how the curator loved to show off the royal memorabilia item by item: tot-size wicker chairs from K Mart, faded board games, dusty airplane models, children's books from A. A. Milne to Sid Fleischman. The room always made her feel as though she were peering into the open grave of a child named Michael Pritcher whose resurrection was expected any second.

She needn't have worried. "Sit here," the woman said, motioning to the old velvet sofa. "I made tea. You still drink tea, don't you, Lael?"

She nodded. Waiting apprehensively with Ace's allergy record on her lap, she decided that the inside of the house looked a little run down. Odd, she thought. Catherine is a meticulous woman, neat to a fault. She had an overnight warning that I was coming. Why the film of dust on all the picture frames?

Why the dead azaleas on the table?

She associated slovenly houses with depressed and deprived people, but what did Mike's mother have to be depressed about? It hit her with a chill that they'd both lost sons. She was used to seeing Mike two or three times a week. His absence must be painful.

The woman returned with a tray that had obviously been prepared in advance. When she had finished pouring a half cup for each of them, she pointed to the only sunny corner of the room and said, "There! Recognize that? You gave it to me for my birthday last year."

Lael turned and saw a stunted ficus, its roots imprisoned in too small a pot. "Nice," she said politely. The tree didn't look an inch bigger than the year before. The classic brown thumb. Plants know when you really don't care about them, she thought. Plants know people better than people know plants.

A mantelpiece clock chimed the quarter hour in descending notes. Catherine Pritcher ran through a few more forced cordialities and then lowered her voice to an intimate level. Lael felt her own muscles tense.

"You know I've always liked you," the woman said, insinuating herself an inch or two closer. She went on as though the closeness of their relationship had been established long ago. "Of course I love my son more than anybody. That's only natural. As a mother you can appreciate that." The soft words didn't go with the hard, unblinking eyes, but Lael nodded.

"And I love Alex, too. Ace, I mean." Maybe she does, Lael thought, but in a relationship as sick as hers and Mike's even a beautiful child like Ace would eventually be an interloper. "So when I talk about this—this little problem, you'll understand that I'm trying to see it from all sides."

"If you love Ace," Lael said, "why don't you tell me where he is?"

The woman went on as though she hadn't heard. "I have no idea *what* got into Mike. I'd give anything if we could roll back the clock, bring him and Alex home. But I've lectured him till I'm blue in the face, and he swears he's not coming back, unless—"

She paused, and Lael sensed it was for emphasis. She could imagine Catherine in front of her mirror, rehearsing her speech with gestures. "Lael, have you ever thought that there's a solution to this mess? Something . . . obvious?"

"Yes. Give me the address and let me bring Ace home.

Where he belongs. With his mother."

Once again the woman ignored the plea. "Suppose," she said, "just suppose you signed Alex away. Now wait! Hear me out! Suppose you were to release him to Mike for good?"

"How would I do that?" she heard herself ask.

"I'm sure your lawyer could tell you."

"Release him to Mike? For life? Does that strike you as fair?"

"We're not discussing what's fair, Lael. We're discussing what's possible." The woman hurried into an explanation of the benefits for both sides. Mike and the boy could come out of hiding and return to the island, "where they belong." Alexander could resume his treatment with his regular doctor. And of course, Mike would grant generous visitation rights. Unlimited, in fact. . . .

Lael was dazed. "You mean I could see Ace, but I couldn't— I couldn't raise him."

"Well, uh, Michael and I would raise him."

"Mike and *you?*"

"I know how to raise a boy."

Lael's mind flashed back to one of the rare days when she'd left Ace alone at his grandmother's. He had angered the woman with one of his favorite songs, sung to the tune of "Row Row Row Your Boat":

> Suck, suck, suck your toes
> All the way to Mexico.
> While you're there,
> Cut your hair
> And stick it in your underwear.

Lael had first heard him and Big Jeremy sing it at school. Susan Sievertson had said, "The boys are in a little scatalogical phase now, Lael. Don't worry. It only lasts about fifteen years." Catherine Pritcher was less tolerant. She had called Ace dirty and made him sit on the couch for the last hour of his visit. This was the woman who knew how to raise a boy.

"I must have missed something," Lael said now. "Why doesn't Mike just come home? Why do I have to sign Ace away to get him back?"

The woman threw up her thin, veiny hands. "Lord knows I've *tried* to talk him into it. Tried *everything!* But you know Mike. Once he sets his mind . . . I'm just trying to break the logjam, Lael. If you give up custody, he'll relax a little. He'll bring Alex back right away, I know he will. He's *told* me he will." She leaned closer and smiled. "It's a first step."

Lael wondered if the woman had the slightest idea of her own transparency. A first step! It would be a *last* step. They must have her pegged for a complete imbecile.

"You made him angry, Lael. Really ticked him off. That's not wise with Mike, I'm sure you know that." There was a note of pride in her voice: *See what a vengeful boy I've raised. Just like his mom.*

"How did I tick him off?"

"Hunting him down like a—a mongrel dog. Now wait! Don't get mad. I'm not accusing you. But—"

"I hunted *him* down?"

"Why, *yes!* To Port Angeles. To Victoria. And you're still after him, aren't you?" The tone was righteous. Lael recognized a peculiar Pritcher technique: Commit a flagrant injustice, and then blame the victim for reacting. Mike had worked the routine on her for eight years.

"How long can you keep it up, Lael?" the dry voice droned on. "Where'll you get the money to hound him from one state to another?"

"I run a business," Lael said.

"Oh, yes, I forgot."

Catherine's lips compressed, as though smiling had become too burdensome. She came across as an aging actress nearing the end of an overlong scene. Watching her intently, Lael suddenly wondered if the woman was losing touch with reality. She seemed to be the same driven, compulsive person as before, but was it possible that a part of the mechanism had broken down deep inside? She wondered about Mike. There was a French term: *folie à deux*, mutual insanity. For the first time she realized that the child snatching might have been Catherine's idea all along. In her mind she could hear the two of them plotting. Mike had always been overly influenced by his mother.

"I'll never give him up," Lael said, edging away on the sofa.

"You've already given him up. I'm just trying to help you get together again." The dead smile cracked like a mud pack as she spoke. The pale gray-blue eyes stared with unconcealed hatred. Lael's first reaction was relief. She felt more comfortable with the Catherine Pritcher she had always known.

"I came here because Mike needs Ace's allergy record and you know where they are," she said. "I didn't come to bargain for rights that're already mine." She held out the manila envelope. "Here. Mike says he needs this fast."

The woman made no attempt to accept the envelope, and it dropped to the sofa between them. "I'd like to know a few things before I leave," Lael said. "Ace. Is he bad?"

Catherine crossed the room and lit a cigarette, blowing the smoke at the wall. "The inhaler isn't doing the job anymore," she said. "He's been using a refill every few days. The doctor—"

"Every few days? That's too much epinephrine! His heart—"

"That's what the doctor said."

"What doctor? Where?"

"Stop prying."

"Why don't you just go to the Island Clinic and get his vaccine and send it directly? Why have a new one made up?"

"Because the clinic won't give me the vaccine without signing a bunch of papers." No, they won't, Lael thought, because you're not his mother. So you need me after all.

"Catherine, where's Ace?" she demanded. "If you have a shred of decency, tell me that."

"I won't."

"He's my son!"

"He *was*." The woman blew a thin flume of smoke across the room.

"Why did Mike do this?"

"You and your Jew lawyer," the woman was muttering. "When are you going to stop? You know what's making my grandson so nervous? *You!* The insecurity you're forcing on them. Strange places, strange people. As soon as they put down a few roots, they have to pull up and move again. *Because of you!*" She said it like a curse, her voice trembling.

Lael tried again, this time in a carefully controlled voice. "Why did he take Ace? Give me one good reason, Catherine. What did I do?"

"It's what you didn't do, girl."

"What didn't I do?"

"You didn't stand by your husband." The accusing words flew from her mouth. "Too busy with your mustard greens, I guess. Your so-called business. Michael needed a full-time wife. That's what you couldn't be."

Lael bit her lip. "Did he say that?"

"Remember what you told him when the shopping center went broke? The dream of his life? You said, 'Oh, did it? Say, my parsley came up today.' That was your idea of consolation. Blame yourself, girl. You and your damned herbs."

The quote wasn't even close. She had cried with Mike when the shopping center failed. She felt falsely accused. She had no idea how to handle such a personal attack and no experience on which to draw. "Please, Catherine," she said softly, "don't call me girl. I'm not a child."

"Oh? What are you?"

Her heart pounded, but her skin felt cold. Her teeth began to chatter. She tried to answer, but at first nothing came out. Then she blurted, "I didn't steal a child! I didn't ignore a baby's suffering!"

"You drove him away. You don't want to bring him back." Catherine's voice had risen; she sounded almost hysterical. "He'll be down there the rest of his life!"

Lael blotted her eyes with a handkerchief and caught a look at the woman's pinched face. It had turned a ghostly white. Wasn't there a case for pity toward a disturbed creature like this? She wondered what had happened to her own forgiving instincts. Hatred and contempt had taken over her heart—alien emotions, unacceptable, inappropriate. She headed for the door. She had to get away fast.

"Selfish bitch."

The words floated across the room like poison gas. She wasn't even sure they were intended for her ears. She took a deep breath and turned and started to talk even as she realized that she should just leave, get away, remove herself from the contaminated area before she herself did something stupid. "You're sick, Catherine," she said. "You need help."

The woman laughed. "We'll see who needs help, girl."

Lael rushed across the room and grabbed the bony upper arms. She saw the fear in the smaller woman's eyes, but she couldn't stop. "Don't call me girl!" she yelled. "Damn you, I'm a twenty-eight-year-old woman. If you call me girl again I'll—I'll—" She flung her against the wall and for the first time saw those cold eyes blink. *"Where's Ace?"* she screamed. *"Where're you hiding my son?"*

The sight of Catherine Pritcher holding up her spidery fore-arm like a shield made her feel suddenly ashamed. The woman had felt empty, weightless, as though thirty years of waiting on tables had dried her from the inside out. Such an unfair fight.

"I'm sorry," she mumbled. She felt confused. "Oh, Catherine, please, *please*. . . . I don't know what to say."

She barely heard the response: "Get out! *This second!*" She obeyed without protest. All she could do in these four walls was make things worse. She should have known that from the start.

Driving home, she shook all over. She turned on the heater and still felt cold. She wondered if this was the "fight or flight" syndrome. She had never experienced it before. How had she lost control so completely? Even as a child she had avoided physical encounters. The thought of touching someone in anger was enough to make her sick.

She stopped the truck in her driveway and tried to calm down. Somehow her whole world had changed with one small physical act. A part of her felt exhilarated, blazing with life, but she also felt threatened and anxious, as though she had left the protection of civilization and wandered into the jungle and now would be exposed to alien rules and forces.

She was still trying to sort out her reactions when she entered the empty house. The hall mirror provided a good view of a beast who would attack a woman of fifty. When Ace came back, would he recognize his own mother? She saw a haggard young woman whose skin was beginning to loosen and whose long blond hair needed work.

Something else caught her eye. She squinted and pushed closer to the mirror. She found it half hidden in the glints and gleams. Her first gray hair.

25

"YOU . . . DID . . . *WHAT?*" The lawyer's words came over the phone like puffs from a blow gun. She imagined him in his office, jumping up from a slouched position, coils of red hair bobbing wildly.

"I grabbed her by the shoulders and shook her and . . . oh, Van, I feel awful."

He didn't respond. "Van," she said, "did you hear me?"

"I'm trying to imagine you muscling somebody. Maybe you're learning too fast."

"Learning what?"

"Some of the things I've been telling you. But assault isn't what I had in mind."

"I hate myself. I don't know what I was proving. I just lost it. Something she said."

"Like what?"

"She called me girl. As though I was a naughty child or something. As though I was hers to discipline."

"Way to go, girl."

She ignored his flipness. "Van, is it irretrievable?"

"Depends. You broke a couple rules, yeah. But"—he stretched the word out—"it's good to see you doing something for yourself."

"I've never stopped looking for Ace, Van. Isn't that doing something for myself?"

"Yes, but you've been so goddamn *polite* about it, so understanding. Listen, Lael, you can't understand people like those Pritchers any more than you can understand rabid dogs. While you're trying to understand them, they're tearing out your liver. Don't you see that?"

"Beginning to."

"Think back. Did she give you any ideas?"

"You mean—?"

"About where they're hiding Ace."

Her mind was mush. "She said Mike was 'down there,' wherever that is."

"Usually means to the south. But the whole damned United States is to the south. Hey, that reminds me. I played that cassette for a guy from Ma Bell. He said the background noise is—wait a minute, I got it written down here somewhere—'transient radio-telephone static.'"

"What's that mean?"

"It means that at some point Mike's voice was being relayed by shortwave. That means he was calling from a place that's served by radio—a mountaintop, a jungle, someplace like that. Maybe even clear out of the country. Hawaii, Mexico, the South Pacific, maybe Alaska. Who the hell knows? But definitely not a city."

She closed her eyes and felt guilty. She'd had a chance to pry valuable information out of Catherine Pritcher and instead indulged in a childish temper tantrum. Her self-image ebbed. "Oh, God, what next?" she said wearily.

"Hey, don't worry. We'll find them."

"It's been five months."

"We'll find them!" He sounded as though there were no room for doubt.

After their talk was over, she leaned forward till her forehead touched the wooden table and her finespun caramel hair with its single strand of gray spilled around her face in a circle. A recurrent fantasy flashed into her mind: Ace's body blows up like a balloon and slowly lifts into the air, expanding till the Oshkosh B'gosh label is as big as a billboard across his waist. Higher and higher he soars, catching the wind and picking up speed, waving elephantine arms and calling, "Mom, *Mom!* Get me down! *Get me down!*" twisting and waving, rising and screaming till his voice fades away and he's beyond her reach forever.

Hawaii, Mexico, the South Pacific, maybe Alaska—all light-years away, and she didn't know where to start.

26

EARLY ONE MORNING she awoke from a frazzled half sleep, released at last from the soggy grip of the sheets. She wondered what had kept her body heat so high even though it was a cool night and both windows were open. Hormones, she supposed. The female condition.

It had been four months since her last period. She'd started spotting again, faint rust-colored streaks that revived bittersweet memories of her pregnancy. The specialist in Seattle had diagnosed suppressed hysteria and reminded her that the word itself derived from the Greek for "womb." Her condition was understandable, he'd said, giving her the feeling that she had wandered into a confessional and been absolved. Why had all her gynecologists patronized her, and why had they all been men?

She lifted herself on an elbow and squinted to read the time. Four-fifteen. She had slept less than five hours, off and on. A good night's sleep, considering. She rolled onto the other elbow and saw that the curtain was opaque. The sun wouldn't rise for another hour.

She decided to run her regular predawn circuit. It was a little early, but the punch line of one of Van's silly jokes popped into her head: *"What's time to a pig?"* She wondered why she was thinking about him.

There was something cleansing about the runs she'd been making lately—not mere jogs, but efforts so intense that the final sprint down her driveway almost wiped her out. She had tried to make the run a habit ever since the confrontation with her ex-mother-in-law. In some mysterious metabolic way the morning workouts were restoring her pride.

She tiptoed across the bedroom and opened her closet door slowly so it wouldn't creak and then reminded herself that there was no one in the house to awaken. She wondered how many months would have to pass before she woke up thinking of herself as a solitary woman instead of as the mother of a sleeping child.

She snapped on a light and grabbed a pair of Day-Glo orange warm-ups and a threadbare sweat shirt imprinted with "U of W." Her running bra was hanging from the hook; she decided not to strap herself down for a change. No one would be on the road to notice her undisciplined breasts. She started lacing up her Nikes, noticed that they clashed with the pants, and laced them up anyway.

Out in the open she encountered a fine mist. She thought about turning back for her rain hat and Gore-tex jacket, but she knew she would be running till the sweat came in rivulets, and what difference would a little fresh rain make?

She turned left at the head of her long driveway and realized she had neglected to loosen up. Too late now, she told herself. What's the worst I can do? Pull a muscle? On a scale of one to ten, how much of a problem would a pulled muscle represent in my life? About one and five-eighths.

She heard the burble of fast-running water as she approached the wooden bridge that passed over Karkainen Inlet, a mile east on the beach road. The long creosoted trestle pinched the road to a pair of narrow lanes. She ran in the middle as though she were alone on earth. Far away she saw bobbing headlights, pinkish in the heavy mist, and wondered who might be approaching at this hour, but the car turned off.

As she picked up speed across the bridge, she listened for the plop of a migrating salmon or the hiss and splatter of schooled herring or candlefish, but the only sound was the gurgling of the tidal bore as it rammed up the inlet, flattening and broadening, reversing its earlier flow. She and Ace had caught tomcod and flounder off this bridge, dipped smelt with a long-handled net, dangled their bare feet from the side, and watched silver salmon wriggle up Karkainen Creek to replenish their race.

She thought of the bald eagles that perched in dead trees along the floodway and the day she and Ace had seen an osprey swoop from a hemlock and snag a small octopus with its claws. "Will he eat it?" Ace had asked, his eyes wide beneath his glasses, and when she'd said, "Sure," he'd made a face and said, "Yuck!"

She opened her stride, trying to outrun her memories. Her eyes picked up the edges of the cannery backlighted by the night glow of Seattle. She sent up splats of water as she ran across the puddled parking lot and leaped to the narrow wooden pier that extended into the bay. She jogged to the end and ran in place under a reddish light bulb that hung as a warning to approaching boats. The smell of iodine and salt soothed her lungs. Then she headed back.

She was sprinting the last few yards of beach road when she saw a dark car—maroon or dark red—parked at the head of her driveway, facing toward the house, motor idling. She skidded to a stop on the gritty shoulder.

As though the driver had seen her, the small dark station wagon backed out, throwing gravel and shells. It passed in a stench of diesel fumes, and she strained to see inside. In the darkness she had the impression of an averted face, cadaverous, vaguely luminescent in the reflection from the dash.

Catherine Pritcher? No. She drove an old Ford.

FALL

27

ON A SOGGY, gray November day a deeply devitalized Lael sipped a cup of strong tea on the ferry crossing Puget Sound. Against her better judgment she was being shanghaied to the Seattle Opera House to see *Petrouchka* with her sister. "You can't keep sitting around that damned house wondering what you've left undone," Julie had insisted. "And you can't guard the place every second. Nobody's come snooping for a month now, and we both need a break. Besides, I already bought the tickets."

As they sat quietly, Lael noticed a woman walk to the head of the line and pour herself coffee, then take a seat in the smoking section several aisles away. Somehow she looked familiar. She wore a tight suede-skin skirt and wobbled on stiletto heels. Her face was geisha white around the edges of her blusher, giving the effect of a double-printed picture, and her purplish eye shadow looked dug from a child's watercolor box. She looked like a go-go dancer commuting to work.

To the east, thunder rumbled softly in the Cascades. The woman sipped her coffee, shuddering lightly as though it were bitter. She engaged Lael's eyes, frowned, and jerked away.

In that instant Lael recognized her. She didn't know what made her so sure—she had barely glimpsed the woman's face before—but she was certain. "Julie!" she said, grabbing her sister's arm tightly. "That's—that's—"

"Take it easy, Sis. What is it?"

"The first booth in the smoking section. That's the woman on the ferry!"

"Huh?"

"The one in the, uh, the b-b-black truck." She couldn't keep from stammering.

Julie's eyes snapped open wide. "You sure? I thought you didn't get much of a look at her."

"I didn't, but *that's her!* Doc, we can't let her get away."

She peeked again as the woman lifted her head and sniffed the air like a wary deer. *Whoever you are, don't try to run for it*, Lael said to herself.

The woman walked off, tottering on her heels. Lael caught up on the staircase that led to the car deck below. "Wait!" she called out. "Stop!"

The woman didn't slow down.

"I'm his mother."

The woman stopped abruptly and turned. "What?"

"I said I'm his mother! The boy you stole."

The woman batted half inch lashes that accentuated the smallness of her hazel eyes. "You crazy or something?" she said, her thin voice squeaking a little.

Lael grabbed her by the shoulder and spun her around. "I won't let this drop. So you might as well stop right here."

"Please?" The childlike voice barely carried. It sounded like a plea for mercy. The woman dug her knuckles into her eyes, smearing her mascara. "Please," she said again. "Let me go. I didn't do anything to you."

Lael grabbed her by the wrist. "You took my son!" Her voice bounced off the walls of the narrow passageway. She slid her grip up to the elbow. "For God's sake, don't cry," she said, steering them both toward the car deck.

The creature barely resisted. "But I didn't *do* anything," she whined. "You can't—"

"Come ON!" Lael said.

"Where are you taking me? I told you—"

"To my truck. My black Luv. Remember? The one just like yours?"

As the woman walked, she kept up a steady blubbering and moaning and fell into a dramatic slump at the sight of the truck. Lael had never felt colder or harder. "You kidnapped my son," she said in a flat voice. "Now get in. Tell the truth, or I swear I'll have you arrested."

The threat brought a torrent of words and tears and moans. ". . . I'll kill myself . . . oh, God, please, God . . . I didn't mean it . . . you gotta believe me. . . ."

Lael squeezed the woman's upper arm hard and thought how fast brutishness becomes a habit. "Get in!" The woman stepped clumsily into the passenger's seat, and Lael slammed the door like a professional jailer. She came around and clambered into the truck, throwing questions as she entered. "Now who are you? *What* are you?"

"I'm—I'm the bartendress at the Inn. Thunder Bay. Is that what you wanted to know?" She smiled wanly through her stained eyes as though she hoped they'd be friends.

"Where's my son?" Lael snapped. She didn't want to give the woman a chance to make up a story. This—what had she called herself? *bartendress?*—this bartendress had a lot to explain.

"I wish I knew. I only wish I knew. But Mike, he—he dumped me the same as he dumped you."

"He didn't dump me," Lael said, and wondered why it mattered anymore.

The woman looked surprised. "He told me he was the one that left. He said it was because"—she cowered as though afraid to be struck—"because you were bad for the kid."

"Bad *for Ace?*" Lael looked hard at the woman's face and then at her own in the mirror. This wasn't a dream.

"That's what he said," the woman repeated. "Was he lying to me about that, too? He always lied."

"What do you mean, 'always'?"

"Well, I mean since we first started, uh, dating."

"Dating?" The word spun her sideways toward the woman. "You mean, like sleeping together?"

The bartendress bit her lip and didn't answer.

Lael turned her head so her face couldn't be seen. The ferry was in mid-sound—fifteen or twenty minutes to go. She tried to compose herself, but she was so shocked that her eyesight blurred. Her husband had been sleeping with this woman from the Thunder Bay Inn? Where his mother worked as a waitress? But how had he kept it secret? Or *had* he? Who knew? The whole island?

She looked at her rival and thought: Anyone passing by would think we're having a pleasant conversation. An ordinary scene on an ordinary fall Saturday. I am the only person on this boat who has just been hit by a falling building. "Who told you how to fool Ace?" she asked. "I mean, that day. Stopping at the mailbox the way I always did."

"Mike. I knew your house. Mike and me stayed there overnight once when you were, uh, out." Lael realized that it must have been the night he had spent at Ace's bedside in the asthma ward of Conant Hospital. *One solid year ago.*

"You were inside my house?" she asked.

"It was his idea." The woman's voice had taken on a truculent tone, as though it were unfair of Lael to question her too closely. "I—I loved him." The childlike whining noises began again.

"Did you . . . I mean, *in my bed?*"

The woman turned tearfully to Lael. "He said you didn't care. He said you...." She completed the destruction of her eye makeup with her knuckles. "You won't be mad at me if I tell you, will you?"

"I won't be mad." Lael had begun to realize she was dealing with another grown-up infant. Mike preyed on the naive and gullible, herself foremost.

"He said you were probably, uh, shacked up with somebody else."

"I *what?*"

"He said you had kind of an open marriage. He said you accepted things. That was a lie, too, huh?"

"Accepted things?"

"Things he did. Like you loved him so much it didn't matter. He said you were ... *you* know. Laid-back."

Lael touched her own hot cheeks with her fingertips. I don't know about laid-back, she thought, but stupid—yes. Unobservant, too. And a fool and a dupe and a ... what was the word? Cuckold? Can a woman be a cuckold? I'm a cuckoldess sitting next to a bartendress. I wonder if he ever came to me from her, still not quite satisfied. Was that what turned me off? Was that what made me ... frigid? Oh, God, how inadequate I must have been for him. "It went on for a year?"

"Sixteen months. I loved him. I wasn't just his, *you* know, his, uh...." Her voice dropped demurely.

"No, I'm sure you weren't," she said gently. It was her natural courtesy returning, but she doubted her own words. Maybe he'd considered them both his whores. Maybe there were others. Maybe that was the explanation for the cot in the back room of his office in Nisbet and the double lock that he'd installed for "security."

She asked herself who would have known about this woman and Mike. Catherine Pritcher, for sure. It's too big a coincidence, the two women working side by side. She might even have put them up to it. There's nothing Catherine wouldn't do, I know that now. Maybe she figured it was a way to destroy the marriage and retrieve her son. What was it she said when I was at her house? That I wasn't there when he needed me? Maybe I made it too easy. I trusted him. What's the use of being married if you can't trust each other? I didn't check his shorts and shirt collars. I believed him when he said he was working late. *Stupid!*

Ace was what mattered now. Her pride and her self-respect

were minor concerns. "Where's my son?" she demanded.

"I don't know. Honest to God. The last I saw them was in Bellingham."

"Doing what?"

"Driving around. Checking in and out of motels. Looking for a cabin or something. He tried to stay close to the steelhead rivers. He likes to fish." Lael thought how bizarre it was to be hearing about Mike from his mistress, as though the marriage and its history had been expunged and now she had to learn from a stranger that the man she had lived with for eight years liked to fish.

"Why aren't you with them now?"

"He ditched me." The woman started to sob again. "Got up one morning, he said the car wasn't running right. That little yellow thing? Told me to wait in the motel while he drove downtown to get it fixed. Him and the kid, they never come back."

"When was that?"

"Coupla months ago. Right after we left Canada."

"But what made you kidnap my son?"

The woman looked horrified. "Not kidnap! *Child-snatch.* They told me it was okay, it happened all the time, Mike would take the responsibility. Oh, God, you won't call the cops, will you?"

Lael ignored the request. *"They* told you it was okay? Who's they?"

"Mike and . . . his mom."

Once the news would have surprised her, but now it seemed redundant. "Where'd you get the truck?"

"A demo. From Seattle."

Lael felt her anger returning. "Why did you let all this time go by? That was my son you took! That wasn't a sack of groceries!"

"I kept waiting to hear from Mike. His mom promised he'd send for me. She'd say, 'Be patient, be patient. He's gotta find a new place, a new identity.' But now she hangs up when I call. Won't talk to me at work. They're Suck City, those damned Pritchers." She reached across the car seat and touched the sleeve of Lael's raincoat. "I'm sorry, honey, I'm really sorry. If I'd of only known what they were really like. . . . They used me. Now I gross them out."

They used us both, Lael thought, but you and I are adults; you and I can fight back. Right now he's using a defenseless child who loves him. And that's loathsome, even for Mike.

"Ace," she said. "How'd he act?"

"What do you mean?"

"How *was* he?" She felt an impulse to dig her nails into the smeared face. "Was he happy? Did he make jokes the way he used to? Did he talk about me?" Nearly in tears, she asked herself: Do I have to come right out and ask? DID HE MISS ME, YOU DENSE THING? DID THE ONLY SON I HAVE IN THE WORLD MISS ME?

"Oh, you mean Alex. Well, uh, Mike told him you didn't want him anymore, you were going to—to hurt him." The bartendress spoke as though her words didn't reflect against her personally, as though everything that had happened was someone else's fault. "He kept telling him, 'Run if you see your mom! Don't let her catch you!' No, Alex didn't talk about you. Not that I remember. Prob'ly he was afraid to." She sighed and said, "Can I please go now?"

Lael nodded, still seeing the two of them intertwined in her bed.

The woman stepped onto the deck. "Your name," Lael called through the window. "How can I get in touch with you?"

The ruined kabuki face gathered itself into a pleasant smile. The skewed make-up looked better now than when it had been in place. "Just call the inn. Any night but Sunday and Monday."

"Who shall I ask for?"

"Chastity," the woman said.

Lael walked behind the bartendress up the metal stairs, feeling unsatisfied with the conversation. She hated to plead, hated to admit that her forcefulness had been mostly an act. "Chastity, please, look at me," she said, stopping halfway up the staircase. "I've lost my son. Do you know how that feels? Please, *please,* where's my baby?"

The woman turned abruptly and dabbed at her eyes. Her thin lips moved at the corners, crinkling her lipstick into pink flakes. Lael had the sinking feeling that it was all put on, that she was being duped by a B actress playing dumb. Mike's old girl friend resembled a child listening to a sad story: the Death of Tabby; Shep's Last Hunt. She looked up and down the staircase and whispered, "He kept talking about going to Oregon. Some river. I forget the name."

Oregon. No surprise. He runs to places he already knows, places with good fishing and warm memories, not too far from his mother. Port Angeles. Victoria. Now somewhere in Ore-

gon. She had placed twenty or thirty HAVE YOU SEEN MY SON? posters in Portland. It was good to know he was on a river.
And she thought she knew which one.

28

One month before Christmas, Lael drove south across the Columbia river bridge to look for her son and his father. At every restaurant and gas station the sound of carols poured from loudspeakers. The hymns had always touched her. This year they also reminded her that she was alone.

Before the talk with Chastity she had intended to avoid the Christmas mopes by going shelling on the Washington coast—some wind-swept place like Moclips or Neah Bay—and pretend that it was just another weekend. Her family knew and understood. But on the road in Oregon every note of every carol held Ace's voice. She thought how much is lost when a child is taken. Pleasant memories turn painful; holidays become sentences to be served. The world spins backwards. She thought: how awful of God to let it happen.

Driving south, she checked in with her sister from roadside phones, and Julie kept begging her to come home. She always answered, "When I find Ace." She skipped meals or nibbled at fast food that sat on her stomach like clay.

She thought often about her last conversation with Van. "Look, don't go chasing rainbows," he had warned her. "Mike must've known all along he was gonna shake this woman. Why would he tell her where he was gonna hide?"

"Oh, Van—"

"Another thing. The kid's asthma's kicking up, right? Didn't you say it comes from spring grasses? How the hell's that match up with Oregon in December?"

It didn't, but everything else about Oregon made sense. Mike loved steelheading, a masochist's sport, at its best when snow and ice covered the riverbanks. She remembered all those impulsive trips to Oregon, how Mike would leave her and the baby in their room at the Anglers Roost Motel in Roseburg while he fished his favorite steelhead stream, the Umpqua. He and Ace were probably holed up in a town near the river: Roseburg or Glide, Riddle, maybe Tyee or Elkton. The idea of living near steelhead waters and hiding out at the same time would appeal to him.

126

She searched from the Umpqua's headwaters to the sea, called on town police and county sheriffs, tramped in and out of school offices, showing her poster and pictures of Ace and Mike and demanding information about new enrollees. She hung around schoolyards and looked at faces; visited nursery schools, churches, medical clinics, realtors, rental agents; asked pharmacists if a father and son had been in for medicine.

The Oregon seacoast turned out to be as dramatic and desolate as Washington's: miles and miles of gray beach covered with rounded pebbles and streaks of kelp and scraps of wood worn as smooth as doeskin; needle-shaped offshore islands with a single madrona or cedar on top; dark skies. At another time she might have found the seascapes beautiful, but now they filled her with foreboding. *What if I don't find Ace?* The fear was a constant.

The daily jumble of experiences began to run together: twisting roads, wrong turns, black ice, dense green woods, cardboard motels with individual packets of coffee and creamer, on-ramps and off-ramps, log-trucks that filled the rear-view mirror of her little Luv and blared "shave 'n' a haircut two bits" as they careened past.

In the soggy December weather she caught a virus. Her temperature climbed so high that she was afraid to find out what it was, and when she awoke one morning without a voice, she penned a hasty note in block printing on a piece of Red Rim Motor Hotel stationery:

I'M LAEL (PRONOUNCED LALE) & I HAVE A BAD CASE OF LARYNGITIS. I AM LOOKING FOR MY MISSING SON AND HUSBAND, ALEXANDER AND MICHAEL PRITCHER. ALEXANDER GOES BY THE NICKNAME ACE AND JUST TURNED SIX. HE HAS ASTHMA AND OFTEN WHEEZES. PLEASE TAKE A REAL GOOD LOOK AT THESE PICTURES AND TELL ME IF YOU HAVE SEEN EITHER OF THEM. OR IF YOU HAVE HEARD OF ANY NEW LITTLE BOYS IN TOWN. THIS IS VERY, VERY IMPORTANT TO ME. THANKS

She spent two cold, dismal days thrusting the note at strangers on the streets of Roseburg. A few hurried off, but most were relaxed, approachable, like her neighbors back home. She could tell that they wanted to help. She phoned Julie in despair and found that Van was trying to reach her.

"No, nothing new, hon," he told her when she called him at home that night. "Worried about you, that's all." His words came in the usual rush. "You're pushing yourself too hard. Julie told me. Gotta slow down."

"I can't," she croaked.

"Yes, you can!" His bossy concern made her feel better. In this mildewed motel room with the pink Olympia Beer sign flashing outside, she had begun to feel hollow and lost. Thanks, Van, she wanted to say, for caring enough to yell at me, but he was still talking. "Julie told me about the laryngitis. Listen, knock off the Wonder Woman act, will ya? You think you can help Ace by killing yourself? Huh?"

"I need another day or two," she whispered.

"You've been saying that for a month."

"Oh, Van, don't exaggerate. I haven't even been here two weeks."

"Two weeks tomorrow." His voice had softened. "Lael," he said, "can I tell you something, uh, selfish?" She wasn't sure she should say yes, but as usual he rushed ahead. "I, uh, miss you," he said. "I mean, I didn't think I would, but I do. You know what I mean? I, uh—"

"Van, stop!" Her throat ached when she talked, but she had to head him off. "Listen to me once, will you? You and I— we don't have the right to miss each other. Understand? That's not for now."

He spoke slowly for a change. "You got a bad case of overthink, you know it, Lael? You think you can reason your way through everything. Who're you, the Ice Queen?"

The words were uncomfortably close to something Mike had said. "I'm sorry, Van," she said. "Okay, I miss you. But— I can't. The situation doesn't allow for it."

"What situation?"

"Ace. Missing you trivializes the whole thing, don't you see that?"

"You're resigning from the human race till he comes back? No emotions permitted on premises?" She tried to improve on his wording but couldn't. "For how long?" he asked. "Forever?"

"He won't be gone forever."

"He might be."

"It's rotten of you to put it like that."

"Somebody has to be realistic around here."

"Van, do you—do you think I'm kidding myself?"

There was a long hesitation. "I don't know." His voice came back softly. "All I know is I care about you, Lael. I mean, I got . . . feelings. Okay? *Comprenez?* You're not just another goddamn client. Keep that in mind while you're down there trying to self-destruct."

The conversation left her upset. For hours she lay awake, thinking about Van and listening to passing trucks rattle the motel windows as they dropped into compound low for the long climb out of the Umpqua Valley. She missed him; yes, she did. She missed her herbs, her house by the bay, her sister; she missed her parents, Trang, her cat Larry Allen and her watch frogs and even the raccoons that ate them. But mostly she missed Ace.

After a few more days she gave up on the Umpqua. She drove south to Grants Pass and Mike's second favorite river, the Rogue. A plain-clothes deputy sheriff looked her up and down and told her he was "on a personal basis with every crow that flies over Jackson and Josephine County and every pissant from Gold Beach to Crater Lake." He just happened to be going off duty and invited her to a bar for a strategy discussion and a hot buttered rum. She slipped away from his friendly taps and touches at midnight, her stomach awash with Calistoga water and her reunion with Ace no closer.

Three more fruitless days passed before she headed back north. Her Rand McNally road atlas showed so many Oregon rivers running to the sea: the Siuslaw, Coquille, Smith, Coos, Elk, Siletz, Nehalem, a half-dozen others. Every one held salmon and steelhead. What would she do when she had exhausted the list? Follow the Columbia to Canada?

She stopped at a motel restaurant in Douglaston, just south of the Washington border, and phoned home in a foul mood. Julie told her, "Chastity called. Said to tell you she remembered. It's the Little Ridley."

Lael was too tired to make the connection. "The Little Ridley what?"

"River, I think."

She checked into a room and uncreased her atlas. With her fingernail she traced the Oregon beachline from Fort Stevens south to Brookings and back up again. There was no Ridley

River, Little or Big. She called the front desk and asked the
teen-age clerk if he'd heard of it. "Are you kiddin' me?" the
youthful voice asked.

"No."

"Ma'am, you could spit on the Little Ridley from here."

"How far?"

"Would you believe six miles?"

"Is it a fishing river?"

"Used to be better. Still good for winter steelhead."

"Why can't I find it on my map?" she asked. "I checked
every river that goes to the ocean."

"It empties into the Columbia," the clerk answered patiently.

She thanked him and looked again at the map. There it was,
the Little Ridley River, running north for ten or twelve miles
from its headwaters to the Columbia. She circled the com-
munities along its banks: Silver Doctor, Ridley Rip, Frazer
Falls, Ridley Bridge. They all were small; they wouldn't be
hard to check out. Back-country people were acutely aware of
new arrivals like fathers and sons.

The next morning the principal of an elementary school in
Silver Doctor told her that a man resembling Mike's picture
had enrolled his son in the first grade and removed him two
days later without explanation. It was his impression that the
man worked in the pulp mill near Cedarville. Lael drove to the
personnel office and received grudging permission to peep
through a thick glass panel at a new employee in the shredding
mill. He looked like Mike, but he was fifty pounds heavier.

She headed north along the river on Route 278, showing
her pictures at stores and schools festooned for Christmas.
Every now and then the twisty two-lane road ran along the
banks of the stream, and she saw flashes of viridian and silver
below the foaming green surface. She drove by dairy farms,
filbert orchards, commercial greenhouses that made her nos-
talgic for her herbs, a U-pick blueberry farm, fields bordered
in blackberry bushes still speckled with dried-up fruit. Under
a covered bridge a fisherman made long parabolic casts, a scene
from an Orvis catalogue. She slowed and stared. He wasn't
Mike. A small boy teetered along the shoulder of the road on
a bicycle with training wheels. She slowed and stared again.
He wasn't Ace.

She bought a hamburger and a carton of milk and parked
in a glade down a dirt road to get away from the log trucks.
Wild plants twice as tall as her Luv loomed on either side. She

recognized hoary nettle and the spindly, spiny branches of devil's claw. A dying alder was scarred with deep black scratches, a bear's territorial scratchings. Dark green Douglas firs met in an arch above. A few shafts of sunlight pierced the canopy and gave her the feeling she had blundered into a cathedral.

She unwrapped the soggy burger and remembered her father's simple blessing—"Dear heavenly Father, we thank thee for this and all thy gifts"—and how the habit of saying grace had been one of the first she had discarded when she moved away. Tell me something, God, she said under her breath, what have I done? Is this some kind of biblical test? She thought of the tragedy of Job, of Abraham sacrificing his son Isaac, of Joseph's brothers selling him as a slave. "Listen to me, God," she cried out in the car. "I'm not some name in the Bible. I'm a live person! How can you take my son like this? *You have no right!*"

She covered her blasphemy with her hand and thought how often her prayers had run to recriminations and questionings and doubts lately. She asked herself what kind of Christian would let her faith slip away at the first adversity. Her parents would be so upset. "Lord, I take it back," she prayed. "I'm not myself." She thought what an ugly time Christmas would be if she were still on the outs with God.

The blue-gray hamburger meat was inedible; she threw it into the weeds for the birds. She drove a few more miles till she passed a small soupy-green pond and a sign that said RIDLEY RIP, POP. 203. The village seemed to consist of a grocery store, a gas station, a post office, and a few stores. A cardboard poster in the grocery window caught her eye:

The children of Miss Bachman's Grades 1-3 proudly present their annual Christmas play PETER PAN FOR TOTS, adapted from the J. M. Barrie classic. Christmas Eve at 4 P.M. Ridley Rip School Gym. Tickets $1.

Peter Pan: Ace's all-time favorite. She could hear his gasp of wonder when Peter explained how to fly: "You just think lovely wonderful thoughts and they lift you up in the air!" How long had it been since she'd thought lovely wonderful thoughts?

The sun slid behind a fluffy overcast. She sniffed and caught the scent of snow. She wondered what the weather was like back home. Mild, probably. It was almost always mild on the island. It had snowed once in the last two years. She remembered how excited Ace had been as he ran outside to see.

Her eye was attracted to a hanging wooden sign in the shape of a fish in front of a maroon bungalow. She squinted and read SOLOMON JOHN, LICENSED GUIDE, RIDLEY RIP, ORE.

She knocked at a door wreathed in holly and cranberries. When no one answered, she walked around the house and found a well-defined path leading to the river, fifty or sixty feet away. At a short dock in a calm eddy someone hammered at the insides of a green wooden dory. At her call he stood up, a thin old collection of gristle and skin. His white hair and sparse white beard rippled in the breeze. He was chewing on a short, lumpy pipe.

"I'm looking for a man and a boy," she said for the X-hundredth time, thinking that she was beginning to sound like one of those Safeway commercials where the woman singsongs the latest prices like a talking machine. She walked to the boat and held out a dog-eared old poster and her little gallery of pictures: Mike smiling at his desk, black hair gleaming; Ace glaring behind his heavy glasses, eager to return to play; a few others.

The old man pushed a pair of rimless glasses up his peeling pink forehead and held the pictures close to his peeling pink nose. Rip Van Winkle, Lael thought. "This fella," he said, frowning. "What's he done?"

She had been traipsing Oregon for almost a month, and she was too worn-out for niceties of expression. "He stole my son," she said.

The man whistled softly through his teeth. "I'll be switched," he said, and clambered out of the boat, blowing wood shavings off the sleeves of his checked wool shirt. He started up the path and beckoned her to follow.

"Better come on inside," he said when they reached the back door of the old frame house. "I think I know these folks."

29

"VAN!" SHE SHRIEKED into the pay phone alongside the gas station. "They're here! I found them!"

"You *what?*"

"Mike, Ace—a little place called Ridley Rip. The, uh, the Little Ridley River." Her words ran together. "I, uh, talked to Solomon John? This guide? He took Mike fishing two—no, three days ago. And they're going again Thursday morning!"

"Day after tomorrow?" Stein said. "Christmas Eve?"

"Yes. At seven."

"Where're they living? I mean what kind of place?"

"Mr. John doesn't have the address. But it can't be far. There's only a few villages on the river. I could check them out."

"No! Stay put. How sure are you about Thursday?"

"Mike left a twenty-five-dollar deposit."

Stein said he couldn't believe their luck, couldn't believe her persistence. She was the first person he'd ever known who'd gone on a wild-goose chase and caught the goose. He demanded full details. When she told how she'd found the Little Ridley, he broke in and said, "You're lying!"

"Van, it's a miracle. I don't even know what made me stop in this place."

"I'm quitting bacon. Going back to *shul.*"

"Let's wait till we see what happens Thursday."

"Oh, ye of little faith." He sounded excited. "This is our shot, Lael." A dark cloud scudded in and out of her mind. Hadn't he used those words before? When they'd almost caught Mike in Canada? "Let's not screw up," he went on as though he'd read her thought. "You staying in Douglaston?"

"The Cedar Inn. Van?" She had a favor to ask, and she didn't want to be coquettish about it. But he'd already done so much for her; it was hard to ask for more, especially since he refused to send a bill. "Van, is there any chance . . . I mean, do you think you could get away long enough—"

"What's tomorrow? Wednesday? I got a Forest Service hear-

133

ing in the morning. They're messing with the Dungeness again.
I'll head for Douglaston after lunch. How long a drive is it?"

"Three or four hours."

"I'll be there for dinner. The Cedar Inn?"

"Just north of town. You can see the sign from the highway.
Room twenty-four."

"We'll talk some more when I get there. Is there any chance
what's-his-name, the guide—"

"Solomon John."

"Any chance he'll drop the dime?"

"'Drop the dime'?"

"Tip off Mike?"

"He's on our side. He said he'd never heard of a steelhead
fisherman stealing a kid."

"You got the custody papers?"

"Sure do."

"Okay. And, Lael?"

"Yes?"

"I still miss ya—*hey, wait!* Don't hang up!" He laughed.
"Strike that. Maybe I miss you and maybe I don't. Now listen,
be cool, okay?" He sounded as though he should take his own
advice. "Get a stack of magazines. Then stay in your room
and eat room service."

"Ugh!"

"Look at it this way. With any luck we'll have Christmas
dinner at my house. Ace and Trang and you and me. Trang'll
cook. Turkey. Lobster sauce. Litchi nuts—"

"Slugs."

They laughed at each other and hung up. Christmas was
three days away. She wished he hadn't said that he missed her.

A few hours after the conversation her customary appre-
hensiveness began to set in. A slogan ran through her mind:
If there's any way something can go bad, it will. One of Mur-
phy's laws, she thought. Somebody should have drowned Mur-
phy at birth.

She fell to her knees alongside the bed. "Please, Lord," she
prayed, "not this time. Not this time. Amen." She got up and
tried another expression aloud. This one came easily to her
lips.

"Merry Christmas, Ace."

30

AT 3:00 A.M. she quit trying to sleep and turned on the TV. A cable network was showing a porno film. She watched for a few minutes and wondered if any real-life couples actually made love with so much unconcealed debasement of the woman. What normal female would permit her body to be used with such contempt? Maybe that's what Mike had wanted, his own personal slave dog. Maybe that's what had attracted him to his bartendress. There'd never been much love in Mike's love-making.

She decided she would stay celibate for life if she had to go through maneuvers like that. She'd never had much taste for sex without love. Something made her think of Van. She liked him a lot, maybe even loved him a little, but the idea of joining with him or anyone else in the thrashings of sex seemed unappealing.

She concluded that her body was still on hold. And just as well.

There was a more immediate problem. How was she supposed to get through the rest of this night and all day Wednesday and all Wednesday night? She wished she had a few Tuinals. The thought of Mr. Guacamole kept her wide awake. She saw him as an infant, hair emerging in a black military friz, dark liquid baby eyes locked into hers, the corners of his rose-colored lips trying out a tentative smile as though testing to see if it was a safe practice, then grinning and gurgling and rolling his tongue in his mouth in an effort to speak. What an international triumph he had scored at ten months: *"Ommmm. Om-ma. Omma. Momma!"*

She reached for the phone and pulled back. Who would be awake at this hour? Julie, who not only had her full load of classes but had been running the herb farm for three weeks? Van? He would pretend he was happy to hear from her, but he'd already said that he had a court date in the morning, and she would never forgive herself for interfering with one of his causes.

She wondered what it would be like to love a man who spent so much of his compassion on strangers. Strictly a hypothetical question, of course. To love is to risk loss, tragedy, degradation, like those pathetic women in the porn film. She could see herself in the future, shrinking, turning wizened and dry, slowly shedding friends, avoiding relationships, till she stood solitary and aloof, answerable only to her own emotions. Shrinking down to an analgesic central core of being: herself alone, impervious to others. *Unhurtable*.

That's what she had learned from the theft of her son.

But Van was . . . nice.

Just before dawn she slid the window open and looked out on the motel parking lot. Moist air caressed her face. The day before she'd overheard talk about an unseasonal drought; it looked to be coming to an end. Thick wisps of fog, opaque, unmoving, hung over the concrete like meringue. She thought: This is how the air must feel in a mausoleum, and slammed the window shut.

She stared at well-worn photographs of Ace. She wondered how he would look when they picked him up in two days. *If we pick him up*, she reminded herself. Don't get yourself too high. It's that much farther to fall.

The confrontation would be on Thursday, the twenty-fourth, Christmas Eve, almost eight months to the day since he had left. How different would he be? She wondered if Mike had altered his looks as well as his name. What could he have done? Bleached his hair, possibly, and cut it short. Plastic surgery? Oh, God, he wouldn't have gone that far. Not even Mike.

The thought of Ace's soft features under a scalpel made her hold her stomach. She snapped her head sharply as though to fling away the thought and then realized it was ridiculous. Solomon John had recognized Ace and Mike instantly from their pictures. So much for the possibility of plastic surgery. She wondered what made her mind reach for the blackest possibilities. The habit of fear, she decided. My new hobbies: worry and panic.

She awoke at seven. Exactly twenty-four hours to go. Van had insisted she use room service, but luckily she had no appetite. She reached in her purse and found a package of organic peanuts. Munching distractedly, she peeked outside.

A hard rain beat on the parking lot. She wondered why she hadn't heard it before.

She fumbled in her purse for the brown card with Solomon John's phone number. She dialed the number in the village of Ridley Rip six miles away. "Mr. John!" she said when he answered. "This is Lael Pritcher. Uh, we talked yesterday? About my son?"

"Miz Pritcher?" The calmness in his voice put her at ease. It was like talking to a favorite uncle. "Somethin' the matter?"

"No, nothing. I mean, Mr. John, do your float trips ever get called off?"

"Well, yes, ma'am, now 'n' then." Her heart sank. God was toying with her again, testing her. "Weather's a factor, surely is."

"What kind of weather?"

"Well, a real bad lightning storm, for one thing, but that's mostly in the summer. This time of year we have to cancel sometimes for high water. River gets kinda muddy. Fish can't see the fly."

"You mean a storm"—she held her breath—"like this one?"

"Storm? She's not stormin' here, missus. Kinda wish she would. We're low on water. Where you at? Douglaston?"

"The Cedar Inn. And it's raining hard."

"Impression I got from Pritcher, it'd take a typhoon to make him cancel," the old man said. "Don't fret, we'll get the little fella back. Know what my missus said? She said, 'Solomon, imagine if this was your own sweet son.'"

By noon the rain had subsided. She looked at her watch. Nineteen hours to go. If the trip were canceled, how long would it be before Mike scheduled another one? *Suppose it rained for weeks?*

Then I would wait for weeks. Right here in this motel room. Without Ace, Christmas is just another December day.

Late in the afternoon the rain resumed in hard slants, and by nightfall a brisk wind was flinging the drops against her window like gravel. She dialed Ridley Rip and got a busy signal, tried again two or three times with the same result.

By 10:00 P.M. she had found another worry to help occupy the time. Where was Van? He said he'd be here for dinner. If he'd been delayed in court, wouldn't he have called? A truck could have jumped the centerline on I-5 and flattened him. A river might have overflown its banks and carried him away. Mount Saint Helen's could have blown again. She berated herself for undervaluing him from the beginning. Now she'd never get a chance to admit it to his face.

He showed up just before midnight, handlebar mustache dripping, face stiff with cold, hands splotched with grease. "The goddamn bike! Burnt out the front wheel bearings. Took me three hours to find a set. Called you once, but the line was busy."

"Van," she said, forgetting all her good intentions toward him. "It looks bad. The rain."

"Huh? Oh, yeah." He slumped on the plastic-covered couch and wiped the water from his blue eyes. His red hair hung in rats. "Worries me, too. Can't fish steelhead in dirty water. What's the guide say?"

"I haven't been able to get him."

"Why not?"

"Busy."

"All *night?* Let me try." She gave him the number, and he dialed. After a minute he disconnected and dialed a single digit. This time he said, "Operator? Verify a BY for me, will you?" He repeated the guide's number, then said, "You're sure? Got any idea what the problem is?... For sure?... Thanks. Thanks a lot." He slammed the phone down and turned to Lael. "Circuits are out. Big storm."

"Oh, Van, I knew we wouldn't, we wouldn't—" The light faded, and she began to lose her balance. She felt him pick her up and lower her gently to the bed.

"I got dizzy," she said. She sat up so he wouldn't mistake her for a bigger fool than she was. She realized she was still fighting the feeling that physical contact with others, however innocent, was somehow disloyal to Ace.

Van was looking at her intently. "What'd you eat today?"

"Eat? Oh, uh, some nuts. Some coffee."

"And yesterday?"

"A hamburger." She didn't mention that she had thrown it away.

"You'll eat tomorrow. By God, I'll force-feed you. What are you trying to prove, Lael?"

She was too weak to answer. He backed to the table by the window and slid a clipboard from his pack. She remembered how he had planned for the expedition to Canada, with lists of assignments for each of them. The methodical mind. She wished he would instill some orderliness in her. She tried to pay attention as he outlined a plan for the morning, but she kept seeing the Little Ridley River, brown and roily and unfishable.

"This time we won't screw up," he was saying. "The second

you identify Mike, we call the sheriff, let him do the rest. That way we won't collect Ace in the morning and lose him in the afternoon in court."

It was all an exercise; they'd never get a chance to collect Ace. The rain rattled against the window, dampening her hopes. How many more near misses would there be? Five? Ten? A hundred?

She pointed to an oily blue-black streak at his hairline and said, "You're a mess." She realized how unremittingly critical she must seem to him. Why did he put up with her?

"My good woman, you underestimate me." He lifted his heavy pack. "My wig is within. Fresh from the cleaner's. I have a clean frock coat and striped pants. Wet but clean."

His good humor almost made her forget the rain. Who else would go through what he'd just gone through and then bother to cheer up a grump like her? She wished she had paid more attention to the plans he'd spelled out. "What did you say you'll tell Mike?" she asked.

"Give up the kid or he'll go to jail till his hair grows to his ass."

It sounded as though he had figured everything out. Except the weather. "Thanks, Van," she said.

"Huh? For what?"

"For sticking by me."

"That's my job. Wait till you see my bill. I'm trying to hold it under fifty thou. But it's tough. Maybe we can work out a barter deal."

"For herbs?"

He opened his eyes wide and flicked imaginary ashes from the tip of his pencil. "Hoibs? That wasn't what I had in mind, goilie."

She looked across the room at him. His face still wore the Groucho leer, but he was plainly exhausted. She didn't know what was involved in replacing wheel bearings, but he looked like a man who'd spent a week in a grease pit at hard labor. "What room are you in?" she asked.

"Room?" He looked surprised. "The joint's full. A Christmas basketball tournament. Figured I'd crash on your couch."

"Van," she said, "wouldn't it be better—"

"For Christ's sake, Lael, you don't think—"

She waved her hand to cut him off. "No," she said, "of course I don't. I'm sorry. I was just worried about . . . how it would look."

"To who?"

"I *said* I was sorry. Sleep on the other bed. That's one good thing about paying twenty-eight dollars a day. You get an extra bed for gentleman callers."

"I saw that play," he said, bending over to unlace his motorcycle boots. "'Oh, Mama, you done broke mah unicorn. Lawdy *lawdy*, Ah feel so neurotic Ah'll just dah!'"

She was too tired to tell him he'd mangled another quote.

"Let's try the Volga boatman one last time," he said when he came out of the steamy bathroom smelling of soap, a bath towel knotted nonchalantly about his waist. His muscles were surprisingly well defined and his chest was a jungle of tight reddish coils. She wondered why she had expected him to look soft. "After that we'll grab some sleep," he promised.

She handed him the phone and listened as he talked in his businesslike tone to an operator who apparently passed him to a supervisor. "Still no circuits," he said when he hung up. "The lines are down. Winds and rain."

Ace, oh, Ace, she said to herself. It was just too good to be true.

At five-thirty in the morning Solomon John called apologetically and said that Mike had just canceled. "I says let's go anyway—heck with the rain. He says no. I made him a deal—no fish, no pay. But he's stubborn. Said he'd call back as soon as the water clears. Told me to hang onto the deposit, so I guess he means business."

She wasn't surprised. Bad news had become the norm in her life. As Van slept on, she mumbled a soft good-bye to the riverman and fell back into bed, cursing the God who made the rain. He was dead to her now and forever.

She was dozing when the motel door burst open and a pimply desk clerk entered behind two policemen with drawn guns. "Yep, that's them!" he said, shaking his finger. Somehow Van had found his way into her bed and now slept with his arm across her chest. "That there Jewboy come in and never come out. I knowed she weren't no local whore." The two adulterers were dragged off to court—Van clad only in a T-shirt and Lael naked. A skeleton in a judge's robes was reaching for her nipples when she woke up, her hand clenched tightly over her mouth.

She looked at the other bed to see if Van was awake. She heard a light sonorous hum, rising and falling. He was facing away from her, the covers moving lightly above his chest.

She decided not to risk another nightmare. She slipped a housecoat over her flannel granny gown and tiptoed to the window. A few thin snowflakes drifted among the raindrops and tempered her mood. Snow! On Christmas Eve! She realized she was anticipating Ace's thrill when he discovered it. As she watched, the flakes dissolved in a steady rain. Oh, Ace, she thought, I'm so sorry, angel. You'll wake up and never know it snowed.

She lay atop the covers and tried to figure how to find him now that Mike had canceled the float trip. She could take the Luv and look around up-river. But what good would it do to check faces in a few country villages? No more than it had on the Umpqua and the Rogue and the others. She told herself to relax, to stop wasting time on—what had Van called it?— *overthink.*

After a while her roommate stirred. He lay facing her, his red hair tangled, his eyes tightly shut, a bare arm dangling to the floor. As she watched, his lips moved, and he mumbled something. She leaned across the space between the two beds, the sheet pressed tightly to her chest.

He babbled a string of half-spoken words. One of them sounded like her name. She leaned closer. He was humming under his breath, an unrecognizable off-key tune. Then, as clearly as though he were arguing in court, he said, "I love you beyond a reasonable doubt." He smiled with his eyes closed and rolled into a ball like her cat, Larry Allen.

She hoped he was dreaming.

31

At 8.00 a.m. she was standing wide awake and naked just outside the small bathroom when Van burst in from the coffee shop with the milk and orange juice he'd promised to bring back from his breakfast. "Don't you know to knock?" she asked, ducking for cover.

"Don't you know to lock?" he asked.

"I wasn't expecting you for a while."

"I eat fast."

"Sure you do," she said, sounding more angry than she felt.

"Jeez, Lael, you're acting paranoid."

"I wonder why." She hated sarcasm, especially her own, but she felt a little out of control this morning. The long string of sleepless nights was showing. And the latest missed connection.

She heard him say, "Uh, listen," but his voice dropped out of range.

"What?"

"Oh, nothing."

"Don't do that to me! Nothing aggravates me more than that."

"Than what?"

"Starting to talk and then saying, 'Oh, nothing.'"

"How much do you weigh now?" he asked.

"Why?"

"I just wondered. Lael, don't get mad, okay? I saw you naked, and you know what caught my eye? *Your ribs!* I could count 'em. I mean, it's nice to be slender, but this is—this is sick!" He sounded uncomfortable. "Don't get me wrong, you've got a terrific figure, but *how much weight have you lost?*"

"I don't know," she answered. She hadn't stepped on a scale for months. She guessed she was down to about 100 from a top of 125. What difference did it make? She wasn't entering beauty contests, she wasn't in the marriage market, and she didn't have anyone to cook for or impress. When Ace came home, her weight would normalize fast.

"When was your last checkup?" he persisted.

"Oh, come on, Van! You're not my doctor."

"God damn it, I'm your friend!"

"For God's sake, let's not yell at each other." She wanted peace. He was a decent human being, and he cared. She couldn't afford to take such relationships lightly. She came out of the bathroom in well-worn Frye boots and jeans that hung loosely on her hips and a blue plaid Pendleton shirt. "I don't know how long it's been," she said. "A while."

"What'd the doctor say?"

"That I'd outlive the world."

"*Hmph.* Was that within the last six months?"

She almost lied and said yes. "No," she said. "It was . . . before Ace."

"I thought so."

"I, uh, haven't felt much like eating."

"When were you gonna start again? No, don't tell me. When Ace gets home. What if that's not for a while? Hey, he won't recognize you!"

"Okay, okay, I'll try. I can always force down an extra glass of milk."

"An extra steak, too. Potatoes. Salad. How about—?"

"Okay, *okay.*" Peace at any price.

She winced at the metallic flavor of the canned orange juice. She shut her eyes and slugged it down. "Happy days," she said grimly, and did the same with the carton of milk he handed her.

"Way to go. Eat already. Listen to Uncle Ivan. Remember, every Jew has a Jewish mama."

"What ever happened to chicken soup?"

"When I was sick, Mom used to feed me vichyssoise. She hated stereotyping. Hey, you know the recipe for vichyssoise? 'First, take a leek.'"

"Are you trying to cheer me up?"

"Vouldn't hoit."

"Huh?"

"My grandmother used to say, 'Vouldn't help, vouldn't hoit.'"

"What'd she say that about?"

"Everything."

She didn't think he was being very understanding, considering how her plans had been shattered. Did he think a comedy routine would help the situation? "Van, listen—relax. What do we do next? *That's* the question."

"I dunno, that's the answer. Mike wouldn't go fishing tomorrow, would he?"

"Why not?" she said.

"*Why not?* Tomorrow's Christmas."

"Mike would go fishing on Christmas, yes. He would, and he has. But Mr. John says the river won't be in shape for a few days. So where does that leave us, I mean in your expert opinion?"

"Tell ya the truth, I think the best thing we can do is nothing. Just wait. Besides—" He stopped as though he found the words hard to say.

"Go on," she insisted.

"Trang. I hate to leave him alone on Christmas."

She was stunned. What a case of tunnel vision she'd had! "Oh, Van," she said. "I must be the most selfish bitch in the world." She reached out and hugged him hard.

"You're not selfish, and you're not a bitch," he said. He stroked her hair and kissed the top of her head and stepped back. "You've got every right to ask your friends for help, Christmastime or not. Hey, Ace is part of my reality, Lael, don't you realize that? I feel like I'm his uncle or something."

They faced each other, and he put both hands on her waist. A minty toothpaste smell filled the air between them. "It's just that right now we're spinning our wheels," he went on. "We should drive home for Christmas, and when what's-his-face the guide hears something definite, we can come back down. That make sense?"

She pulled gently away. "It makes sense," she said. "But I want to do one thing first."

"What's that?"

"Some kids are putting on *Peter Pan* this afternoon. I want to go."

"*Peter Pan?* Where?"

"A school in Ridley Rip."

"Ridley Rip?" He sounded aghast. "You'd drive up there and risk being seen? Why?"

"It was Ace's favorite play. The Middle School gave it last year, and he made me take him twice. We have it on tape; we have the book. I don't know, I just thought he might show up. Just—you know—a hunch."

"A hunch?" Van glowered. His sleepless nights were showing. "Do you have some kind of wish-fulfillment thing that he'll come flying across the stage at you? Is that it?"

"He's too little to learn a part. You know that."

"So he's gonna turn up in the audience? Did Mike ever take him to see anything like that—*ever?*"

"Uh, no." She felt a certain desperation. "I guess I just need to feel—you know. . . ." She let the sentence die. How could she explain that the storm and the postponed trip had aggravated a suspicion that God had chosen sides against her, that maybe she would never see her son again? She knew Ace wouldn't be there, but she felt a desperate need to make contact with his memory, even if it was just to watch a play they both loved. It would be like writing him nightly letters. But Van would never understand. "Let's drop it," she said. "It's just something I have to do, okay? Do I have to have a reason?" She swallowed hard. "Try to understand."

"You don't understand, but I'm supposed to? Listen, Lael, you got a spooky ex-husband up in those hills, and if he sees you, he's gonna grab that kid and take off like a scalded cat. It's gonna be Victoria all over again." She took a few steps toward the window, and his strident voice followed. "And for what? Do you really think *Peter Pan*'s gonna make you feel better? That sick nostalgia trip? It's gonna be the worst bummer of your life. It's gonna *hurt,* Lael. This is Christmas Eve. You're already—"

"Quit trying to tell me how I feel." She turned, and they stared hard at each other. "Quit treating me like a space case."

He threw up his hands. "Can't you see this is your self-flagellation act again? Lael, listen—you're losing touch."

The discussion had gone too far. She remembered another one like it, when they'd ended up screaming at each other. She bristled at his self-appointed role of therapist. How could he presume to understand what she was going through, what she had to do to survive? How could anyone? "Stop trying to protect me," she said, aware of the shrillness in her voice. "I don't need you or anybody else to protect me." She rubbed a palm across her eyes.

"Lael, honey, don't." He stepped toward her, his arms outstretched.

She put up her hands and backed away. "Don't call me honey! Don't touch me! I'M NOT CRYING!"

"I'll stay here with you," he said in a resigned voice. "I'll just call Trang and—"

"No!" The tears formed at the corners of her eyes. "I want

to be by myself." She couldn't let him see her cry. It was so weak. She felt like the world's biggest fool.

"Go!" she yelled. *"Go!* Get out of here!" Her sobs came in whoops and wails. "I don't want you here, can't you see that? For God's sake, leave! Who asked you here? Get out!" She pushed at his chest. "Go...on. Get...*out!"*

He reached for her, but she jerked away and ran into the bathroom and locked the door. A few minutes later she heard a faint tap. "I'm going now, Lael," he said softly. "If you hear anything, call me right away. Trang'll know where I am every second, and I can be back in three hours. Okay, hon? And listen—don't be so hard on yourself. Okay? Okay, Lael?"

She didn't answer. When she heard the outer door close, she started to cry all over again. He hadn't even wished her a merry Christmas.

32

SHE STOOD JUST outside till the lights were lowered, then slipped into the dimly lit gym with its familiar smell of children and socks. Her eyes were hidden behind dark glasses, her hair and most of her face under a magenta kerchief. She wore newly purchased coral red lipstick, pink blusher, mauve eye shadow and kohl mascara. How could anyone possibly recognize her in the poor light? She had looked in the motel mirror and barely recognized herself.

She stood against a brick wall, getting her bearings. In front of a few long benches, children were sprawled on the floor, chomping popcorn and candy apples. She edged to a seat at the end of a bench, hoping that no one would try to get friendly.

As the curtain started to rise, her mind teemed with memories. Sometimes she and Ace used to pretend he was Mr. Darling, or she would be Peter and he would be his favorite character of all, Tinker Bell. Dear Father in heaven, she prayed in the half darkness, let me get through this play without proving Van right.

Onstage a child in a Newfoundland dog suit—Nana the combination pet and nursemaid—lay on the floor of the stage. A cuckoo clock sounded six times, and the dog jumped up and began turning down beds, its furry backside wagging madly. A boy in pajamas stumbled onstage as though shoved by an unseen hand. He regained his balance and yelled at the dog through a gap in his teeth, "I won't go to bed! I won't, Nana. It, uh, it ishn't shix o'clock yet. Two minutesh more?"

The child playing Nana busied himself about the stage. Behind the muzzle and the shaggy fur, Lael could make out the glint of glasses and dark hair. Something about his movements reminded her of her son: the little extra twists and skips. She had nicknamed Ace Mr. Skippyfrisk because of the same energetic motions. Whoever this boy was, he was perfect in the role. He made the other children look lethargic.

Nana finished preparing the nursery and looked across the footlights in her direction. The dog seemed to tilt its head in surprise, then straighten up and tilt again. She let herself imagine that Ace was under all that fur, recognizing her, pining for her, wishing he could jump from the stage into her arms. Oh, Ace! *It's Mom, angel!* You're such a good actor, sweet baby. You're the star!

A small girl in three-inch pumps scuffed across the stage, wearing a pink bonnet and a lilac-colored dress that dusted the floor. Before speaking her first lines, she turned toward someone in the audience and smiled. Then she remarked in a peculiar accent that she had just seen a "strange little face outside mah window and a hand groping as if it wonted to come in."

The line reminded Lael of the dark night when she had seen herself in Ace's window and how she had fallen back in terror. She'd been a child at heart in those days. She asked herself what she was now. A woman alone, she decided, lost, deserted, bereft, with no more reason to live than poor Mrs. Darling will have in a few more minutes. Van was right again. This play isn't helping my morale a bit. Van is always so damned right.

She lowered her head and tried to figure out how she could feel warm toward him one minute and hateful the next. She wondered if the tissues of the brain could be damaged by grief, abraded like a skinned knee. Would it heal? Or would she keep on switching from mood to mood, snapping and snarling at people who were only trying to help? She looked back at the stage. Nana seemed to be staring at her again. She wondered if she shouldn't just slip away.

She pushed her dark glasses up her forehead so she could check out the audience. Her heart leaped when she noticed a boy with black hair and black-rimmed glasses, but he was too small to be Ace. Did boys shrink? She glanced again. Not Ace.

She looked down the long bench and saw that the woman nearest her was watching. Lael smiled and slid a few inches closer in friendly body language. The woman smiled back and nodded, and she returned the nod: two proud mothers watching their talented children.

By the time she turned back toward the stage Mr. Darling had made his appearance: a tall boy wearing a dark suit, a derby, and shiny plastic spats. He waved his arm imperiously toward the stage children and shouted like a hog caller, "There is not their equal on earth! AND THEY ARE OURS, OURS!"

Nana waddled to stage front and collided with Mr. Darling. The dog head flapped backward on its hinges, and a face flashed in and out of sight.

It was Ace.

She gathered her scarf across her cheeks as Mr. Darling bellowed, "I refuse to allow that dog to lord it in my nursery for one hour longer!" Ace began to nuzzle the other boy. "In vain, in vain," Mr. Darling yelled down. "The proper place for you is, uh, the proper place for you is—"

"The yard," the prompter's voice whispered.

"THE YARD!" the boy shrieked. "And there you go to be tied up! THIS INSTANT!"

Lael was immobilized. She couldn't run up and grab her son in front of all these protective parents. There would be pandemonium. Oh, God, why wasn't Van here?

Nana waddled toward the wings. Lael's brain was numb. She bit a knuckle and ordered herself to calm down and think. Let's see now, Mike has coached him to run if he sees me. But I can't go after him. Not yet. These people are already suspicious. I can't call his name.

But if I wait too long. . . .

Nana exited to her left. The stage emptied, and a slender child in a belled cap and green leotards peeked out and said, "Tinker Bell, Tink, are you there? Oh, do come out of that jug. . . ."

She didn't join in the whistles and applause when Peter made his entrance held high aloft by a male adult or when the other children soared across the stage in the same rudimentary way. She barely heard the familiar lines. She gulped when she heard the boy playing Michael cry out, "I flewed!" but only because it sounded so much like Ace.

One of the actors asked, "Where am I?" and another answered, "In Never-never Land." We all are, Lael said to herself. I have just seen my son, but any second I'll be back in the real world and he'll be gone again. She sat rigid, afraid to break the spell, waiting for the object of her despair to return to the stage. She tried to recall the plot of the play and realized that Nana wouldn't appear again till the last scene.

At the intermission she thought how risky it was to wait. Mike might arrive any minute. What would she do? Fight him with her fists? She wished she had brought his old .38 Chiefs Special, locked up at home, and quickly discarded the wish as the measure of her desperation. What would she do with it— challenge him to a duel?

She decided to grab Ace right now. He was hers by court order; there was no need to feel guilty about taking him back.

He might be a little upset at first, but Mr. Guacamole would always trust his mom.

She spotted the door to backstage. While most of the play-goers were clotting in the hall, she walked up nonchalantly and turned the knob.

Locked!

She wrenched hard, but the door held. She looked around for another. "Can I help you, miss?" a plummy voice asked. She turned and saw a hen-shaped young woman wearing a worn velvet Empire dress and flats.

"Oh, the, uh, ladies' room?" Lael said.

The woman beckoned toward the hall, and Lael followed her instructions. She would have to be patient.

When the play resumed, she slid off her dark glasses and discreetly double-checked the audience. No Mike. Maybe he'd show up late to collect Ace. All she needed were a few seconds at the end of the performance.

She devised a simple plan. At the final curtain she would rush up and grab her son. If Mike or anyone else tried to intervene, she would hold on and refuse to let go. She hadn't come this far to lose him again. She would raise the ruckus of all times. Let them call the police; that would suit her fine.

The play droned on toward the end. Her favorite line passed almost unnoticed: "Whenever a child says, 'I don't believe in fairies,' there is a little fairy somewhere that falls down dead." The dog trotted back on the stage, every extremity in motion, her own dear Mr. Skippyfrisk. She inched forward on the bench for a better look. No other child on earth moved with such animation and energy. It was as individual as a fingerprint.

The curtain would fall in a few minutes. Every cell of her body was ready. It wasn't too late to be home by Christmas.

There! The curtain unwound in jerks and squeaks. The children began forming in front. As she stood up at her front-row bench, the door to backstage opened from the inside and a small face peeked out. She pushed through before it could be locked again.

Three or four adults were standing in the wings, clapping and looking pleased. Teachers, probably. She grinned at them happily, as though she were related to one of the actors. She didn't know where she was getting her poise. Experience maybe. Or desperation. She'd been tested and passed; she was tempered steel. As Van had said, *no mistakes this time.*

She heard bursts of applause; the actors were taking individual curtain calls. It seemed they would never end. Then the little room was alive with screeching children in painted faces and diaphanous wings and tutus. Nana tramped in last.

Lael walked across the room and grabbed a strangely cold paw. "Ace," she said, fighting back unexpected tears. "It's Mommy."

The paw pulled away, and she got a glimpse of a frightened face staring at her through holes in the furry head.

"Ace, baby, it's me," she said softly. "Mom."

The child edged away on all fours, as though still in character. "Don't run, angel," she said. "I won't hurt you. You and I, we're going home."

He backed away till he came to a wall lined with hooks and costumes. Two or three of the other children had turned to watch. Suddenly she realized the problem. How stupid she was!

She yanked off the glasses and the kerchief and let her hair spill across her shoulders. "Ace!" She was oblivious of the onlookers. "It's me!" He spun as though to leave. "Baby, it's *me! Mommy!*" She dropped to her knees and held out her arms. "Listen, baby! *Rotten rabbit guts!*"

The child started to run. She lunged for a furry paw and held on. He resisted with surprising strength, and they slid to the floor. A woman's voice cried out, "Nettie! *Don't go near that woman!*"

"Let me go," a frightened voice said from under the dog suit. "You're hurting me!"

"I don't want to hurt you," she said. "Please, Ace. Come on. *Come on now!*"

"Let . . . *go!*" he cried.

"I'm not letting go!"

People edged closer. Lael looked up and said, "Call the police. He's my son. I won't let go! You might as well call the police."

Ace whimpered, and she relaxed her hold. He wrenched hard and left her holding a furry leg. She scrambled to her feet and chased him into a warm room full of pipes and ducts. She heard a sound behind a furnace. "Come out, Ace," she said softly. "I won't hurt you, baby. I love you, Ace. I'd never hurt you, angel."

She circled the boiler and found him crouched against a

wall, trying to shed the lower half of his dog suit. "We're going home, baby," she said, approaching slowly so he wouldn't panic again.

He ran around a furnace and through another door. She followed and came out on a long hallway papered with primitive drawings. The boy wasn't in sight. Red exit signs were equidistant left and right. "Ace!" she called. "Wait!"

A short, bald man in rimless glasses came up, puffing. "What's this all about?"

She ran outside. It was just turning dark. All she could see was a line of cars and pickup trucks parked along a driveway, her own among them. "ACE!" she yelled.

The little man lumbered after her. "Lady, miss, what's going on here?" She ignored him and stood on her tiptoes to see beyond the cars.

Something moved in the fringe of underbrush behind the school. She sprinted forward and flushed a crow. She wondered if he could be hiding in a parked car. It would take forever to search every one. From the corner of her eye she caught a moving spot of color on the far side of Route 278. She ran across and felt a rush of air as a truck swerved to miss her. Excited voices carried from the schoolyard.

"Over there, over there!"

"She cursed, and they run off. That's all I know."

"It's that little Lee McQuinn."

McQuinn. So that was the name Mike was using.

She ran up a rutted dirt road. Mud sucked a loafer off her foot. She pulled it loose and sat hard on a ridge of moss. Her feet were caked, her kneesocks ruined. She pulled them off, stuffed them in the deep pocket of her parka, and noticed for the first time that the only footprints in sight were her own.

Ace was gone. He had run from her as though from one of his dream monsters back home. She decided to ask the other parents for help. Maybe someone knew where he lived.

Still breathing hard, she reached in a pocket and pulled out her kerchief and dark glasses. She had established too high a profile; she didn't dare expose her face again. She crossed the highway more carefully this time, barely able to see in the gathering shadows. A dozen strangers stared at her from the front schoolyard, some of them gripping their children.

"The boy who played Nana?" she said, holding her arms open as she stepped onto the asphalt. "He's my son. Does anybody know where he lives?"

The same bald man who had followed her out of the school exit stepped from the group. "Just hold it right here, ma'am," he said.

"That's her," a female voice called from the crowd. "Said, 'God damn your rotten guts,' somethin' like that. Like to scairt the living daylights out the poor thing."

The man smiled and took her arm. She knew how crazy she must look. But Ace mustn't get away. The poor child had been brainwashed. How could she explain this to a crowd of people who only knew what they'd seen?

The man's grip tightened. She whirled and broke loose. "Where did you hide him?" she demanded, backing away with both hands outstretched.

"Just take it easy," he said, catching her wrist after several swipes. "Somebody'll be along in just a minute."

Another man stepped up and grabbed her other arm. "Let go!" she screamed. "I don't need help! I want my son. Where is he? *Where's my baby?*"

In the distance she heard a siren.

33

THE WINDOWLESS ROOM was a six-foot cube. Flakes of gray paint lay like dandruff on the scatched desk top in front of her chair. On the wall X had defeated O in a game of tic-tac-toe below a graffito: ORAL SEX SUCKS. The pervading smells were tobacco, sweat, leather, and a few she didn't want to identify.

A chunky arresting officer with the name tag "WILSON" had booked her and fingerprinted her and read her a message from the back of a card. She had wasted her single phone call; Van didn't answer. Then the same deputy, bulging in his uniform like a kielbasa, had put her in this room and locked the door from the outside. The solid walls made the room worse than a cell. She had to fight off a feeling that she had been entombed for her sins.

After a few hours she passed into torpor. It was a feeling she remembered from home. More and more lately lassitude had overcome her and she would doze for an hour or two. Then she would awaken and sit up half the night, worrying about her lack of energy, her lack of initiative. The latest stage. She wondered how many more she would have to work through.

In the cubicle she heard nothing—not even a passing truck or the clack of a typewriter. She felt like war prisoners she had seen on TV: pale and drawn, uncoordinated, eyes glazed as they shuffled along. There was nothing as demoralizing as being restrained by another's hand. She couldn't escape the feeling that since she was in jail, she deserved to be in jail.

Now that it was over, her mistakes stood out. She had acted without judgment, without common sense. She should have planned her actions the way Van planned his, with legal paper and sharpened pencils and a neat column of As, Bs and Cs. She should have realized how she would look, barging into the school gym made up like a $10 hooker. Now she was paying the price for her carelessness.

And so was Ace, she reminded herself. Poor baby. How upset he must be, how confused. He still must have deep feelings about me. We loved each other so much. How he fought to get away! Poor angel. Poor troubled baby. What a Christmas present Mommy brought you.

By now the boy and his father could be miles away, the little Escort filled with whatever they had grabbed on short notice. Oh, Ace, she thought, I hope he didn't take you away. She doubled over at the thought of the pain she had inflicted on her son. Sharp fingernails biting into his arm. Hands flinging him to the concrete floor. What a reconciliation. What a mother.

At last the deputy named Wilson returned and squeezed behind the small table. During the ten-minute drive from the school to this substation he had refused to acknowledge her existence. She had sat in the back of the patrol car behind a grate, and he had locked both her doors with a click by touching something on the dash. Now he looked slightly friendlier.

"Okay, Lael, we're holding you on suspicion of child molesting. Like I said, you got a right to a lawyer and you got a right not to talk. Let's take it from the top, okay? Cigarette?" He slid a crumpled pack of Camels across the desk, and she shook her head. He lit up and filled the room with acrid blue smoke. He gave the impression that he was trying to establish an intimate superiority. It didn't matter what he established; she had only one story to tell.

"Child molesting?" she asked.

"Suspicion of."

"How did I molest him? He's my own son. *How did I molest him?*"

He shook his head like a teacher whose prize pupil has disappointed him. "Gimme a break, will ya, Lael? Don't yell at me. This room's too small."

"I yelled because nobody listens."

"Hey, don't sweat it. If you're clean, you'll walk. We're running you through the computer right now." She saw herself being fed feet first into a machine, pale worms of flesh wiggling out the other end. The deputy raised his pencil and asked, "How many falls does this make, hon?"

"How many what?"

"How many times you been arrested?"

"You mean, like speeding?"

Wilson stared at her from dull yellow eyes. He was built in the general shape of a casket, but he had a soft face with clear skin and fatty folds around his chin like an overnursed infant. "I mean arrests," he said after she looked away. "Look, we're gonna find out anyway."

"I've never been arrested. Unless you count this time. And I was only trying to find my son."

"How long's that story gonna fly, Lael?" He sounded as if he were trying to keep her from making a mistake.

"It's true," she said. She found her equanimity slowly returning. She had always been at her best with children. His Sam Browne belt shone so brightly that she could see the overhead neon light in it. She resisted the temptation to congratulate him on his neatness. He tapped a freshly sharpened pencil on the table next to his opened notebook, but he hadn't taken any notes.

"How about giving it to me straight?" he said.

"I've been trying to." She began with her arrival in Douglaston, and she had reached Tinker Bell's first appearance onstage when the deputy laid down his pencil and leaned across the desk.

"Can I make a suggestion, Lael?" he said, frowning. His breath was a blend of tobacco and wintergreen. "More assault, less Tinker Bell?"

Assault? So he still didn't believe her. She hadn't assaulted anybody. How she wished she hadn't driven Van away with her foul temper.

"He's my son," she said. "I have the court papers. They're in my truck. I—"

"A court awarded custody to *you?*" He spaced his words evenly.

"Yes. I told you that in the car. You wouldn't listen."

He stared again. "I dunno, Lael, you don't look all that motherly."

"That's—that's an awful thing to say!" She realized she had raised her voice again. She rubbed her eyes and drew back a smear of black. My God, she thought, how did my eyes get so filthy? Then she realized that it was mascara. The deputy was talking down to her because she looked like a tramp. And he wasn't listening. What was the use of telling her story if he wouldn't listen?

He walked around the desk and stood next to her, his shiny pant leg inches from her face. He laid his hand on her shoulder and squeezed gently. "I'll give you a chance to think things over." He stepped toward the door. "Holler when you feel like telling it straight. How long you figure? A couple hours?"

"Please," she said, "if I could only make a call."

"You already made your one and only, hon."

"But I didn't get any—"

The door eased shut. More hours passed before the door opened and a policewoman with a black beehive hairdo and a lovely doll-like face entered and said, "You want to come with me, miss?"

On their way down the hall the policewoman leaned close and said, "Don't worry, you'll be okay. I can see you're different than the others." Lael wondered if she was about to undergo the famous good-cop bad-cop routine. They stopped at a pay phone, and she had to beg for a coin.

This time Trang was home to accept the charges. "Lael!" he said excitedly. "Where you?"

"Trang, get your dad!" she said rapidly, as though the phone might be ripped from her hand any second.

"Dad phone a few minutes ago, say please take numbers. What happen, Lael? Can Trang help? I got bike."

"Trang, listen, tell your dad I'm being held by police. Ridley County sheriff's department."

"Ripley County?"

"Ridley. R-I-D-L-E-Y. In Oregon. Have him call as soon as he can."

"Okay. You not worry, Lael." Everyone was telling her not to worry. Then why was she so scared?

The policewoman led her to another small room and pointed through a semitransparent window. On a scarred maple bench a frightened-looking girl of six or seven snuggled between a man and a woman.

"They insisted on seeing you," the policewoman said. "It's unusual, but the lieutenant thought under the circumstances—"

"Who are they?" Lael whispered. The trio looked like a habitat group, "Homo Sapiens Family, Rural U.S., 1950s." The man wore a crew cut and a skimpy wool suit with an off-center red tie, the woman a gray flip hair-do and a dress that looked made from flour sacks. The child was dressed in khaki shorts and long brown stockings. Something gave Lael the impression they were mutes.

The policewoman led her through the door. "This is Pete and Eloise McQuinn," she said, "and this is their daughter, Lee." No one offered to shake hands. "Lee was in the play you saw."

The names didn't register. She noticed that the child wore dark plastic-rimmed glasses and had a small nose and long black hair. Lael said, "Hello. I, uh, I don't remember you. What part did you play?"

"The doag," the man said in a flat voice.

"You mean Nana?" Lael looked from father to child.

All three nodded.

Staring at the cowering child, she saw at once how she had made the mistake. On the poorly lighted stage there had been a superficial resemblance; a tired imagination had done the rest. "I'm sorry," she said. "You looked just like my son." She realized how ridiculous her words must sound. "I mean under the costume." She reached into a pocket and shoved a crumpled picture of Ace at the father.

"Don't look a bit like Lee," he said, his stone face still noncommittal. "You scairt her real bad."

"I didn't mean it. I thought. . . ." Her words dribbled away. She didn't even convince herself.

"Where ya from, lady?" Evidently the father was going to speak for the family."

"Washington. Uh, Puget Sound."

"Puget Sound?"

"I live on an island." She tried for a show of respectability. "My father's senior chaplain at Bremerton."

"You say you're looking for your son?"

"Yes. My husband stole him. In April. I have legal custody."

The man nodded. "Heerd of things like that." It was impossible to tell if he believed her. He beckoned to the policewoman and whispered in her ear.

"Wait here, will you, please?" the officer said. All four stepped into the hall, out of earshot.

Once again Lael found herself alone in a small room, waiting. She wondered if she would be put in jail with prostitutes and psychos. Who would believe that she hadn't meant to molest the poor child? Some of her earlier lethargy began to return. She recognized it as a protective mechanism, a technique to help endure the unbearable.

Ten or fifteen minutes later the door opened, and the chunky deputy who had arrested her beckoned her outside. Without a word he led her to the property desk, where she signed for her parka, watch, and purse. "This way," he said, guiding her through a door with a sign that said, "Garage."

He motioned her into a police car next to him. She imagined they were going to the women's jail, wherever that was. In Douglaston probably. She hoped he wouldn't have to handcuff her. The car skidded around a corner. The deputy's heavy jaw was set, and the pouches of fat on his neck wobbled with each jerky movement of the car. She imagined him standing at a bar over a dice cup and a bottle of Coors, fragments of hard-boiled egg spraying from his mouth as he spoke. She sat as far away as she could.

They had sped a mile or two up Route 278, siren and lights piercing the darkness, when she summoned the courage to ask where they were headed.

"Back to your truck," he said.

"You mean I can go?" She hardly dared say the words.

"I don't make the rules." He sounded as though he wanted to distance himself from a gross miscarriage of justice.

She gathered that the McQuinn family had declined to prosecute, but she was afraid to ask for details. There might be another charge this Wilson could bring against her: disrespect to an officer, talking back, resisting arrest. She was a submissive child again, uncertain of the rules.

They sat silently in the speeding car till he slowed at the outskirts of Ridley Rip. She hoped her Luv was still parked in the school lot. "Thanks for the ride," she said stiffly.

"If it was up to me," he said, blowing a cloud of smoke at the headlining, "you'd be in jail."

Her feeling of being unfairly accused overcame her fear. "For what?" she asked. "I'm a mother looking for her son. Isn't that obvious by now?" Even as she spoke, she knew it was useless to try to justify herself. As the arresting officer Wilson had a vested interest in her guilt.

He turned and gave her a sly smile. "A mother looking for her son, huh? Is that what you were last night at the motel?"

My God, she thought, I dreamed something like this days ago! Do dreams anticipate life? "What's that supposed to mean?" she asked, dreading the answer.

"That yayhoo you spent the night with. I heard all about him. A biker, huh, Lael?"

Her throat tightened. "That was completely innocent! He's my lawyer. How do you even know about that?"

"Your lawyer, huh? Listen, desk clerks don't miss much in small motels. Your line of work, you oughta known that. Lemme tip ya. Next time make the john register, pay a little extra room rent. That way everybody gets a piece of the action, see what I mean?"

He stopped the car abruptly. The parking lot was in deep

shadow behind the boxy black shape of the school, but he wasn't going to give her the courtesy of driving around. Before she could open the door, he reached across her and pulled the handle and nudged her into the street with the back of his hand. "Take my advice, Lael," he said. "Point that truck north and don't stop. Next time you lay your hands on a little girl, make goddamn sure it's not in Ridley County, Oregon."

"But—"

"Your type make me sick."

The siren whooped and the door slammed before she could answer. She felt like a rape victim—pained, demoralized, ashamed. The police car made a U-turn and sped west, its whirling red light reflecting on porches and trees. So my type make him sick, she said to herself. I must have done something awful.

She looked around, confused. She was alone on a black night in front of a country school. She had to think hard to recall the names: Ridley Rip, the Little Ridley River.

She looked toward the crossroads where she had first seen the poster announcing *Peter Pan for Tots*. A pale violet light blinked in the store window. She walked around the corner of the school, and a splat of cold rain caught her in the eye. As she trudged across the parking lot toward her truck, she summoned the strength to wriggle her sleeve and look at her watch.

Three minutes past midnight.

Christmas.

34

SHE AWOKE CONFUSED in the pre-dawn darkness, wondering where she was. Then she remembered that she'd checked out of the Cedar Inn with its leering personnel and moved a mile down the highway to the Woodlander the night before. The room had only one small bed, but that was all she needed, and the price was $23.50. Julie had been glad to hear from her and learn the new address, even at one o'clock on Christmas morning.

In the closet-sized bathroom she splashed cold water on her face and brushed her teeth. A fallen woman stared back from the mirror; she couldn't engage her eyes. The title of a book she had read in college kept repeating in her mind: *Been Down So Long It Looks Like Up to Me.* Over an oily cup of instant coffee mixed with tap water, she decided that from now on everything would look like up to her. What could be worse than being hauled off to a police station as a child molester and mistaken for a whore?

Groggy from the short night of sleep, she tried to emulate Peter Pan and think lovely, wonderful thoughts. The loveliest thought of all was that Mike's $25 deposit was still in place. That could only mean he would be coming back to the river, maybe this time with Ace. All I have to do, she told herself, is sit tight, wait for word from Solomon John, and summon good old dependable Van. I won't leave this room if it takes a month! I'll eat the room service food. I'll watch "Days of Our Weeks" till I can follow the plot. Hang in there, Mr. Guacamole, help is on the way!

She sat on the lopsided bed and tried not to worry about his asthma. By now Catherine Pritcher must have delivered the allergy chart. Why had his condition flared up? Probably because Mike had let the immunization program lapse. Ace *needed* those shots. That damned Mike. . . .

She reached across the bed and turned on the radio. A children's choir sang, *"Natum videte, regen angelorum."* She snapped it off. I can get through Christmas, she reminded herself, but not by listening to carols. What a shame to have to blank out the whole holiday, but when Ace comes home, it'll be different. I'll buy him so many bikes and skateboards and scooters and sleds he'll think it's Christmas every day.

Just before 11:00 A.M. there was a single knock on her door. She thought she heard a giggle as she turned the knob. She opened it a crack and was enveloped in arms. Amid cries of "Merry Christmas!" and *"Gud Jul!"* her mother, father, and sister shoved inside as though there were a prize for whoever hugged her the hardest, and the scene wound up as a rugby scrum.

She shrieked, "I can't believe it!" a half dozen times, then asked, "Doc, who's watching the farm?"

Her sister said, "Trang, the famous herb sitter."

"Trang?"

"With a little help from Van. They're having a high old time making tussie-mussies."

The intruders insisted on an instant briefing about Ace, and she gave them the short version. When she came to *Peter Pan* and her arrest, she thought she saw her mother and father exchange knowing glances. Her father asked, "Why didn't you just come home, hon?"

"I have to wait for Mike to show up. It could happen any minute."

"Do you *know* this fisherman person is Mike?" her mother asked.

"I'm positive."

"But weren't you positive about Ace? In the play?" Lael bit her lip. Her mother went on, "I just hope you're not building yourself up for another—"

"I'm not, Mom."

Her father took her hand. "We're with you, hon. It's just—"

"Say, whatever happened to Christmas?" Julie interrupted.

Her father smiled and held out his hands, palms up, as though adjuring his congregation to rise. "Christmas will now begin. You ladies follow me."

"Where?" Lael asked.

"Have faith."

They trooped down the hall and entered a small suite above the motel office. Boughs of cedar and fir had been draped across the doorway. Stockings hung in front of a false fireplace that was almost hidden from sight by brightly wrapped packages. A pair of card tables sagged under her mother's traditional Swedish Christmas dishes: *gravlaxås,* the savory dumplings called *kroppkakor,* the pungent sausage *potatiskorv.*

Lael lifted the silver lid from a tureen and inhaled the sweet scent of *bruna bonör,* baked beans with spices and brown sugar. The breadbowl held fennel-scented dark *limpa.* There were four or five herring dishes in gleaming silver salvers, a bowl of lingonberries so wetly scarlet that they looked luminous, a dish of pickled cucumbers and another of pickled mushrooms, a silver bowl of potato salad with whole peeled hard-boiled eggs, and at the center of everything a pitcher of hot glögg and a full bottle of the aquavit that gave it bite.

She gawked. Her mouth stayed in a wide O and wouldn't shut. The three of them must have spent *days.* She kept looking from the tables to her parents and back again, saying, "Oh, Dad. Oh, Mom." She repeated herself till she knew she must sound like an imbecile, but it beat bawling. "Oh, Dad," she said once more. "How on earth did you get it all here?"

"Julie had to ride on the roof."

"Nice view," her sister said.

Her father disappeared into the other room and returned with a tinsel-draped tree that brushed the ceiling. "Don't tell me you brought *that* from home," Lael said.

"Found it this morning on a street corner in Douglaston. Too big to sell, I guess. I looked around for somebody to pay, but nobody was there. So I said, 'Thy will be done,' and took off."

"Like a shot," Julie put in.

They sat for the traditional feast, and he asked for a blessing on the food and on all of them "and most especially on our absent son and grandson, Ace." Oh, Acey, she thought, you should be here to see this. You almost *were.*

Van should be here, too, she said to herself as she reached across the table for a third helping of *kropps* and potato sausage. He won't stare at my ribs the next time.

After dinner she sat on the rug and opened her gifts. As she unwrapped a new *Organic Gardening* book on mulching, inscribed "To Sis with all my love, from Doc," she started to cry. Her mother rushed over and hugged her. She looked up into three concerned faces. These perfectly decent human beings had sacrificed their own Christmas to help her survive hers, and she was rewarding them by squawling like a self-centered brat. "It's all right, Mom," she said, wiping her eyes. "Dad, it's *okay!* I mean, I would've cried anyway. But this crying is different. I mean, I think it helps."

"Just what you need," Julie said, looking as though she might cry herself. "You hold too much inside." She turned away.

"I feel better," Lael said, brushing at her eyes with the back of her hand. They all smiled again. She thought: Families! No one can help or hurt like families. The day before she had felt that since she was in jail, she deserved to be in jail. Now she felt that since she was loved, she deserved to be loved. The best Christmas presents couldn't be wrapped.

Toward evening Julie and her mother went for a walk, and Lael was left on the plastic-covered sofa with her father. "Dad," she said, "if you only knew what this means to me."

He was silent. Then he said, "It's awful to lose a child."

His words revived her deepest fears. "Dad, don't put it like that. Ace isn't lost. It's just a matter—"

"He may be gone for good, honey," he said. He put the flat of his hand across his chest and inhaled deeply, as though summoning his strength. "Your mother and I, we've accepted the possibility. With the Lord's help. He'll help you, too."

She told herself: They just don't understand. Nobody does. She balked at the idea of asking God for anything. The God she'd come to know lately was uncompromising, unyielding, implacable, mean. Let others worship a God like that. But she knew how her parents felt. They loved Ace, too. And they loved her. It must have hurt them deeply to see her suffer— and frightened them that she might suffer more.

"I'm not suggesting you stop looking," he went on. "I'm just asking you to accept the possibility. You'll never start to heal till you do. Can you take that on faith, angel?"

"I can try, Dad." But she knew she never would.

Her family said good-bye at nine o'clock Christmas night, carrying leftovers in plastic bags from the motel's coffee shop. Lael was afraid she might cry again as the Pontiac chugged away on its worn-out shocks, but she didn't. She shut the door of her room and thought: Hooray for them and hooray for me! I survived Christmas.

She had just slid one slender foot into a steaming tub when Van called to see if there was any news. The conversation turned to their acrimonious parting two nights before, and he said, "Look. Lael, I'm not gonna play cute, okay? I wanted to stay. But you gave me a choice of spending Christmas where

I wasn't wanted or where I was."

She caught the hurt in his voice. "I hope you know better than that," she said.

"Better than what?"

"You *were* wanted. And needed. Oh, Van, I don't know my own mind anymore. I start to say something, and I say the opposite. I lose control of myself ten times a day. I wanted you to stay, but—but I'm glad you left." She heard her own contradiction and yelped, "See what I mean? I can't make up my mind! No, I mean—I just meant—thanks for taking care of the farm. I'm glad you spent Christmas with Trang. I hope you had as nice a time as I had."

"We did." He sounded more like himself. "Hold on a minute. Somebody wants to say something."

Trang said, "Happy Christmas, Lael." They talked for a while. He said he had enjoyed making tussie-mussies and sachets. She told him he was hired: three hours a day at $3.50 an hour. He said he would start at dawn.

She went to bed early, feeling almost at peace. The curtain had just gone up on her first dream—a baby lies sleeping under a blue woolen blanket—when she snapped awake. Something was wrong. Yes! She'd forgotten to tell Solomon John where to contact her. The most important thing.

She dialed his number and was relieved to hear his unhurried voice. "Been trying to get you at the Cedar Inn. Thought I oughta pass somethin' along. I got to talking to Doc Fuquay outside church this evening. Said he's been treating a new kid for asthma. Six, seven years old. Name of Al. Doc says he's been living with his dad up to the old Roadway Courts, about a quarter mile north of my place."

Her fingers shook as she scribbled "Rdwy Crts 1/4 mi N" on a motel scratch pad. She said, "Mr. John, please, don't mention this to anyone."

"Course not." He paused. "Well, g'night, Miz Pritcher, uh—Lael."

"Good night, Mr. John. I don't know how to thank you."

As she started to dial Van's number, she wondered if God would ever forgive all her faithless thoughts. Yes, he would, she decided. He was famous for that.

35

AT SEVEN-TWENTY the next morning, she shivered on a steep hillside covered with brown bracken fern so tall that she'd had to stomp some of it down to see the cluster of buildings below. The pale December sun had just begun to touch the highest peaks of the Cascades to the east; it would be another hour before it edged over the jagged ridgeline to start one of the shortest and coldest days of the year. When she and Van had driven away from the Woodlander Motel an hour earlier, the thermometer outside the office had read 16.

The Roadway Courts appeared in the shadows below as seven or eight lumps, distinctive as rabbit hutches. The walls of the cabins buckled outward. A yellow light bulb hung from a pole. The light shone directly on a gutted station wagon that sat rusting in a shallow trough as though laid to rest by a hurried gravedigger. It seemed odd to come across a slum in a beautiful place like Ridley Rip and to find her son a resident. Or had Mike hustled him off to a new hiding place already? She would know soon. If word had spread about her madwoman act two days before, the two of them would be long gone.

She blew warm air into her hands and wondered how the shacks were heated. Probably with wood. Inside, it would be as smoky as a tepee and always too hot or too cold—the worst possible conditions for an asthmatic. Ace mustn't spend one more night here.

Van was sighting through the binoculars. "See anything?" she asked. Her words pulsed across the cold air between them as little clouds of frost.

"No."

"Look for a yellow Ford Escort with about three antennas on the roof."

"Antennas?"

"He's a CB freak."

Stretched out on his stomach, Van watched silently. "Nope," he said at last. "Still too dark. It's like an abandoned recon post down there. They should give this hill a number." His voice sounded strained, thin. When she'd summoned him a few hours before, he'd still been up, writing a brief on nuclear dumping. He couldn't have slept.

"I wish old John had known the exact cabin," he said, his voice quaking from cold. "It'd be a lot easier to focus on one place."

An owl hooted in the woods behind them, and a few seconds later she heard the slippery whisk of wings. Van rolled on his side, and handed the Bushnell glasses to her. She swept the area quickly. The light had improved since her last turn, and this time she could make out three or four vehicles, all too big to be Escorts. But she also saw overhangs and outbuildings that might hide a compact car.

As she watched, a light flashed in a cabin. She squinted and saw a silhouette pass a window and then pass it again in the other direction.

"Somebody's up," she said. "Third house from the left."

He interrupted a deep yawn. "Gimme a look." After a few seconds he said, "A beagle. They just let him out." She felt apologetic as he handed the binoculars back.

By eight-forty the light was almost full and there was no movement below. The overcast sky looked like leftover oatmeal. She was glad she had two sweaters under her parka, but she was worried about Van. He was wearing a biker's down-filled vest with a light wool shirt. She could imagine him grabbing whatever clothes were handy. Now he must be freezing.

They had been handing off the 7x35 wide-angle binoculars every fifteen or twenty minutes, and she was on her third tour of duty when she saw the door open in a unit at the center of the court. A small figure emerged and walked in a familiar light-footed style toward the end of the sagging porch, leaned over a small box and extricated something, and stood up in the full light, facing her.

She felt her heart beat under her clothes. She wiped her eyes with a sleeve as her son skipped back to the door with a container of milk. She tried to spot the cowlick where she had cut away the bubble gum almost a year ago. It was gone. His luxuriant black hair had been trimmed almost to a crew cut. He was dressed only in Jockey shorts. My God, she thought, no wonder he's having asthma. How can Mike let him go out in the cold like that?

"Van," she whispered. He lay on his back, not moving. "Van!"

"Huh? I must've dropped off."

"*Sssssh*. He's there. The middle cabin. The one with the shed."

He sat up and grabbed the binoculars. "Did you get a good look?"

"Perfect. It's Ace."

He watched for a while. "They're up," he said. "Smoke's coming out of the chimney." He lowered the glasses and grabbed her hand. "Lael, you're sure?"

"I'm sure." She spoke in a whisper, afraid that her voice might carry to the cabins a few hundred feet below. On the drive up from Ridley Rip, Van must have warned her a half dozen times that they couldn't afford another mistake.

They inched back up the slope till they reached the cover of the untrampled fern, then jogged a half mile to the corduroy skid road where the Luv was stashed. Van had trouble starting the cold engine; every whine and wheeze made Lael cringe in fear that Mike would recognize the familiar sound. She hunched out of sight on the floorboards till they were safely away from Ridley Rip. "Let me do the talking," Van said as they approached the sheriff's substation. "Cops are different."

The place appeared empty except for a middle-aged policewoman working under a humming fluorescent light. A fat black fly buzzed around a plastic Christmas tree hung with candy canes.

Van asked for the watch commander. The policewoman blew a wisp of graying hair off her face and asked, "What's it about?"

"Officer, this is Mrs. Lael Pritcher," he said pleasantly. "I'm Ivan Stein, her attorney." He slid his business card across the Formica desk, reached in his briefcase, and pulled out a paper. "This is a certified copy of a Washington superior court order. You'll see that it awards custody of Mrs. Pritcher's son, Alexander, to his mother. We've located the father and son, and we want the boy picked up. Today. Now."

The policewoman peered at the papers, then up at Van and back at the papers. "Washington matter, huh?" she said, her casual tone of voice indicating her feelings about the offense. She turned to Lael and said, "You got an Oregon order?"

"I, uh—"

"We don't need an Oregon order," Van intervened. Lael

could see by the policewoman's bobbing eyebrows that she was having trouble relating Van to his gear. "There's federal legislation," he went on. "I'm sure you've heard of it. This order is valid in every state."

"Uh, wait here, please."

Lael couldn't keep her hands still. They brushed imaginary loose hairs from her forehead, tapped the Formica counter, rubbed downward across her cheeks, and forced her lower lip flat. Her breathing was as quick as a sparrow's. Van grabbed her by the arm. "Be cool," he whispered.

"What's taking so *long?*"

"It's called due process," he explained, "and this is no time to ignore it."

After a few minutes the policewoman returned and said, "Where's the subject now? District Two?"

"He's in Ridley Rip," Van said.

"Oh, God, the lieutenant'll love it."

"Can we see him?" Van asked.

"Would you just wait over there?"

They sat on a worn bench with wooden armrests hollowed out by their predecessors in trouble. Lael squirmed and sighed and clucked till Van grabbed her hands and told her again to relax. "How?" she asked. "Ace is right up that road!"

"Take some deep breaths."

"I did."

"Take some more." He enclosed her hands tightly. His were warm, hers were ice. She was thankful he was here.

It was nearly 10:00 A.M. when they were ushered into the presence of a smiling policeman with rimless bifocals and silver bars on his collar points. A plastic nameplate advertised "CURCIO."

Van reached to shake hands, but the telephone interrupted and then interrupted again, and soon all three console lights were on. The balding cop shoved the buttons one by one like a man killing ants and spoke in a soft, controlled voice. At last he hung up and addressed the two of them as though he'd known them all his life. "I got a four-car pileup on the interstate. One car's stolen, the driver rabbited. State police borrowed four of my units. What's left couldn't handle a riot at a nursery school." He smiled at Lael, shook hands with both, and said, "Whatcha got, Counselor?"

Van sketched in the details and handed over the custody papers. "I know about this case," the watch commander said, taking a long look at Lael. "No problem." He punched a button, and the policewoman appeared. "Betty, call Wilson at home and get him to come in."

"He worked late—"

"Didn't we all. He made the arrest; this is his baby. Besides, I'm out of warm bodies. Unless you want to—"

"I'll call Wilson." She beckoned to Van and Lael. "If you'll just step this way."

"I know you're busy, Lieutenant," Van said, remaining in his seat, "but could we talk a minute?"

Curcio stopped in mid-dial, put down the phone, and said, "About what? We're gonna go out and pick up a six-year-old kid, isn't that it?"

"We've had the boy and his father cornered before. The child's been led to believe that his mother hates him. They'll both run. And they're slippery."

"Meaning—?"

"Meaning your man's gonna need help. We've been chasing Mike Pritcher since April. The next time they get away, it could be for good."

The watch commander took off his glasses and rubbed hard at his light brown eyes. "Listen, Mr. Stein, if this was an ax murderer doing his thing at a Christmas mass, I'd have to handle it the same way." He motioned to the policewoman, standing in the doorway, listening. "Go ahead. Call Wilson."

"Code Three?"

"No. But tell him to shake it."

Van wouldn't let up. "There's thick woods up there, Lieutenant. If—"

Curcio smiled wanly and held up a hand. A small moonstone on his little finger caught the fluorescent light. "Don't break my chops, okay, Counselor? This is a custody case, right? A routine pickup."

Lael heard herself exclaim, "It certainly is *not!*"

The watch commander looked at the ceiling. "Strike what I said," he told her. "I know it's not a routine case to you, missus." He held out his hand. "Am I forgiven?"

She took his hand, and he stood up and gently guided her toward the door as though he were leading her onto a dance floor. "Now if you'll just wait a few minutes, the officer'll be right along."

"Lieutenant," Van said, "how about letting us help out? Me

and Mrs. Pritcher. I mean, just in case."

"I'd have to be bughouse. You're not even residents. Give us a little credit. I've sent one-man cars out to pick up escaped felons."

He left the two of them at a bench outside. Now Van was the one who tapped his feet as they waited. "Be cool," she said, throwing his own words at him. "He seems competent." She was apprehensive about seeing Deputy Wilson again, but this time he would be on her side. Theoretically anyway.

At noon the policewoman came out of a small office and said, "Do you know where the grocery is in Ridley Rip?"

"At the crossroads," Lael said.

"The officer wants you to meet him there. Park in back. He'll find you."

"And then we'll pick up the boy?" Van asked.

"You'll have to talk to the deputy about that."

They took the Luv to Ridley Rip. It was after one o'clock when a brown and white cruiser marked "SHERIFF" pulled up alongside. "Jesus, man, what took you?" Van called through the open window.

"One thing after another," Wilson said through the open window. By now Mike and Ace could have driven away for the day, Lael thought, or gone fishing, or heard about my performance at *Peter Pan* and left the county, left the state, left the whole Northwest. And we have to rely on a baby-faced deputy who thinks I'm a hooker or a pedophile or both.

She slumped in the seat. Wilson had given no sign of recognition. Maybe he was happy to forget his behavior. He hadn't exactly covered himself with glory.

"Just tell me which cabin it is," he ordered. "I know the Roadway Courts backwards."

"It's almost in the center," Van said. "Asphalt shingles, brick chimney, one window broken and taped. It's the only cabin with a painted front porch. Green."

"Car parked outside?"

"He drives a little yellow Escort, but we didn't see it. It might be in a shed."

"Let's get it over with," Wilson said. "You and the, uh, lady stick right here. I might need you for something."

"We can't help out?" Van asked. "Watch the exits or something?"

"It's against procedure."

The police car left with a squeal of tires. "I hope he doesn't make all that noise when he pulls up," Van said. "As spooky as Mike is."

They waited. Lael's tight lungs felt as though she were suffering sympathetic asthma. She was trying to prepare herself emotionally for the sight of Ace's head in the patrol car. How well would he remember her after eight months? She'd read that young children lose much of their bonding to parents after six months of separation and all but forget them after a year. She wanted to pull him from the car and crush him in her arms. But how would he react to her?

"Van?" she said.

"Yeah?"

"Ummm . . . nothing."

He took her hand again. "Hang in," he said. "It can't be much longer."

"I'm scared." She pressed the back of his hand to her forehead and leaned forward. "Oh, Van, I'm scared."

"Hey, this is Mike's day to be scared."

Minutes passed. "Christ, what's happening?" Van said.

"Can't we go see?" She bit back the sharp taste of orange juice. Her whole breakfast seemed to be in her throat.

Van said, "He told us to wait."

"But how long?"

He kicked in the clutch and turned the key. "We'll drive by. Vouldn't help, vouldn't hoit."

They slowed in front of the Roadway Courts. Up close she could see that the one-story houses were built on cinder-block foundations like sharecroppers' shacks. The asphalt roofs were streaked with moss, the sagging porches littered with junk. A three-legged dog nibbled at a bone.

The patrol car was parked in front of the house where she had spotted Ace. Its roof lights were still spinning. Wilson stood on the porch. Two adults in work clothes and a cluster of scrawny children watched from down the row.

"Van," Lael shrieked, "you don't suppose—"

"Let's go!"

He drove straight up the rutted driveway across slicks of ice. The two of them piled out of the truck together and ran up on the porch. "Where are they?" Van asked.

"Not home," Wilson said. "I was getting ready to see what the neighbors know."

"Not home? Did you try the door?"

"It's locked," he said, raising both palms.

"Well, break it down, man!"

"Not without authorization. Not on a case like this." He added something under his breath. Lael caught the last few words, "only acting like a father." He looked blankly at her.

She knew where his sympathies lay. He had made that obvious the other night. Now what could they do? Wait around like that night in Canada? She felt like crying. She had found Ace again and lost him again. She could see no end to it. She would still be tracking him when she was an old woman. He wouldn't know her and she wouldn't know him.

Van shoved at the scarred old door.

"Hey!" Wilson called out. "Back off!"

Van's boot crashed into the knob. The door held, but a panel splintered lengthwise. His hand snaked through the jagged hole, and the door opened.

Lael ran past the two men and inside. The front room was as dark as a cave, lit only by a few embers in a tiny fireplace. "Ace!" she called out. "Acey, are you here? It's Mommy, baby. Don't be afraid."

She stumbled toward a slash of light down a short hallway and came to a small kitchen. A roach retreated from a pair of eggshells on the counter. The room was surprisingly warm.

Van disappeared in the rear. A few seconds later he stomped back through the small house, his boots hitting the floor like hammer blows. She followed him till he reached the deputy, standing in the living room. "How in the goddamn hell'd this happen?" Van snapped, jutting out his lower jaw.

"How'd *what* happen?"

"What did you do after you left us?"

"I, uh, I went to the place next door."

"But we told you—"

"You gave me bad directions," Wilson said. "What's the difference? They weren't home anyway. We'll grab the kid later."

"No, you won't," Van said. "Come here." He led the way to the rear of the cabin. The back door hung open on rusty hinges. A few feet away, beyond a break in the woven wire fence, thick underbrush gloomed dark and impenetrable. There was no sign of Mike or Ace.

36

LAEL LOOKED AROUND the empty cabin. At this moment she was supposed to be cradling Ace in her arms, quieting his fears and buttoning him up against the chill, not peeking under tables and looking in musty closets. She wondered when the shock of this latest loss would begin. She always felt it first in her stomach.

The place was thick with dust. No wonder his asthma had been kicking up; house dust was a 4 on his chart. In a bathroom without a door she found a claw-footed tub filled with soapy water. She reached in, fighting a feeling that she was intruding. The water was warm. In a small back room she found a double bed. Father and son must have bunked together. Alongside a dresser with one missing drawer she stepped on a Seattle Mariners baseball cap. She picked it up and sniffed.

Ace.

She flattened it against her breast. The plastic strap in back was cinched up to the smallest size. Oh, Ace, she thought, why would you run from your mom?

She heard the men returning from the woods and met them on the sloping back steps of the house, folding and refolding the cap in her hands. "They got too big a lead," Wilson said, his paunch heaving.

"Call in a dog," Van said.

"I wonder if there's a phone in this dump," Wilson grumbled.

There was, a dull-black wall model that looked as though Ma Bell hadn't upgraded it in twenty years. She heard him ask for Lieutenant Curcio. It was easy to tell how the conversation was going. The deputy asked for a tracking dog and then kept saying, " Right . . . right. . . ."

Van tapped him on the shoulder and asked with his hands what was happening. Wilson pointed a thumb at the floor.

Van yanked the phone away. "Lieutenant? We need a dog fast. . . . Well, *you* listen to *me!* I don't give a good goddamn how silly you'd look using dogs in a custody case." His head

174

moved in angry jerks, shaking his red curly hair. "You sat there this morning and told us not to worry, didn't you?... Your man blew it, *that's* what happened. My thirteen-year-old kid could've done better...."

Lael looked for the deputy. He was walking back toward his car, as though seeking cover. "First he goes to the wrong house and alerts the whole goddamn place," Van continued loudly, "and then he lets the guy back-door him.... What?... Bet your ass!... Goddamn right.... Okay, we'll wait. But they're getting farther away every second."

Two minutes later the phone rang, and Van picked it up. "Good," he said. He turned to Lael. "A dog's on the way."

A low-slung German shepherd arrived in thirty minutes with its handler, a middle-aged man who kept scrooching up his nose and testing the air. He let the animal sniff around the inside of the house and then released it. The dog ran out the back door, nosed the ground, and rushed headlong into the woods, exhaling steam. It reappeared a few houses away and trotted along the border of the Roadway Courts to the highway. "He's trained to wait at roads," the handler explained as they ran to catch up.

On the far side of Route 278 they followed the shepherd through an orchard and along a ditch bordered by thick blackberry bushes. The dog stopped at a small dock on the Little Ridley. Feathery borders of ice rimmed the pilings and the shoreline, but the main current of the river flowed strongly. Van held up a pair of limp mooring ropes that had dangled into the pale green water. "Call in a chopper, Wilson! They stole a boat. We got 'em trapped on the river."

"The state's got choppers," the deputy said, "but they're only for emergencies."

"What can we do?" Lael asked, turning from one to the other.

"I dunno," Wilson said. "By the time we get a boat up here from town—I dunno. They already got a big jump. They coulda already taken out by now."

"Solomon John!" she said. "He has boats."

"How far's this river go?" Van asked as they ran back toward their vehicles.

"Three and a half miles. To the Columbia."

"Is it dangerous?"

"A little." The deputy didn't seem eager to talk.

"What kind of boat's Solomon John got? Fast?"

"Same as everybody else," Wilson said. "A double ender float boat."

"What's between here and the Columbia?" Van asked.

"Some good water, some bad. Him and the kid, they probably already went ashore and walked up to the highway."

The hunt party found Solomon John running a model railroad train under his Christmas tree for two small children. "My grandbabies," he introduced them, but Van was already asking if he could catch a boat with a thirty-minute lead.

"That Pritcher fella?" John said, struggling to his feet. "I don't think so. Not unless they hung up"—he lowered his voice—"or broke up."

"What's that mean?" Lael asked.

"Well, they coulda high-centered on a rock or tore the bottom out in a chute. We could take a look down to Jagurtha Pool. That's, uh, that's where most of the bodies turn up." He looked away from Lael, as though he had revealed more than he intended.

She bit her lip as Van told the deputy, "Why don't you go check the takeouts." It wasn't a question.

Wilson said, "I told you, mister, they probably took out by now—"

"I don't care what you told me," Van said. He turned to the guide. "Can you take me down-river?"

"You bet."

He gave her a quick hug. "We won't be long," he promised. He called to the deputy, disappearing through the front door. "The man's a kidnapper! Try to remember that."

Outside he held up his arms while Solomon John strapped him into a flotation jacket and hurriedly got into one himself. The guide pulled on a floppy pair of hip boots and started untying the mooring knots. Lael felt panicky at being left. She stepped into the boat. "Hey!" Van said. "You can't—"

"It's her son," the riverman said evenly.

He flipped her a plastic jacket and poled the boat into a wide span of water that rippled and sparkled in the clear cold air. The wind came straight upstream; flecks of icy spray lashed her face like sleet. "Who'd fish on a day like this?" Van asked.

"A steelheader," the guide answered.

For a while the watercourse squeezed between high clay banks and they moved a little faster than walking speed. But then the boat hit a wide deep stretch and inched along. A pair of birds followed, too high to identify.

The river narrowed again, and they bobbed past a tall pair of needle rocks glazed with ice. Lael noticed the old boatman's economy with the oars, using the current to do the work. Mike didn't have the experience or the skill to handle a boat that way. She prayed to herself, *Dear Lord, let them be safe. Protect my son from his father.* She wondered if there was any chance of catching up. *What will we do then? Grapple like pirates?*

In a few minutes they had curved away from the highway and were running under towering slabs of columnar basalt. Most of the rock was vitrified, polished. Spray had thrown up sculptures and glazes, smoothed edges, created a frosting that softened the scene.

She jumped at a loud noise. The guide had banged one of the oars against the side of the boat. "Ice," he explained. She could see it on the long, thin shaft. The wind seemed stronger. The moisture in her breath reappeared as frost on the collar of her parka, irritating her face each time she turned. She tried to tuck down into the heavy material but found she couldn't see ahead.

She pulled the strap across her chin for warmth and looked at Van. He knelt in the bow, her Jewish-Viking mariner, keeping watch downstream through the binoculars. The sleeves of his thin plaid shirt flattened out against his skin, and she wondered how he and the guide could stand the cold in such skimpy clothes. As she watched, Van fumbled for his binoculars and focused. "Up ahead," he said. "A man."

"That's Steam Bend," the riverman said. "The first takeout after Ridley Rip."

The boat moved with agonizing slowness. "Please," she said, "can't you row faster?"

"Don't much matter how fast I row," he said calmly. "I'm mostly just steering."

After a few minutes Van lowered his binoculars. "Goddamn," he said. A fisherman in chest-high waders stood in the river.

Solomon John said, "Hey, Lefty, you seen anybody on the water?"

"About twenty minutes ago," the man called back as he lowered a scarf from his face. "A man and a kid. They wasn't fishing, though. Hey, Sol, you shoulda seen the steelie that just come through here. I thought it was a Roosian sub." He threw back his head and cackled like a chicken, revealing pink gums.

After the boat had floated out of earshot, the guide said, "See what he was casting? Metal. There's always one or two." He sounded ashamed. Lael didn't know what he was talking about, or care. Four billion people would keep on with their daily lives no matter how long Ace was gone, but she didn't see how.

They bumped down a whitewater chute that made her bounce on the seat and came to a stretch marked by intermittent gravel bars jutting into the river like fingers. Whenever it looked as though they would go aground, the boatman flicked an oar and steered them clear. She hoped the deputy was doing as good a job. Back at the Roadway Courts he hadn't even bothered to get the directions straight. Laws had changed, but not this lawman. What was it he'd said about Mike? "Only acting like a father." *And I'm just another stubborn woman, I suppose. Dad came close to saying so yesterday. Thank God for Van.*

The boat rounded a corner and came to a broad clear-cut area that was just beginning to recover. Wild huckleberry bushes poked from the tops of fir stumps. Baby cedars grew in threes and fours from mother logs. She noticed that Van's attention had wandered momentarily from the river ahead to the no man's land on both sides.

The current picked up as the river squeezed between low rolling hills. She felt disoriented. The sun had been behind them when they started; now it was ahead, shining like a silver button through a thin layer of clouds. She imagined them floating for days, freezing in the sunlight, moving in a helpless circle like creatures from Jules Verne. In her mind she saw Mike scrambling up the cliffside, stopping to laugh at her as they floated aimlessly on the river below. She said, *"Hmmmm,"* dimly aware that someone had spoken.

"I said, 'Are you cold?'" Van's voice came back.

"I'm f-fine."

The boat bumped along the rapids between cutover woods and piles of half-burned stumps and slash. A water ouzel waded into the shallows till its head disappeared beneath the surface. High above, the same two unidentifiable birds rode the shock waves of the wind. A small deer peeked from the interior of a thimbleberry bush and trotted discreetly away, its black tail signaling. The boat reached a slow stretch and almost seemed to stop. "My God," Lael said, "I can walk faster than this."

"Along that bank?" Solomon John asked patiently, the corded muscles standing out on his lower arms. On both sides of the river the blackberry brambles and devil's club formed a wall at the water's edge. Ropes of vine maple lay in mats, and stranded logs and stumps were scattered about as though someone had emptied a box of huge toothpicks. Now she knew why the float boats could be taken out only at certain points. A person would slash himself to death trying to pierce that vegetation.

"Can't outrow anybody," the guide said between strokes. "These wood boats aren't made for speed."

"How far've we gone?" Van asked from the bow.

"Halfway."

"Does it get better or worse?"

"One bad chute left. Split Run, it's called. You have to stay to the left of the marker rock. Go to the right and—it's a bad drop."

Lael said, "My son. . . ."

"Your husband'll know how to handle Split Run—he done it with me a couple of times." Yes, Lael thought, but nobody was chasing him then. *Hounding* him, as Catherine would say.

At the end of a reach of bubbly water that kept the boat jiggling, the river entered a long channel through crumbling volcanic pumice. At the edges of the scree a few sugar pines and shaggy-skinned madronas groped for a footing, and the bottom of the gorge was a tangle of bushes and herbs in their late fall format: mazzard cherry, youth-on-age, sticky cinquefoil, rattlesnake plantain, frozen specimens of yellow monkeyflower, so tasty in salads, and purple foxglove, so deadly. There was still no escape for Mike and Ace except straight ahead. Maybe the deputy had reached the takeout in time.

Solomon John gave a heave on the oars, and the boat bumped around a sand bar and came to another long stretch of holding water. "This is the last flat spot before Split Run," the guide called out. "It's half a mile ahead. If we were gonna catch 'em, it shoulda been here."

Lael saw color a couple of hundred yards downstream. "Van!" she said, motioning for the binoculars hanging from his neck. A fish hawk lifted off an alder snag and soared up and over the boat as she fumbled with the glasses. She couldn't feel her fingers as she tried to focus.

At first she saw two disembodied heads. Then a boat bobbed into view beneath them: another double ender. She took a firm hold on the binoculars.

Mike and Ace came in sight as clearly as though they were

a few feet ahead. They were both bareheaded, lightly dressed.
Ace was wearing his black plastic-rimmed glasses, but one of
the lenses looked cracked. She had the feeling that he would
wave and call, "Hi, Mom!"

"It's them," she whispered without lowering the binoculars.
The child turned full face, and she saw that his cheek bore a
bloody scratch. Oh, my baby, she thought. You were running
from Mom and you hurt yourself. She thrust the glasses at the
guide. "Take a look. How close are they to the—the rapids?"

"Split Run?" The old man let the oars swing in the current
while he refocused the binoculars. "Jesus oh my *gosh!*" he
cried. "He's headed for the wrong side." He lowered the glasses
and yelled, "Look out!" as though his voice could carry 200
yards down-river. "Oh, Lord," he muttered. "He done it
wrong."

God in heaven, she prayed, don't let them drown! Give Ace
a chance. Please, Lord, take the father, *take the father!*

"Let me see," Van said. He raised the glasses and said,
"They're out of sight."

"Over and gone," the boatman said, one palm flattened
across his forehead. He turned to Lael. The color had drained
from his leathery face. "I'm sorry if I scairt you, Mrs. Pritcher,"
he said. "They might of made it." He sounded as though he
didn't believe his own words.

Her fingers were sore from gripping the gunwales. The boat
floated with maddening slowness along the long stretch of
water. A party of crows lifted from a snag and flew across the
river, raining curses. The cliffs and banks fell away on the
right side and became a sandy slope leading to dark patches
of leopard lilies and horsetail ferns. Every few minutes she
heard the whir of a car or truck and realized the river had
circled back to the highway, just past the ferns to the right.
She felt the boat jerk. The guide was pulling hard on one oar,
positioning them for the rapids.

"Nothing to it," he said. "See that rock?" He pointed to a
flatiron shape parting the current. "We steer to the left. Nice
little chute in there. Floats you right down to the takeout."

"What's on the right side?" Van asked.

"A thirty-foot drop to the rocks."

She let her head flop backward on her shoulders and peered
into the sky. The two birds that had tracked them down the
river dipped closer. They were buzzards.

The boat made a quarter turn and picked up speed. The tips

of the oars made Vs in the water as the riverman moved them gently. She strained to see ahead. It looked as though the stream dropped off into space. She realized that she was looking at the upper edge of Split Run.

Solomon John hauled hard on the right oar, and the heavy wooden boat moved to the left. A few more strokes, and they were in the grip of the current. "Hang on!" he shouted.

The boat passed the marker rock and angled forward and down. They skidded and bumped through whitewater for fifty or sixty feet and then coasted into a twisted line of brownish scum and leaves and froth in the rough shape of a spiral. "Jagurtha Pool," the guide said. Floating at its edge was a broken, overturned boat.

The old man said, "Look down! See if they're in the water. I'll hold us here as long as I can." She leaned over the side and stared. Leaves, weeds, wood chips, sticks rotated slowly beneath her gaze. A line of bubbles fizzled up from the bottom like a necklace. A shadowy form the length of a body caught her eye: a sunken log. Then they were spinning out of the whirlpool like riders at an amusement park.

The riverman pointed to the takeout just around a sharp bend. Lael stared back into the water, afraid of what she might see: a thin little leg, an outstretched arm, a pale face staring upward, unseeing brown eyes, a thin stream of bubbles rising from a mouth. Oh, my God, she thought, those bubbles! Were they from my baby? She stared at shadows and glints and gleams, looking for her son.

The deputy was waiting onshore. "See 'em on the river?" he called out.

She jumped from the boat and splashed through the shallow water. "Help!" she said. "My son . . . they went over . . . oh, please! *Send for help!*" She remembered reading about drowning victims being brought back from the dead after—how long was it? Four minutes? Forty? She felt guilty for not knowing more. "It's just happened," she said, uncertain if Wilson understood. "He's still alive. Help, please help! *It just happened.*"

The deputy unbelted his portable radio. "William Two," he said. "Request a Frog team. Jagurtha Pool. Code Three."

Van came up behind her and held her by the elbows as though she needed support. She broke loose and ran toward the water. She was in up to her thighs when she heard someone shout, "Stop! *Don't!*"

The water hit her face like a slap. A hand grabbed at her

ankle, but she kicked loose. She swam in her strong crawl toward the center of the river. After ten or twelve strokes she turned her head sideways and gulped air. Then she headed down.

She breaststroked five or six feet below the surface, eyes open, till she was near the middle of the pool. She came up for air and wondered why she wasn't cold. She sucked her lungs full and made another surface dive, deeper this time, slicing through shiny specks of suspended sediment.

Ace, she kept saying to herself, are you down here? It's Mommy, angel! *Mommy's coming.* She kicked till she was so deep that the water looked like cold green paint.

She couldn't see bottom. The water closed around her, gelatinous and thick. She reached far down and found only more water. She would have to go up for air and try again.

Suddenly her stomach muscles contracted, and the strength left her arms and legs. She recognized the massive cramp and went limp. When she thought her body had floated to the surface, she raised her head and took a deep breath and sucked in water, then more water.

The green depths turned gray, then black. A voice screamed, *You've killed the baby...it was your fault...you shouldn't have chased them...you've killed the baby.* She wondered what her mother-in-law was doing here.

In the darkness she heard hollow cackles and giggles, the clown sounds of a fun house. A voice that sounded like her own soared above the others. "Don't you see the humor? I came here to get him back, and I'm getting him back! As soon as they drag the river. *Can't you see the humor?*"

She opened her eyes but no light entered. She wished she knew where Van was. *Van, Van, don't leave.* She wondered if this was death. *Oh, Van, please. Have I lost you too?*

They were supposed to be together at the end.

37

SHE AWOKE UNDER cool white sheets in a room with white walls and a white ceiling. She closed her eyes tightly and opened them again. More white. A form swam in and out of focus at her bedside. "How're you feeling?" a sepulchral voice asked.

She tried to decide what to answer and settled for *"Hmmmm?"* Were the dead expected to have feelings? Memories, yes, but physical feelings? She wished she knew the protocol, but she had never been dead before. She told herself to look on the good side. Ace must be near.

A hand touched her face lightly. "I didn't think you were *ever* gonna wake up." She knew the voice from somewhere. She shut her eyes hard and tried to think.

Van! He hadn't deserted her after all. Or was he dead, too? "Be cool," he said. "You're in the emergency room. They gave you a shot. You were raising hell."

"Raising . . . hell?"

"Screaming, raving. You grabbed a nurse by the neck and wouldn't let go. They gave you something heavy."

"What—what happened?" She wasn't dead. She wouldn't be seeing Ace. Both thoughts were depressing.

"Well, we brought you here in the aid car and—"

"What did I do? Why did you have to bring me here?"

"You don't know?" She shook her head and he told her she had almost drowned in the Little Ridley River. She remembered being grabbed by the foot. Then she remembered everything.

"Ace!" she said. "Did they find—"

He shook his head.

"But they're still looking?"

"They're, uh, dragging."

So he was gone. How had her parents known to prepare for the worst before it happened? Now she could test her father's theories about getting over grief. Would she live long enough? She hoped not. "Oh, Van," she moaned, "why didn't you let me die?"

"Don't talk like that." He sounded in pain. "You'll be fine, you'll be great." His hand stroked her hair. "Hey, come on now. Lael, lean on me, lean on your friends. We all love you, honey."

She yanked her head away. "If you were my friend, you wouldn't have saved me."

"It wasn't me, Lael. I'm a lousy swimmer."

She wondered what it would be like to live in a world without Ace. Her herbs would wither and die. No more puns, no more songs about sucking your toes all the way to Mexico, no more tricks and pranks, no more sand tracked through the house. Nothing would have meaning. God above, how could you let it happen? A little boy floating face up in that awful river. You call yourself a just God, a merciful God? And you gave him a death like that? So violent? So cruel?

She felt someone touch her cheeks with a Kleenex. She heard words. "Wilson dived right in. Snagged your arm on his second or third try."

She blinked and turned. It was Van. "What?"

"I said Wilson saved you."

"The—the deputy?"

"Yeah."

"Why?"

Van shrugged. "It's his job."

"Is he okay?"

"Last I knew, he was being interviewed by a reporter. He kept telling the guy to interview you. He—" Van jumped up and headed for the door. "What's that racket?" he said.

"Don't leave," she said. "Van! Please! *Don't leave!*" She was afraid to be alone.

Solomon John burst through the door ahead of a red-faced nurse. "I'll get the security guard, mister!" the woman said.

"Get him then," the old man gasped. "Hey, pay attention. We found tracks."

"Tracks?" Van said.

The riverman took a deep breath and lifted his tractor cap from his white mane. "Just upstream of Split Run...fresh tracks...deep tracks, like they was made by somebody heavy. Started in the sand and went all the way up to the highway."

He hesitated, then lowered his voice. "A few spots of blood, too. We lost the trail in the ferns, but the dog picked 'em up again. In the dust by the highway. Only they was two sets of tracks up there, one big and one little. The boy and his daddy, they musta hitched a ride."

Lael didn't comprehend. "Ace?" she asked. "Did you find my baby?"

"No, ma'am," Solomon John said as Van gently pushed her back down on the bed. "Not the boy. Just his tracks."

Van said, "How do you figure it?"

"Pritcher and the boy musta jumped out on that last sand bar before Split Run. Then they shoved the boat back in the river and beat through the swamp to the road. My guess is he carried the boy in his arms as far as he could, maybe because—" He glanced at Lael and stopped. She finished the sentence in her mind: maybe because he was sick. His asthma again. Or . . . loss of blood? She remembered the long scratch down his face.

"Ace," she said weakly. "He's—he's. . . ."

"Alive," Van's voice answered. She turned and looked into his smile. "And miles away by now. We'll have to start over."

WINTER

38

JANUARY ARRIVED WITH its short days and its smudgy skies, a drain on her spirits. The Oregon authorities were silent about Ace. Mike's car was on the "wanted" lists but hadn't turned up.

With Trang and Julie helping, Lael went through the motions of collecting the seeds from the bags of seed heads hang-drying in the attic, added salt hay mulch to the perennial garden, and hacked at blackberry runners with a growing feeling that they would outlast the world. When Channel 5 forecast a hard frost, she washed the sweet marjoram and bay with warm soapy water to kill off aphids and red spiders, then brought the plants into the shelter of the greenhouse.

The island's annual snowfall arrived in the first week of February, and she called her father to ask him to preserve it with his movie camera. "I need pictures of snow on the trees, on the ground, some coming down. Okay, Dad?"

"Well, sure, honey, but why? What's so special about this snow?"

"It's for Ace," she told him, wondering why she had to explain. She ran outside in her pajamas and filled an ice tray with snow for the freezer. Within a few hours the thin white overlay swirled into the storm drains and gutters under a warm rain that raised steamy clouds of fog. The dismal winter weather had always been a trial. This year, at least, it seemed appropriate.

Late one night she was at her desk, writing the last few paragraphs of her daily letter. "Trang works for the farm now, and we talk a lot. You two will be great friends. He has black shiny hair just like you, and once in a while he has trouble saying his Ls. Once he called me Rare! A long time ago you used to call me Layoo! Well, that's all for tonight, dear Mr. Guacamole. I hope you're getting your shots every week wherever you are. Here's a thousand kisses and a hundred bear hugs! I LOVE YOU!!!"

She paused and added, "Love, Mom." She scanned her

words and wondered if she hadn't overworked the word love. Impossible. She added a whole sheet of Xs and Os. Silly woman, she thought. Writing letters to a child you may never see again. A child who runs from you. Silly, pathetic, gushy, mushy woman. . . .

After she fell asleep, she was awakened by intermittent gurgling and cooing. She tried to pinpoint the direction. The sounds seemed to be coming from down the hall. Ace's little sighs and moans!

She ran to his room. Poor baby, she thought, he hasn't made those sweet noises since he was in diapers. The doorknob wouldn't turn. She'd forgotten that it had been locked for almost ten months. Gulled by another dream.

She tried to get back to sleep, but she kept feeling his presence in the old house. It seemed unfair that he should be so conspicuous in her memory. She looked at the clock. Almost 4:00 A.M. She lay back against the pillow and tried to concentrate. Something was wrong. Larry Allen! Where was her favorite neckpiece? She hadn't seen him all day, or was it two days? She was losing track. First Ace and now her watchcat.

A week later Larry Allen was still gone—probably for good, she had to admit to herself—and she was walking in the garden, pondering her losses, when she realized that she had passed a swatch of dormant thistle without yanking it out. A day or two before, she had ignored some early Himalayan blackberry runners creeping murderously toward the sage. She wondered what was happening to her. Didn't she care about her herbs, her business? She decided that she cared, but the weeds would have to wait till her spirits improved.

One morning Julie arrived before daylight and disappeared into the greenhouse. Lael dawdled over coffee at the kitchen table; lately she had been drinking six or eight cups of coffee a day instead of her usual two or three cups of herb tea. She was still at the table, deep in thought, when she realized that Juliet had come inside and was talking.

"Hmm?"

"I said I've got to get the nine o'clock boat," her sister said. "Big test. Generics. Could you put the lovage seeds in the sod cups? They soaked all night."

Lael heard herself mutter, "If I get a chance."

"They'll rot."

"I said I'll do it! Do you want it in writing?"

Julie muttered, "Gee, Sis. . . ." Her voice fell off.

Lael thought how hard her sister had worked, how she had held the business together, and she felt ashamed beyond words. She shoved back her chair and held out her arms. "Doc, Doc, how could I talk like that to you? I'm so selfish!"

They held each other for a few seconds, then stepped back and came together again. "I understand," Julie said. "Listen, Sis, don't you *ever* call yourself selfish. And don't you *ever* apologize to me. Damn it, I love you!" She took Lael's face in both her hands and pressed her cheeks. "Another thing. We're not giving up on Ace. Understand? Whatever you have to do, go out and do it! I can run this place blindfolded."

After Julie had driven off in her old MG with the flapping fenders, Lael flopped down on the corduroy couch in the living room and sighed. All you need, she told herself, is a broom and a pointed hat. You've become a world-class grump, a walking headache. You're wretching everybody out: Doc, Mom, Dad, Van, Trang, even some of your customers.

But then she asked herself: What do they expect? Am I supposed to do a happy-face number like some empty-headed anchorman on the six o'clock news?

I *can't*.

For a month she tried to solve the problem by keeping to herself. She made excuses to be away from the house, avoided family gatherings, shopped across the bridge so she wouldn't bump into friends. She wrote run-on letters to Ace, started and finished her long jogs before daylight, spent hours perched on her dock communing with the cormorants, hiked through the woods on faintly marked trails.

She made a few attempts at becoming a nighttime movie-goer, but too many of the scenes brought Ace back. TV was better: less realistic, more anesthetizing. Julie suggested she start dating—"It doesn't have to be a big heavy thing, Sis; it can just be fun"—but she remained dead to the opposite sex. Van talked to her every few days, but he was different. She felt as though she had known him forever, but she also felt guilty about taking his time. Nothing could come of it.

In her self-imposed isolation she noticed that she was losing her old decisiveness, her confidence. She would study the apples at the market for ten minutes and walk away empty-handed. She would start to turn the mulch under in one of the raised beds and then decide to add a few inches more—and end up doing neither. One minute she was positive that she would find

Ace, and the next that he was gone forever.

Sometimes she wondered if there was any point in going on without him. Every personal triumph, every little satisfaction for the rest of her days would be made meaningless by her loss. No matter how successful she was at life, she would always be behind in the game. Why play?

She threw challenges at God, dared and denied him. She would sit up in bed and yell, "Listen to me, if you're there, if you've got one shred of decency, send him back! At least, give me a sign. Anything, a hint, a whisper. *Give me something!*" Late one night she dialed her father to berate him for the religious lies he had told her as a child, but she hung up in tears when she heard his voice. She decided she must be losing her mind to do a thing like that.

But Ace had been gone for *so* long.

One dismal February morning she checked the Havahart trap that had replaced Larry Allen. A calico mouse ran back and forth in the cage, across the pan, up and down the sides. It stopped to rest for seconds at a time, tiny chest palpitating, then returned to its task of finding a way out. She watched, fascinated. There was no brooding, no despair. Only man wasted time on those emotions. *Maybe there's a lesson here*.

She took the trap to a grove of firs on the highest ridge of the island. When she opened the metal doors, the mouse skittered into the cool winter sunlight, turned, and stared back at her. The shiny oversize eyes made her look away; they were as brown as Ace's. A Teasdale couplet popped into her head:

> ... What we never have, remains.
> It is the things we have that go.

She looked back. The mouse was gone.

39

INSPIRED BY A mouse, she packed her bag and climbed into the Luv and spent two weeks on the road. She distributed HAVE YOU SEEN MY SON? posters in Bellingham, Wenatchee, and Spokane, took a sidetrip across the Idaho border to Coeur d'Alene and Moscow, then drove home by way of Richland and Yakima and Tacoma. Some of the storekeepers remembered her. A few still kept the sun-bleached placards in their windows. "Heard from your li'l boy?" a soul food proprietor in Tacoma asked as she walked in, and when she shook her head, he poured out a few fingers of a clear fluid and told her, "Siddown here a second. This'll keep up your strenth." Her eyes watered as she drank; she hoped it was from the gin.

By the time her trip was over March had arrived, and an amateur radio operator called and told her he'd heard about her case and wanted to spread the word. Soon she was collecting information from far-off places: a black-haired boy of twelve or thirteen seen with a man in Mandeville, Louisiana; a child crying "Mommy" on a front porch in Fulton, Missouri; a gray-haired man chasing a boy across a mall in Pasadena, Texas. She checked out the most promising tips by phone, calling at hours when the rates were cheapest. Her phone rang often, sometimes at three in the morning, and her tape recorder saved the messages she missed.

When the shortwave action slowed, she looked around for another way to emulate her trapped mouse. She pulled old lists from the middle drawer of her desk and phoned her media contacts again. A Spokane columnist said, "Let's see, how long's he been gone now?"

"Almost eleven months."

"You picked a good time to call. The ME just killed my Thursday column. Can we talk?"

The telephone interview lasted twenty minutes, and the column appeared under a headline:

SON MISSING A YEAR,
MOM PROMISES TO
'SEARCH TILL I DIE'

It opened with statistics, quantifying her struggle:

> She has written 1,000 letters to newspapers and broad-
> casting stations, tacked up 2,000 posters, driven 10,000
> miles in the United States, Canada and Mexico, checking
> out tips and handing out fliers. She has also lost some
> 30 pounds, and there is a sadness about the corners of
> her eyes that time may not erase.

The column made her out to be a modern Joan of Arc. If she'd
read the same overstatements about another woman, she'd have
put her down as obsessed, quirky, out of touch. There was no
mention of Julie's role—precious Doc, without whom there
would have been no time to search for Ace. And not a word
about the most important helper of all: Van. The column ended:

> We asked this courageous woman how long she could
> afford the expense of scouring the earth for her lost son.
> "As long as herbs grow," she smiled. That could be a
> while.

A few days after the column embarrassment, a Seattle pro-
ducer offered her time on a radio interview show. She was
frightened at first, but she couldn't turn down an opportunity
to reach someone who might have seen Ace. Julie buoyed her
up as they rode across on the ferry. "You'll be g-r-r-eat! Just
tell your story straight and loud."

"Oh, Doc, you know how I am. I'll start talking and go to
pieces."

"No, you won't! This is for Ace."

The interviewer asked Lael to tell the story in her own words
and broke in before it was half-completed. "Forgive me for
asking, Mrs. Pritcher, but have you ever thought of just con-
ceding the loss? It's been—how long? Eight months?"

"Almost eleven," Lael answered.

"Your son, uh, Allen—"

"Alexander. Ace."

"Correct me if I'm wrong, but he's had to make some
difficult adjustments already, has he not? How can you ask

him to make another? He's—how old? Four?"

"He's six, and I only hope I get the chance."

The sisters caught the eleven o'clock boat back to the island. "I shouldn't have let him get to me," Lael said.

"But he was wrong on all his facts, Sis. He didn't care!"

"His son isn't missing. Why should he care?"

For a while they were silent under the cloud of her cynicism. "They're nowhere near here," she mused, more to herself than to her sister.

"Huh? Who's nowhere near here?"

"Mike and Ace. They're a thousand miles away."

"That's what you thought the first time. And they turned up just across the Strait."

Lael dropped Julie off in Nisbet and drove home. Her house seemed like a tomb, even at noon. The day was coming when she would have to sell, and the prospect no longer upset her.

A light breeze had sprung up in the warming March air. She heard the *slpp-slpp* of water against the dock. A pair of goldfinches squirted from the dandelions, lifting up and down as they flew, as though riding waves. Her flickers flew the same way, with one squawk per dip. From the little woods alongside the house she heard pileated woodpeckers slashing and ripping at bark. They were so big they looked like red-headed chickens climbing up and down the trunks. We don't lack for birds around here, she said to herself. And I'll bet every single one of them misses him.

As she walked across the lawn, the phone rang. She stepped into the warm greenhouse and picked up the extension.

"Mrs. Pritcher?" a voice asked. "This is Chastity. Remember me?"

"Oh, yes," she said. *The other woman.* She tightened her grip on the phone.

"I got news." Behind the little-girl voice, music played and glasses clinked. The bartendress must be working lunch. "Catherine gave notice yesterday. I been trying to get you. It's suppose to be a big secret. She had a roof rack put on her new car, so maybe she's planning a trip. We're giving her a party Thursday night. After the bar closes."

Something clicked in Lael's head. "She bought a car?"

"Coupla months ago. A Volvo station wagon. Dark red."

A station wagon. Yes! The one that had been parked at the end of her driveway. Spying on the house at 5:00 A.M.

"Hey, gotta run!" Chastity was saying. "Catch ya later."

Lael sat on the tall stool in the greenhouse and tried to think. She noticed that someone had planted anise and borage seeds in small peat pots. A mistake. In no time their long taproots would break through. Had she done it herself? Possibly. She made a lot of mental errors these days.

She wondered where Catherine was headed after so many years on the island. I'll follow her, she thought. Could I do that? She took a deep gulp of the earthy greenhouse air to counteract a touch of panic. The woman was her last contact with Ace. Somewhere in that ugly tract house his address must be filed away. But how to get it before Thursday night?

She dialed Van. A familiar voice said, "Hello!"

"Trang? What're you doing home from school?"

"Hi, Lael! You okay?"

"I'm okay, Trang." She was touched by the compassion he always showed. He'd probably learned it on the South China Sea, watching his family die. "Is your dad there?"

"Out in back. With Serbia."

"Serbia?"

"Serbia—no, *Serl*via." She could hear him straining to say the Ls.

She took a stab. "Sylvia?" she asked.

"Right."

Lael frowned. Van had never mentioned a Sylvia. "Get him for me, would you, Trang?"

Van's deeper voice came on the line. "Hi, Lael. What's happening?" He sounded as though he had been exercising.

"Van, I didn't mean to interrupt. It's just—"

"Hey, no problem! Trang's with her now. She's having a rough time. Looks like she's carrying twins."

"Who?"

"Sylvia! Our goat. Purebred Angora. She's...."

Why did she feel relieved? "Van, listen," she said. "She's taking off. Catherine. She quit her job and got a new car with a roof rack."

He gave a long whistle. "Where's she going?"

"Where else? To be with Mike and Ace."

"God*damn!* We need her here."

"Maybe it's for the best. I can follow her straight to Ace."

"You can what?"

"Follow her. You know, tail her car."

"She's probably going hundreds of miles. Maybe thousands."

"So?"

"So how do you refuel the truck? Stop and buy gas and then speed to catch up to her?"

"I hadn't thought of—"

"And how're you gonna know when she leaves? Wait outside her house for maybe a week?"

"I'll figure out a way."

"There's *no* way, hon. You know how many cops it would take to run a tail like that? Across state lines and all? Four teams, maybe five—and choppers."

Oh, God, he was so damned sure of himself. "What can we do?" she asked. There was a long silence on the line. "Van?" she said.

"First thing we can do is calm down, okay? Lemme think a minute. . . . No, that wouldn't work either."

"What wouldn't work?"

"A lawsuit. I was thinking we could serve the papers fast, keep a legal hold on her. Some silly action: outrageous behavior, alienation, violation of your parental rights. But it's hopeless. Not enough evidence. Not *any* evidence, really."

"But she's helped him all along. She admitted she knows where they are."

"*I* know that, *you* know that, but we'd have a bitch of a time proving it. Wait! Maybe we could make her a material witness." He was silent. She let him consider his own proposal. "No way," he said. "In a murder case, yeah. But they'd laugh us out of court on this one."

"It's still just a domestic matter, isn't it, Van?"

He paused. "That's the sad truth, hon."

"I can't bear to think of that woman driving away to spend the rest of her life with my son. As if—as if she deserves him. And me staying behind. Alone."

"You're not alone."

She didn't have the heart to argue.

40

SHE STEPPED FROM the greenhouse and walked with her head down across the small lawn. Trang would be here in a few hours, if he could disengage himself from his pregnant goat. Halfway across the grass she stopped and sniffed the air. Something was wrong. It was the damned old house again. The place was beginning to give her the whim-whams.

She took a side trip to the herb garden, strolled a few feet between the raised beds and sniffed. She reached over and squeezed a ball of earth. It held its shape. The ground was still too wet to set out the savory. There was an unusual scent in the air—or was it a lack of scent? Even this late in March her herbs produced a light bouquet. But it was missing, and she smelled—what did she smell?

A thick cloud replaced a thin one in front of the sun, like a new gel in a spotlight, reducing the early-afternoon light. She walked toward the sage, and the smell grew stronger. She dropped to her haunches and touched one of the gray-green leaves. It was wet, greasy. The smell was unmistakable: gasoline. She rushed to the next bed: lamb's ears, her favorite. The tiny plants were bent as though choking for breath.

She dashed up and down the rows, sniffing like a mad bloodhound. She whirled about, checked the same row two or three times, lost track of where she'd been, and finally told herself to start at the beginning and take the sickening inventory row by row.

Five beds had been drenched: sage, lamb's ear, dill, parsley, and thyme. Five out of sixteen. She thought of the chemicals seeping through the root systems of her plants, poisoning the soil that she had built up through the years. No herbs would ever grow in these beds. A third of her farm was gone.

A lone patrol car responded to her emergency call. A hatless young deputy jogged across her lawn with gun drawn and called out, "Is he still inside?"

Her hands shook in front of her face. "My herbs," she said. "They've been poisoned."

"Herbs?" he said, sheathing his weapon. "The dispatcher said it was a break-in." He sounded disappointed.

"I was upset when I called."

He followed her down the row, feeling the leaves, shaking his head. "Kids," he said. He looked about eighteen himself. "Any idea when this happened?"

"This morning," she said. "It had to be this morning. Is there anything you can do?" Once she would have expected swarms of lawmen to descend on the place—deputies, state policemen, FBI agents, brushing the leaves for fingerprints, taking samples for forensic testing, fanning out into the surrounding areas to interview neighbors. Now she was neither surprised nor offended when the young deputy told her politely that he would file a report.

"Thanks for coming," she said. He was probably the only officer patrolling the whole island. Why get excited about a few dead plants?

She was certain that kids hadn't been the culprits. What was the teen-age thrill in pouring gasoline on plants? Kids would have thrown in a match and enjoyed the blaze from the bluff. A different sort of vandal came more readily to mind. She remembered how the newspaper columnist had quoted her: "I'll never stop looking for him as long as herbs grow." Herbs wouldn't grow around here much longer.

She walked slowly into the house and made a cup of instant coffee. Pacing her living room with the cup in her hand, she told herself that she was dealing with twisted flesh of twisted flesh. The Pritchers held an insurmountable advantage: They felt no need to play by the rules. Weighed down by foolish morality, how could she win?

Anyway, it was absurd to talk about winning or losing. The Pritchers had already won. Now they were rubbing it in. *Oh, God, to kill my herbs!* "Damn you, Catherine!" she yelled. "That sage stayed green all winter, and you murdered it!"

She screamed at Mike. "You've got my baby! That's my flesh and blood! Give him back! *Mike Pritcher, you give him back this minute!*"

After a while her rage lost its edge and turned to sorrow and then despair. She thought about the bottle of sleeping pills in the medicine cabinet. There were eight or ten capsules, not enough. I can go to Dr. Haggen and tell him I'm having trouble sleeping, but he's so cautious—he'll only prescribe a few at a time. Maybe I could buy some on the street. But where?

"Ace?" she called out. "If I killed myself, would somebody sit down with you and explain? Would they tell you that *Mommy couldn't help it?*" She sank onto the ratty old corduroy couch and dug at her scalp with her fingernails. Who would tell him for her? Julie? She would have to make some careful plans.

Her eyes opened, and she looked around the room. She was still sprawled on her couch. She didn't know how long she'd slept. The wind had died. Late afternoon sunlight shone at the windows. The house was still.

She reached for the phone to call Van and pulled her hand back. A plan was forming in her mind, and it didn't require his assistance or his approval. Besides, she'd been taking advantage of him lately. It was time to do something on her own.

She felt unusually calm. Was this another of her famous mood swings, signifying nothing, to be replaced in forty-five minutes or an hour by depression? God, she hoped not.

She wondered how she had ever been able to entertain the thought of suicide. Her new plan might land her in jail, but she had been in jail in Oregon. It wasn't so bad.

It wasn't nearly as bad as giving up.

41

WHEN TRANG ARRIVED up the next day on his bike, Lael beckoned him inside. He was full of talk about Sylvia the goat and her false pregnancy. Lael wished she could be amused, but the proprietor and part-time employees of the Salt-Water Herb Farm had to shovel out the gasoline-drenched soil and haul it to the dump. A sad job. On the phone her mother had suggested they refill the empty beds with new earth, but Lael insisted she could never sell "organic" herbs that had grown in such a contaminated place.

A glass of apple juice and a piece of carrot cake loosened Trang's tongue, and she steered him to one of his favorite subjects. After a second piece of cake he began to reveal some of his old secrets, and when she showed interest, his brown eyes lit up as he talked about the career that had kept his family alive in Saigon.

Above all, he told her, a burglar must be patient and painstaking. Plan each job carefully. Map at least two escape routes. Wear plenty of pockets to free the hands. Carry a flat piece of plastic to insert between door and lock, a glasscutter and a cutoff toilet plunger to remove window panes, a stiff length of wire to unhook door chains, a sliver of soap to grease stubborn window tracks. And always use the smallest possible flashlight. "Why?" she asked.

"Big one make too much light," he explained patiently. "Too much glow on window shades. Why you ask? You gonna be burglar?"

"The best," she said, slicing another piece of cake.

He clapped his hands and laughed, showing his gold-edged teeth. But after a few minutes he said in a serious tone, "Lael, come on now, why you ask so many question?"

"Just . . . interested."

He stared at her with slitted eyes. She hoped he was satisfied. If Van learned that she'd developed an interest in housebreaking, he would make the connection fast. It wasn't time for him to know. Him—or anyone.

42

AT ELEVEN O'CLOCK on the night of Catherine Pritcher's farewell party Lael called the Thunder Bay Inn and spoke through a doubled-up handkerchief like a character she'd seen on TV. "What time's the bar close?" she asked.

"Excuse me?" a male voice said.

She spoke louder. "What time does your bar close tonight?"

"I'm sorry, sir. We got a bad connection."

She whipped the handkerchief away and repeated the question. This time the voice answered, "Oh. Midnight."

Her mind spinning, she started dressing two hours before it was time to leave. No mistakes, she told herself, this isn't a children's game. Except maybe in Saigon. Poor Trang, he's been through so much. I'm so glad I didn't have to involve him. What was the phrase that private detective used? "Brown bag job." He said the FBI did them all the time.

She put on her gray warm-ups, her oldest Nike jogging shoes with smooth soles coated with Shoe Goo, a black nylon bandanna to conceal the lightness of her hair, a worn pair of brown gardening gloves, and an indigo rain jacket she had worn sailing with Mike.

She spread her kit on the bed before assigning the tools to the pockets one by one. She had lined up every item Trang had mentioned except the glasscutter and toilet plunger, and she had added a pocketknife with twenty-four blades, an extra penlight in case the first one burned out, and a small screwdriver set in a plastic pouch. Her first and last brown bag job wasn't going to fail for lack of materiel.

She left in the Luv at ten minutes before midnight. The air was soft and moist, with a Stilton moon and a breeze that was light for March. She had anticipated a more somber ambiance: a storm, dark clouds scudding across Puget Sound, moaning winds.

First she headed for the Thunder Bay Inn. Catherine might slip home between shifts or on a break, but she couldn't very well sneak away from a farewell party in her honor. Still, it wouldn't hurt to make sure she was pinned down.

A maroon Volvo station wagon with a roof rack was parked by the main entrance. It was midnight, party time. She wondered if the woman might have left houseguests at home. Not likely. A burglar alarm? That was a worry.

Ten minutes later she was cruising the streets of the subdivision to refresh her memory about the layout. Cabezon Way. Geoduck Lane. Moon Snail Circle. Was there a single "street" or "road" in this cutesy place? She doubted it. Just as she'd recalled, a wide alley bisected each block in a north-south direction. She inched the Luv into the alley behind the Pritcher house, engine barely ticking over, parked behind a garage, and stepped into the night.

From inside a fence a dog whimpered and then growled. She shut the door of the truck quietly, but the click sent the animal into a frenzy. She could imagine the bared teeth, the two-footed attack stance at the end of a chain.

A window slammed open. She stopped dead. "Can it, Prince!" an angry voice stage-whispered. The dog barked louder than ever, as though trying to tell its master that this was no false alarm. She backed slowly toward the truck. Her mission was going to fail because of a mutt named Prince. She drove off in a clash of gears.

She had gone three blocks when she calmed and thought of another approach. Catherine's house was shielded in front by shaggy growths of arbor vitae and bramble. Once inside the gate she would be invisible from the street. Then she could force the front door. Maybe.

She parked the truck on a shell road four blocks away and strolled toward the house as though she owned the night. She was prepared to break into a jog at the first sign of a human being. Just another fitness fanatic. Perfectly credible.

A car drifted into sight a block ahead. She wondered why she hadn't heard it. The driver slowed at the corner as though he were lost, then turned in her direction. She began running at an even pace, her rain jacket clinking with every stride. She pressed her elbows against the pockets and ran past the car. She thought it slowed slightly, but she didn't dare turn and look.

She turned the corner and broke into a sprint. At the shrubby entrance to the Pritcher house she stepped sideways into the vegetation. She didn't move for five minutes.

Just as she was about to head for the porch, a car entered

the street and stopped. She heard the clunk of its shutting door and froze. No car passed. She vaulted lightly over the low fence, hitting the ground with a metallic rattle that sounded like an explosion in the quiet night. She waited again, squinting her eyes to see into the street. No one appeared.

A rustling sound made her jump. Something small and low to the ground ran across the bark mulch and disappeared under a bush. She decided it had been a rat. Another hunter of the night.

At the front door she had the feeling that she was being watched or followed. She put her fear aside as normal for the circumstances, the mind's way of keeping alert. She looked through a small window of leaded glass. A greenish glow shone from inside. She assumed it was from a night light. If not, she would know soon enough.

She tried to squeeze her Bankamericard between the door and the jamb to force the lock, but the crack was too narrow. She put her weight against the door to widen the space. The door gave a fraction of an inch, and the card dropped inside. Trang hadn't mentioned this possibility. Lael, you klutz, she admonished herself, you've left your calling card. Brilliant! Now you've *got* to get in!

She took out the screwdriver set. There was an interchangeable plastic handle for all six blades, but it squirted from her hand and fell into the shrubs alongside. In the dull moonlight she would never find it without using her flash, and she didn't dare make a light outside the house. She tried to slide the thinnest screwdriver blade between the door and the jamb, but she couldn't get enough purchase on the thin metal shaft. She reached into her pocket to see what she could find.

The knife.

A car crawled by, its lights illuminating the outer fringes of the shrubs. She ducked, even though she was sure she couldn't be seen. Was it the same car that had passed before? It had slowed again. A deputy, making his rounds?

She set herself to jump into the bushes. The engine noise faded away, but she was left with the impression that the police were filming this entire break-in with infrared light: an instructional, a how-not-to. Any second now a helicopter would appear for the overhead shots.

She opened blade after blade till it felt as though she had opened all twenty-four. At last she came to the screwdriver. She tried to use it as a chisel, but thin strips of metal on both door and jamb defeated her. She decided to unscrew the lock and lift it out intact, one of Trang's techniques. The first screw wouldn't turn. With a *ping,* the knife blade snapped.

She wrenched the big glass knob in disgust. The door opened. Who would have expected a suspicious person like Catherine Pritcher to leave her front door unlocked?

Her watch said ten to one. The farewell party was almost an hour old. She had bumbled away valuable time. How long would it take for a toast or two and a few pleasantries? Not much longer.

She stepped into a room full of shapes and shadows and edges. She thought: Is this me? Inside somebody's house? So many real events had seemed like dreams in the last few months, and so many dreams like reality. Her sleeping and waking lives were blending. Wasn't that called schizophrenia?

She flicked on her penlight. The living room walls were bare except for pale rectangular imprints that showed where pictures had hung. A large outline was etched against one wall, a remembrance of the desk she had hoped to ransack. Catherine's favorite knickknacks were gone; so were *The Handyman's Encyclopedia* and the *History of the U.S.* The sofa where the two of them had sparred with words was covered with a lemon-colored sheet. The lifelike Christ on the cross had ascended from its alcove, and all that remained of the votive candle was a light scent of wax.

In this room she had hoped to find a connection to Ace: a discarded envelope, an address book, phone records—some insignificant clue to start her on her way. But there wasn't even a wastebasket.

She heard a sound. Someone was coming down the hall. She flicked off the little flashlight and held her breath. The newcomer was taking pains not to be heard, making his presence known not so much by sound as by a pressure, a feeling. Then she realized the sounds were too faint to be caused by a human. What then? Dear Lord, she thought, my first attempt at housebreaking, and the place turns out to be haunted.

She pressed against the wall, wondering what to do. Trang had told her a good burglar always had two escape routes in mind. But she couldn't move. The presence was in the room. She gulped and snapped on the flash.

Yellow eyes glowed like dying flames. A ratty-furred angora cat jumped up on the sofa, yawned, and closed its eyes. Cedric, Catherine's ageless cat. Did he know where Ace was, too? The address was somewhere in this house. She felt like shaking the cat and demanding the answer.

Mike's old room turned out to be as empty as the living room. She had a mental picture of Catherine taking down the airplane models and dusting them carefully with a handkerchief, packing his old books one by one, stopping to smile at a familiar title, sorting out his trophies and ribbons and holding them to her breast as the memories flooded in, packing them all for shipment to . . . where?

In the kitchen a greenish night light revealed the tip of an envelope under a breadboard. She lifted the board and found other envelopes. Today's mail. Apparently Catherine hadn't had time to read it before leaving for the restaurant. Please, God, she thought, let one letter be from Mike.

A bill from Puget Power was unopened. So were a couple of letters that looked like solicitations. In a small manila envelope with neither address nor stamps she found a flat plastic box of color photographs. She spread out a selection of typical summer vacation shots: a caramel-colored ketch running before the wind under candy-striped sails, four or five working boats tied up behind a semicircular rock breakwater that sheltered a small untidy marina, a stretch of desert with straggly bushes whose bare branches reached upward like the fingers of the dead, a silver-colored mobile home with a small boy staring forlornly from the window.

A small boy. . . .

She looked closer.

Ace! My God, she thought, that's Ace!

She shone the wavering light on the picture. Her son looked at her through his black-rimmed glasses. The broken lens had been repaired. His wide brown eyes were half-closed, and he was wearing a cowboy hat that covered his hair.

She picked up the picture and dropped it, picked it up again and dropped it again. She lowered the flashlight till it almost touched the photograph. The deep scratch was gone from his face, but he seemed wan, drawn. Where were his eyebrows? She recognized the pale cast of the chronic asthmatic, the tired look that comes from walking through life uphill. In his asthmatic periods Ace had never shown well in photographs, but he had always managed a grin or a smile. Now he looked like a ventriloquist's dummy.

She shuffled through the rest of the pictures. It was a boring selection, typical of Mike's impatient photography. His aim had always seemed to be to get through one roll of film and start another, as though loading were more interesting than lighting and composition. She found another picture of Ace, standing in front of an animal in a homemade cage. A fox? No, a coyote. Where could it have been taken? Coyotes lived everywhere. She had seen one caged at a gas station in upstate New York and a whole dead family from parents to pups spiked to a barbed-wire fence in Craig, Colorado.

The lights went on. Everything in the kitchen sprang into sharp relief. For an instant she wished she'd brought the gun. She waited for the announcement. *All right, sister, up against the wall! Spread 'em, SPREAD 'EM!*

No one spoke. The shades were up. The next-door neighbors could see right in. She broke from her stance and turned.

The room was empty. At the door she found a curious round switch with numbers on it. She shoved it with the heel of her hand, and the lights went off. A timer! Exactly what a working woman would use to make burglars think she was home when she wasn't. But then why the unlocked front door?

A trap?

If it was, she was caught.

She took one more glance at the picture of Ace. A few open-faced shacks were visible beyond the animal cage. There was a sign on one, but she couldn't understand the word. She slipped the pictures into the pocket of her rain jacket. Maybe Catherine would think she'd mislaid them. Who gave a damn what the woman thought?

She stepped into the master bedroom, feeling unexpectedly smarmy. The double bed was piled high with clothes, towels, bedding. Two plastic suitcases and an overnight bag rested in front of the empty closet. She hefted one. Full. Catherine was ready to go.

Oh, please, God, she said under her breath, let me find his address. Some indication of where he is. This is my last chance. A little hint, Lord. . . .

Something rattled behind the house. More spooks? The cat? She held her body stiff and motionless at the entrance to Catherine's bedroom and listened.

She thought she heard footsteps.

She tiptoed to the rear window and looked down at the alley. Two indistinct figures were approaching the house in a crouch. They disappeared behind a clump of bushes and reappeared at the steps to the back door.

She thought of making a break, but she could hear the back doorknob turning. Where was her alternate exit route? Through the window? She should have opened it earlier or at least unlocked it. Trang would have. Now she was trapped. The house was so damned small. She'd never make it as a burglar. Maybe she'd be more successful as a prisoner.

Hushed voices came from the kitchen. What were they whispering about? "These goddamn silent alarms . . . whattaya wanna bet it's the dog? . . . this is the third one tonight."

She must have tripped an alarm. God, how amateurish! The two men would reach the bedroom in seconds. She reached up to unlock the window and found that it was already unlocked. Why was Catherine so inconsistent? Doors and windows unlocked, but a silent alarm cocked and ready, as though she had hoped to catch somebody. Well, her plan had worked.

She raised the window a few inches. The cops were moving around in the next room. She rammed it open and dropped to the ground.

She had just reached the alley when she heard a shout: "Hold it right there, buddy!"

She ran.

Heavy footsteps pounded behind her. "Stop!" a voice yelled. "I'll shoot!"

Go ahead and shoot! she screamed inside. What the hell do I care if you shoot? *Shoot, damn you, shoot!* She was armored by indifference. There was nothing on earth as inconsequential as her life.

She ran faster but with no serious thought of getting away. It was something to do before the bullets cut her down. She realized she was outdistancing her pursuer. Before long she would reach the street. From there she could choose a direction, and the deputy would have to guess which one. She stepped up her pace. Getting shot in the back had ceased to be an option.

A gun went off. She twisted her head and looked back down the alley. A light beam hit her in the face from fifty or sixty feet. "Freeze!" a voice cried out.

She did a scissors leap over a low wall behind a house. Her night vision had been diminished, but she ran through the yards, dodging shadows. She saw a white picket fence just in time to clear it with an awkward hurdle. A dog rushed at her as she passed through a yard but whined and slunk off when she raised her arms. She clomped through the soft earth of a garden, barely breaking stride. She was young and strong and in perfect shape. The Gingerbread Woman! No cop on earth could catch her.

The end of the block had to be near. She splashed in and out of a backyard pond, scattering ducks. She ran through a row of brambles and felt the stickers draw dotted lines across her thighs. Why do people grow those damned things, she wondered, when they can grow lamb's ears or sage? *My murdered plants.*

She burst through a hedge and found herself under a bluish streetlight. She sprinted halfway down the block and slipped back into the yards, leaving a wake of yipping dogs.

She had almost reached the shell road that led to her truck when a clothesline dug into her neck and slammed her to the ground. She picked herself up and felt her heart pounding in her Adam's apple. She ran a few steps, half-blinded by pain, and knocked over a sundial. She got up and tried to run, but she fell to her knees on a velvety lawn and bit back vomit.

Control, *control!* she told herself. Pain is a state of mind. You have the advantage. It's dark, you know where you're headed, and the cops don't. Stay...in...control!

She lurched the last few yards to the shell road. She looked in all directions. No one was in sight.

She jumped in her truck. The starter coughed and she eased into the night, headed for—where?

She couldn't go home. One of the deputies had spotted her, and even if he didn't know who she was, Catherine Pritcher would soon put him wise.

She didn't dare involve Julie or her parents.

She reached the highway, flicked on her headlights, and held her speed at thirty-five so she wouldn't be stopped for speeding. At Old Mill Road she snapped the wheel sharply, rammed the Luv into four-wheel drive, and headed for the cabin in the hills.

Van would know what to do.

43

THE ROUGH-TEXTURED slab creaked open to her knock, and his tall, gangly silhouette appeared against a yellowish light from inside. Thank God, Lael said to herself, I've got the right cabin. "Van," she said, "look! Pictures!"

"Pictures?" He opened the door wide. His eyes were almost as red as his unruly hair. Somehow she had expected him to be dressed, but all he wore was a pair of checked undershorts that looked as though they'd been washed a thousand times. He clung tightly to a thick open book. She remembered that he'd said something about driving to the court of appeals in Tacoma in the morning. This was the man she'd once typed as indifferent.

"Pictures," she repeated, breathing hard. "Ace."

She brushed past him into the cabin. The big open-raftered room smelled of fir and cedar. Heat radiated from a Jotul wood stove, its black firebox embossed with an elk and a bear. A large bed with a reddish plaid blanket occupied one corner, a neatly arranged kitchenette another. Legal papers littered a large oaken table illuminated by a gooseneck lamp. She spread out her photographs.

"Where'd you get these?" he asked, leaning over the table.

"They . . . just arrived," she said.

He straightened up and looked at her curiously. "In the mail?"

"Uh, yes." How easily the lies came after a little practice.

"That's Ace?" he asked, picking up the shot of the boy looking out the window of a trailer. "Lael, he doesn't look good."

"He's sick. Van, look closely. Where were they taken?"

He adjusted his Ben Franklin glasses and held each picture to the light. "None of these tell us much," he said at last. "Ace staring out a window, a caged coyote, a couple of scenes from *Yachting* magazine. Could be Asia, Africa, could be right here on the island. Where'd you say you got 'em?" He squinted hard at her.

"In the mail."

"Anonymous? Lemme see the envelope."

"I left it home."

He stared again at the picture of the boy and the coyote. His head dipped forward till his eyes were inches above the print. "Hey," he said, "see the sign on that shack in the background? *Almejas?* That's clams. Goddamn, they're in Mexico!"

It took a few seconds for the news to sink in. Then she grinned broadly and said, "We found my baby!"

"Mexico's a big country," he reminded her.

She studied the photographs again. "This marina," she said. "Do you think it's in the same town as the clam shack?"

"Possibly. Look. Shrimp boats." He lifted the picture to the light.

"What about the ketch?"

"My guess is these pictures all came off the same roll of film."

"So this is a fishing village with a small marina, some working boats and at least one sailboat. Van, it's something to go on!" She felt like dancing him around the warm room. "Oh, Van, how many fishing villages can there be in Mexico?"

"Zillions." Where was his enthusiasm?

"I don't care. I found him in Oregon, and I'll find him in Mexico."

He was looking at her closely. She thought she could feel his disapproval, but it really didn't matter. The only advice she wanted now was her own.

"Find him?" he asked. "How?"

"Patience. Work. Whatever it takes."

"Where'll you start?"

She thought about Mexico's geography. "The nearest place, I guess. Baja."

He shook his head. "You got a short memory, Lael. Think how you found them in Oregon. You searched till you were ready to drop, remember? And got nowhere. Then that woman came up with the name of the river."

"Yes. I remember."

"Who'll tip you off this time? Your mother-in-law's leaving, and Mike's gone. Who's left to feed you information?"

When she didn't answer, he walked over to a two-burner hot plate and lifted a baby blue porcelain pot. She watched him pour the steaming liquid into two heavy mugs. "I'll leave tomorrow," she said. "I'll—"

"You'll be making a hell of a mistake."

"I'm *not* going to be trampled by those people." She almost yelled the words. "I've had it, Van. I've got to do something."

"You're high as an owl, Lael. How can you make a rational decision?"

"I don't claim it's a rational decision. I don't make rational decisions about breathing, do I? But I breathe, don't I? The whole damned world doesn't run on your damned lawyer's logic."

"You're sure stubborn."

"Maybe I am. As stubborn as Mike. He stole my son to get even with me for—for nothing. Now that's *stubborn!*" She realized she was being unreasonably loud.

He pulled up two hard-backed chairs and beckoned her to sit at the table. She glanced at one of the sheets lying there: legal papers. She was distracting him from his law practice again. "You've got a trial tomorrow, don't you?" she asked, trying not to wince at the taste of the coffee.

"I'm as ready as I'll ever be." He fixed her with his intense blue eyes. "Lael, where'd you get these pictures?"

"I told you. In the mail."

"A midnight delivery?"

"I, uh, they came this morning. I just opened them."

"You let your mail sit around all day?"

She squirmed in her chair. "Am I being cross-examined?"

"Yeah. Now where'd you get 'em?"

She had to get him off the subject. Talk about stubborn! "Where's Trang?" she asked.

"Out back with Sylvia. Now—"

"The sheep? Was she really pregnant?"

"Goat," he said, tracking her eyes. "She's gonna deliver tonight. Where'd you get the pictures, Lael?"

"I can't tell you."

"You can tell me *anything*. I'm your attorney. We have a confidential relationship. By law."

"But I don't want to involve you."

"I'm already involved. I *want* to be involved. Now god damn it, where'd you get those pictures? Did you send that detective inside Catherine's house? What's his name? Nyren?"

"Uh, no. I, uh, I"—she turned away from his eyes—"I did it myself."

When he didn't blow up, she looked back. He was staring at her as though she were a wayward teen. "You didn't," he said. He sounded deeply disappointed.

"I did," she said. She recounted the story, leaving out Trang's innocent role. "And I'd do it again," she ended up.

He went to the stove and refilled both their cups. "Your father said he was afraid of something like this."

"My father? When did you see my father?"

"We . . . talk."

She felt betrayed. What right did they have to discuss her as though she were a thing, an amoeba? "You sit around and talk about poor crazy Lael, do you? Behind my back?"

He turned and raised his voice. "We worry about you. Does that surprise you? We *care* about you, Lael. Did you get away clean?" His tone of anger had changed to a tone of urgency.

"I—I think so."

"Nobody made you? Or the truck?"

"'Made me'?"

"Saw you. Well enough to identify you."

"I don't think so."

"Maybe we have some time then."

"To do what?"

"To lie in the weeds. Once your mother-in-law leaves, there'll be nobody here to bring charges. And no evidence."

"What about the pictures? Aren't they evidence?"

"The DA doesn't have the pictures; *we* do. They'd have a hell of a time proving burglary. Besides, those pictures don't tell much. That's probably why she left them around."

There was a scratching at the door. He opened it and let in a parade of animals: a one-eyed dog and two cats. "This is Van Lingle Mungo," he said as though introducing friends from high society. "These are my cats, Groucho and Chico. The coyotes ate Harpo and Zeppo."

"I didn't know you liked cats," she said.

"One of my clients gave them to me. In lieu of a fee."

"Do you ever get paid in money?" she asked.

"It's no big deal," he said as though he wanted to drop the subject.

"What do you mean I can lie in the weeds? Where?"

"Right here. When the Pritcher woman splits, you can go back home."

"And where would I sleep?"

"Trang took his *futon* out back with Sylvia. You can have the bed. I'll take the couch."

Déjà vu. "Like Oregon, huh?" she said. "Could you sleep

on that thing?" She pointed to the old leather couch with the stuffing leaking out. It looked like something else taken in lieu of a fee.

"Sure," he said. "Why not?"

"I'll sleep on the couch."

"We could, uh, share. The bed's a queen. I could lay out my sleeping bag on top."

She considered the idea and asked, "What would Trang think?"

He laughed. "The unflappable Trang?"

"It's a nervy idea."

"Look who's talking about nervy ideas. A confessed burglar!" He laughed again.

She showered in a cedar stall with duckboards and a nozzle that ran hot and cold at its own whim. She toweled off and slid under the covers in her warm-ups. "Will you go to my house and get me some clothes tomorrow?" she asked.

"I'll send Trang first thing," he said, spreading his sleeping shell alongside. Something about the arrangement seemed silly and old-fashioned and insulting to both of them—as though they had to put up artificial barriers to curb their unbridled lust—but she was too exhausted to worry the thought to its conclusion. He didn't look much livelier, standing there trying to gouge out his eyes with his knuckles. "Thanks, Van," she said.

"You can pay me in herbs."

"A lifetime supply of Good-King-Henry. You'll love what it does to a casserole."

He disappeared out the back door, returned with the news that Sylvia was still expecting, and turned out the lights. Her body was drained, but her brain wouldn't slow down. *So Acey's in Mexico. I can hire a Mexican detective agency. No, I won't hire a soul. This is too important to leave to others. Look what those deputies did in Oregon. Besides, I'd go broke paying private detectives, even in pesos. Maybe they'll take a credit card.*

Dear God in heaven. "Van!" She sat straight up.

"Huh? What?"

"I left my Bankamericard on her floor."

"You *what?*"

"At her house. I dropped it through the front-door crack."

"You didn't."

"I did."

"You *couldn't* have."

"Van, I *did*."

A light went on. He stood alongside the bed in his shorts. "That's hard evidence, Lael," he said, his clear blue eyes blinking. "How the hell did you—"

"I dropped it. I was nervous. I'm new at burglary."

"I'd never know."

"I'll just get out of here," she said, annoyed at herself. "I'll leave for Mexico before they can find me."

"In your warm-ups? With no money? On no sleep?" She looked at her watch. It was eighteen after two.

"I can sleep a few hours. There won't be any planes till nine or ten anyway."

He whistled through his teeth. "Mexico isn't Oregon, Lael. Got any idea what could happen to you down there?"

"I can take care of myself."

"There was a story in *Time* last week. An American *turista* took a stroll in a campground, and they found her hands half a mile from her body. I'm telling you, Lael, there's no law in Mexico."

"There's no law here either."

"Compared to Mexico, there's tons."

"Come on, Van, not another lecture."

"What do you think Mike's gonna do while you're trying to snatch Ace? You can only corner a rat so many times, Lael. Then he goes for your throat."

She swung her bare legs over the side of the bed. "I hear what you're saying. Maybe you're right, but I'm going. If you'd ever lost a son, you'd understand why."

He took her hand. "I—I—Lael, don't! Think about it awhile." She pulled the hand away. He said, "Don't act . . . crazy."

There it was, the word that had been on everyone's lips. "We'll see who's crazy," she muttered.

"You can't go home tonight. They'll be waiting for you."

"With butterfly nets? Wet packs? To take care of the poor crazy lady?"

"Lael." His voice was hushed. "I didn't mean it that way. I was just trying to make you see."

"You made me see, all right." She turned away.

He sat alongside her on the bed. "Listen to me, hon. Did you ever stop to think you could go all the way to Mexico and strike out? I mean, there's no guarantee you'll even find the town, let alone find Ace. Then what?"

She started to answer and realized that the question was senseless. There were numerous possibilities, but striking out wasn't one of them.

He said, "I don't want you to be hurt. I—I—" He hesitated. "I worry."

"Don't bother. I'm none of your concern. I'm a client, that's all. Send me a bill."

"You *are* my concern. You'll always be my concern."

"Why?"

"Because I love you."

Oh, God, she thought, how unfair. How rotten! If only he had kept quiet, or called me crazy again, or said anything except what he'd said. "Please," she said. "Take it back, Van."

"Why?"

"Because—because it's wrong. I mean—oh, Van, why'd you say that?"

"Are there rules?"

"Van, stop. You're like a kid sometimes." Her voice broke. "You just don't consider your words. You—"

He leaned across and put his arms around her. She raised her face, and he kissed her nose. "I love you, Lael," he said. "It can't be wrong."

"Oh, Van," she said, feeling stupid again. How had she let things reach this point? A perfectly decent man, and she had to put him off like a sixteen-year-old tease. He kissed her lips, and she kissed him back. If he tried again, she would have to turn away.

"Oh, Van," she repeated. She swallowed tears. Far in the back of her mind she was thinking: The last man I loved told me I was frigid and found another woman and stole my child.

"Don't talk," Van said. His hushed voice shook and made her shake. He held her tight till she stopped quivering.

When he let go, she said, "Please, Van, hold me."

They clung to each other on the sagging old bed. "Van," she murmured, "I never dreamed—"

"I did," he said, holding her tighter. "I mean . . . I dreamed." A vein pulsed in his neck. His skin warmed hers. When she started to talk, he laid his index finger on her lips.

She didn't know how long they'd held each other close when a door banged open and a high-pitched voice yelled, "Dad! *Dad!* Hurry! We having—oh, hi, Lael!"

Van was already off the bed. "What happened?" he asked.

"I think Sylvia making twins," the boy said, flashing his golden smile. "Three of them."

"Three twins," Van echoed. He cast a sorrowful look toward Lael. "Get some sleep," he said, pulling on a pair of jeans. "I won't wake you when I get up."

Oh, Van, she thought, I love you. I hope I can tell you someday.

44

THE DOOR CREAKED behind her as she stepped into the cedar-scented air. She hoped the sound didn't alert the obstetrical team of Van and Trang, but she had to take the opportunity to get away.

She picked her way carefully through the clearing that surrounded the hillside cabin. Alternating ribbons of light pierced the fence around the maternity shed and flashed across her face. She imagined Sylvia resting comfortably, the new arrivals nuzzling her soft belly. A cat meowed in the distance, and Van Lingle Mungo chugged out of the darkness, wagging his backside. The place put her in mind of the children's zoo in Seattle: "Please pet." She wondered why God made plant people and animal people and if they were compatible.

The Luv was parked slantwise on the steep slope. She released the hand brake and coasted silently down the steep hill. At the road she started the engine and sped away. With luck they hadn't even heard.

A quarter mile from home she spotted a gleam of light. She slowed and looked hard. A sheriff's car was parked at the head of her driveway. She turned away and sped toward Nisbet. No lights showed in her rear-view mirror. She tried to decide what to do. She couldn't make a move without clothes and money. Both were in her house.

She followed the beach road in a long arc till she was directly across the bay from her house. A mist had formed in the cool morning air. The night light outlined the end of the Port Nisbet Yacht Club pier like a corona.

She parked and looked out on the scene. The club was an artifact, the subject of jokes by the young fashionables who docked their plastic yawls and cabin cruisers far across the island at Thunder Bay. The moorages in this undredged shallow bay went dry at low tide, and the boats flopped sideways in the mud on their keels. She peered down at the undistinguished collection of vessels, from rowboats to tugs. They were floating free. The tide was in.

She hid the Luv behind the yacht club office, in case any deputies came calling, and ran toward the docks. She undid the bowline that secured the club's seven-foot dinghy and stepped aboard. Icy water filled her Nikes. She picked up the plastic bailer and worked till the blue and white Livingston was almost dry. Then she grabbed the oars and pushed off.

Her house was two miles across the bay. She figured she would be able to row the boat at just under walking speed, depending on the tide. That meant—she tried to figure—an hour over and an hour back, plus a half hour or so in her house, plus a half hour cushion for error. If everything went smoothly, she would be driving off the island before the sun came up. *Just* before. She had to hurry.

She wished she'd had more practice rowing. At first the long splintery oars slapped the water like a beaver's tail or missed entirely, making the boat heel and yaw and veer off course. The mild outgoing tide presented no problems, but halfway across the bay she began to wonder if she would be able to find her dock in the poor light. Her only navigational references were far-off specks on the land, and she wasn't always sure which was which. She felt suspended between the black water and the black sky, rowing through space like some celestial sculler of mythology. By the time she reached her dock her hands were sore, and her shoulders and arms felt as though someone had been jumping on them.

She tied up the pram and clambered onto her rickety dock. The house was dark, the lawn damp with dew. She walked across the grass, keeping the house between herself and the head of the driveway. She entered through the back door and stood silently for a few seconds. The only noise was the soft whir of the refrigerator motor.

Working without light, she changed into a denim wash-and-wear pantsuit that could be rinsed out and dried overnight. She stuffed warm-weather clothing into a small suitcase, threw in a pair of sandals and her tennis hat, grabbed her custody papers and her checkbook and $11 from the herb farm's petty cash fund and dashed off a note to Julie:

Sis. Gone to Mexico to get Ace. We'll both see you soon! V. has details. Tell Mom and Dad NOT TO WORRY!
  Love you all. Lael.

She was halfway through the back door when she remembered something. She hurried to her room and unlocked the bottom drawer of her dresser. The ugly lump came coldly to hand. She had always considered pistols the ultimate pollution, obscene clumps of metal manufactured for the sole purpose of piercing human organs and shattering human bones. But her world was skewed now; her world was upside down and inside out. If someone got between her and Ace, she would shoot without hesitation. A year was too long.

She packed the .38 Chief's Special and peeked out the window. A lone vehicle sped past, illuminating the beach road. No police car lay in wait. Would they be back to arrest her later? As Van would say, the point was now moot. Dear Van. . . . Did he feel betrayed? Someday she would make things right.

She wedged her suitcase under the stern seat and cast off. Barnacles were beginning to come into sight as the tide dropped down the pilings. She wished she'd had time to check a tide table, but all she could do now was row. She imagined herself bobbing helplessly around the bay, waiting for the tide to flow back into the Nisbet marina while the sun climbed higher and the deputies stood onshore with hands on hips and cigarettes dangling from their mouths. No one could wade more than a few feet through the soft bay ooze. The prospect of getting ignominiously stuck in the mud made her flail at the water.

By the time the yacht club's navigation light came into sight again, her hands were sore and raw. The little boat scraped bottom a hundred feet out, but she poled a narrow channel to the tip of the longest dock.

As she drove away, she tried to foresee what the deputies would do. Would they watch the ferries? The bridges? The airports?

She decided to leave by the back side of the island, drive west across the two-lane bridge and then south to Bremerton. The bridge was empty, its topmost steel girders looking like tinsel where they caught the first rays of the morning sun. She held her breath as she crossed, waiting for sirens and roof lights, but all she saw was the empty shack where some of Van's Indian clients sold fireworks and firewater tax-free.

Thirty minutes later she passed the curved prow of the battleship *Missouri* and the other capital ships off to her left and decided to make a dash for Portland. The cops might be waiting for her at Seattle-Tacoma Airport, but they would never be looking for her in another state. She wasn't Son of Sam.

Interstate 5 was choked with morning traffic as she drove south through the dark green forests outside Olympia. She thought of Van. He must be on his way to Tacoma by now, taking the same route she had taken. She couldn't escape a feeling that her behavior had been tawdry. How capricious, kissing him and then sneaking away like a thief. But how else was a thief to behave? She consoled herself: Van will forgive, Van will understand. Saint Ivan, the first Jewish candidate for canonization. Almost too good to be true. Once she had felt the same about Mike. . . .

She was ten miles south of the state capital when the sound of a horn jerked her head to the left. The state trooper was pointing toward the shoulder. She thought of running, but the Luv wouldn't stand a chance in a chase. What had given her the idea? Desperation, she supposed. And rage. What about fright? She felt none. The emotion of fear was as absent as Ace. She wondered what that signified.

She eased into the right lane. The big white car had slipped in behind her. Whatever happened, the trip to Mexico wasn't off; it was just postponed. For how long? One to five years at hard labor? She stopped on the gravelly shoulder. Maybe she could jump out the passenger door and lose herself in the tall grass sloping down from the roadway. But how far would she get? She'd seen a tracking dog in action.

The trooper took his time about leaving his car. She watched in her mirror as he spoke into a microphone. If he didn't know who I was before, he does now, she told herself. *Wanted for burglary: Lael Estes Pritcher, 29, former mother, armed and dangerous. . . .*

In her side mirror she saw him strolling slowly toward her: Mr. Coolcop, right off TV. She wondered if he would handcuff her. "Morning, ma'am," he said, touching the front brim of his Boy Scout hat with his index finger. "May I see your license and registration, please?"

She passed them over without speaking. "Miz Pritcher," he said, "I clocked you at sixty-four."

"You did?" she rasped. Her throat was raw from Van's coffee. Her larynx felt as though it had been scraped with a curette.

He wrote a ticket on his clipboard and handed it across along with her car papers. "This is a warning, Miz Pritcher. Take it a little easy, okay?"

"Y-yes," she said,

"And have a nice day," he said as he backed away.

45

WATCHING HER SPEED, Lael reached Portland International Airport at 9:50 A.M. and checked the Mexicana Airlines board. A plane would be leaving for Tijuana, La Paz, and Cabo San Lucas in ninety minutes. The clerk said it was wait-listed. "You can try for stand-by," he told her in a soft Mexican accent. "But I don't think you'll get on."

"When's the next flight?"

"Tomorrow."

She bought a ticket and waited. There were six stand-bys ahead of her. Two made the flight. She hurried to the Western Airlines counter. A 707 would be leaving for San Diego at 4:00 P.M. She decided to take it.

She had four hours to kill. Her throat throbbed where she had hit the clothesline. She had a carpet-tack headache at the back of each eye socket. Her arm muscles ached from her long row across the bay. When she walked away from the counter, she felt faint.

She found a chair in a lounge and curled herself up like a pill bug. When she awoke, her mouth tasted sour and her eyes felt as though they'd been sanded. Across the aisle a man in a dun-colored felt hat peeked around his *Oregonian*.

She shook out her hair and teetered to the bathroom. She brushed her teeth and scrubbed her face and drew her hands down hard over her face till some of the circulation returned. When she exited, the man was waiting. Oh, God, she said to herself, let him be anything but a cop.

She walked past him to the Western Airlines counter and asked if her plane was on time. The clerk looked at her ticket and said, "Yes, Mrs. Estes." She started to correct him and then remembered that she was flying under her maiden name. This was no time for another stupid mistake.

She found a restaurant and ordered coffee. When she left, she almost bumped into the man in the hat. She hurried toward the street exit as though trying to make a getaway. If he was a cop, let him make his move now. She stopped suddenly at the door and turned around. There he was. "Buy you a drink?" he asked. The words insinuated themselves softly into her ear.

"Why?" she asked, looking around.

"Why not?"

She turned and stared at him. His hat was off, revealing gleaming gray hair in perfect waves. His nose was straight, his mouth a sensuous bow, his eyes as honest blue as Van's. She whispered in his ear, "If you follow me one more step, I'll kick you in the balls." The last she saw of him, he was disappearing around a corner.

She dozed on the two-hour flight to San Diego, but when the plane landed, she found she was sleepier than ever. Cumulative fatigue, she decided. It was too late to show her stolen photographs to the Mexican Tourist Bureau, as she had planned, so she took a motel room on Pacific Highway and went to bed just after dark.

When she awoke, the sun was up. She looked at her watch. For twelve hours she had been dreaming nonstop, finishing with a Technicolor production about the *almejas* stand and the curving stone breakwater.

She pulled the double curtains aside. The view was familiar; her father had been stationed at North Island for two years when she was in junior high. Out on San Diego Bay a fat gray tender the size of six or eight Puget Sound ferries nursed identical-twin submarines, and a flotilla of sailboats beat around them as though passing an island. She squinted till she made out the Coast Guard registration number on one of the boats: CA3721.

She frowned, trying to remember something. The caramel-colored ketch with the candy-striped sails. . . . Of course! That must have had a number, too! Why hadn't she and Van seen it? She got out the pictures and took another look. Now she knew. The number was a squiggle—far too small to read.

She patted down her suit, slapped at her hair with a brush, and ran outside for a cab. A cool breeze streamed across the bay from Point Loma, and the sun was bright in an unblemished sky. How many such days she recalled! The air-conditioned city was living up to its billing. She told the driver to take her to the nearest store that sold magnifying glasses.

They tried three, ending with a stationery shop in Mission Hills. "Where next, lady?" the driver asked when she emerged emptyhanded. The meter read $12.30.

"The main library," she said.

A young blond librarian who looked as though she'd just posed for the cover of *Playboy* handed her a large rectangular magnifying glass with an offset black plastic handle. The boat number seemed to jump from the photograph and into the lens: A22121. She scribbled it down in a raggedy handwriting that she could barely read herself, then double-checked the small letters and found that she had made a mistake in her excitement. The second digit was a Z, not a 2. She could hear Van, perched on her shoulder: *No more mistakes, hon. We can't afford any more mistakes.*

Yes, Van, she said to herself. That's why I double-checked. AZ2121.

WN was Washington. CA was California. OR was Oregon. AZ was . . . Arizona!

She rushed outside to the cab. "Coast Guard headquarters," she said.

"It's Saturday, lady."

"Let's try."

The big woven-wire gate was padlocked. She rattled the lock and called out, "Open up! *Somebody open this gate!*"

A woman in a blue and white uniform appeared from a side door and told her to come back Monday morning. Lael said, "Do you handle boat registrations?"

"I'm sorry, ma'am, we're closed to the public on weekends."

"Don't call me ma'am!" she snapped. She was sick of being called ma'am; it made her feel forty. "I'm sorry. I just need you to look up a number. It's terribly important."

"I'm sorry, ma'am," the woman said. "You'll have to come back Monday." She ducked inside the door.

The drive to the motel took forever. She couldn't wait two days to find out who AZ2121 was. Her father answered her frantic telephone call and made her spend ten minutes convincing him that she was alive and well. "Dad," she said, "I need your help."

"Just ask," he said.

Forty minutes later he called back. "It's a ketch, thirty-two feet. Diesel-powered, U.S. registry, listed to Howard Holling, Scottsdale, Arizona. And I owe the Coast Guard duty officer a bottle of scotch."

"Holling? Not Hollings?"

"Holling. H-O-double L-I-N-G. He must be a singular man."

"Thanks, Dad!" she cried into the phone.

"Honey," he said, "you're not getting yourself into any tight spots down there, are you?"

"Behaving myself, Dad."

"Everybody's worried about you. Couldn't one of us fly down and help you? Whatever you're doing?"

Exactly what she didn't want. He travels fastest who travels alone, she thought, and so does she. "Please, Dad, no. Trust me on this one, okay? And Dad? Will you tell Van I'm fine and—oh, that's enough. Just that I'm fine."

"Sure, honey." He wouldn't let her off the phone till she made a solemn promise to keep in close touch.

The information operator came up with the numbers of three Hollings in the Greater Phoenix area. The first didn't answer, and the second didn't own a boat. A youthful male voice answered at the third number. "Mr. Holling?" Lael asked.

"This is Howie," the voice said. "Dad's operating. Who's this?"

"Uh, my name is Lael Pritcher. I wonder . . . could I speak to your mother?"

She heard a loud "Mom! It's Mrs. Pritcher!"

Her pencil made drum rolls on the glassed surface of the motel table. After what seemed like hours, a female voice said brusquely, "Alice Holling, Mrs. Pritcher. Are you one of Doctor's patients?"

"No," she said nervously. "Actually you don't know me. Actually I—"

"Please!" the voice interrupted. "Could you slow down? Is this an emergency?"

"No—I mean, yes. I mean, in a way. Mrs. Holling, do you own a boat? A tan ketch? With striped sails?"

"Past tense. *Owned*. Dear old *Placebo*. She was wrecked in a storm. Swept from our moorage, you see. Is this the Pru?"

Lael had heard the same drawn-out diphthongs and overused "you see's" back East. The women at Mount Holyoke had called it Brooks Brothers English.

"Was your boat in Mexico recently?"

"Yes, that's where it happened."

"Where? Would you mind telling me?"

"At our winter home in—Mrs., uh, Pritcher, may I ask what this is about?"

Lael explained briefly, and the doctor's wife said, "Was your son four or five years old? A tad underweight, thick glasses?"

She grabbed the mouthpiece of the phone with her other hand to keep it from shaking. "Yes," she managed to say. "Do you know—"

"Let me think," the woman interrupted. "Doctor saw so many, you see. The boy's father brought him to the wharf if I remember correctly. *If* I've got the right boy. It's hard to remember them all. Doctor saw *so* many."

The woman sounded as though she were making a sincere effort to be helpful, and Lael had an insight into what it must be like to be an M.D.'s wife, so involved with death and disorder that names and diagnoses and prognoses blended. She asked, "Do you remember if—"

"Wait," the woman said. "Oh, dear, was he the little American boy? The one who—"

There was a long pause. "Who what?"

There was another hesitation, and Lael thought she could hear the woman talking behind her hand. When the voice came back on the phone, it sounded cool and distant. "Mrs. Pritcher, I do wish I could help you, but I just can't. Would you mind enormously waiting till Doctor's here? I'm afraid I've said too much already, I mean really. Call back in an hour or two, would you? Would that inconvenience you terribly?"

"Please, Mrs. Holling. Can't you remember what was wrong with my son?"

"I—no, I can't. I probably have it all wrong, you see. I'm just *ever* so sorry. Call back, would you, dear? Gotta run now. Thanks *so* much for calling."

In a panic Lael started to ask where their winter home was. It would be a start. "Where—" she said, but she cut herself off. She couldn't risk alienating the woman. "I'll try later," she said. "And thank *you*, Mrs. Holling. You've been very kind."

She redialed the number in exactly sixty minutes. "Oh, yes—Mrs. Pritcher," a resonant male voice answered. "How can I help you?"

"Dr. Holling? Didn't your wife explain?"

"Explain? Explain what?"

"Why I called?"

"Well, uh—oh, yes. Something about a boy?"

"Something about my son," Lael said, trying to keep from sounding annoyed. It must annoy surgeons to have to deal constantly with overwrought relatives. "Alexander Pritcher," she said in an even voice. "Ace. I understand you treated him."

Dr. Holling gave a rambling speech to the effect that his wife had spoken without authorization and that it was unethical and downright irresponsible to give medical information over the telephone. He said he treated many sick children at his winter home from time to time, strictly gratis, a favor to his Mexican friends, but he couldn't be expected to remember specific cases. He might have seen a child named Alexander Pritcher, and he might not. He didn't remember him by name.

"An American boy," Lael said. "An asthmatic—"

"Mrs. Pritcher," the doctor interrupted, "you're a voice on the phone. I have no way of knowing who you are. There are legal considerations, possible lawsuits. These matters are strictly confidential."

Lael bit her lip. "Doctor," she said, "my husband kidnapped my little boy last—"

"Please, *please*, don't go on! I did everything I could for those children. I don't think it's fair to blame me—"

"Blame you?"

"That's really all I have to say."

"Blame you for what?"

There was no answer, but she heard a short, sharp intake of breath.

"Please!" she said, her voice shaking. "Can't you just tell me where your winter home is?" She would go straight there and find out what had happened. It was only her son's life they were discussing.

"I'm sorry," he said. "I—"

A female broke in and for a few seconds the two voices ran together. She caught something that sounded like "Puerto," followed by another Spanish-sounding word that she missed.

"Where?" she asked.

"God damn it, Alice, get off!" the doctor ordered. Then the line went dead.

When her heart stopped pounding, she dialed the number again. A woman's voice gave a tentative "Hello?"

"Mrs. Holling, please don't hang up. Puerto *where?*"

"I'm enormously sorry." There was a click and a pause and the low buzz of the long-distance dial-tone.

The line was busy on her next call, and no one answered on her next and her next. She could imagine the high-strung Dr. Holling excoriating his wife. Physician, heal thyself. She was sure her short relationship with the Holling family of Scottsdale, Arizona, was at an end.

She went to an American Express office to draw cash on her credit card. A clerk who looked like a high school cheerleader asked for three different forms of ID and disappeared into the rear for what seemed hours. Would the American Express people know that she had dropped her Bankamericard in a burglary? One phone call and the San Diego PD would be on its way. She had to take the chance. The young clerk returned with a sweet-faced older woman who smiled and said, "Two thousand dollars. That's a substantial cash advance. Wouldn't you like it in traveler's checks?"

Lael said she would like it in cash. She was afraid that somehow the authorities could punch a few computer buttons and render her traveler's checks void. She hid the money in the bottom of her oversize purse and went to a bookshop just off Fifth Avenue. She picked out a Fodor's guide to Mexico, a Rand McNally road atlas, and a pocket Spanish dictionary.

Back in her room she opened the atlas to Mexico and looked for towns beginning with "Puerto." The nearest to Scottsdale, Arizona, was Puerto Peñasco, a hundred miles down the slanting shoreline of the Gulf of California. Eighty or ninety miles farther—over a dotted line that signified "unimproved roads"—was Puerto Totuava and then Puerto de la Libertad. It was six or eight inches down the map to the next Puerto—Vallarta.

She tried to think. Puerto de la Libertad was too big a mouthful for Mrs. Holling to have blurted into the phone; the Puerto she had mentioned was a single word. Elizabeth Taylor and Richard Burton had made Puerto Vallarta a familiar name; she probably would have caught it. That left Puerto Totuava and Puerto Peñasco, unless the Holling family preferred to winter far from the nearby Gulf of California, in which case—she leaned over the map again—their vacation home could be in Puerto Escondido or Puerto Angel, both at the southern tip of Mexico, or, God forbid, Puerto Arista, almost at the Guatemalan border a thousand miles away.

She took out the stolen photographs and spread them on the motel table, trying to rule out some of the places. Without an expert assistant like a travel agent or a Mexican national, the task was impossible. Every Puerto seemed to qualify, even the ones on the Gulf of Mexico side. As Van had told her, there were clams and coyotes and shrimp boats at every town and village on the Mexican coast. But only one with a boy named Ace. A sick boy, maybe a dying boy.

A dead boy?

She called Greyhound and Trailways for bus schedules, packed her suitcase, and checked out. It was early afternoon. She couldn't wait another minute.

46

SHE READ HER Mexican travel guide from San Deigo to Jacumba on the bus and fell into a crumpled sleep for the rest of the run, fighting off bad thoughts about the Holling's remarks. At seven o'clock on Saturday night she was still more asleep than awake when she wobbled off the air-conditioned bus.

Calexico smelled like old cantaloupes. Hot air blew her damp hair dry as she hurried from the bus station to the nearest drugstore. She bought a nebulizer and a bottle of epinephrine tablets for Ace and asked a cabdriver to take her to the border crossing. By the time she reached the customs shed on the Mexican side her beige cotton blouse was limp, and she wondered if she had brought enough clothes.

As she approached her first encounter with a Mexican official, she decided not to try to speak Spanish. She had studied the language on phonograph records—for a trip to Mexico that had never come off, like so many of Mike's vacation ideas—but about all she could remember was *Buenas días.* Or was it *Buenos días?*

A semi-uniformed inspector with a flat Indian nose and a body shaped like a jalapeño pepper returned her yawn with a smile and a yawn of his own and began groping in her suitcase with both hands. She remembered the gun. It was under her tennis hat and there was no way he could miss it.

He lifted a corner of the canvas hat with thumb and forefinger so that the blue-black metal was visible only to the two of them, then smiled at her again. She smiled back. Let him confiscate the damned thing. It had been stupid to bring it.

"Porpose?" he asked.

"Excuse me?"

"The porpose. What is the porpose of the *pistola?*"

"Oh. Uh, protection. Personal protection."

"You not here to start another *revolución,* eh, lady?" he asked, still smiling.

"Heavens, no." What a pleasure to be able to tell the whole truth about something.

He held out his hand, and she smiled and shook it. He responded weakly and continued smiling. "Oh," she said. The guidebook had mentioned this quaint custom, but that didn't make it any easier.

She glanced around the customs shed. No one was looking. She pulled a $5 bill from her wallet and passed it palm to palm. He made the bill disappear and looked up expectantly. She produced another wrinkled five, and he nodded. Next time she'd know the going rate.

Their business relationship now established, he slapped a seal on her suitcase and asked her destination. "Puerto, uh, Peñasco," she said. "And then Puerto Totuava." She hoped her pronunciation was close.

"Ah, *sí*. You know how to get to?"

"No. I mean, not exactly."

"Come." He beckoned her into a cubicle where cigar smoke hovered like smog. A map of the state of Sonora was overprinted with the words *Tome Coca-Cola*. A black line ran in shallow sine waves from Mexicali southeast, here and there touching the Gulf of California. *"Ferrocarril,"* he said, tracing the line with his finger.

"I'm sorry," she said, feeling stupid. An all-purpose phrase was working its way through her memory. Suddenly it surfaced like a bubble. *"No comprendo,"* she said. Now at least she could tell Mexicans that she didn't understand, instead of constantly repeating, "I'm sorry."

"Sonora-Baja California Railroad," he said. "You take straight to here." His chubby index finger pointed to Puerto Peñasco; it appeared to be about six stops down the wavy black line. "To get to Totuava from Peñasco, you take bus—if it runs."

"If it runs?"

"They had a big storm down there. A *chubasco*. Wash out roads."

A tall man in uniform yelled something from the customs shed. "I go now," the inspector said. He whistled shrilly through his teeth and waved his stubby arm over his head. A magenta Ford taxi spurted into sight with a burst of engine noise, and the driver made a lavish production of opening the back door while the inspector placed her suitcase in the trunk. She held a dollar bill through the window, but he raised his hand in mock reproach. Apparently a flat rate covered his services. "Enjoy jor trip!" he called out.

A *chubasco*. Something else to worry about. But storms gave plenty of warning, even in Mexico. Wouldn't Mike have taken Ace inside, protected him? Ships and sailboats and docks and beach houses got hurt in storms, but not boys. Did they?

The sun was gone, but the heat waves shimmered above the streets and sidewalks like the air above a bonfire. At the railroad station she bought a coach ticket and was told that the train left at 9:45 P.M. and reached Puerto Peñasco at 2 in the morning, *"más o menos."* She asked what *más o menos* meant, and the ticket seller held his hand flat with the palm down and tilted it gently from side to side. *"¿Comprenda?"* he asked.

"Sí," she answered. Her first two-way conversation in Spanish.

The great hulk of the train lay still and silent on its siding, each coach in its own bright color, like a giant row of children's blocks. As she watched, a rickety old boxcar hooked on with a crash, the sound running down the train in diminishing jolts.

She had an hour to kill, but Mexicali was an oven, and her mind wasn't on sightseeing. She put a five-peso coin in a soft-drink machine and pushed a button with a picture of a lemon on it. A paper cup descended and filled with shredded ice as a swarthy old man in long braids stood alongside watching. When she walked away, he was staring at the machine and crossing himself.

She sipped the oversweetened lemonade and climbed on the coach. Soon she would retrace this journey with Ace, and these border towns would look better.

She wondered what Dr. Holling had been afraid to tell her and if maybe she shouldn't be in Arizona arguing with him, screaming at him, threatening to take him to court, instead of boarding an empty train in Mexico. Well, she could always go back if she didn't find Ace. *Chubasco.* Could something have happened to Ace in the storm? But why wouldn't the doctor have told her?

She took a seat on a napless green cushion. The pungent smell of woodsmoke wafted through her window. A persistent fly attempted a landing on her lemon-scented lips. Every now and then a package would slide through an open window— burlap sacks, bundles of sticks, cardboard suitcases, chickens and small beady-eyed animals in reed cages. She felt as though she had blundered into a freight car.

A heavy woman in a flowered dress dropped into the seat alongside with a thud. *"Hola,"* the woman said wearily.

"Hola," Lael answered, smiling and nodding. She hoped her new companion wouldn't attempt a casual conversation in Spanish. She was relieved when the woman busied herself arranging the collection of bags and sacks that dangled from her shoulders and arms like saddlebags.

The train lurched away at ten-thirty while her seatmate was halfway through an evening meal of tortillas and cold beans extracted from glass jars with a plastic fork that looked like a gift from Ronald McDonald. Lael shut her eyes and tried to doze but soon had to give up in the combined noise of the train and a portable radio playing native music, all trumpets and bass guitars. Just outside Mexicali the train made its first stop, and a gang of young men climbed aboard. They looked like the stoop laborers she had often seen sitting in Van's office.

"Pistoleros," her seatmate grumbled, edging nearer.

Yes, Lael thought, aren't we all? The train rattled and groaned through places she'd never heard of and couldn't find in her travel guide: Riito, Médanos, El Doctor, López Collada. The newcomers lurched up and down the aisle, singing dolorous songs and passing a bottle of pink liquid. *"¡Bonita Rosita!"* one of them shouted in her direction, but he made no attempt to get acquainted.

The locomotive's horn died in a long descending tail of sound. It sounded miles away and made her think of Ace and the little *ffft* he made with his lips. A drunk shouted, "Jalisco!" and flopped into the seat across the aisle. When she peeked across at him after a proper interval, he was holding his face in his open hands. Hopelessly drunk or just sad? You're someone's own precious son, she thought, but please, stay on your side of the aisle.

The revelers stumbled off at a stop marked "Gustavo Sotelo," where they were met by a band of dogs that seemed to know them personally. She fell asleep and dreamed of a dog town with a dog mayor and dog taxis and dogs that walked people in the park, crying, "Heel!" When she awoke, her seatmate was gone and the train had stopped in the middle of a black void. Through the open window she thought she heard the pounding of surf. A faint howling and yipping made her remember the picture of the coyote in the cage.

Are you out there, Acey?

The train rumbled back into motion but soon jerked to a stop. "Puerto Peñasco," a voice called from behind, making her jump. She picked her way along the littered aisle and

allowed the conductor to help her down the dimpled metal stairs.

She sat on a wooden bench and waited for daylight. It arrived along with an old car bearing the word TAXI in red plastic letters on the trunk. She pulled out the picture of the marina and showed it to the oily-haired man behind the wheel. "Please," she said very slowly, "you . . . take me . . . to this . . . place. Okay?"

"I spik good English, lady," he said, looking offended. He held the picture in the morning light. "Where's this?"

"Isn't it here?"

"There's noteen like this," he said. "Punta Peñasco's a few mile down the road—plenty American fishermen—but sometimes the tide go way out and leave everteen high and dry." She thought of the Port Nisbet Yacht Club's similar problem as he passed the pictures back. "No way we got a marina like this."

"American fishermen?" she repeated. The magic words. "Would you mind if we just drove out there and looked around?"

"You the boss," he said, smiling with a face that resembled the surface of the moon.

On the way through town the cab passed spavined Oldsmobiles and Buicks and Chryslers with tires splayed outward and sagging springs, clunking along without mufflers, sending up plumes of bluish smoke. She read the names across their grilles: Ernesto. Pepito. Mi Consentida. An old wooden-sided station wagon passed at high speed, its roof rack lashed with live chickens, feet trussed skyward.

The taxi left the city limits and followed a sand road across tidal barrens hummocked with saw grass. After a while the driver asked, "You got business here? I mean with the local people?"

"Uh, yes," she answered. At least she hoped so.

"Funny people," he said.

"How do you mean?" she asked politely, intent on getting to the coast.

"Too *plácido*. Too—how you say?—too contented. You ask one of these guys, 'Hey, man, you wan' make some money?' He say, 'No, man, I already got six pesos.'"

She tried to listen, but she was worrying about the storm. If Ace wasn't here, there was a chance he was in Puerto Totuava, the town with the washed-out roads. Please, God, she said under her breath, let him be here, where there'd been no storm.

She remembered the words of the doctor's wife. "Oh, dear, was he the little American boy? The one who—" Why hadn't Mrs. Holling completed her sentence? The one who what? Couldn't she see how important it was?

The driver babbled non-stop. Lael had the feeling that this was a standard monologue to sell his Mexican colorfulness to the *turistas*. She wished he would just drive. The trip from the town to the fishing village had already taken fifteen minutes. Maybe he was going the long way to run up the meter. She peeked. There was no meter. Maybe they would round the next bend and find a skinny little boy with black hair and glasses.

"Guy from here had two windmills," the driver said in his singsong voice. "Last year he took one down. Not enough wind. *Poco loco,* hey, lady?"

"*Um-hmm.*"

They steered around a sand dune and over a ridge dotted with brown grass. A vast sprawl of houses and shacks came into sight below. There was no marina in sight, let alone a curving stone breakwater like the one in the photograph. The gouged roads were caked with oil and salt, the sandy yards littered with the dried carcasses of stingrays and sharks. A place consecrated to fishing. She'd known a few in her years with Mike.

Oh, God, she thought, I've wasted my time. But then she realized she should be grateful. The loquacious taxi driver had saved her hours of wandering shyly around Puerto Peñasco and Punta Peñasco looking for a marina that wasn't there.

"*Señor,*" she said, "where can I get the bus to Puerto Totuava?"

"Totuava?" He jerked his head around.

"Yes."

His flat wet eyes opened wide, and he shook his fingers as though he had just touched a stove. "You Red Cross?"

"No. Why?"

He said nothing and seemed to be waiting for her to volunteer more information. When she didn't, he said, "I show you bus stop."

She tried to question him again about his reaction, but he had launched another nonstop monologue. All the way to town he recounted the saga of his life in what he referred to as the Uni' States, where he had made many moneys picking lettuce and fruit before a manslaughter conviction—an unfortunate misunderstanding—had caused his jailing and deportation.

They rumbled through the city streets and stopped. "Wait over there," he told her as he opened the door and pointed to a shady spot under a billboard advertising Llantas Goodrich. "When the yellow *cooperativa* bus come along, give the driver forty-two pesos and tell him take you Totuava. Not one peso more! If he ask for more, tell him Ramón Sánchez Padilla stick him like a pig."

"How much do I owe you?" she asked nervously.

"Three hundred twenty pesos plus teep. I suggest eighty pesos teep. You tell me when you comeen back, I meet you." He smiled and flipped a wavy lock of greased hair into place like a pockmarked Caesar Romero.

"Is it a dangerous ride to Puerto Totuava?" she asked.

"Dangerous?" His eyebrows came together, as though he were trying to decide whether to answer. At last he said, "No. The bus go every day."

"Didn't they have a storm?"

"Very bad," he said quickly. "But road is okay now." He seemed in a hurry to leave.

She counted out 400 pesos and watched as the cab moved off in a cloud of fine dust. Why had he given her the clear impression that he preferred not to talk about the second Puerto on her list? The *chubasco?* Or another reason? She hoped no American women had been murdered there lately.

47

IN AN HOUR or so a fat yellow bus stopped with a squeaking of brakes. It was still early morning, but the thickly moist air clung to her body like syrup. She remembered reading that the human organism took four days to adjust to abrupt changes in climate. She wondered if she would have to buy lighter clothes and where she would find the shops.

She climbed up the rusty steps and held out forty-two pesos. "Puerto Totuava, *por favor,*" she said.

The undershirted driver gave her a long look and said, "*¿Donde?*"

¿Donde? Where? "Puer-to To-tua-va," she repeated.

He studied her without responding. She could imagine how she looked after the overnight train ride. She turned and noticed that two squat passengers were also peering at her through heavy-lidded eyes. A pig squealed from a wicker container on the roof, and she gave a nervous twitch. Why are they staring? she wondered. Surely I'm not the first confused American they've seen? She couldn't help thinking of the Mexico of D. H. Lawrence and Graham Greene: the spooks and spirits, *brujos* and *curanderos,* the *naguales* who could turn themselves into goats and dogs.

The driver slid her suitcase up on the railed roof with the pig and chickens and other freight. The bus ground out of town on a twisting dirt road that kept edging back toward the gulf as though drawn to water. Far across the brown sand she saw two coyotes digging by an outcropping of rock and wondered if they were the ones she'd heard in the night. How could they stand this gathering heat in their furs?

The bus passed the bloated body of a cow, lying in a ditch like an outsize russet balloon. The driver sucked at a beer as he drove. The road bent inland, and the desert began to turn from light brown to a redder shade. Whenever the bus slowed or stopped, a cloud of dust sifted through the open windows, infiltrating the weave of her clothes.

They stopped at crossings, burro paths, groupings of reed

houses, at unheard sounds and unseen signals. New passengers seemed to rise from the earth. The door opened and shut every few minutes, and straw-hatted peasants in bare feet or huaraches climbed in and out like clowns in a circus act. She wondered where they all lived. Nothing that she saw through the window appeared congenial to human life. She closed her eyes and inhaled deeply and smelled the acrid smoke that had followed her all the way from Mexicali.

Just before noon the driver pulled to a halt in the middle of the desert and lit a black *cigarro*. His break, she supposed. He found shelter from the sun beneath a monumental old cardon cactus—green only at the tip, dying from the ground up like an old man—while the passengers waited with blank Sonoran faces. After a few minutes a barefooted man in a big sombrero rode over the nearest dune on a burro, slapped the big-eyed animal hard on the rump, and climbed aboard. The trip continued.

She asked herself what kind of life Ace could be living in this country. Maybe it was cooler, more pleasant, *civilized* where he was. God, let it be.

By early afternoon she despaired of ever reaching Puerto Totuava. Her bikini underpants had ridden up, and she didn't dare rearrange them. She tried to nap but gave up after waking with her sweaty head touching the shoulder of a young Indian.

At a whitewashed rock marked with a wooden cross her seatmate got off with a low wave of his straw hat. The bus lurched ahead to a small range of mountains, and the gears clanged as the driver shifted in and out of compound low. They went over the ridge at last and rolled toward a broad desert valley.

She watched for a while and then dozed again. The angry face of Dr. H. Holling materialized in front of her face. He had straight black hair and a toothbrush mustache and he was making an outdoor speech to a crowd of helmeted men dressed in jackboots and medals. When he pounded the podium and said, "I did everything I could!" the soldiers roared their approval.

She awoke and found she was the only passenger. The driver had pulled into a hardscrabble turnout and was refilling the bus's radiator from a cloth-covered bag on the roof. She looked out the window. The desert floor was scored by fresh ravines littered with uprooted cactus and tumbleweed. An adobe house had been blown flat, the bricks dissolved into shapeless lumps.

A car was submerged upside down in the soft sand, its wheels raised skyward like a playful puppy's feet. Dust devils vacuumed the broad valley; she counted four spinning at once. She was glad she wasn't trying to make a living here as an herb farmer. Or anything else. The place reminded her of the dead gray landscape below Mount Saint Helen's.

She was half-asleep again when the driver called out the name of a town. She looked around and saw that she was still the only passenger.

"Totuava," he repeated.

Her watch said one-forty. She stepped down into a searing sun. The driver retrieved her suitcase from the roof and pointed to a cobblestone street that led toward the gulf. "Hotel," he said. Then he stepped back into the bus and started the engine as though he couldn't get away soon enough.

"*Gracias,*" she said. No one was in sight. She walked past flat-roofed adobe houses cloaked in fading bougainvillaea and hibiscus and jacaranda, and all she could think of were the other Puertos she would have to visit, the other *cooperativa* buses she would have to ride, the other trains and taxis. She dragged her suitcase around a corner and came to a wide paved street with a few people in sight. A scrawny dog the color of salt pork lay in the shade of a flame tree, its belly rising and falling to the rhythm of distant surf as a swarm of tiny flies reconnoitered its backside.

She turned and saw a curving line of rocks stretching into the gulf. The wreckage of a small fishing boat bleached in the sun and spray on the breakwater. A shrimper lay on its side, its wooden flanks holed. Inside the rock wall a few smaller boats bobbed at anchor, and three or four others were docked.

She pulled out the stolen picture to be sure. The boats were different, but the breakwater and the marina were the same. Exactly.

Ace was here. Somewhere.

48

HER WRINKLED BEIGE skirt caught the onshore breeze and curled over her knee as she walked the embarcadero, breathing a quiet prayer of thanks. When she stepped into the shade of an arcade, someone reached from behind and grabbed her suitcase. She yanked back and looked down at a frightened boy with the face of a dusty brown Botticelli angel. *"¿Por favor?"* he squealed.

She felt like a certified child molester. *"Sí, sí, certainamento,"* she said, not even sure there was such a word. She handed the suitcase over and wondered where to instruct him to take it.

An old aquamarine jeep chugged to the curb in a cloud of smoke, and a driver with a lopsided face poked his head out. One eye was almost completely shut, an ear was twisted out of shape, and his nose was flat. He looked as though he had endured a torturous trip down the birth canal. He made her feel even more guilty than the boy.

"Hotel, *señorita?*" he asked in a muffled voice.

No other vehicle was in sight. She climbed into the flat-hooded Willys Jeep and hoped to God the two of them weren't a father-and-son bandit team. The boy flipped her bag into the back and joined it with a nimble jump.

"¡Andale!" he yelled in a soprano voice, as though he had taken command. He was barely audible over a radio announcer who spoke rapid Spanish and interrupted himself with frequent buzzes and bongs.

The aqua-colored "taxi" shook and jiggled its way along the embarcadero at a majestically slow pace, as though the driver were afraid it would break like crystal. The cobblestone street was full of potholes and washouts. The *chubasco* again. She tried to make herself comfortable on the sloping front seat.

She looked for English-language signs in the shop windows and found none. The town looked unreceptive to visitors. Somehow the tourist boom had passed it by. The business section consisted of places like the Farmacia mi Consentida and a turquoise-splashed bar bearing a sign saying CERVEZA

DOS Y TRES EQUIS and a small market called Mercado Garibay.

Almost every place had a sign in its window saying CER-
RADO. She looked it up in her pocket dictionary: "Closed." A
small tank truck with *Aguador* on its side was parked across
the street from a dusty plaza dominated by a dry fountain in
the shape of a fish. A ring of painted rocks encircled a small
barrel cactus in a garden of sand. She couldn't imagine Ace
or any other child living in this barren place. The fishing had
brought Mike here, she decided. But what about the schools,
the playgrounds, the hospitals? They were unimportant as long
as the fishing was good.

The other two cast occasional glances at her as the open
Jeep limped along dusty streets lined with one-story adobe
houses with corrugated roofs. After a few minutes they turned
again and headed uphill into a warren of rutted dirt streets
bordered by shacks of thatch and tar paper. Stunted and dead
plants were everywhere—mostly hibiscuses and morning glories, a few jacarandas. Something was wrong. The poorest
Mexicans treated their flowers as she treated her herbs. When
she tried to question the driver, he wiggled his hands and shook
his head.

A few townspeople stared hard: an old man leading a bony
mule, a woman balancing a jar on her head, a boy pushing a
cart piled with driftwood. Were light-haired women such an
oddity here? She reminded herself that Mike might come strolling down the street and see her, and she slid lower in the seat.

The boy tapped her lightly on the shoulder and said *"¿Señorita?"* as though beseeching her indulgence. His face wore a
wide grin, and she noticed how much he resembled a deeply
tanned Ace. *"¿Señorita?"* he asked. *"¿Está Usted* moobie star?"

"Heavens, no," she said, thinking that only a little Mexican
boy could take her for an actress.

His brown eyes flashed, and he said, *"Muy guapa dama."*

"Juancito!" the driver exclaimed, but the child's open smile
showed that he'd meant no disrespect. With the radio blaring
"Deep Purple," they drove over the words *HIJOS DE LA
CHINGADA* painted on the pavement. A glance at her *dic-
cionario* showed that *hijos* meant "sons," but *chingada* wasn't
listed; she supposed it meant something like "pioneers." She
was pleased at how fast her Spanish was coming back. It
might come in handy if she had to deal with the authorities.

On the southern outskirts of town her eyes widened at the
sight of a coyote pacing a cage alongside a market. She looked

beyond and saw the *almeja* shack exactly where it had been in the photo. She felt like jumping out of the car and kissing the bare earth where Ace had stood. My baby! How long ago? Not more than a month or two. Angel Ace, how far are you?

The taxi moved past a school playground. A few scrawny children peeked from the rusting carcasses of cars. A gearbox protruded from the dirt with the metal teeth painted in alternating colors. Small boys curled up inside tires and rolled down a pile of dirt, yelling. She scanned the whirling bodies one by one, but he wasn't among them.

The driver took a lazy right turn down a long lane lined with trees that looked like tamaracks and headed for a low-slung building glowing hot white in the afternoon sun. "What's that?" she asked.

The driver pointed upward toward the name: *Hotel Totuava*.

Two rectangular wings reached to a set of dunes that fronted on the gulf. The place looked like a naval recruit depot. A pair of dipper ducks pecked at the green scum on the surface of a small swimming pool. A sign on the front walk warned, NO PISE LA HERBA, but she could see no *herba*, not even a blade of grass. Everything was gravel and sand and reddish dirt.

The driver steered to the shade of an overhang and opened her door, keeping his face averted. She followed the man and boy through a plaster-walled lobby with a white textured ceiling marred by a pair of brown spots. She looked closer and saw that they were bats.

She referred to her guidebook and asked the desk clerk, "*¿Tiene un habitación?*"

"*Sí señorita,*" the overweight young man answered in a high nasal voice, his shiny black eyes showing excitement. "*¿Quizá Usted habla inglés?*"

"*Pardoname.*" she answered. "*No tengo español.* No, wait! I mean, *No* hablo *español.*"

"Ah, but I spik *inglés!*" he said triumphantly, leaning forward and rubbing his hands. His dark face looked as if it had been gently patted for hours by a sculptor working in cocoa butter. He waddled around from behind the counter to bow and shake her hand. He wore tennis shoes that turned outward from his ankles and tight white pants a couple of inches short. He was a rarity in her brief experience: a fat Sonoran. "Tell me sunfeen," he said, showing bright white teeth. "Joo like rock?"

She wondered what she should answer and settled for a curt nod.

"Suntine I play my *discos* for joo," he said, running back behind the counter. "Rulling Stuns, Bittles, joo name eet." His English was so bad it was almost funny, but then she thought guiltily: Who am I to pass judgment? My Spanish would put them in stitches.

It took all three of them to conduct her to her room, the clerk leading the way, the child carrying her bag, and the taxi driver protecting the rear. Apparently her arrival was an event. "Anyteen joo want, joo call Luis," the fat man said, pointing to his own middle. "I am at the service! Thank you for spikking *inglés;* it is my job to spik *inglés* at my peoples. If joo like, I help jor Sponish. *Yo soy, tu es, el es.* I ám, joo am, he is. Easy, no?"

She thanked him and stépped into the room. She hadn't bathed since San Diego; if the room had no shower or tub, she intended to make a dash for the gulf, clothes and all. It turned out to be a dark cubicle with a shower stall in one corner. Alongside was a handlettered sign: NOT TO RUN WATER WITH-OUT CHECK-IN WITH DESK.

"May I shower?" she asked the clerk.

"My great pleasure," he said, bowing again.

She studied the rest of her *habitación*. The walls were plain plaster with faded accents of red and aqua. A simple set of wooden furniture focused on a maroon sofa that had been ripped down the middle and resewn with pink thread. Above the concave bed hung a hammered aluminum Aztec sunburst encrusted with colored bits of glass, most of them missing. The door to a narrow balcony was slightly ajar; a fine sifting of dust had collected in a miniature dune.

"Okay?" the clerk said as the boy put her suitcase on the bed and the Jeep driver loitered near the door, his blind eye turned away.

"Very much," she said, wishing they would leave. She wanted to ask about the storm, but she would have to find someone who spoke better English. She opened her wallet to pay the driver and the boy, and a picture of Ace dropped out. It was an old one, taken in the bathtub when he was four, his coal black hair slick with shampoo. The taxi driver picked it up, and the clerk peered over his shoulder. She thought she saw a look pass between them.

"Do you know him?" she asked.

"Never see heem," the clerk said. "*¿Tú, Temo?*" he asked the driver.

"*Nunca,*" the man answered, shaking his head emphatically.

Something unsaid hung in the warm afternoon air. She felt deceived. She wouldn't have been surprised if the baggage boy and the man with the damaged face had come from Central Casting and the hotel was a set. Or maybe a night and day of desert travel had softened her brain. But she couldn't afford to pass up the least chance to pinpoint Ace. "Listen to me," she said slowly. "I'm looking for this boy. He is my son. If you have seen him, please tell me."

"Joo pay mawneys?" the clerk asked. He had an open-eyed fat man's look that made him appear jovial, but he was deadly serious about money.

"I pay," she said.

"How many?"

"Uh, a thousand pesos." She was willing to pay far more, but she didn't want to sound like someone worth robbing in the middle of the night.

"I find!" Luis blurted out.

She asked, "Do you know what a Ford Escort is?"

"The baby Ford?" he said. "Chure. I teenk they make here. *Hecho de Mexico.*"

"I'm looking for a yellow one. A two-door. Washington plates—white with green letters."

"We find for joo," the desk clerk said, and rattled off a Spanish phrase to the others. After a while the three of them backed slowly out the door, the taxi driver leaving last, tilting his misshapen head and looking intently at her with his one green eye as though wishing he had the nerve to speak. When they were gone, she realized that she hadn't paid him. She wondered why he hadn't insisted.

She closed the red plastic curtains and flopped on the sofa. Dr. Holling was on her mind again. "I did everything I could. I don't think it's fair to blame me."

She peeled off her clothes and found a lining of rust-colored grit behind her elbows and knees, around each toe, and caked in a burnt sienna V between her breasts. As she bathed, a noise like an air compressor came from the rusty shower head and the narrow stall filled with the aroma of sulfur. After two or three minutes hot water poured from the nozzle and quickly changed to steam. She turned the knob, but the steam continued.

She jumped out and glared at the shower head as though it

were alive. The tiny sink produced a trickle of warm water. She brushed her teeth and looked down into a bowl of used toothpaste and spit. It looked as though it would take all day to drain.

She opened her suitcase and unfolded a navy jersey dress with a conservative stand neckline and a pin-tucked bodice that flowed into the skirt. It wasn't Mexican, but it wasn't an eye catcher either. She toyed with the idea of wearing nothing underneath but changed her mind in favor of her lightest bra and panties. The hotel hall was cool, considering the temperature outside, but she felt the perspiration begin to form as soon as she took a few steps. Three days to go before her body's thermostat clicked on.

A passageway off the lobby led to a row of shops. One by one she checked the doors: all locked. She looked at her watch. It was 5:30 P.M. She was surprised. She had read that Mexican shops reopened after the siesta and stayed open till 7 or 8 at night.

She came to an alcove at the end of the hall and a narrow show window bearing the words *English Spoken*. There was barely room for a modest display: two seashells resting in pink sand and copies of *The People's Guide to Mexico* and *The Sea of Cortez*. A sign said, LIBROS. BOOKS.

She pushed against the door and was surprised when it gave. A petite woman with doll-like features and old-fashioned wire-rim glasses like Van's greeted her with a puzzled look and a smile, *"¡Buenas tardes! Como—"*

"You speak English?" Lael asked, pointing to the sign.

"Oh, yes! Do *you?* How nice!" The woman emphasized her words with birdlike flutterings of both hands. She looked like someone who seldom ventured out.

"I'm an American," Lael said. "I just checked in. I'm— I'm—" She couldn't think of the right word and settled for "confused."

"About what?"

"Puerto Totuava."

The woman said, "Oh?" and walked from around the counter on tiny feet encased in open leather sandals. Two reed chairs rested in a corner alongside a caged parrot; she motioned Lael into one. "Tea?" she asked. *"¿Café?"*

"Neither, thanks," Lael said, sitting on her bare legs.

"It's been so quiet here since the *chubasco*."

"Was it . . . bad?" Her heart pounded. She desperately wanted to know, and she desperately wanted not to know.

"Very bad," the woman said, shaking her head. "The tourist agents are warning people to stay away. You are the first *turista* in three weeks. Our valley ran ten feet deep. It washed out the aqueducts that brought down our water. It washed out most of our roads. It washed out *todo.*"

Dr. Holling leaped into Lael's mind. "Were any children hurt?" she asked, sitting so far forward that the chair started to tip.

"*¡Por Dios!*" the little shopkeeper exclaimed, her small hand fluttering up to cover her mouth. "You haven't heard?"

Lael felt the blood leave her face. "No."

"No one was hurt at first," the woman said in a voice that sounded pained. "We had plenty of warning."

"You mean . . . children died later?"

The woman bit a tiny knuckle with white niblet teeth and spoke faster. "Our water went bad. It turned—oh, what is the word?—toxic. But nobody knew till babies began dying at the *orfanatorio.* They were already undernourished. Then a four-year-old died in town. My niece, Anita. After that, they began dropping everywhere. Terrible. So—so *triste.* Altogether we lost one hundred and thirty-six—one death for every ten people in town—mostly the very young but a few *viejos.* My mother said it was like the old days when smallpox would come and the weak ones would be dead in a week."

Lael gripped the edges of the chair. "Oh, God, what can I do?"

"Leave, *señorita.* Most of our people have gone. The government keeps the hotel open to pretend nothing happened. Myself, I will leave when my fiancé returns from Arizona. I have a cot in the back. I am surprised you didn't hear about the storm. Didn't the American papers. . . ."

Lael had stopped listening. She was trying to remember what Mrs. Holling had said. *Was your son four or five years old? A tad underweight, thick glasses. . . . Doctor saw so many. . . . It's hard to remember them all. Doctor saw so many. . . .*

She swallowed her panic. "Miss, Miss—"

"Ortega."

"Miss Ortega, do you know an American boy named Alexander Pritcher? Ace Pritcher? About so high, black hair, glasses? He might have been wheezing, he—"

"He's yours, isn't he?" A sad smile crossed the tan features.

"Yes. Please. Tell me the truth. Was he—?"

"I don't know," the woman said, reaching out and touching her arm. "We lost so many. I don't know if any were from your country."

"Do you know if my son was living here?"

"I have no knowledge. There are Americans at the Meriwether place—house-sitting, I think you call it—but I never see them."

"Where's that?"

"Fifteen kilometers north. Laguna Gris."

She thanked the woman and walked blindly from the shop, ran through the silent halls, and collapsed on the bed. He's alive, she said over and over. He's alive, isn't he, God? He's living at that laguna place with his father. Please, God, isn't he living at the laguna with his father?

There was a soft knock.

"Yes?" she mumbled through the thin wooden panel.

"Open, pleece," a voice said.

"Who is it?"

"Luis! Clerk of the desk. I have phone message."

"Can't you just slip it under the door, Luis? I'm sleeping."

"Hokay." He sounded disappointed. When he spoke again, his voice came from floor level. "Joo mus' go to room two of the *municipio* in the morneen. Eight o'clock charp!"

She felt angry at herself. After all these months of hunting for Ace she was still making mistakes. She should have kept a low profile instead of baring her soul to people she didn't even know. Now they were ordering her around.

"Eight o'clock?" she asked. "Who says so?"

"The police."

49

ALL NIGHT LONG the damp sheet kept sticking to her skin. As she floundered around, trying to sleep, it gradually worked loose from its tucks and slid to the floor. A faint smell of mildew exuded from the mattress, and she got up in the darkness and refastened the sheet, only to have it pull loose again. She tried to sleep uncovered and rolled into the middle of the concave bed. Her finger came to rest in a hole in the mattress big enough to admit a family of rats. She wondered if any were in residence.

At five forty-five a cock crowed. She weighed it in her mind: one pound of meat, two pounds of feathers, three pounds of voice. She walked across the hemp carpet to the rust-stained sink. Who on earth would practice violin at this hour of the morning? She realized she was hearing the water pipes. She sponged quickly, lest she awaken the town.

The squat off-white building looked as *cerrado* as every place else when she arrived in the same Jeep taxi a few minutes before eight, clutching her court papers for protection. A Ford Fairlane with a faded red finish was parked in the shade of an olive tree, an unevenly lettered sign on one of the doors saying, DELEGADO. The car had two spotlights, one of them cracked, and a police light bar on the roof. A brass plate next to the gracefully arched doorway of the building proclaimed, MUNICIPIO. SUB-DELEGACIÓN MUNICIPAL VALLE DE TOTUAVA.

She shoved through a flimsy wooden door and into a narrow hall. A reception desk was unmanned. A sepia lithograph titled *"Hay Hombres que Respiran Luz"* hung from the flaking wall. She'd forgotten what *Hay* meant, but the rest sounded like "Men who breathe light." Below were cameo pictures of Rivera, Orozco, Ricardo Montalban, Lopéz-Portillo, a dozen other famous Mexicans. Next to the lithograph hung the reception room's only other decoration, an unstrung guitar.

The door to Room 2 was slightly ajar. She tapped lightly with her fingernails, and a voice said, "Come in, you are expected." He sounded like an American businessman with a slight unassignable accent.

She clamped a smile on her face and entered. At first she was blinded by streaks of silvery light streaming through the window. A silhouette took form as a man of her own height with a dark face crisscrossed with scars like a butcher block, brown eyes behind steel-rimmed glasses, and black stringy hair worn in a bowl shape, Indian style. He looked like a still life in sandstone or dust. A heavy chrome-handled automatic was stuck inside his belt and fastened by a big metal clip. "You're the chief?" she asked, hoping she didn't sound dubious.

"If you wish," he said, nodding disarmingly. "I am *delegado, guardia de policia, carabinero, gendarme, comisario de policia,* however it pleases you, and I also take care of the building. Hernández." He stuck out a smooth, cool palm and shook her hand. "Ramón Hernández Hernan. I went six months to Compton JC."

"I'm Lael Pritcher." She wondered if she should say she went four years to Mount Holyoke.

He motioned her into a spavined wooden chair. "Your papers, please?"

She handed over her tourist card and her Washington driver's license with the unflattering photograph. He glanced at them, glowered, handed them back, and said, "Why are you here?" She was just as glad the niceties were over.

"To find my son," she said, pushing her court papers across the littered surface. *If I have a son left to find.*

He scanned them quickly. "I see. How can I help you?" He set the papers aside and tilted backward in body language that said he was harmless to mothers and children. His abrupt changes of attitude caught her off guard. She had been primed for harassment, truculent opposition, at best a bored dismissal. Mike had had plenty of time to make friends with the town establishment, even to buy a few officials if necessary. What wouldn't the inhabitants of a place like this do for a $10 bill?

"You could enforce my custody decree," she said. "I'm told it's as valid here as in the States."

"Perhaps," he said, "but first there are formalities."

"Such as?"

"Going before a Mexican judge. The nearest one is in Caborca. The road disappeared in the *chubasco.* To get here from Caborca is now a two-day trip. Judges are not pleased by two-day trips."

"Couldn't I take my papers to the court?" Even as she was making the suggestion, she didn't think much of it. It would give Mike too much time to get away.

"No. Under our laws the matter must be tried where the child is found."

"Is that the only problem?"

"No. The other is that I don't know where your husband and your son were—*are*."

"I was told they might be at Laguna something."

"*¿En verdad?*" He seemed surprised.

"That's what I heard."

"Laguna Gris?"

"Yes, that's it."

"Is possible. There's a big house up there."

"How do you get to it?"

"On the main road east there is a turnoff next to a sign that says TORTILLERIA LA ÚNICA. The tortilla factory was washed away, but the sign stayed. After the turn it's fifteen or sixteen kilometers up the coast—over dunes and tide flats, very bad. I strongly recommend you not to attempt it. For many reason."

"I don't intend to. But I was hoping *you*—"

He held up his hands. "I can do nothing, *señora*. You can see the situation here. Maybe you can wait. It has been—how long now?"

"Almost a year."

He shook his head sadly. "It is cruel even to say the word wait. Please—accept my pardon."

"I heard that some children, uh, died. Do you have records?" She wondered if he would jump up and lead her to a filing card with Ace's name. And how she would react.

"Everyone keeps the records here and here," he said, pointing to his head and his heart. She wanted to ask if he had lost children himself, but she was afraid the answer would be yes.

"Do you know if a boy named Alexander—"

"I don't," he interrupted, as though he wanted to get off the subject. "But it is possible. There was many confusion."

His uncertainty eased her mind. She was sure he would have heard of the death of an American boy. So would the others she had talked to. Six months ago she wouldn't have jumped to this conclusion; her mind would have locked onto the possibility that Ace was dead. But she could no longer live in a full-time state of despair. It took too much strength and endurance, and her stamina was low. She asked, "What do you suggest I do next?"

"Please," he said, "allow me a day or two, maybe three, to see what I can find."

"And then?"

"That is up to *nuestro Señor*." She must have looked puzzled; he quickly translated, "God in heaven," and crossed himself. "Maybe we wait two or three more days, and two or three more after that. Some things, they cannot be hurried."

"I—I can't wait."

He looked at her intently. *"Señora,* do not try to do the work of the *delegado,* please. I wouldn't want anything unpleasant to happen to a visitor. We would be so ashamed." She wondered if she had just heard a threat.

As she walked to the waiting taxi, she said to herself, I'm doing exactly what I swore I'd never do again—leaving things up to somebody else. But what choice do I have? I can't take a step without being seen. If I tried snooping around on my own, I wouldn't get out of the lobby. And where would I start?

She wondered how she could endure three or five or eight days of doing nothing in this Godforsaken place. In Oregon, living on hope and coffee, she had had her fill of playing the passive mother waiting for the big heroic men to find her child. It hadn't worked then, and it wouldn't work now.

Just before her Jeep taxi reached the long lane of tamaracks leading back to the hotel, it passed a one-story white building bearing the word *Funeraria*. She asked the broken-faced driver to stop. It wouldn't hurt to check the funeral register. It would be one more proof that Ace hadn't died.

A green and white sign on the door said, PARA INFORMES EN LA PESCADERIA LA TOTUAVA. She translated word by word from her dictionary and followed instructions. The round little man in the fish store next door smiled and said that he was indeed the funeral director, that he spoke a small English, and that he would have only too much happiness to show her the registry of the dead. He led her to the back of the mortuary, where an ancient Cadillac hearse bore ornately scripted green letters spelling *María Madre* across its battered front bumper. Black paint flaked from a fender; the side mirror was broken off. As they passed the hearse, her nostrils twitched, and she blurted out, "Was there a funeral today?"

The man laughed. "Did I say something funny?" she asked.

"Your nose *muy sensitivo,*" he said, laughing again. "This

morning my hearse is carry *camarones* and *langostes.*"

"Shrimp and—"

"Lobsters," he said, grinning. "Hwhy you wan' know? You wan' rent it? Fi' hundred pesos a day—and I don' ask no question."

"No," she said. "No, *gracias.*"

They went inside. She wished he would stop giggling and snorting to himself. He led her through a cool room where the shriveled body of a old woman lay on a slab. Her face looked as though it had been painted with flat white enamel, and she was dressed in an ivory silk dress with ruffles and pleats down the front. "My wife's wedding dress," he explained. "Ees also for rent." He laughed uproariously. She wondered how he contained himself at funerals.

They passed through a small room stacked floor to ceiling with caskets. A Styrofoam box with a fitted lid bore the inscription: *"600 pesos. Para niños."* She looked closer. A label read, "Plastic chaise pad for webbed chaise lounge, made in Calif." Amazing. A discarded shipping box had metamorphosed into a cheap coffin for Mexican children. The mortician lived in a seller's market. No wonder he laughed and snorted. He was stroking an adult-sized fiberglass coffin with a tufted blue finish, a silky white liner, silver-painted plastic sides and handles. *"El mejor,"* he said proudly. "Twenty thousand pesos. Eet make you hoppy to die."

She followed into a chapel the size of her room at the Hotel Totuava. Six lounge chairs protected by split burlap faced a small white altar decorated with soiled gauze. A roughly whittled Madonna and Child in Day-Glo orange and aqua looked down from the altar. An inscription on a Bible said, "Distributed by the Gideons." In a corner of the room the proprietor showed her a thick book on a pedestal: *Registro de los Muertos.* "I may look?" she asked.

"Mi funeraria," he said with a bow, *"su funeraria."*

He stepped out the front door, giving her a glimpse of the Jeep driver smoking a cigarette. She began turning the thick pages.

God spare me seeing his precious name now, she said under her breath. After another few minutes she realized she'd been spared. She tiptoed out the front door to find the cabdriver sitting behind the wheel of his aquamarine Jeep, his ruined face turned away. They continued on, barely above walking speed, toward the hotel.

"*Señor*," she said on a sudden impulse, "how do you get
to the cemetery?" The cab continued; she had forgotten that
the one-eyed driver barely spoke English. She opened her
purse to find the Fodor. "*Momentito*," she said as she groped.
The old Jeep lumbered to the curb and parked in its own
pollution.

Under "Useful Phrases and Vocabulary" she found the words
she needed. "*¿Cómo se va a? . . .*" She looked up "cemetery"
in her pocket dictionary and started over, "*¿Cómo se va a
cementerio?*"

The driver pointed left with his thumb. "*Izquierda*," he
said. She had no idea what he meant.

"*¿Andale?*" she said, hoping it meant "Can we go?"

"*¿A . . . cementerio?*"

"Yes. Uh, *sí*."

He blinked as though hesitant, and she noticed that his one
good eye was dark green. "*Señora*, pleece—"

"I will pay," she said again. "*Mucho dinero, mucho pesos.*"

"Mawney ees no *importante*," he said, rubbing his scarred
cheek with his hand and shaking his head slowly.

"Please," she begged him.

He turned and looked straight at her, then turned back and
sat silently. She dug in her purse and waved Ace's picture
under his nose. "My son," she said. "I have to find him."

The jeep crunched into gear and made a U-turn back past
the breakwater. An old green fishing boat rode low at a dock
as two men strained under the weight of an oversize burlap bag
that almost slipped from their hands. "Isn't that Luis?" she said
aloud.

"*No*," the driver snapped. "*No es Luis.*"

She looked again. It was either the room clerk or the second
fat man she had seen in Sonora. What would Luis be doing at
the embarcadero loading a boat? Moonlighting? He didn't look
the type.

She slouched in the seat as the Jeep moved through the
empty streets. The *delegado* was probably still in his office—
it was barely 9 A.M.—but she didn't know who else might spot
her and turn in a report on her activities. Who had tipped him
off yesterday? Luis probably. Desk clerks were notorious in-
formers. She remembered the one in Oregon who had reported
her as a whore. It seemed a lifetime ago.

The taxi turned east along a road she remembered from her
bus trip. A few women in rags stooped in the sparse landscape.

She couldn't imagine what they were picking. Brightly colored clothes hung from cactus spines, and a horse with ribs like a zebra's stripes was tethered to a large stone. As the taxi passed, the animal lifted both front feet sharply to jerk the stone to a new grazing area a few inches away. Farther along the dusty road a dead dog lay under a thick black mat. She looked closer and saw that it was made of flies.

After a few minutes the driver stopped the Jeep, opened her door, and pointed. Then he hurriedly climbed back into his own seat to wait. *"¿Aquí?"* she asked, practicing her Fodor's Spanish.

He nodded.

She looked out and saw the same barren landscape. *"Usted . . .* come with?" she asked.   .

"No!" he said as though horrified at the suggestion. She walked over a low rise and saw the *cementerio*. She was already sorry she had come. The driver probably thought she was a silly *turista* getting her kicks from the local color. The *delegado* would hear the whole story. She would say she had misunderstood his instructions.

There was no gate. The graveyard looked like a corral that had been abandoned to the sun and sand. She wouldn't have known it was a cemetery except for the crosses of sticks and scrap, pieces of whitewashed wood bearing clumsily painted names, and an odor that made her gasp and rub her eyes. It was a shantytown of the dead, and the gravediggers hadn't dug deep.

She stepped into one of the rows with the same ashamed feeling she had felt entering Catherine Pritcher's house. The first grave was a shallow trough in the hard red dirt behind a portion of orange crate with "Jaime Cruz" scratched on it in crayon.

A few steps farther a rat peeked from a hole below a hand-lettered piece of cardboard reading "Silvia Hernández, 3 *años.*" She pictured the rat family living in the child's body, its own babies sleeping inside the fur-lined skull, the older ones playing in the ribs like gerbils in a pet-shop window. Was that God's purpose in taking this infant? To provide a domicile for rats? No wonder the driver hadn't wanted to come. She glanced toward the Jeep and saw the back of his head.

As she walked on, an empty Montejo beer bottle almost sent her sprawling. She came to another grave under a latticework arch of thin wood. The back of a cigar box bore an inscription in primitive capitals and small letters: *"REcUErdO dE NUEstrO HIjO YsIdrO GÓmEz, 6 AñOs, FAllEcItO. En PAz DEscAnsE."* She felt a sudden chill as she looked up the words in her dictionary. Was there an inscription like that for another six-year-old? "Alexander Charles Estes Pritcher, Rest in Peace"?

She came to a grave that seemed atop another. The survivors must have been desperate. Bodies had been buried everywhere, at angles, in the walkway, under the wood scrap fence. Something jutted from the dirt. She reached down and touched the remains of a tiny finger, as thin and dry as a wishbone. She started to kick dirt over it, then knelt and filled the bowl of her hands with reddish dust and completed the reinterment.

The final resting place of Silverio Gutiérrez, 84, was surrounded by a border of oil cans, and the grave of Enrico Armas, 8, by Crisco containers, every third one wrapped in tinfoil. The monument of Martín Vásquez, 2, was a ripped portion of bed slat. Alejandro Núñez, 1, slept under a cross made of broom handles; Benito Poret, 9, under a cross of lead pipe and elbow joints, and *"El niño Pedro, a los II meses,"* under a pyramid made of six beer cans. A layer of dust covered everything.

The longer she walked under the hot sun, the less sure she was that Ace wasn't here. There were so *many*. Why all the others and not him? She wished Van were with her, or Julie, or Trang, to help check off the names. *"El niño Pedro."* She wondered why his parents hadn't inscribed his full name and then realized that strangers must have buried this body. Had there been mix-ups in identification? She trembled at the prospect of rounding a corner and finding a simple placard: *"El niño americano,"* or *"El niño Ace."* What would she do?

She knelt to read a scrap of paper skewered to a sharpened stick in front of the grave of Rosa Suarez, 2. *"Nuestra hija ... corazón ... hasta morir...."* The words meant nothing, but she could tell it was a poem. Would there be one on Ace's grave? What would be a suitable epitaph for a five-year-old—a six-year-old now—who loved to play with words as much as he loved to play with toys? How about

> Suck suck your toes
> All the way to Mexico.

> While you're there,
> Cut your hair
> And stick it in your
>   underwear.

It was all she could think of at the moment. She finished the row and then another. How many to go? Maybe two, maybe three. The inscriptions ran together before her eyes: "Juana García *nuestra ángel* Diego Sánchez Emiliano Rincón *en paz decanse* Paco Jiménez 8 *meses* Juana Garcia 2 años E.P.D. José Alvarez FloraGonzálesJoséDíaz*fallecito*Diego-Salazar. . . ." She stopped and looked at the red ball of the sun. No tombstone offered shelter from the hot rays.

She began to talk to herself. Ace, you aren't here! *You aren't here!* Can't stop. Mustn't miss a single grave. Wouldn't sleep another minute if I did. Will he be in one of those plastic boxes made in California? Or did Mike splurge and buy the best. Something nice, with a tufted finish? *Make you hoppy you die.*

She brushed the back of her hand across her forehead and pushed on. A burned fringe of weed surrounded the final resting place of Franco Delcampo, 2. José Fuerte's larger plot was adorned with aqua-colored pismo shells and a cross made of broken dishes set in clay. A luxury setting for a man of seventy-four.

Only half a row to go. . . .

She stepped ahead, planting her foot solidly so she wouldn't lose her balance if she saw something shocking. Mournful cries seemed to seep from the earth and drift like woodsmoke toward the gulf. What was one little boy's death compared to so many? She felt as though she were committing an outrageous sin, praying to God that the next name and all the remaining names would be Mexican. Murder by race, murder by the process of elimination.

She turned guiltily toward the old Willys Jeep. The driver stared hard at her. His hand came up to shield his disfigured face, and this time she was the one who looked away.

She heard a drone. High above the fetid air an invisible jet drew a white ribbon across the sky. Bound for another Mexico, she supposed, full of loud Americans burping complimentary margaritas. For the first time she felt close to the soul of this pitiful country. So many children dead because of contaminated

water. Could that have happened in the States? She doubted
it. Would a Mexican have stolen a child from his mother? She
doubted that, too.

A few more graves to go. Another Sánchez. Another Sal-
azar, *fallecito*. Miguelito Hernández, 6, E.P.D. Then the last
grave of the last row.

The plot was small and neatly kept, the hard brown soil
scratched by the marks of a broom. Two cutaway Purex bottles
were filled with nearly fresh flowers, and a white plaster statue
of the Virgin was protected by a cage made of coat hanger
wire.

She couldn't bring herself to read the name. She raised her
eyes and lowered them and covered her face with her hands.
It was all too much.

Someone tapped her shoulder. She whirled and pulled her
hands away. Small wet runnels creased the dusty wreckage of
the driver's face. "'Bustamente,'" he read aloud. "'Juan y
Ezekiel Bustamente. *Cinco años.*'"

He took her arm in a firm but gentle grip. *"Es todo,"* he
said. *"No más."* They walked to the Jeep in silence.

50

THE *DELEGADO* CALLED on her the next morning as she sat in her room, picking at a breakfast of *huevos rancheros* that tasted like the *chiles rellenos* of the meal before and the *carne asada* of the meal before that. She wondered if she would ever regain her interest in food.

"Only to remind you," he said as he entered. "Please do not intrude the case." He gripped and twisted a light straw hat. "Already I am learning a few things."

She held up the carafe to ask if he wanted a cup of coffee. "No, *gracias,*" he said, refusing to leave the door. "These days there is no time for *nada.*"

"I understand," she said, thinking of the cemetery. "Have you learned anything?"

"The Americans at Laguna Gris, they arrive two months ago. Every week the man comes to the *mercado* and buys a few things. No one sees him otherwise."

"What's he look like?"

"The *mercader* says only, 'He is American.' Pays in dollars and leaves in a little yellow Ford. Talks to no one."

She tried not to betray her excitement. "Has he been in this week?" As she spoke, she was thinking: When Mike's in town. Ace must be back at the house. Alone.

"No. He come today or tomorrow. The *mercader* promise to tell me. Soon you will know."

Soon soon *soon.* She'd been hearing about "soon" for almost a year. "Soon my son'll be dead!"

The *delegado* frowned. "Dead?"

"He has asthma. My husband doesn't take care of him. The last I heard—"

"I know that condition. An annoyance. No one dies from it."

She wondered again about human insensitivity. Before the doctors had started the shot program and the nebulizers, she had seen Ace turn a yellowish blue from asthma attacks, had seen his eyes roll up in his head in fear of suffocation. She

259

had heard of asthmatic children suffering heart attacks and strokes from sheer fright. An annoyance?

"*Señor*—" She was embarrassed. She couldn't remember his name.

"Hernández," he said.

"Forgive me." She couldn't afford to offend. "*Señor* Hernández, why can't you just drive out there and pick him up?"

He looked thoughtful as he stood in her open doorway. "For now—too many complication. You tell me your husband has run before. That doesn't sound like a man who will say, '*¡Bienvenida! Here is my son. ¡Vaya con mia bendición!*' "

"But you're the law! He's—he's a guest in your country."

"We will be patient, *señora*. He will come to town and maybe bring Alejandro with him. Everything simple then, no?"

"But when will that be?"

"Only *nuestro Señor* knows that."

She wondered if he was stalling for a bribe offer. Maybe he was in touch with Mike, playing both sides. But twice he had spoken piously of "our Lord." A truly religious man wouldn't be for sale.

The *delegado* left, and Luis arrived to pick up her breakfast tray. "Well," he asked, "hwhat do joo doing today?"

"I am sitting today," she said. "By order of the police." He started to leave. "I saw you yesterday at the embarcadero," she said.

"Not Luis," he said emphatically.

"Helping load a boat."

"Oh, *sí!*" he said, as though he had forgotten. He lowered his voice and said, "*Especial* sheepment for Uni' States. Jor favorite fruit!"

"My favorite fruit?"

"Uni' States' favorite fruit." He held his thumb and two fingers to his lips and made a hissing noise. Marijuana? Was that what he meant? It aggravated her that he had taken her into his confidence. Another worry. She already had a full supply.

51

SHE SAT IN the room for two more days, picking at hand-carried meals and trying not to think about Ace. Luis accepted her pencilled cable to Julie—"ALL OKAY. DON'T WORRY. COMING HOME SOON WITH ACE. TELL VAN"—and promised to give it to the driver of the bus for delivery to the telegraph office in Puerto Peñasco. "But I saw a shortwave antenna at the *municipio*," she pleaded.

The clerk hesitated. "Not workeen."

The main trouble with the chubby Luis, she told herself, was that he was always around. Once she opened the door of her room and found him standing in the corridor. "Joo called?" he asked, his face cloaked in innocence.

"No." She slammed the door and regretted it. Was he assigned to watch her? Probably. Then why antagonize him? Would that help her cause?

Her little room had neither air conditioner nor fan, and showers were limited to two five-minute periods a day. Her inner thighs and upper arms itched from prickly heat. While she was dressing after a nap, her foot crunched something inside her blue canvas espadrille. A scorpion dropped out and crawled haphazardly on the hemp rug. Luis advised her to probe her shoes first with a coat hanger. She didn't have the heart to complain about the other occupants of her room: crickets, mosquitoes, roaches that skittered around the shower stall, whirring green-shelled beetles that bounced off her face as she tried to rest.

She dreamed that Luis and the one-eyed cabdriver set off a fumigant bomb on her bed. Mother insects led long parades of babies from holes in the mattress and the walls. Crickets and beetles and flies and mosquitoes dropped from the ceiling, and infant mice dragged their tiny legs behind them as they tried to escape. She woke up and looked at the floor in horror, expecting to find an inch of dead wildlife from wall to wall. Thus she passed her time.

At the end of the third day of waiting she stepped out of

her hothouse room onto the narrow balcony. In the west the sky looked like a sheet of glass splashed with purple ink, but the eastern mountains were exchanging salvos of cadmium scarlet lightning. A few drops of rain spattered into the dust on her narrow slab of porch. She stuck out her hand and caught a drop.

God sent this rain to make me feel at home, she told herself. And maybe to apologize a little. God wants me to be patient, to cooperate with the *delegado*. She went back inside and wondered why God was a male in every culture. *Nuestro Señor*. Sometimes it would be easier to deal with *nuestra Señora*.

The rainfall never developed, and after a while she heard a less welcome sound. She opened the plastic curtains and saw Luis strumming his guitar on the walk by the pool. For an hour words like *corazón, esperanza, mi vida, mi amor* floated up from the steamy courtyard in heart-rending tremolo. If he had to serenade her, she wished he would try something allegretto. She was the last person on earth who needed to hear mournful tunes about broken hearts.

The next morning he was all smiles as he brought her a steaming plate of poached *huachinango* and a tall glass of fresh orange juice. "Joo hear my *serenata?*" he asked.

"Very nice," she said politely.

"I sing for joo," he explained. "Joo are my star. I weel call you Estrella."

"Thank you," she said, picking at the fish. "I will call you Luis."

He leaned slightly forward in a strained fat man's bow. "At the service."

There was no word from the *delegado*.

52

ON THE FOURTH afternoon she changed into shorts, a flowered nylon halter and her tennis hat and took off on a stroll between the dunes. Soon she was on a stretch of beach swept by long lines of breakers that made the stones and sand dollars and shells click together like castanets. She saw clam spouts like the ones at home. The smell of salt and iodine made her gulp. She wondered if she was getting homesick. No. Home was where Ace was.

A frigate bird dived close enough to show its blood red throat and its hooked beak. A flight of pelicans rode the breeze above the waves, rising and falling so that they were always a few feet above the water. She thought of Ace and their mornings by the bay.

Far down the beach the figure of a man came into sight. Even though his face was a dot, she was sure it was the taxi driver. What had Luis called him? "Temo." She wondered how his face had become damaged.

She stopped and looked, then continued on her walk. He kept his distance. She stopped again, and his silhouette disappeared up and over the dune. A few seconds later she caught the glint of sun on glass. She jogged back to the hotel, her bare heels digging into the sand.

The *delegado* was waiting outside her room, his straw hat tipped over his dust-colored face. This time he made no effort to greet her. "I have told you not to leave," he said.

"I just went for a walk," she said, throwing a robe around her bare shoulders.

He followed her inside without an invitation. "Your meals are being sent to your room?"

"Yes."

"Then you have no cause to leave. I order you not to."

"You mean I'm under house arrest?"

"If you like that phrase."

"For what?"

His dark brown eyes narrowed. "If you leave here, I think

263

you maybe try to kidnap your child."

"I won't." She started to promise but held back.

"Please, *señora*. Do not destroy the work I am making."

"You mean you've seen my ex-husband?"

There was a slight pause. "No."

"Then what *are* you doing?"

He was already walking down the hall, his boots pounding the tiles. "Talking," he said over his shoulder.

She closed the door and went to her window. The dunes were deserted. She threw on a robe and went down the hall to check the entrance to the hotel. The Jeep was parked at the curb, the driver slumped behind the wheel as though he had been sitting all day waiting for a fare. There are no fares, she thought. I'm the fare. Is he on permanent call for me?

Footsteps sounded behind her. She turned and saw the woman from the bookstore. "Hello!" Señorita Ortega greeted her. "How are you? I've been in Peñasco."

They walked together to the lobby and sat side by side in cowhide-covered chairs. A beaming Luis brought them steaming cups of *café crema*. Something about the woman elicited trust. "Do you know the taxi driver?" Lael asked in a hushed voice.

"Everybody knows Temo."

Lael started to mention the encounter on the beach but thought better of it. "What happened to him?" she asked out of mild curiosity.

"His face? A gun blew up. He was the best wing shot in Sonora. *Palomas*, doves. Now he is the best taxi driver. Well, tell me, how have you been entertaining yourself?"

"Looking at the cemetery," Lael admitted.

"Didn't you find it interesting? Did you see the antique graves? The English sailor from 1830 with the Bible verse on his stone?"

Stone? She'd seen no stones in the *cementerio*. Or any grave older than a few months. She gasped and covered her mouth with her hand.

"You went to the new one!" the woman said, leaning forward. *"Por Dios,* you must have been shocked."

Lael heard herself ask, "There's another cemetery?"

"Our old one. Todos Santos. On the road to Laguna Gris. We used it till—till there were no more places."

"Are children buried there?"

"Oh, yes."

Lael drank the searing *café* to the bottom. She thought: You've always got a loophole, don't you, God? Something up your sleeve, some little surprise. "Excuse me," she said. "I forgot something."

"You look upset. Did I—?"

"No, no. Thank you." She rushed to her room. It was one-thirty, siesta time. She changed into the most conservative outfit she could find: a sand-colored skirt of light cotton and a long-sleeved high-necked white blouse and a pair of brown De Elisse flats. She dropped her purse in a Bon Marché tote bag and added her Nike running shoes in case she had to cover ground. Halfway out the door she remembered Van's warning about solitary American women in Mexico. She fished the .38 Chief's Special from the bottom of her suitcase.

Through a narrow window she saw that the aquamarine Jeep was still on station. She tiptoed the length of the hall and out the rear exit. Using the bulk of the building as a screen, she hurried to the nearby *funeraria*. If the *delegado* saw her now, what was the worst he could do? Throw her in jail? No punishment could be as painful as sitting around wondering if her son's body was in the earth.

The rear door of the *funeraria* was slightly ajar. She stepped inside and saw a body on the embalming table. She touched its arm, and the funeral director sat straight up. "*¿Cómo?*" he said. When he saw her, he said, "Ah, *buenas tardes*, lady. I was jus' resteen my back."

"The hearse," she said, trying to appear calm and businesslike. "Is it available today?"

"María Madre?" She had forgotten that the old Cadillac had a name. "The holy mother is always for rent," he said. "One t'ousand pesos."

"You said five hundred the other day."

"Eight hundred pesos. *Especial* to you."

She counted out the money and allowed herself to be led through the side door. The place smelled like sandalwood and old feet; there must have been a funeral in the morning. He told her that second gear no longer functioned, but she would find first and third dependable, *más o menos*. "Where do you go?" he asked.

"Oh, around town. See the sights."

"And back by dark, okay? María Madre have no lights. Only candles." He tittered at his little joke.

"Yes, yes. Okay."

The engine pounded as she backed out of the sandy parking space onto the embarcadero. She couldn't imagine a funeral procession led by this belching old wreck. She was convinced that every citizen of Puerto Totuava was already running to report her to the *delegado*. She looked at the dash; the gas tank was full.

At the first intersection she turned right and drove a few blocks till she was on rutted back streets that looked as though they hadn't been used since the *chubasco*. The Cadillac bobbed and wobbled. By dead reckoning she came to the main road north of town and turned inland. She passed the new children's cemetery and continued to the ruins of the *tortilleria*. A tilted sign at a northbound side road said, LAGUNA GRIS. 15 KMS.

The old cemetery was just beyond the first sand hill. An iron fence surrounded the plot. Tombstones and monuments and a few mausoleums were plainly visible.

She parked the hearse and walked under a wrought-iron arch bearing the words *Cementerio Todos Santos*. She studied a few tombstones bearing Mexican names and one with a tilting flat tablet reading "In loving memory John Rawlins Hensley of Fersfield, Norfolk, and Puerto Totuava, died July 6, 1830. He only is my rock and my salvation. Psalms ix II."

It was midafternoon; the sun was falling toward the gulf, but the air was still hot. She looked at a few more tombstones and stopped to fan herself with her hands. The earth at her feet was soft and loose. She dropped to her haunches and realized she was on a fresh grave.

Light rose-colored sunlight filtered through the volcanic dust. Still crouched down, she saw a simple granite tombstone topped by a carved cross. The plot was fringed in ice plant and morning glory, and a cobalt blue vase was stuffed with plastic daisies like the real ones that grew on the bluffs at home. She read, "Alexander C. E. Pritcher, 6 *años. En paz descanse.*"

53

SHE KNELT IN front of the tombstone. Dazed and bewildered, she rubbed hard at the name with her knuckles, but the stonemason had cut deep. A drop of blood seeped from her hand and fell atop her son's grave.

A hollow feeling spread upward from her stomach. She felt as though she would float away like Ace in a dream she had once had. The sky went black, the air cold. She opened her eyes and saw that she was lying on her side in the dust.

She tried to remember where she was. Her bare wrist was inches in front of her eyes. A vein expanded and contracted in spasms. Her skin felt damp, her eyelids heavy. She called weakly, "Van!" but the word died away.

She found herself sitting on the ground. It was as though no time had passed. The cold air had heated up again. Her right cheek was coated with grit. She planted both fists in the warm sand and pushed herself up, embarrassed that someone might have been watching. Her son's name caught her eye.

She jerked backward and looked at the depression in the redbrown earth. "Ace," she whispered. "You're not . . . down there?"

She squeezed her hair into a painful bun. She told herself there'd been a mistake. Children can't be buried until they die. The grave's a fake, a hoax. She looked at the date on her watch. April 1. It was God's idea of an April Fool's joke. How cruel! Or had Mike set the scene to torment her, to drive her back home for good? Anyone could buy a stone and cross.

She dropped to her knees and clawed at the soft sand. It yielded easily. "You're not there," she said as she dug. "DON'T YOU DARE BE THERE, ACEY!"

She tore a nail against a flat surface and flicked away the dirt with her fingers. White Styrofoam came into view. Would it say, "Plastic chaise pad for webbed chaise lounge, made in Calif."? Was that all they could find to bury her baby?

She fell to all fours and pressed her forehead to the plastic lid. It was as close as she could get to him. Then she stood up

and brushed herself off. A vision of Mike Pritcher floated
before her eyes and shut out everything else. She wanted to
scream into his face, "How? *Why?*"

She wondered if it was murder under Mexican law to neglect
a child to death. Why had he been dragged to this Godforsaken
place? *For the fishing?* She thought of his year of rootlessness:
missing his mother and his friends, fighting asthma and loss
and loneliness. Six years old! And at the end . . . an epitaph in
foreign words, a thousand miles from home.

She paced back and forth between the graves, yelling. "You
terrible, horrible, *weak* man! I'll find you, I'll look you straight
in the eye, I'll make you admit what you did." She knew she
was out of control, but it didn't matter now. "You killed our
son. *Murdered* him! You'll be called to account. *Yes, you will!*"

That would be her parting gift to Ace; she hadn't sent flowers. She thought of the gun in her tote bag. "You'll be called
to account, you rotten thing! Now! *Today!*"

She ran through dusty motes of sunlight, every step kicking
up dirt. She climbed in the hearse and slammed the door. All
her emotions had short-circuited into rage. She saw herself
grabbing Mike by the collar and shaking his head till his eye-
balls bulged and his purple tongue rolled around in his mouth.

She talked out loud as she fought the steering wheel on the
soft sand road toward Laguna Gris. "What kind of man would
let his son die to spite his wife? I'll never rest till I find you!
And if you're not at that Laguna place, I'll find you wherever
you are. I'll sell my house, I'll sell my business, I'll sell myself.
I'll never stop. . . ."

The narrow road skirted dunes, low hills of shale and rock,
a few large cardon cactuses standing like guard towers. She
tried to remember what she had heard about the house at Gray
Lagoon. The *delegado* had said it was ten or fifteen kilometers
from the main road. He also had warned her not to attempt the
drive. Why? So far the road was good enough. María Madre's
big balloon tires floated over the sand, the undercarriage clearing the bumps that might have high-centered a smaller car. The
gas needle still pointed to "F."

She wondered when the grief would set in. How would she
handle it? Defiantly, like John Donne? ". . . Death, thou shalt
die." But three hundred years had passed, and death was alive
and well in Mexico.

She drove through a cut in a shale hill, a man-made inden-
tation barely wide enough for the hearse. At the far end she

looked down on a broad vista of sand and dust, salt flats and gulches, grooved and scarred from east to west by the marks of rushing water. Off to the left the gulf licked at the desert in irregular pools and bays. Where was Laguna Gris?

She eased the hearse into first gear and headed into the bottom land. Her eye caught a small brownish cloud a mile or two ahead. At first she thought it was a dust devil, then a galloping horse, and finally realized it was an approaching car. She stopped and rammed the hearse into reverse and backed into the middle of the narrow cut to wait.

She wished she had Van's binoculars. Mike was due for a grocery trip to town, but maybe other people lived in this sandy wilderness. At the least they might be able to point her in the right direction.

Minutes passed. Locked in the narrow pass through the hill, she could make out nothing but sky. She took the pistol from the bottom of her tote bag and laid it on the seat, then tucked her blond hair under a green scarf so she wouldn't be instantly recognizable. Just in case.

"Be Mike," she whispered. "Don't be some damned stranger. *Be Mike!*" She wondered if he'd seen her car. Would he turn and go back to Laguna Gris? She would wait a few more minutes and give chase. Sooner or later he would run out of gas or road.

A vision of Ace's body in his new blue suit passed before her eyes. The shock was so intense she couldn't catch her breath. She screamed and started breathing again.

Don't think about him, she ordered herself. There is something you *must* do. Mourning comes later.

She wondered if she should rev up María Madre and head into the valley. No! Hidden in the middle of the pass, she had the advantage of surprise.

A dust cloud boiled up at the entrance. A car materialized in the swirls of sand and dirt and slid to a halt inches from her bumper.

A yellow Escort.

She slid down in the seat so that only her eyes and forehead showed above the windshield.

A man's voice yelled, "Hey! What—"

She pressed the horn. She knew the effect the reverberating blast would have on an immature man like Mike.

The Escort's front door opened, and he jumped out. He was slender and sunburned and wore a typical peasant's straw hat tied at the back with a cord. His shirt was a thin white *camisa*, his pants tattered chinos, his shoes huaraches with thick soles.

He sauntered toward the hearse. She opened the door a crack and held her left hand on the handle and her right on the gun. When he was six or eight feet away, she jumped out and yelled, "Stop!"

"What—?"

"Stop!" Her gun hand wavered, and she supported it with the other.

"Lael!" a high-pitched voice called from the car. "What—what are *you* doing here?" The dry, flat tones were unmistakable.

Before she could answer, Mike shuffled forward. "For Christ's sake, Lael," he snapped, "put that thing down before you hurt somebody."

"If you take one more step," she said, "I'll shoot you." She called to the car, "Catherine? Come out!"

The woman climbed slowly into sight, thin lips twitching, pale blue-gray eyes fixed on the gun. She wore a thin sundress that showed her sinewy arms and legs. She looked like a Bouvier sister in advanced age: all bone and ligaments and tan.

When mother and son stood side by side, Lael said very slowly, "Why did you steal my son?"

Mike glanced at his mother as though expecting her to answer. When she didn't, he said, "It was, uh, it was best for him."

Lael fought to maintain her self-control. She knew she was trembling but hoped it didn't show. *"Best for him?* You can still say that?"

"What does that mean?" the mother asked.

"I found the grave."

Mike's eyes widened. "We were—we were going to tell you," he sputtered. "It's just that . . . it's hard to reach you from here." One of his sandals inched forward. "Come on, Lael," he said soothingly. "Let's talk." He stretched out his palm for the gun. "This is no way."

"I told you to stop," she said in an even voice. Slowly she raised the heavy pistol. "Now *stop!*"

He moved. She aimed at his face and fired.

The kick jerked her gun hand upward and the explosion rang in her ears. The bullet lifted a dusting of rock just behind Mike's head. Mother and son reeled backward, hands outstretched.

"Don't, Lael, *don't!*" the woman yelled. In a loud aside to her son, she said, "For God's sake, don't antagonize her. She's crazy."

"That's right, Catherine," Lael said, lowering the weapon. "If you're sane, I'm crazy."

Mike spoke from behind open hands thrown up in front of his mouth. "It's not the way it looks," he called out, twisting his body sideways. "Come on, sweetie, give us a chance. You're not yourself. You're—"

"Crazy?" she said.

The mother pulled her gray skirt below her knees in an odd show of modesty and said, "Lael . . . please."

"Do what I tell you," she said. "I won't miss the next time." Nothing mattered, neither their lives nor hers. She knew what the Chief's Special could do; Mike had shown her how it splintered two-inch planks. Thanks for the training, she said to herself. Thanks for being so paranoid about the muggers and rapists and robbers that don't exist on our island. At last your paranoia makes sense. Because in a few minutes I'm going to commit the most moral, responsible act of my life. I'm going to kill you both.

"Lie on your stomachs," she ordered.

"Lael," Mike pleaded, "you don't understand—"

"I do understand. That's the trouble." She stepped closer. "Turn over!"

"Lael, don't!" Catherine begged again. "Listen, there's something—"

Mike started to interrupt, but his mother stretched out her bony hand and gripped his arm. "Lael, please, look inside our car," she said.

Why? she asked herself. What could be in the car? Her gunsight tracked the cowering figures as she stepped sideways toward the Escort. "If you move," she said, "I'll shoot."

"We know," Mike said in a small voice. "We understand."

She peered through a grimy rear window. A Mexican boy in short pants and white *camisa* was sprawled on a sleeping bag on the storage deck. He looked like a photographic negative of Ace. His face was the color of melted caramel. His eyebrows and lashes were so bleached by the sun they were almost invisible. He wore a baseball cap.

"Who—" she started to ask. The boy turned from her and buried his face in the sleeping bag. She opened the rear-deck door and reached inside. The skin around his ankle was cold.

He jerked his bare foot away. "Don't," he said weakly. Her jaw sagged at the sound of his voice, and she almost dropped the gun.

Out of the corner of her eye she saw movement. "Get down!" she yelled, waving the muzzle. Mike subsided to a sitting position. *"All the way!"* she said, punching the gun toward him as though it were a club. He lay in the dust beside his mother, and their fingers joined.

Lael opened the car door. "Come out," she said.

The boy obeyed stiffly, as though leaving a sickbed. When he stood before her, she reached out slowly and raised his hat. His short, curly hair was such a vivid white that it made him look like a shriveled old man. He held his skinny forearm in front of his face as though expecting to be hit. A thin line of perspiration dappled his upper lip. He was wheezing.

"Ace," she whispered.

The brown eyes widened. He raised both hands and turned away. She took his wrist with her free hand. He started to cry. "Don't you know me?" she asked.

He gave no sign of recognition. "Are you...gonna ...hurt...me?" he asked in a shaky voice. His sobs came in short gasps, as though he lacked the strength to cry normally.

"No," she said. "Never. Is that what they told you?"

Mike called out, "We didn't—"

"SHUT UP! I'm talking to my son!" She let him sit on the tailgate and turned toward the others. "You don't have to explain how you treated him," she said. "It's all on his face. You went to a lot of trouble, didn't you? Why? Why the grave and the tomb and—and the daisies?"

Mike gave her the tight-lipped look that she knew so well from the days when he neither apologized nor explained. She walked toward him till she was a few feet away and lowered her voice so the boy couldn't hear. "Tell me right now, or I'll shoot you in the ear."

"I—I—"

"For God's sake, tell her!" the woman croaked.

He mumbled a few inaudible words. "What?" Lael insisted, *"Speak up!"*

"I said we had to."

"Had to?" She kicked him in the bare shin as hard as she could. "Why?"

"We—we knew you'd never stop looking."

She was still confused. "But how? I mean, a grave and a casket?"

He held up the fingers of his free hand and rubbed them with his thumb.

"Who did you buy?" she asked. "The funeral director? The *delegado?*"

"Everyone's for sale," he muttered.

"Not everyone," she said. She had a sickening thought. "Who's in that grave?"

She couldn't hear his answer. She yelled, "Who's in that grave?" and drew back as though to kick him again.

In a low voice he answered, "Nobody. A Mexican kid. Just a body we, uh, bought."

"A body you *bought?*"

"There were plenty."

She looked at Ace. He had wriggled back on the sleeping bag and stopped crying. His head bobbed up and down as he breathed in puffs. She looked down at the other two: Madonna and Child. Catherine whimpered, and Mike rubbed the back of her hand. "Don't worry, Mother," he said. "Lael wouldn't hurt us."

She stared at the two weak faces that had flitted though her nightmares for a year. She had already executed them a thousand times. Once more shouldn't be hard.

Mike wiped his mother's sweating forehead with the sleeve of his white shirt. They seemed such weak, pathetic figures. Running so far, and to such an inhospitable place. Bleaching Ace's hair. Lying. Going to so much trouble to throw her off. Why? In furtherance of what? She wished she didn't need to understand. Hatred and revenge were so much simpler.

She felt the weight of the gun. Wedged in her fingers, it looked like a prop in a cheap movie. She had to fight the feeling that she had drifted into another dream. Everything had changed so fast. She was with Ace. Everything was new again.

She reached inside the Escort and pulled the hood latch. The distributor cap came off with a twist, and she dropped it in her pocket.

"Hold Mommy's hand," she told her son.

He didn't respond. She reached inside the Escort and eased his skinny body out. She took another look at the cringing figures in the sand and led her son away.

Catherine called out, "You—you hate us, don't you?" Lael almost laughed. It struck her as the last word in fatuous Pritcher remarks. Maybe she should apologize for inconveniencing them.

"You're not worth hating," she said.

She opened the Cadillac door and gave Ace a boost.

"What are you doing?" Mike asked.

She raised the revolver and sighted on his face. The range was six or eight feet. She held the heavy lump steady for several seconds and then lowered it. "Think of yourselves as dead," she said. "That's what you'll be if you ever come near us again."

She twisted the key. The old V-12 sputtered and coughed and settled down to a rackety drone. She backed forty or fifty feet till the car was below the lip of the cut, then waited a few seconds and drove straight toward the Pritchers.

They lay face-down, still holding hands. The life seemed squeezed from them. They were so flattened to the dirt that they put her in mind of cutout dolls.

As she rammed the hearse into reverse again, she saw the woman glance backward. There was a look in her eyes, abject, pitiable. Lael recognized the look of defeat. Mike lay so still that he looked dead. In a way, he was.

She drove out of the cut and turned toward town.

54

SHE WONDERED WHAT awaited her in Puerto Totuava. The Pritchers might be defeated, but the *delegado* wasn't. That hard, unyielding man had given her strict orders not to leave the hotel. She remembered everything Van had told her about Mexican justice. The *delegado* might throw her in jail, and where would Ace be when she finally got out? With the Pritchers. Mike had bought a child's dead body; he would be willing to pay dearly for his own son.

She checked the fuel gauge again; the needle was on F. Ace seemed lost at the edge of the worn leather seat, as far away as he could get. His head drooped sideways. His brown eyes under his strange white brows peered at her in fright. She wondered how long he would consider her a threat. Forever? She leaned across the seat and listened for a few seconds. His breathing was still jerky.

As she steered María Madre around a dune, he shuddered the length of his body. She stopped and turned off the ignition. His eyes were closed, and he was panting. It took her a long time to find his pulse, fluttery and weak. How long had he been like this? *God damn those awful people!*

She had to risk driving back to the hotel for his nebulizer and the bottle of epinephrine tablets. Why hadn't she had the sense to carry them with her? From now on she would carry extra inhalers. A year of untreated asthma was enough. If his heart wasn't damaged already. . . .

They passed the old cemetery and reached the road that led back to town. A small brown boy who looked popped from a toaster waved at the car and smiled. Another survivor. Father in heaven, she prayed to herself, help me get my own survivor home safely, just lead us to the border, God, and I'll do the rest. You'll never have to lift a finger for me again.

She tried to decide what to do after she picked up the medicine. Could they make an escape in this old heap? Without lights? She was beginning to realize that the gas gauge would always register full. Where could she buy more?

She looked at her watch: ten after six. The funeral director wouldn't be expecting her for another three hours. If no one sounded the alarm, they could be miles away by then, headed— where?

The only feasible escape route was north to Puerto Peñasco. She wished she'd paid more attention on the bus ride. All she remembered were switchbacks and detours and swales of sand and salt. How could she find the way?

The black roof of the hearse absorbed the late afternoon sun, and engine heat poured through the fire wall. She looked upward through the cracked windshield; the sky was the deepest blue, almost ultramarine. The color seemed silly, a flagrant mistake. On a day like this the sky should be a fiery scarlet, with sparks and flames and smoke. Then this heat would make sense.

She thought of Mike and his mother, stranded in the open. *My God, I aimed at him and fired! I tried to kill Mike!*

She told herself it was a case of temporary insanity. What if she'd shot straight? One of Ace's parents would be dead and the other on the way to prison. That would leave . . . Catherine. Thank you, God, she said. Oh, thank you for jerking my hand.

The town looked empty as she steered the big car along the gouged-out back streets. She passed the *funeraria* and turned into the long lane that led to the hotel entrance. She had reached the next to last tamarack when she saw a mottled red Ford lurching to a stop at the porte-cochere.

She yanked the wheel sharply and U-turned across the divider. Had the *delegado* come to arrest her? She sped past the *municipio* with its roof cluster of antennas and suddenly realized what must have happened. Mike's CB radio. One of his toys. She hadn't disabled enough of his car.

At the next intersection she turned into a side street. Something caught her eye. A car was a block or two behind. She floored the bare-metal accelerator, and the hearse rocked along deserted streets as lumpy as creek beds between rows of windowless one-story houses in faded pastels. Dying vines hung in tatters. There were no yards and no people. These must have been the homes of those who'd fled. Or died. How lucky that Ace had survived.

She glanced at him as she fought the mushy steering. He was taking shallow breaths, interrupted by shudders. He started to sniffle but apparently didn't have enough strength. "Ace," she said, "don't be afraid. Mommy'll take care of you." She wished she knew how.

The engine sounded like cannon fire. The speedometer registered "o," but the Cadillac was doing about thirty-five. Top speed. She made a wide, sliding turn onto the road that led out of town. A pair of hogs grazed on the shoulder ahead. She couldn't risk hitting one. What had the guidebooks said? "If the animal's head is lowered, it probably won't step into the road. If its head is raised, look out!"

She slowed and passed safely. In her mirror she caught a flash of blue or aquamarine. The *delegado's* Ford was a splotchy red. Maybe this was his deputy. Did he have deputies? Ace started to cry.

"Sleep, baby," she said softly, hoping that her tone and her voice would touch something deep in his memory. His brown eyes slowly closed. She pulled his head and shoulders toward her so that he lay crosswise on the seat. He didn't resist. She wondered if he was becoming reconciled to her or just growing weaker. She heard his wheezing over the engine.

They bumped past the ruins of the *tortilleria*, crossed a long stretch of salt-streaked lowland and turned north into the devastated region of the flood. The bluish car was no longer in sight; she was thankful for one less aggravation. But the road presented problems.

It wasn't a single track but three or four, all more or less parallel, all rejoining when the newest washout or dune or pileup of flood debris had been by-passed. Sometimes she lucked into the right choice; sometimes she had to jam on the brakes at a gulch or a wall and back out to try a different fork. She was constantly hauling on the wooden steering wheel to avoid deep sand traps and swerving around uprisings of shale and rock.

She passed a warning sign bent almost to the ground. She twisted her head and read: CAMINO SINUOSO. She sighed. It was *camino sinuoso* all the way to Puerto Peñasco; why single out this stretch? Another sign said, NO HAY PASO. Don't pass what? she wondered. There were no vehicles in sight. She double-checked in the mirror. A swirl of dust appeared about a hundred yards back.

A high dune with wisps of fine sand curling from its ridge loomed straight ahead, and the road forked and went around it on both sides. She took the right fork and almost drove into an arroyo. She tried to make a U-turn and realized there wasn't enough room, threw María Madre into reverse, and plowed backward through the sand till she noticed that her rear-view mirror was filled with blue.

The taxi driver's aqua Jeep blocked the road. Sweat glistened on the wreckage of his face. She grabbed the gun. *Why didn't this creature mind his own business?* Now she would have to kill a human being. Could she? No. Not even for Ace. The shot at Mike had been an aberration, an act born of despair and desperation.

But she could try another bluff.

He walked toward her in runty steps and kept jabbing a finger at himself as though insisting that she get out of the hearse and join him.

Her finger slid back and forth along the crosshatch pattern on the trigger. Would a warning shot fend him off? Or just make matters worse? Ace sat straight up, his dark eyes open wide. She pushed her door open and stood behind it for cover.

The man was a few feet away, smiling with his twisted face. She raised the pistol and said, "Stop!"

He stopped and squinted out of one green eye. "No, *señora,*" he said, tilting his head quizzically.

"Get that Jeep out of my way! ¡Vamos! ¡Andale!"

He turned slowly, as though to obey, and then flung himself backward at the heavy door. She was knocked to the sand, and he was on her before she could twist away.

She clawed at his face, punched, tried to bite his wrists, but his knees pressed down on her upper arms and immobilized her. "No, no, *señora,*" he repeated, as though making a polite request.

She spotted the gun a few feet away. He grabbed it and flung it halfway up the dune. *"No quiero pistolas,"* he said.

She twisted and heaved and couldn't move. He was small but wiry. She tried to kick him, but her legs wouldn't reach. She was finished. The gun had been her only chance.

The man spoke rapidly. She had heard him talk both English and Spanish and barely understood him in either. *"¡Vamonos!"* he said in that strange muffled voice that seemed to come from his throat instead of his mouth. He pointed to his Jeep.

She turned her head in the sand and saw Ace watching from the driver's seat of the hearse. He looked like a long-distance runner at the finish line. *"Sí, sí, vamonos,"* she said. At least they could get him some medicine.

The cabdriver picked up the child as though he were a doll. "Joo in front!" he said to Lael, and yanked open the door of his Jeep. The floor was gritty with sand, the seat a mass of lumps. He laid Ace's limp body in her arms.

Her mind raced. She abandoned escape plans one after another. Without a vehicle or a gun she was helpless. She decided to try another tack: She would beg; she would implore; she would promise the *delegado* money or whatever he wanted if he would just let her take her papers and her son before a judge. If justice were for sale in this country, she would give every cent she had to buy her share—and her son's.

"*¡Abajo!*" the man said, pointing at the bare floor. Why did he want them to get down? Was he afraid they might encounter a *federal* or a highway policeman, some legitimate law officer who would come to their aid? She slid to the floorboards and pulled Ace with her. Peeking out the sides of the open Jeep, she tensed for the sight of a passing car.

Soon she noticed that they had turned onto a narrow, bumpy road. They drove across gray-white sand through stunted brush and saw grass till they came to a shack on stilts. The surf crashed nearby. A bare yard was littered with tires and two abandoned automobiles. The Jeep pulled into a shed of woven reeds and stopped.

"*Mi casa,*" the driver said politely. "Please. Joo sit."

A green-eyed woman with a thin face walked down a ribbed wooden gangplank and listened with tilted head as the man spoke in Spanish. Lael remembered reading about a nomadic race of Mexican Indians with clear green eyes, hunters and fishermen of the gulf, lately reduced to poverty. The man took the woman by the hand, led her to Lael and said, "*Mi esposa,*" as though introducing her at a formal affair.

"*Gracias,*" Lael said, not knowing the correct response.

"*Mucho gusto,*" the woman said. "Joo come een?" She tittered with embarrassment as she spoke. Two thick auburn braids dangled down the back of her unadorned cotton dress.

The cabdriver reached into the Jeep and gently lifted Ace. "*Mi hijo,*" Lael said, remembering the word for "son" from another time.

"*¡Güero!*" the woman cried, touching the child's blond hair, "*¡Un ángel de cielo!*" She pointed up the rickety gangplank. Lael supposed they were going to be held in the shack till the *delegado* came. Or Mike. She wondered why the cabdriver hadn't driven them straight to the *municipio*. Her hand reached out to touch her son. These might be their last minutes together. They climbed the ramp like refugees.

The interior was nearly dark. When her eyes adjusted she saw that the walls were of driftwood and the roof of tar paper and palm fronds. One narrow window was fashioned from flat scraps of broken glass, another from bottle bottoms. An adobe oven was slightly ajar; a jungle cock peeked inside as though looking at its future. The air hung heavy with smoke.

The woman unrolled a straw mat, and her husband put Ace on it. She disappeared down the stairs and returned with a Coke bottle full of water. *"¡Fría!"* she said, sprinkling the child's forehead. He drew a deep breath, his eyes squeezing shut and his chin wobbling from the effort. A few small children entered the house, and the woman shooed them out.

Lael reached in her tote bag and pulled out her University of Chicago paperback dictionary. *"Mi hijo,"* she said, frantically turning pages by the light of a candle, *"el es . . . enfermo. Muy enfermo. El . . .* must have *medicina."*

The woman said, *"¿Estómago?"*

"No, no," Lael said impatiently. "Not stomach." She raced through the pages. There was no entry for "asthma." She held her hands on her chest and made a wheezing sound.

"Ah, *sí!*" the woman said, her slender brown hands covering gaunt cheekbones. *"¡Pulmonia!"*

"No!" Lael said, and wheezed again for lack of a better idea.

"Asma," the husband said softly. No wonder it hadn't been in the dictionary. It sounded the same as in English.

"Quiero medicina," Lael said. She thanked God that Fodor's had taught her the all-purpose verb that meant "I want," "I like," "I need," "I love"— indispensable. *"Muy importante,"* she added.

The couple chattered together. She understood the main point: The drugstore was *cerrado*. She looked at her watch: 7:35. Didn't the stores stay open late? Then she realized that the drugstore was probably boarded up like most of the other shops along the embarcadero. A nebulizer and a bottle of epinephrine lay in her room at the hotel, but how could she get them? Any second now the *delegado* would be arriving. She would beg him to give Ace his medicine before he took them away.

She leaned over the sleeping child and listened to his breathing. His skin was cool. Oh, God, she said to herself, don't let him be dying. He gave a sudden jerk. She hoped he wasn't starting to convulse. If she could only get him to a hospital, or a doctor, or even a *farmacia*.

The cabdriver pointed to her tote bag and rattled off a long phrase in Spanish. When she shrugged, he said, "No got *medicina?*"

"*Sí,*" she said. "*En hotel.*"

"*¿Hotel?*"

"*¡Sí!*" Frantically she tried to make him understand. "*¡Sí! Medicina* es en mi, uh, room." She pointed to herself. "*Medicina es* on *mi* dresser."

The couple looked blank. Lael walked across the room to a pair of stacked orange crates and mimed opening and closing drawers.

"*¡Sí!*" the wife said. "*Medicina en hotel en cómoda.*"

"No!" Lael said. "On . . . dresser."

"*¡Comprendo, comprendo!*" the woman said, and spoke to her husband in Spanish. He hurried down the stairs, and a few seconds later she heard the Jeep pull away. Was it possible?

Three or four green-eyed children climbed into the house and stared at the visitors. "*Hora de dormir, niños,*" the mother said, waving them out. Lael looked through a slit in the wall. One by one the children lay down on the seats of the abandoned cars.

She wondered what was happening. Was this little family planning to shelter her and Ace? Why? A piglet waddled up the incline and into the room, looked around, and vanished behind a cardboard box. She looked at her son, sprawled on a mat, his nose bent against his thin tanned forearm. How long could he keep breathing this dense, smoky air? Everything about him showed signs of neglect, if not abuse. He was thinner than he had been a year before, and he hadn't grown an inch. How could a man do this to his own son, or a woman to her own grandchild?

After thirty or forty minutes she heard a burst of engine noise. The cabdriver ran into the room and blew out the two candles on the table. "*¡Silencio!*" he whispered.

Another car drove up, stopped for a few seconds, then sped on with a clash of gears. When the sound had died away, Temo relit one of the candles and extracted two small packages from the pockets of his worn jacket. His crooked face was set in a smile as he handed them over. "How did you do it?" she said, forgetting that he barely spoke English.

He smiled but didn't answer. She ripped the cardboard from the nebulizer package and inserted the neck of the pressurized bottle into the plastic mouthpiece. "Ace," she said. "Open, angel."

His eyes rolled in his head as if he were beyond hearing. "Ace!" she said.

His little rose lips parted lazily. She slipped the beige plastic in his mouth and pressed. Wisps of vapor drifted from his lips. Wasted. He was too weak to time the inhalation. She squeezed off another tiny cloud. This time he breathed some of it down. "Please," she said. "Some water. *Aqua*."

The husband went outside and returned with an inch of brownish fluid in a dipper. She wondered if it was safe. She didn't want to hurt the man's feelings, but she didn't want to poison her son either. When he turned away, she pretended to take a drink and set the dipper down so that the water spilled through the floorboards. She opened the bottle of epinephrine tablets and shook one out. "Ace," she said. "Here!"

It had always been a fight to get him to take the bitter white pills, even with orange juice. "Make some spit!" she commanded. "You've got to get this down."

He grimaced and swallowed. Within minutes his eyes closed, and he dropped off to sleep. His breathing was almost regular.

A siren howled in the distance. It veered close and then continued down the beach. "*Delegado* lookeen," Temo said. "Him lookeen till berry dark. *¡Entonces ... nosotros nos fuimos!*"

So the *delegado* would look till it was very dark. But what did those other words mean? Somebody was going somewhere? But who? "After dark, we go?" she asked, making her fingers walk across her palm.

"*Sí señora*," the man said, his good eye glittering in the candlelight. "*Nosotros*." His circling hand marked out himself and Ace and Lael.

"Where? Uh, *donde?*"

"*A Puerto Peñasco. Es muy seguro en Peñasco*."

Seguro seguro. . . . She found it in the little dictionary between *segundo* and *selección*. They would be "safe" in Puerto Peñasco? Maybe Temo was a "coyote"—a smuggler of wetbacks. Maybe he would leave them in the desert for the buzzards. She was carrying more than $1,000 in cash. But he had driven to town for the child's medicine, apparently at great personal risk. Would he have bothered if he intended to rob and kill them?

Once she would have assumed that his act of mercy validated his status as a decent human being. She would have trusted him with her own life, her son's. Now she assumed nothing.

"Joo slip," the woman said, pushing her gently backward by the shoulder.

"Gracias," Lael said. "I sleep."

She lay back and listened to Ace's breathing. It was slightly fast, the normal reaction to the drug. He would breathe easily for a few hours, and then she would have to give him more. When they got home, he would resume his shot program and hardly need the drug. He had been almost free of asthma when Mike had taken him away.

She put her arm around his shoulders. "Thank you, God," she whispered. "I'd almost forgotten how this feels."

The room grew dark. Something rustled in the palm roof. A rat? A bat? A *snake?* She couldn't sleep anyway. Soon she became aware of a glow in the far corner. She heard voices and propped herself on an elbow.

Temo and his wife knelt in front of a guttering stump of candle set in a reddish glass that looked as though it had once done duty in a bar. The ruby light shone on a cardboard triptych of photographs. She squinted to see. Even from ten or twelve feet she could tell that the pictures had been poorly retouched. The twin boys' cheeks were too roundly red, their hair unnaturally blueblack, and their lips bright carmine slits, but they had the green eyes and the thin facial features of the woman. Had the man looked like that once? It was impossible to tell. A line of gold plastic stick-on letters had been pasted above the pictures: JUAN Y EZEKIEL BUSTAMENTE. 5 AÑOS. EN PAZ DESCANSE.

She eased herself back down on the mat without making a sound. What a heavy name for two dead little boys. She tried it on her tongue: Bus-ta-*men*-te. It sounded like an oath, or a threat. She thought she remembered the name from somewhere. Was it in the new graveyard with all those other Spanish names?

Juan y Ezekiel Bustamente. . . . *Yes.* The last grave in the last row. The names the driver had read to her before he'd led her away. That was why he'd cried.

The woman's voice rose in a keening monotone: *"En el nombre del padre, del hijo y del espíritu santo. . . ."* The couple unlocked hands and embraced briefly, the man's brown hand resting lightly on his wife's back.

Lael waited for them to part and called softly, *"¡Por favor? Juan and Ezekiel, es el—?"* She realized she was asking, "Is he?" and stopped herself. How to say "are they?" She began again in English. "The *niños*. Are they . . . were they—"

"Nuestro angeles," the woman said, the planes of her narrow face shadowed in the candlelight. *"Nuestro hijos."*

"Our *bebés*," the man translated.

Lael didn't know what to say. "I'm sorry," she said at last. "I'm so sorry." She wished she knew the words in Spanish.

The cabdriver touched his wife on the cheek and called across the room, *"Buenas noches, señora. Buenas noches,* Ace. Soon we go."

Far off in the Mexican night a trumpet played—thin, pure, silvery notes in the highest register—and a few minutes later a basso sang from the direction of the beach, his voice receding in the distance bellowing, *"Soy puro mexicano. . . ."*

How far it seemed from their island and their own beach house. Oh, Ace, she said under her breath, we're *so* lucky, my baby. She thought of the twins in the triptych. Even a robust name like Bustamente couldn't save them.

He stirred and said something she couldn't hear. She hoped it had been "Mommy," but she was afraid not. "Daddy," more likely. Or "Grandmom." But you'll always be my *bebé*, she murmured into his ear. Her nose twitched and her head slumped backward and her eyes half closed at the sweaty small-boy smell. The sweetest perfume. His room used to reek of it.

55

THEY DROVE AWAY in the still midnight air. Ace sat in front, on the ragged seat with the springs poking up. At Temo's wife's insistence, the child was wrapped in an old blanket and a serape and secured in the seat by a loose nylon rope looped through his belt. Lael sat behind him on the flat board seat as the old Jeep crept past the town limits. He still wasn't responding, but he seemed to pay attention when she spoke.

When they passed the big dune where the cabdriver had intercepted her, she saw that María Madre was gone. She wondered if that meant there would be a roadblock ahead: a shout, gunshots, flashlights stabbing the night, the end of her time with Ace.

They descended into the broad floodlands. The Jeep's weak headlights sent jerky cones of yellowish light fifteen or twenty feet ahead, but the moon bathed the ravaged landscape and highlighted the obstacles as the driver pulled and hauled at the wheel. *"La luna,"* he said, jouncing in his seat and pointing upward. "Suntine God help. No?"

Yes, she thought. Suntine. . . .

After a few hours they began climbing the small mountain range between the two Puertos. The temperature dropped sharply. The open car moved in a cloud of fine dust; she had swallowed so much that she knew there must be a wet clump of it in her stomach. She fitted a handkerchief over Ace's nose and mouth. "Baby," she asked when his eyes opened, "are you okay?"

He inhaled deeply and nodded. His asthma was kicking up again. The dust. It was too soon for more epinephrine.

Just before dawn the Jeep lost its footing on a steep sandy hill and skidded slantwise, its wheels spinning wildly. Temo alternated reverse and forward, but the treadless tires dug in till the underside was almost afloat on the sand.

She jumped out. There was a flinty chill to the desert air, but she could imagine what would happen to Ace if they were stuck here through the heat of the day. "I help?" she asked the driver.

"Ees okay," he said, unclamping a spade from the rear of the Jeep. She watched as the thin brown arms pumped in the fading moonlight. When the sand had been cleared from each wheel, he began to fumble with his pants. *"Excusa, señora,"* he said, turning his back. *"Es necesario."* He went from tire to tire, urinating in the track, whistling *"Cielito Lindo."* Then he disappeared for a few minutes and returned with an armload of mesquite. He motioned her into the car and spread the brush on the dark wet patches in front of the wheels.

He raised his head to the sky, shouted *"¡Por favor, Señor!"* and crossed himself. The jeep crawled over the dune on the first try.

The sun came up, and she picked out a few familiar landmarks. She knew they couldn't be far from Puerto Peñasco, but even on flat stretches Temo drove slowly. Maybe he was stalling to rendezvous with rapists or robbers—or cops. No, that was unfair. If he'd intended to turn them in, he could have done it a long time ago. Anyway, there was nothing she could do about it. They were in his hands.

At a few minutes before nine in the morning the smoky swirls of civilization appeared in the distance. "Peñasco," he said over his shoulder. *Seguro, seguro,* she repeated to herself. Can it really be true?

They passed a wrecked shrimper that had been thrown up on the beach. A string of wash hung from its decks, and a man stood in the wheelhouse as though steering. She was still looking back over her shoulder when the Jeep lurched and she was almost thrown out. She reached for Ace, but he was secured by his nylon rope.

"What—" she asked.

"¡Mira, Mira!" Temo yelled. *"¡Policia!"*

At the beginning of a curve ahead, she saw a pair of black and white cars nose to nose across the highway. She lost sight of them as the Jeep careened down a dirt road and began a zigzag run through corrals and meadows.

"¡Prestar atención!" he said, pointing to his ear. She listened. The sirens were close.

They cut through an alley and a parking lot and slowed to a stately pace at an open area where hundreds of people milled about. The sirens were loud as he grunted, "Take *niño*! Stay *mercado*. I come."

He almost shoved them out of the taxi and disappeared in a cloud of bluish smoke. She picked up Ace and her tote bag and ran into the shelter of the crowd. Children sucked on plastic bags of colored ice. An old crone in a gray dress rubbed Ace's head. *"¡Güero, güero!"* she said excitedly. *"¡Buena suerte!"* Others crowded around to share in the good-luck ritual, and Lael hustled him away. In the shadows between two market stalls she bound his hair in her kerchief, exposing her own.

"We have to walk," she told him. "The bad guys are after us." Mike's sick game. Maybe it would work.

She dragged him along, and he began to lift his feet. She wondered how much of his reluctance to cooperate was mental. From his viewpoint he was in the care of an evil person who wanted to hurt him. Why should he help? She hoped to God he didn't start screaming for his dad or the police.

They followed the crowd past displays of used bicycles, ironing boards, high chairs, repainted tires, ball-point pens, tool sets and typewriters and gewgaws and junk. Loudspeakers screamed for attention. A swarthy man with a silver microphone the size of a quarter taped to his throat yelled, *"¡Tenga! Tenga, señora!"* and pushed plastic statues of the Virgin at dark-eyed women from an Orozco mural.

Two cars pulled up at the end of the row. Men in sharply raked brown caps and light brown uniforms and jodhpurs strode into the crowd. She dragged Ace around the back of a stand displaying used shoes painted a shiny black. In the shade alongside a hardscrabble roadway a baby cooed in a cart. She pulled Ace down and draped the serape high across their faces. After a while she felt the vibrations of a heavy vehicle inching up the road. The sound stopped and a voice called in a loud whisper, *"Señora!"*

She peeked out and saw Temo waving them aboard the tailgate of a truck. A thin leering face, all teeth and black mustache, looked down from the vibrating cab. She read the inscription on the bumper, "AGUILAR." She wondered: eagle— or coyote?

She handed Ace to Temo and scrambled aboard. He pulled up the tailgate and jerked the canvas closed. The air smelled of onions and peppers and overripe produce. She wondered what the truck's next payload would be. Two *norteamericanos*? Was that a richer cargo than a truckload of vegetables?

After a short rumbling run they stopped. Temo put his finger to his lips and motioned for them to stay. With a twist of his narrow body he disappeared over the tailgate. She looked at Ace's face. He was watching her shyly through heavy lids.

His pulse showed in his temple. It looked normal.

They waited and waited. When the child started to cough, she touched a finger to his mouth. The air grew so hot and close she had the feeling she was part of a Spanish omelet. Ace seemed to suffer less. The latest dose of medicine had helped. He sat against an empty crate marked "GONZÁLES— *Las Mejores Cebollas,*" his nose twitching, his eyes opening and shutting in catnaps. "Stay quiet, angel," she whispered in his ear. "Mommy's here."

She wished she knew where they were, what they were waiting for, but she didn't dare peek. She guessed they were parked at a curb. In the hot gray silence, she picked out sounds: the soft slap-slap of someone nearby making tortillas, the clip-clop of a horse on hard ground, a high-pitched voice shouting, *"¡Dulces! ¡Helados! ¡Dulces!"* Bells pealed in the distance, and repeated an hour later. A chicken squawked from under the truck as though laying a large egg. Flies buzzed in and out, and she shooed them away. Over everything was the national smell of Mexico: smoke from burning wood and burning dumps and burning papers and burning bones and burning tires, smoke from charcoal racks and hot engines and adobe ovens and charred fields and trains and buses and boats. She had encountered the smell at the border and ever since. It would always be Mexico to her.

She remembered reading about a "coyote" who had left a truckload of wetbacks to broil to death in Texas. She looked at her watch: four forty-five. How much longer should they wait before making a run for it? The tailgate rattled, and a brown hand appeared. The truck driver vaulted inside.

"I am Miguel," he said, and stuck out a thin hand with fingers like sticks. "We go now. Do you feenk joo can help a leetle wit' the gas?"

"Help?"

"Dinero," he said, holding out his hand.

"Uh, yes. Of course."

She lifted her purse from the tote bag and counted out $200. The thin-faced man looked into her wallet. She hoped this didn't mean their bones would mulch the desert.

"Good," he said. *"Muchas gracias."* She had the impression that he had expected a smaller contribution and that she had blundered by exposing her treasury. He parted the canvas flaps and started to climb down.

She called softly, "Where is Temo?" as though to remind

him that at least one other person knew their whereabouts.

"The *federales* find his Jeep," the driver said. "Take him away. He say tell you *adios* and good lock." She thought of the wife with the long auburn braids, the children sleeping outside in the cars, the dead twins.

"I'm sorry," she said.

Miguel nodded and disappeared. The gearbox clanked and ground, and the truck inched away, but before long it stopped again. "Joo leave," the driver said. "We load now."

He helped her to the dirt floor of an enclosed shed. The walls were stacked with bulging plastic bags. He handed Ace down and led them into a small office decorated with a picture of the three wise men and a full-frontal nude with tawny breasts the size of footballs.

As the driver left, he locked the door. She remembered Van's warning about Mexicans. What would he think now? She was reasonably sure that the bulging bags weren't full of rosemary or valerian or lady's-mantle leaves. She felt no fear for herself, but her knees turned to water when she thought what these strangers might do to a helpless child. She rapped on the glass to call the man back. "Will you do something for me?" she said as he opened the door.

"Een a hurry, lady," he said.

She reached in her purse and conspicuously counted her bankroll. It came to just under $1,600 dollars. She knew there were a few more bills scattered in the purse, but not many. She was holding almost her last liquid capital in the world. "Here," she said. "Give this to Temo, will you? It's all I have. Will you be seeing him soon?"

The man's eyes bugged out. "T-t-temo?" he stammered. "He ees my brawthair-een-law." She studied his face and saw no resemblance to the green-eyed woman in the reed shack. The man hefted the bills in his hand as though evaluating them by weight, *"Muchas gracias,"* he said, alternately smiling and frowning. "I will give." There was no longer any reason to harm her son. The man left, and this time he didn't lock the door.

After a while a dark-skinned young boy brought tepid bottles of orange Fanta and said, "Wait, pleece. Not long."

Another hour passed. Ace dozed in her arms, his breathing thick, and she made him swallow a pill. She pulled aside a shade and peeked out. A man in a priest's cassock was walking around the truck, sprinkling water. She yanked the curtain closed. The driver entered and whispered, "Ready."

The front half of the truck's cargo area was now crammed with the translucent plastic bags. A nest of burlap sacks and greasy pillows had been hollowed out in the middle of the load, and the driver helped them get comfortable. Two bare-chested workers raised a wooden scaffolding just behind the midpoint of the cargo hold and tied it to loops on the walls. Then the rear half of the deck was filled with boxes marked *"Cerveza Dos Equis—Hecho de Mexico."*

The truck moved out. My God, she thought, we're camped on marijuana. She looked at her son in the near darkness. "We're safe, angel," she said. "We're on our way home." She wished she believed it.

56

THE TRUCK SWAYED and lumbered through the Mexican night. Several times it stopped, and once it slowed to a crawl and made a labyrinthine series of turns, as though by-passing towns or using back streets to avoid inspection stations.

A few minutes after 3:00 A.M. she awoke from a doze. Ace lay shivering across her lap. Her bones were creased and twisted and flattened and strained—and she was ravenous. The leftover smell of onions and peppers made juicy quiches dance in the blackness before her eyes. Apparently the smugglers thought the human organism could subsist for hours on pop and pot. Assuming, of course, that they thought about their cargo at all. Who bothered to feed the condemned?

Over the pounding of the engine she began to speak into her son's ear. She knew he probably was asleep and wouldn't believe what she was saying even if he understood every word. He hadn't even acknowledged who she was. Had she changed so much? She remembered reading that a small child could lose almost all bonding to a parent in a year.

"I loved you all the time," she said just above a whisper. "I never stopped looking for you." She felt like a manipulator, taking advantage of a helpless child, but she couldn't stop. "Mommy'll take care of you. Always! You're Mommy's best angel. I love you, Acey." She had to say the words while she had the chance.

At six-thirty in the morning she felt him quivering. Either he was cold, or she had overdone the epinephrine. She pulled him close and tucked Temo's old blanket around their bodies. After a while he stopped shaking, and his eyes opened. She thought she heard him speak.

"What, angel?" she asked, lowering her ear to his mouth.

"Are you gonna hurt me?"

She held him tight and said, "No. Not me. Not anybody."

In a voice just above a whisper he said, "You're my mommy."

"I'm your mommy, baby." She stopped. He was still talking. "What, angel?" she said.

"I always knowed you loved me."

Soon he was asleep again, his faintly medicinal breath passing across her face in fitful puffs. Thank God, she said to herself. Whatever happens, he always knowed I loved him.

Later she awoke to a dim glow. The marijuana express droned on through the morning and into the afternoon with only a few stops. Just before 5 P.M. the truck braked, then moved forward and stopped again, jerked ahead and stopped again, over and over, till she began to feel nauseated. The air filled with exhaust fumes. Street noises pierced the walls: passing cars, yelling children, vendors shouting in Spanish. The starts and stops continued for almost an hour, and then the engine coughed and died. In a few minutes the driver's hushed voice came from the tailgate: "We are here now. Please *excusa*. Joo mus' wait."

She sighed through the sweat and the grime that covered her face like a cheap cosmetic pack. We must wait? This drive began thirty hours ago. Where are we? Mexico City? *Guatemala?* We've had nothing to drink since Puerto Peñasco. But I'm not complaining. *Joo mus' wait.* No problem. I'm with my son.

Another hour passed before she heard the driver's voice again. "Ees time, *señora*. Hwhen I let joo out, jump! And walk fast."

"Walk where?" she whispered.

"Anyhwhere," he answered. He sounded agitated and a little anxious.

How could she jump with a sick child? How could they walk fast? But the man had offered no alternative. Ever since Temo had intercepted them in the desert, they had been without alternatives, their lives in the gnarled brown hands of Mexicans. She wondered what Van would think of the way things had worked out, or if she would ever see him again. Dear Van. Saint Ivan I. She wished she could see him again in his "Nuke the Nukes" T-shirt.

The tailgate dropped with a metallic clunk, and beer cases were shifted aside to form an exit tunnel. She pushed Ace through to waiting arms and slid to the ground after him.

The bright daylight almost blinded her. "Go now!" a male voice said in a loud whisper. She shielded her eyes from the sun and dragged her son to a narrow sidewalk. A long line of trucks stretched both ways. At the front she could make out a shed and a bilingual sign, ADUANA. CUSTOMS. CAMIONES. TRUCKS.

She struck out aimlessly, trying to get away from the truck; but her legs were stiff, and Ace could hardly walk. She picked him up and staggered for another fifty or sixty feet and put him down again.

She looked behind. No one seemed to be following. The late-afternoon sun was the size and color of a newly minted peso, and the air was cooled by a moist breeze. Back at the line of trucks Temo's brother-in-law was lacing the canvas flaps that covered Aguilar's cargo deck.

Mother and son hobbled along toward six or eight lines of automobile traffic lined up at guardposts manned by Mexicans in uniform. Pedestrians flowed toward a doorway marked "To U.S." and disappeared in a closed archway that led north. Everywhere she looked she saw *turistas*. She hoped there were enough to keep the police from noticing a blond boy in a serape and a slatternly woman in rumpled clothes, both reeking of onions and peppers and dope.

She stopped dead when she saw them: three men in dark uniforms striding toward her and the child. They were a half block away, but there was no mistaking their mission. As she watched, they broke into a half trot. Why are they bothering to run? she asked herself. Where do they think we can hide?

The trio approached, jogging abreast. She couldn't help wondering one last time about God and his choice of methods. In any other country, she thought, I would be welcoming these men. I would be throwing myself at them. But not here. Not after what I've seen.

The policemen were almost on them. The tallest one smiled at her, showing gold-edged teeth like Trang's. She knelt and threw her arms around Ace. "I love you, baby," she whispered. She gave him one last hug and stood up, holding his hand tightly. "Please don't hurt him," she said out loud. "I promised. He's only—"

The uniformed men were gone. She spun around and spotted them alongside a blushing-pink truck bearing the name Los Tres Hermanos. They banged on the door of the cab, and when the driver opened up, they hauled him down by his undershirt.

She stood dazed for a moment, then said, "Let's go!" Mother and son merged into the crowd headed for the pedestrian over-pass marked "To U.S." Everyone seemed to be carrying pack-ages, laughing, jostling. She realized that the two of them looked too conspicuously different to get by the border guards without attracting attention. "Come," she said, and led the boy against the grain of the traffic and back to the street.

They walked to a shop marked *"Curios, objetos raros y curiosos"* and emerged with a seascape painted in blazing colors, a tasseled cardboard hat for Ace, and a clay pitcher inscribed "Welcom to Mexico." In the middle of the archway that led toward home, a loud voice boomed from behind them, "Lady! *Hey, lady!*"

She grabbed Ace and started to run. "Hey, *wait!*" An elderly man with an American Gothic face rushed up and handed Ace a hat. "Here, sonny," he said. "You dropped your sombrero."

They walked toward the guards on the U.S. side. A few tourists were being questioned, but most were waved through. If only the two of them weren't so aromatic. She had a mental picture of a dope-sniffing Doberman leaping at their throats.

Now there were four people in the line ahead, now two, now. . . .

"Evenin', ma'am." A soft western accent, a tired smile. "How long you folks been in Mexico?"

"Uh, just shopping."

Some of the smile slid from the square-jawed face. "How *long*, ma'am?"

"Oh. Uh, just today."

The uniformed man stared back and forth between her and Ace. She was sure he could see her heart pounding through her blouse. He said, "Thank you," and waved them on. They had shuffled a few steps when he called out, "Ma'am?" She grabbed Ace's wrist. "The boy," he asked in an embarrassingly loud voice. "Is he all right?"

"Him?" she answered just as loudly. "I sure hope so. He ate everything that wouldn't eat him."

They walked along the shoulder of a broad roadway choked with northbound traffic. In the unexpectedly cool air she began to lose the feeling that a long brown arm would reach out and drag them back to Mexico to face the *delegado* and Mike and the others. Her feet felt as light as a ballerina's. Her thoughts returned to the couple with the three green eyes. She hadn't even said good-bye.

Maybe she would send them some herbs. Tons! One good truckload deserved another: rosemary and sweet cicely and dill and enough lavender and mint to scent their beachfront shack for life. She laughed out loud and smiled at Ace, and when she saw his puzzled look she realized she was acting silly. An elderly couple in matching plaid jump suits turned and stared, and she gave them a wave and giggled again.

She hurried Ace along till they were out of sight of the border crossing. A big green and white highway sign said, SAN DIEGO 15. They came to a parking lot that seemed to hold thousands of cars. A phone booth stood at the entrance.

As the sun tucked behind a potholder cloud, a soft breeze lifted her unkempt hair and swirled it around her neck. Night was coming. To the west, a pale wash of purple and red flowed in long streaks down the sky. She found her telephone credit card and dialed a number. Her other hand gripped Ace's, and his own hand gripped back.

Van answered on the first ring, as though he'd expected the call. "Van!" she yelped. "We're here! I've got him, *I've got him!* Oh, Van, we're safe."

It was over. She wondered why she started to cry.

Bestselling Books

☐ 21889-X	**EXPANDED UNIVERSE**, Robert A. Heinlein	$3.95
☐ 47809-3	**THE LEFT HAND OF DARKNESS,** Ursala K. LeGuin	$2.95
☐ 48519-7	**LIVE LONGER NOW,** Jon. N. Leonard, J. L. Hofer and N. Pritikin	$3.50
☐ 80581-7	**THIEVES' WORLD**, Robert Lynn Asprin, Ed.	$2.95
☐ 02884-5	**ARCHANGEL**, Gerald Seymour	$3.50
☐ 08933-X	**BUSHIDO**, Beresford Osborne	$3.50
☐ 08950-X	**THE BUTCHER'S BOY**, Thomas Perry	$3.50
☐ 78035-0	**STAR COLONY**, Keith Laumer	$2.95
☐ 11503-9	**A COLD BLUE LIGHT,** Marvin Kay and Parke Godwin	$3.50
☐ 24097-6	**THE FLOATING ADMIRAL**, Agatha Christie, Dorothy Sayers, G.K. Chesterton & others	$2.95
☐ 21599-8	**ESCAPE VELOCITY**, Christopher Stasheff	$2.95
☐ 37154-X	**INVASION: EARTH**, Harry Harrison	$2.75

Prices may be slightly higher in Canada.

Available at your local bookstore or return this form to:

 CHARTER BOOKS
Book Mailing Service
P.O. Box 690, Rockville Centre, NY 11571

Please send me the titles checked above. I enclose _____. Include 75¢ for postage and handling if one book is ordered; 25¢ per book for two or more not to exceed $1.75. California, Illinois, New York and Tennessee residents please add sales tax.

NAME _____

ADDRESS _____

CITY _____ STATE/ZIP _____

(allow six weeks for delivery)

A-9